"Tom Wangler takes an obscure landmark of Central Oregon's Cold War history and turns it into the setting for a gripping technical thriller. The result is a fast-paced, entertaining novel set at the intersection of fact and fiction."
—Glenn Voelz is a writer based in Bend, Oregon and the author of *The Gisawi Chronicles*.

"I had no preconceived notion about the story I was reading. The suspense of the events kept me reading on. The characters were neatly tucked into their own chapters until the very end and stayed with me even after I closed the book. This was a good read, nay … it was a great read."
—Connie Souther is a rancher with homes in Tumalo, Oregon and Ft. Worth, Texas.

"This was a fun, well-structured action suspense mystery. The timeline is tight and clearly labeled. Our heroes are relatable and likable. I liked having feminine representation of various shades. I enjoyed working on this story! It was clearly written by someone who understands military procedures and loves helicopters."
—Kelly Lynne Schaub is a professional editor living in Springfield, Oregon.

BACKSKATTER

A Botched Experiment Creates

the Ultimate Weapon

TOM WANGLER

ISBN-13: 978-1-945587-78-8
Library of Congress Control Number: 2022909843

Backskatter: A Botched Experiment Creates the Ultimate Weapon
1. Military; 2. Cold War; 3. Oregon; 4. History

Book Design: Dancing Moon Press
Cover Design: Dancing Moon Press
Illustration Art: Philip McDaniel

Dancing Moon Press
Bend, Oregon USA
Lincoln City, Oregon USA
dancingmoonpress.com

DANCING
MOON
PRESS

The story you are about to read is a historical novel. Technically, it is a work of fiction. The setting and all locations, including the various military installations mentioned exist, or existed at one time, as described. The weapons technology depicted is also real. For obvious reasons, the names of various organizations have been changed. All of the principal characters were inspired by a variety of people the author has met or known. Any resemblance to actual individuals, however, is purely coincidental.

"We have been letting technology run us as if we had no judgment of our own."

—C.P. Snow
Noted British Writer and Scientist

"We have been letting technology run us as if we had no judgment of our own."

—**C.P. Snow**
Noted British Writer and Scientist

PROLOGUE

In the fall of 1999, the world was preparing for the apocalypse.
It was not the "End of Days" in the Biblical sense, merely the end of one century, the beginning of a new one. Nonetheless, it was a time of great uncertainty, anxiety, and confusion.

"Y2K" as it was popularly called, loomed on the horizon. It was a time that would send a substantial number of people into virtual panic mode. An unpredictable event for the entire human race was but a few months away.

At the core of this lay a small electro-magnetic device known as a microchip. Since computers and other similar devices were programmed to read only the last two digits of each year, when their internal clocks clicked over at midnight on New Year's Eve, they would be reading "00". The concern was, computers and other high-tech devices including cell phones, high-definition television sets, and even traffic signal lights would recognize the new century as 1900. That being the case, every device with a microchip would systematically shut down and stay that way.

Doomsayers claimed virtually everything electronic would quit working. Their predictions warned of banking systems and financial markets collapsing. Pensions, IRAs, and other forms of investment would be wiped out or lost altogether. People all over the globe either withdrew money at an alarming rate, cashed out their stocks, bonds and annuities, or planned to do so before December 31. People were led to believe credit cards, along with ATMs, would not work. Many feared even checks would not be accepted. They surmised that cold, hard cash would be the only acceptable means for purchasing goods and services. As a result, people started stashing away all they could.

Speculation included the possibility of computer-controlled or computer-monitored services, which included all utilities, would also stop working. There would be no electricity, no natural gas or fuel, no method of personal or mass communication, no municipal services like potable water or sewage disposal. Portable electric generators sold like hotcakes. Additionally, it was rumored, there would be no way to transport or distribute goods, including food, medicine, and hygiene products. Many even feared that governments, being totally ineffectual, would falter then collapse. The armed forces of all nations would be crippled, and thus be exposed to attack.

These "doomsday" scenarios, real or imagined, were the impetus behind the United States government to spend over $400 million to upgrade its primary computer systems, with the expectation to spend an additional $600 million if necessary. Other countries took similar measures.

"Survivalists" also went into high gear that fall. This group drained their bank accounts, stocked up on food, water, medicine, portable generators, fuel, guns, and ammunition. They transferred everything from their computers to disks for safe storage, then made hard copies of all their important documents and purchased safes to keep everything in. They prepared for the worst. The collapse of all social, political, and legal structures.

Even though the inhabitants of planet Earth had already seen their fair share of strife, turmoil, and changes in 1999, Y2K fears weighed foremost on everyone's mind.

Many forgot, or didn't care, that U.S. President Bill Clinton teetered on the cusp of being impeached. That NATO began a bombing campaign in Yugoslavia. That the Columbine shooting in Colorado left a dozen high schoolers and a teacher dead. That an earthquake in Turkey killed an estimated 13,000 people and left ten times that many homeless. That the newly formed European Union transitioned to the Euro as a means of uniform currency. That the Panama Canal was returned to Panama after eighty-five years of American control. That John F. Kennedy Jr., his wife, and her sister were killed in a private plane crash. That following a messy coup de tat, the African country of Zaire became the new Democratic Republic of Congo.

Everyone seemed oblivious to what had already happened. All mankind was apparently focused on the end of the twentieth century. Year 2000 became the center of all attention.

Hidden among the many events of the year was a little-known and deadly incident which occurred in the high desert area of eastern Oregon during a four-day period in October of 1999.

Something inexplicable had killed wildlife, livestock, and human beings without provocation, without exception, and without mercy. Their grotesque deaths were quickly written off as an isolated event, leaving very few clues and many unanswered questions as to what actually happened and why.

Until now...

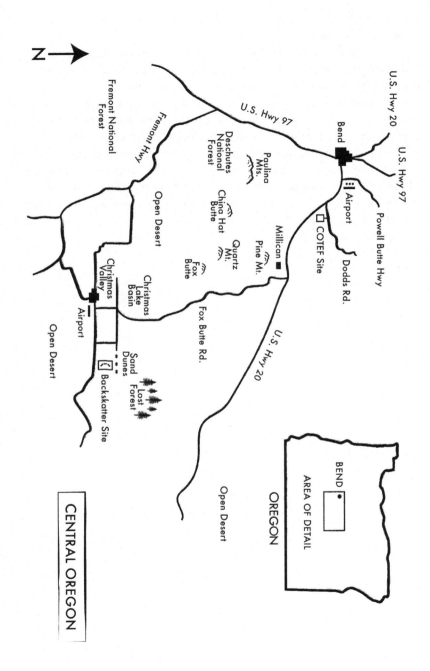

CENTRAL OREGON

N →

Fremont National Forest

Fremont Hwy

U.S. Hwy 97

Deschutes National Forest

Paulina Mts.

China Hat Butte

Open Desert

Quartz Mt.

Fox Butte

Millican

Pine Mt.

Bend

Airport

COTEF Site

U.S. Hwy 20

U.S. Hwy 97

Powell Butte Hwy

Dodds Rd.

Christmas Valley

Airport

Christmas Lake Basin

Open Desert

Fox Butte Rd.

Sand Dunes

Backskatter Site

Lost Forest

U.S. Hwy 20

Open Desert

OREGON

BEND

AREA OF DETAIL

4

DAY 1

Saturday, October 16, 1999

CHAPTER 1

Eastern Oregon
Saturday, Mid-Morning

The sleek LifeAir helicopter made its transitional approach to Central Oregon Regional Medical Center's helipad from the southeast that October morning.

Normally, the pilot of the twin-engine Bell 222 UT would come in hot and fast. Time was everything when a life hung in the balance. It was called the "golden hour," a critical sixty-minute period from accident to the emergency room. A time span which could mean the difference between life and death.

The pilot of the $2.5 million aircraft, with its distinctive red, white, and blue markings, typically altered his flight path whenever approaching the hospital for noise abatement purposes. Coming in fast from different directions as well as using different approach angles was done to minimize its noise "footprint." Pilots performed this routine procedure to prevent complaints from the inhabitants along the helicopter's route. The 222 was deafening when it was flying low and in a hurry.

Years earlier, the standard 22-foot-long main rotor blades of the EMS helicopter had been switched out for the shorter, fatter blades found on the Bell AH-1 Cobra attack helicopter. Because both helicopters were made by the same company and shared similar components, a special waiver from the FAA allowed the hospital to install the more compact blades on its machine. The shorter, more functional, military-style rotors allowed LifeAir to land and takeoff in more confined areas. This strategy made the medevac helicopter much more versatile.

The trade-off, unfortunately, was the noise. The distinctive, ear-splitting wump-wump-wump of the shorter blades could be heard from five or more miles away. A Cobra, or in this case the 222 UT, was not going to sneak up on anyone.

A noise abatement approach was not necessary for this morning's landing. The helicopter's sole patient, an elderly man found naked and alone in the desert region of eastern Oregon, had died while in route to the hospital. Despite being outfitted with advanced trauma and life support systems, two flight EMTs conducting on-going care, and a skilled pilot who could push the sizable helicopter to its limits, the old man could not hold onto life long enough to reach the hospital.

A young couple hiking in the remote area known as the Lost Forest came across the man earlier that morning. The two college students were checking out one of the many rock outcroppings in the forest when their dog discovered the man crouched on his hands and knees behind a boulder. Found muttering something indistinguishable, he was in bad shape to say the least.

Aptly named, the Lost Forest occupies a semi-remote area in the high desert region of eastern Oregon. Located on the northern edge of Lake County, just across the southern boundary of Deschutes County and some sixty-five miles southeast of the resort community of Bend, the forest is a true anomaly. A pine forest should not be in the middle of a desert.

Unbeknownst to many non-Oregonians, the high desert, so named because of its altitude, is a vast and open region that covers approximately 26,000 square miles on the eastern side of the Cascade Mountain Range. It is an area larger than the state of West Virginia. The land is principally flat with a fair number of hills, bluffs, buttes, gullies, ravines, dried-up alkaline lake beds, and an occasional town. The landscape is covered with sagebrush, bitterbrush, desert shrubs, a variety of grasses, flowering plants, juniper trees, and a mixture of desert wildlife. There are some populated areas, however. This remote part of Oregon is understandably rural; dotted with numerous alfalfa farms, cattle ranches, and small hamlets. All things considered; it has remained somewhat locked in time.

How the Lost Forest came to be in this dry region has always been a source of great speculation, especially since the closest timberland of any real consequence is over forty miles away. This isolated stand of Ponderosa pine trees covers approximately 9,000 acres and by all accounts, definitely looks out-of-place among the arid landscape of the area. Because there are no known springs or standing water to support this forest of impressive trees, how it originated and survives will always be one of the great mysteries of the high desert.

Even stranger still was how the old man got there.

Emaciated, without clothing, sunburned, and suffering from exposure, he was also severely dehydrated. The man appeared to be disoriented and looked as if he had been crawling on his hands and knees for some time. Afraid his life was in serious jeopardy, one of the hikers called 911 for help on her cell phone. Her boyfriend gently moved the old man into a sitting position, covered him up with a light hooded sweatshirt, and gave him some water. They kept him as comfortable as possible until help could arrive from the closest town, the small and isolated community of Christmas Valley, located approximately twenty-eight miles to the southwest.

A Lake County sheriff's deputy posted to the little town's field office received the relayed call that morning around 8:45. The deputy subsequently checked his list of local volunteers trained in search and rescue operations then made a couple of quick phone calls. By 9:15, two volunteers were on their way to the location in a Jeep equipped with a CB radio, emergency provisions, medical supplies, and survival gear.

While the two were in route to the site, the deputy made a judgement call and phoned the dispatcher at LifeAir. Then he informed his two volunteers, via CB radio, what was in the works.

Central Oregon Regional Medical Center, the predominant hospital for most of the central/eastern Oregon area, was located on the eastern edge of Bend, the area's largest city with a growing population of 36,210. LifeAir, a separate entity under contract to serve the hospital, supplied the medevac helicopter, dispatchers, mechanics, and pilots.

The twin-engine 222 UT (which stood for "utility transport") used by the hospital was a 1991 model equipped with extra fuel tanks in its side sponsons instead of the standard retractable landing gear. With the extended range this upgrade provided, LifeAir could cover an enormous amount of territory. It was also a fast helicopter, very fast. With a maximum speed of 135 knots (155 mph) it could get to where it was needed and back to the hospital usually within an hour. The powerful twin-turbine machine flew almost daily and was credited with saving dozens of lives every year.

The two search and rescue volunteers reached the Lost Forest at approximately 9:50 and immediately went to work. While one helped the two hikers attended to the old man, the other prepared an "LZ" (landing zone), anticipating the arrival of the medevac helicopter from Bend.

They didn't have long to wait. The swift-acting machinery of the LifeAir staff had the Bell 222 airborne within fifteen minutes of receiving the initial call. The flight time from the hospital to the Lost Forest was a mere twenty minutes.

The pilot skillfully set the big helicopter down on a hard-packed dirt road a scant fifty yards from where the old man was found. LifeAir was on the scene only twelve minutes behind the arrival of the two search and rescue volunteers. It was airborne again in less than fifteen minutes. Typical of the LifeAir organization, the timing of the entire medevac operation was immaculately coordinated.

Despite the immediate and on-going care on the flight back to Bend, the old man didn't survive the trip.

As the helicopter gently settled onto its landing pad at Central Oregon Regional, two orderlies had a gurney waiting in the receiving area. The time was now 10:45 a.m. The helicopter had made the 137-mile round trip, with pickup, in approximately one hour.

Because of the many onlookers stationed outside the fenced-off area of the helipad, LifeAir's flight EMTs and the orderlies elected not to put the man into a body bag. Instead, they carefully unloaded him onto the gurney as the helicopter spooled down and covered him with a sheet and blanket. Leaving his face exposed and the intravenous bag of fluids attached, the group quickly wheeled him into the hospital.

To the many onlookers scattered throughout the parking lot and helipad area that morning, it was quite the sight. LifeAir had once again performed a miraculous, life-saving mission. No one seemed to notice the subdued and solemn movements of the ground and

flight crew as they finished securing the helicopter and that one of the flight EMTs, Emily Spooner, was crying.

Jack Winters, as the senior EMT caregiver on the flight, accompanied the two orderlies as they wheeled the old man into the ER. It took the group a little over a minute to cover the forty yards from LifeAir's helipad to the main entrance of the emergency ward.

Without stopping, the two orderlies wheeled the dead man directly to ER room #19, one of the back examination rooms. This was a specially outfitted room affectionately referred to as the "Resurrection Room" by the staff, a solemn reference to the many people who were literally brought back to life by the extraordinary efforts of the various doctors and nurses at Central Oregon Regional. It was also the hospital's policy not to leave dead people in the hallway or in proximity to those either awaiting treatment or those being attended to, it was not only upsetting, it was also bad PR.

Winters stopped at the reception desk to apprise the two attendants they had lost the patient in route back to the hospital and to start filling out the required DOA forms, one of which was a detailed account of the treatment and measures they took after picking up their patient in the desert.

One of the attending ER doctors was called in to perform an evaluation, fill out the necessary paperwork and sign the death certificate. After finishing with his forms, Winters was directed to room #19, where a staff physician was conducting his post-mortem examination.

"Hello, Jack," Dr. Miles Emerson said as Winters walked into the room. "Tough break. I know how you hate to lose one."

"I was really hoping he would make it, even though he was in pretty bad shape when we picked him up." Winters replied as he pressed his lips together in obvious frustration. "What are you going to list as the cause of death, Doc?"

"Cardiac arrest … probably brought on by acute renal failure." Emerson said as he flowed down the check sheet on his clipboard with a pen. "Standard for someone of his advanced age. We see it all the time. What happened when you picked him up?"

Jack Winters glanced at the report he was still filling out. "When we first got to the victim … excuse me, patient … Emily and I checked his vitals, did a standard triage, hooked up an IV bag of fluids, then loaded him onto the helicopter. We hooked him up to the monitoring equipment as we lifted off and tracked his vitals right up to his first cardiac arrest."

"His first?" Emerson said, looking up and showing more concern. "How many did he have during the return flight?"

Winters unconsciously let out a heavy sigh and responded with "three."

"Let me get this straight." Emerson reflected, furrowing his brow. "His heart stopped a total of three times during your trip back. Was he 'shocked' on all three?"

"Yes ... Spooner and I worked up a good sweat trying to revive him on each stoppage," Winters confessed. "We were successful on the first two, but not on the third. Emily took the loss pretty hard."

"It's amazing you two got him to survive as long as you did." shrugged the doctor, then added: "I guess there really is something to the three strikes and you're out rule."

Winters didn't appreciate the parody but kept his opinion to himself. "Given his age and hardiness, I really thought we could save him."

"Jack." Emerson said, putting a hand on the EMT's shoulder. "I know you and Emily did all you could. I don't think anyone could have possibly saved this man, not at his age and condition."

"Really?" Winters unconsciously stepped closer to the examination table. "Considering what he looked like out in the desert, I would have guessed exposure or dehydration to be the primary cause of death, not old age or a weak heart."

Dr. Emerson narrowed his eyes and spoke with a more curious tone. "Jack, how old would you estimate this man to be?"

Without even looking at the body, Winters said, "oh, I don't know... I would 'guestimate' he was probably in his early sixties or thereabouts."

"Take another look at him, then guess again," prompted the doctor, nodding towards the table.

Winters saw something in the doctor's expression that was unsettling, then took another couple of steps closer to the exam table. Glancing back at the doctor before proceeding further, Winters slowly peeled back the sheet covering the man's head and shoulders.

The seasoned EMT looked down at the dead face and gasped.

"What the hell's going on?" Winters exclaimed, looking back up at the doctor, his voice rising with tension. "This is not the same man we brought in!"

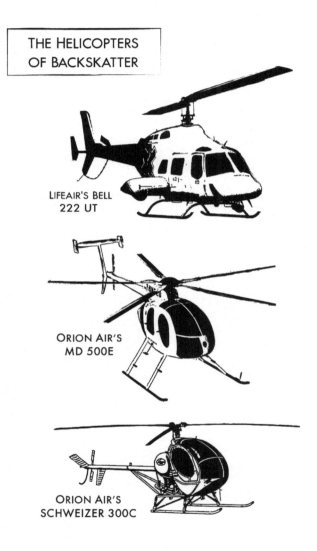

THE HELICOPTERS
OF BACKSKATTER

LIFEAIR'S BELL
222 UT

ORION AIR'S
MD 500E

ORION AIR'S
SCHWEIZER 300C

CHAPTER 2

Bend Municipal Airport
Saturday, Mid-Morning

Chance Barclay looked up from what he was doing in time to see the LifeAir helicopter with its shark-like profile skirt the southern edge of Bend's airport and disappear toward the city to the west.

Barclay let out a wistful sigh as he watched the Bell 222 make its run in the direction of the hospital. Oh, how he would love to get his hands on a machine like that.

It was a typical fall day on the eastern side of Oregon's Cascade Range. The mid-October weather on the high desert was always warm and sunny, what the locals typically referred to as an "Indian Summer." Barclay was the pilot on duty Saturday at the small helicopter service called Orion Air, located on at the southern end of the small municipal airport. He was preparing one of the company's two helicopters for a morning's worth of scenic flights as the EMS helicopter made its east-to-west run.

Chance Barclay, or "CB" to his friends, was a retired Army veteran who began his military career straight out of high school. At five-foot-ten inches tall with a slight but muscular build, Barclay was nothing short of what one would call a "character." Born and raised in the small ranching/farming/logging community of John Day, Barclay was a good-looking, middle-aged man with an outrageous sense of humor and common-sense, "aw shucks," wisdom. Everyone who knew Chance liked him and enjoyed exchanging "war stories," whether it was about growing up in rural eastern Oregon or his experiences in the Army.

After his initial basic training, Chance applied for the Army's

Warrant Officer Candidate School because the notion of flying helicopters appealed to him. Graduating from WOCS with high marks, he was selected to attend flight school and completed the thirty-two weeks of primary training and fourteen weeks of specialized training with distinction. After being assigned to an observation squadron flying the OH-58 "Kiowa," the military version of the Bell 206B Jet Ranger, he wound up flying ground support missions in the Gulf War.

After two tours of duty in Iraq and one in Afghanistan, Barclay finished out his twenty-year commitment as a chief warrant officer and flight instructor at the U.S. Army's Aviation Center in Fort Rucker, Alabama. Upon his retirement from the service at the ripe old age of forty, Barclay and his wife Emma moved back to their home state of Oregon in search of new career and lifestyle opportunities. They finally settled down in the growing community of Bend so Chance could attend a local community college while Emma furthered her career as a school nurse.

Chance Barclay loved to fly, especially helicopters. There was just something magical about what these machines could do and the level of skill it took to fly them. Piloting a helicopter was not only fun for Barclay, but also somewhat intoxicating, if not a downright rush. Barclay was not only an adrenalin junkie, he was also an extreme professional. What one would call a pilot's pilot. In addition to being the company's chief pilot, Barclay was also its certified flight instructor. His passion for flying "whirlybirds" made him an excellent CFI for student pilots.

For the two scenic flights Orion Air had on its schedule this Saturday morning, Barclay was going to use the company's four-passenger McDonnell Douglas 500E. A compact, lightweight, turbine-powered helicopter with remarkable speed and agility. He was in the process of performing his pre-flight safety checks on the aircraft when interrupted by the passing of LifeAir's 222.

"Wishful thinking partner?" Trent Westbrook asked as he strode up to the helicopter Barclay was checking out.

"Whoa, you snuck up on me!" exclaimed a surprised Barclay. "I thought you were taking the day off ... or something like that."

Westbrook, his wife Charlie, and Barclay were all equal partners in the fledgling aviation business. Despite the challenges and the stresses associated with starting and operating a helicopter service, the three worked extremely well together and considered themselves good friends. Westbrook was not only part owner, but also the company's other pilot and compliance officer. The FAA, their insurance carrier and other agencies required a certain amount of "compliance" with the accompanying paperwork regarding various regulations, policies, and laws. Westbrook had a knack for dealing with the ponderous paperwork requirements. Charlie worked the front office, kept the books, and did the marketing for their business.

According to today's schedule, Barclay and their office girl, Becky Irwin, were the only ones scheduled to work on Saturday morning. Understandably, he was surprised to see his friend and partner.

"I was," Westbrook said. "That is, until I got a call from the Beckster saying some phone company technician wants to check out some cell tower sites. I knew you had a couple of scenic flights this morning in the 500, so I'll be taking the Schweizer."

For the principals of Orion Air, operating an "on-call" helicopter service meant flying seven days a week and at all hours. That was the nature of a start-up flight service. One took the business whenever they could. Weekend duty was normal, and October was a busy time for the company. It was the tail-end of the tourist season, and many businesses needed something done from the air before the winter weather set in. Real estate agents especially liked aerial shots of the higher-end properties they were trying to sell.

In fact, business for the little company had really picked up over the course of the summer and fall. So much so, it enabled Orion to add a second machine to its fleet. Though they had started off one-and-a half years earlier with the three-seat, piston-powered Schweizer 300C, the demand for their services had grown to such an extent they could justify leasing the larger, more powerful MD 500E.

"Yep, I just love those little scenic flights," Barclay answered in his typical redneck drawl. "I'm taking a family of three up into the mountains for an hour and then a retired couple on a whirlwind tour of some of our finest sights."

"Which explains why you're taking the hotrod," Westbrook teased, inwardly smiling to himself. On several occasions, passengers whom Barclay had taken on scenic flights in the nimble 500 came back saying Chance not only gave them an informative ride, but a thrilling one as well. Some even went as far as to say he was more of an entertainer than a tour guide or pilot.

"Sounds like it's going to be a busy morning for the both of us, ace."

At forty-five years of age, Westbrook himself decided to learn how to fly helicopters and start a flying business when he was laid off after working eighteen years for a utility company. Like Barclay, Westbrook was a native Oregonian, with the exception he had lived most of his life in the immediate area. Tall and lean with a sharp wit, college-educated Trent Westbrook had a personality like that of Barclay, which probably explained why they were not only business partners, but also best of friends. Along with his wife Charlie, Chance Barclay was who Westbrook leaned on when his parents were killed in a tragic motor vehicle accident three years earlier. The trust fund his parents left behind was the seed money that allowed the group to start up Orion Air.

"Where are you and your technician off to … and how long do you think you'll be out?" Barclay drawled. "Remember, we were going to give our 'birds' their weekly baths this weekend."

"Oh, I haven't forgotten," Westbrook emphasized. "I always look forward to seeing what shenanigans you have up your sleeve when it's time to clean up our babies!"

The two friends had a long-standing habit of having as much fun as possible when they "spiffed up" their helicopters. They typically waited until the end of a weekend flying day so they could party while getting their machines ready for a new work week. A couple of beers and a water fight made the occasion more fun than work, and both looked forward to it. It was not only the nature of their individual personalities, but also a bonding time that helped relieve the tension after a long week of flying.

"My customer wants to scout out some potential cell tower locations south of Pine Mountain."

"Really? That's the direction LifeAir just came from." Barclay casually pointed toward the southeast. "Maybe you'll get to see what they were up to."

"I doubt it. Could be anything from a farming accident in Christmas Valley to a traffic accident on Highway 20," reflected

Westbrook. "They sure have been busy lately."

"Too busy, actually." Barclay observed, rubbing his chin. "Do you realize every time they fly, we get a call to do something? It's like a reminder to the public we're out here and ready to do business. Sometimes it makes me feel like we're some kind of bottom feeders."

The off-hand remark struck a somber chord with Westbrook. His parents both died in an open road accident to the north because LifeAir could not respond. The life-saving machine had already been dispatched to the south for another accident. The responding EMTs and their ambulances couldn't get to his parents for over an hour. The circumstances of that delay in getting help to his mom and dad always made Trent wonder, "What if ...?"

It was at that moment the petite and bubbly Becky Irwin strode out of the company's hanger and walked over to the helipad where the two pilots were talking.

"Hey, CB!" She said with a voice that oozed congeniality. "Your eleven o'clock party is here. I'll finish up with the paperwork if you give them the pre-flight."

The "paperwork" was a straightforward task for the spirited Miss Irwin. It consisted of explaining the various forms the passengers were required to read and sign, as well as collecting payment. Bright and eager, the adorable little redhead was taking a "gap year" to earn money for college. Orion Air paid Becky above minimum wage, not only because she deserved it, but also because her upbeat personality brought in repeat business. Something that Chance and Trent greatly appreciated. To show how grateful they were, the boys had set up a tip jar on the counter with a couple of ten-dollar bills stuffed inside as seed money. The gesture was intended to be a subtle suggestion that satisfied customers should appreciate her efforts as well.

The "pre-flight" was the company's standard safety briefing all passengers received before boarding a helicopter. Not only was this company policy, but also a requirement of the FAA and their insurance carrier. The briefing typically consisted of the safest way to approach, board, and exit a helicopter for normal operations as well as in emergencies. Emphasis was always placed on the dangers of approaching the aft end of a running helicopter. The FAA had a ton of accident reports regarding people who came in contact with the spinning tail rotor. The extremely high RPM of the blades made them virtually invisible and would act like a buzz saw if contact were made with them ... with mutilating consequences.

After boarding, the correct way to use the four-point seatbelt/shoulder harness system was demonstrated to the passengers, as was the use of the headsets with their voice-activated microphones. Finally, the PIC, or Pilot-in-Command, would explain what their flight would consist of and answer any questions. Chance could always spot a nervous passenger by how many questions they asked, most of which were downright dumb.

"Oh, and Trent," Becky continued, "your customer just showed up too. Want me to start on his paperwork as well?"

"Yeah ... Bec." Westbrook replied, nodding his head. "That would be great, thanks."

The two pilots watched their perky little office girl walk briskly back into the hanger towards the office area. Although it was a "casual" Saturday, Becky still liked to dress professionally when dealing with the public, which meant bum-hugging slacks and a tight pullover with the company logo embroidered on the front. Both Chance and Trent had, on more than one occasion, regarded Becky's "professional attire" as a contributing factor her tip jar always being full.

"Well," Westbrook finally said, shaking his head and breaking the awkward silence. "I guess it's time to saddle up and go flying."

CHAPTER 3

Central Oregon Regional Medical Center
Saturday, Late Morning

EMT Jack Winters could not believe his eyes or what he had just been told.

There on the examination table was the body of a man who must have been at least eighty years old. The frail and gaunt corpse with the sunken eye sockets was nothing more than a pile of loose, wrinkled skin with protruding bones. He looked nothing like the semi-robust, elderly man the EMT tried to save on the flight in from the desert.

"I don't understand," Winters said, "you say this is the exact same person we just brought in? How can that be? Death doesn't do that to people that quickly!"

Miles Emerson glanced down at the body himself. Then took a second, and then a longer, closer look. Although it had only been a little over twenty minutes since he performed his initial examination, the body did not look the same to him either.

"You're right," said a now-concerned Dr. Emerson. "Normally, a newly-deceased person only turns a pale or a grayish color due to the cessation of blood flow. One doesn't radically age, or even start to decompose, within a few hours of death. This is something I've never seen or heard of before ... I'm somewhat at a loss to explain why or how this is happening."

"This is really creepy," Winters intoned. "Maybe we should call the hospital's pathologist ... or the medical examiner. Have one of them take a look."

"Getting a pathological viewpoint might be a good idea,"

Emerson conceded. "I'll be right back."

The physician quickly walked over to the room's entryway and grabbed the wall phone. He decided to make two calls, one "upstairs" and the second to the county coroner's office. Jack Winters took one final look at the corpse, which he thought had degraded even more during their conversation, shook his head in dismay, then headed back to the LifeAir hangar to finish his report.

Dr. Emerson was developing a growing sense of confusion, mixed with a little dread, over what he and Jack Winters had just witnessed. Out of habit, he glanced up at the wall clock in the exam room as he picked up the phone. It read 11:45 a.m., Pacific Daylight Savings Time.

Emerson's first call was to his supervisor, apprising him of the situation and suggesting they have one of the hospital's pathologists, as well as the county coroner take a look. The supervisor agreed with the suggestion and authorized Emerson to make the calls, which he immediately did. Then Emerson took it upon himself to hang a temporary quarantine sign on the examination room's door and informed the rest of the ER staff of the room's situation.

Although it was the weekend, the semi-urgent call from the hospital intrigued Dr. Michael Clark, the county coroner. After closing his flip-style cell phone, he cut short his less-than-stellar golf game, apologized to his companions, and headed directly to the clubhouse. To the forensic pathologist, the accelerated and unusual degradation of a human body could spell all kinds of problems, especially if some highly viral or bacterial disease were involved.

The hospital's own chief pathologist, Dr. Virginia "Ginny" Thompson, was putting in her typically long week and happened to be in the middle of performing an evaluation on a biopsy when Emerson's call interrupted her. She finished what she was doing, made a few quick notes, then secured the tissue samples she was working on. Donning a fresh lab coat, she walked from the medical diagnostic unit on the southeast side of the building to the ER on the northeast side. Considering the size of Central Oregon Regional with its maze of corridors, it was not a quick journey. Miles Emerson was waiting for her in the ER's reception area and was just beginning to brief her when Michael Clark arrived.

"So ... what do we have, Miles?" Inquired the coroner as he

strode up to the pair in the hallway. Emerson looked at his watch, which read 12:26 p.m. The doctor thought the coroner must have broken a few traffic laws to get to the hospital as quickly as he did.

"Hi Mike, thanks for coming," Emerson said, shaking the coroner's hand. As I was just explaining to Ginny, LifeAir brought in an elderly patient this morning who was emaciated and unresponsive. He was found by a couple of hikers out in the Lost Forest suffering from dehydration, exposure, and shock."

"I assume you called us," Ginny Thompson said, nodding towards the coroner, "because the patient didn't survive, and you have misgivings or concerns about the actual cause of death?"

"I do." Emerson replied, looking a little grim. "It seems like the deceased aged considerably between the time of pickup, the time he was delivered to the ER, and by the time I finished my examination an hour ago."

"What do you mean, aged considerably?" Michael Clark asked, not fully understanding the issue.

"Jack Winters, the senior EMT caregiver on the medevac flight, said the man they picked up looked to be somewhere in his sixties," Emerson began. "The patient expired in route to the hospital and was taken directly to exam room #19 right after they landed. The man I examined for the postmortem report, about twenty-five minutes later, looked to be more in his eighties to me. When Winters had filled out his DOA and flight care report, he checked in with me to verify the exact cause of death, which I said was primarily due to age-related conditions. After looking at the body, Winters was adamant the man I examined was not the same man they brought in earlier on the helicopter."

"There was no positive ID?" the coroner asked, still unsure of the problem.

"That's the mystery." Miles Emerson explained, sounding a little frustrated. "As Winters and I were talking, we both took a second look at the body and inexplicably he looked even older yet … like someone who'd be around ninety or older. That's when I decided something wasn't right here and called you two for an opinion."

The three doctors stood in silence for a minute, each trying to sort out in their minds what all of this could possibly mean. Michael Clark looked at his watch. It read exactly 12:36 p.m. "When did the flight EMT register the time of death?"

"Winters recorded the time of death to be 10:30 this morning … approximately at the mid-point of their return flight back to the hospital." replied Emerson.

"So, our patient expired just two hours ago?" Clark asked. "The state of the body should be somewhere between lividity and the onset of rigor mortis. Except for a slight skin discoloration, our victim should look fairly normal."

Listening to the dialogue between the two male doctors and respecting the fact that Miles Emerson was an experienced ER physician, Virginia Thompson finally spoke up. "Okay, Miles. I've heard enough. Let's go have a look at your mystery man."

The trio walked down the hallway together without saying a word. Each donned a gown, a face mask, a set of latex gloves and protective eyewear from the cart parked outside of the exam room then walked in. The dead man was draped head to toe in an oversized, green hospital sheet. The thermostat in the room had been bumped down to fifty degrees to keep the body cool.

Dr. Miles Emerson pulled the sheet back from the top, exposing the head and upper torso. All three doctors audibly gasped.

The body that came into the hospital as a recently deceased man in his sixties, who appeared to have spent too much time in the sun, was now in the first stages of putrefaction. In the roughly one-hour time period since the body was last observed, it had progressed from livor mortis through rigor mortis to outright decomposition.

The man's skin had gone from a slight ashen color, when Emerson first examined him, to a greenish tinge. Because the body was also beginning to bloat, the skin was in the process of marbling and starting to slough off between the toes and the fingers. The deep-set eyes had turned black, and the now-gaping mouth was locked in a grotesque half-grin.

Michael Clark cleared his throat and spoke up first. "This person could not possibly have died a couple of hours ago. This body, by clinical standards, has been dead for at least two, maybe three days. Miles, are you absolutely sure this is the same man LifeAir brought in? The one you initially examined?"

Momentarily at a loss for words, Miles Emerson was literally appalled at what became of the old man in such a brief period of time. Quickly regaining his composure and trying to be as professional as possible under the circumstances, he provided the only answer that came to mind. "Unless someone is playing a sick, practical joke on us, which I doubt … this is the same man."

CHAPTER 4

Schriever Air Force Base, Colorado
Saturday, Late Morning

U.S. Air Force Lieutenant Logan Davis was hoping to have quiet and uneventful shift this Saturday morning.

The report he received from Oregon this morning had ruined his day, and now he would have to relay the bad news to his superior officer. Because it was the weekend and most of the base's primary officers were off duty, the young lieutenant was apprehensive about notifying his boss, Lt. Colonel T.J. Rutledge, at home. The news regarding the disastrous equipment malfunction at the "Oregon Project," as everyone called it, was not good. Not good at all.

Lt. Davis had been at Schriever for less than a month, having been transferred from the Air Force's Space Research Laboratory at Wright-Patterson Air Force Base in Dayton, Ohio, and was somewhat unfamiliar with the protocols of this base and his new job. He had to consult with one of the non-commissioned airmen on duty that morning, typically an embarrassment to many officers, as to what the off-hour notification procedure was.

Formerly called Falcon Air Force Base, Schriever had been renamed the previous year as result of its new role within the Air Force's Space Command. Located approximately eighteen miles east of Colorado Springs and the Air Force Academy, Schriever AFB was also strategically positioned ten miles east of Peterson Air Force Base on a wide-open, semi-barren plateau. All things considered; the complex was somewhat isolated. With good reason.

Coded as a "highly classified" facility, Schriever was home to the 50th Space Wing, the 310th Space Wing, the Joint National

Integration Center, and the Air Force's Space and Missile Defense Command. The facility provided command and control for over 170 Department of Defense satellites, including early warning, navigational and communications satellites. The base was also home to the command-and-control network for the U.S. military's spy satellites in the Pacific sector. Needless to say, the facility was well fortified.

To the casual observer, Schriever was somewhat non-descript as far as top-secret military bases go, with its block-style buildings and multiple, over-sized satellite dishes and communication towers. But to the trained eye, the double span, eight-foot-high cyclone fence topped with razor wire and the guarded, double entry front gate were pretty much a dead giveaway. Not to mention the multitude of security cameras, ground-level sensors, and roving guards with their M-16s and German shepherds.

Lt. Davis had to make the call. It was his job, his duty. He wasn't sure how well it would be received. Being the messenger of bad news typically did not turn out well for the messenger. He had only worked with his superior officer for a little over a month, with minimal contact, and wasn't sure how the colonel would receive the news he needed to relay. With a heavy sigh, he finally picked up the secure phone and punched the button for Lt. Colonel Rutledge's home number and held his breath.

"Rutledge," was the curt answer.

"Sir, this is Lieutenant Davis in Building 500. We have a serious problem with one of our projects," Davis nervously said, trying to sound as neutral and professional as possible.

After a moment of dead silence, the colonel responded. "Lieutenant Davis, you do know we are talking on an unsecured line at my home ... which is off base."

"Yes, sir. I'm only calling to inform you we have an issue of extremely high importance that will require your immediate attention," Davis announced, trying to keep his composure. He was hoping his call and phraseology weren't a security violation.

"How serious, Lieutenant?" Was the gruff response.

"I think we need to get some people on this right away, sir." Davis wasn't sure how much more he could convey in vague terms without getting into trouble.

"Okay, Lieutenant, I'm on my way in. Has anyone else been apprised?" Rutledge asked.

"Negative, sir." Lt. Davis responded, breathing easier. "I'm awaiting further instructions, sir."

"Good. I'll be there in thirty minutes," announced the Colonel. "Meet me in my office for a detailed briefing at 1230 hours, Lieutenant."

Rutledge abruptly broke the connection before Davis could respond, but decided to say something anyway, even if only for his own piece of mind.

"Will do, sir. Thank you, sir. Have an awesome day, sir."

CHAPTER 5

Bend Municipal Airport
Saturday, Late Morning/Early Afternoon

Chance Barclay was long gone in the MD 500 with his three passengers when Trent Westbrook started his flight briefing with the cell phone technician.

The technician, Johnny Clark, had hired Orion Air to take him out to the desert just south of Pine Mountain in southern Deschutes County. There, almost on the county line that bordered northern Lake County, lay several buttes with sufficient height to accommodate a cell phone tower with substantial reach. Erecting a tower in this area would allow Clark's company, High Desert Cellular, to extend its service further into southeastern Oregon. Clark's assignment was to see if any of these locations would work for his company.

From liftoff to arrival at their first waypoint of China Hat Butte, a thirty-mile distance, took the little Schweizer 300C approximately twenty-five minutes. It was a moderately quick ride. Westbrook kept the small helicopter low, never flying more than two-thousand feet above the ground. At an average speed of 70 miles-per-hour, the little three-person helicopter was not as fast as the turbine-powered 500 Barclay was flying, but it did the job, and the customer was impressed by how quickly they got out to the buttes. He also appreciated the expansive view from the 300's bubble canopy.

From China Hat, the pair flew southeast, taking their time checking out East Butte, Quartz Mountain, Long Butte, and Squaw Butte. Four of the highest landmarks in the area. From their last scouting at Squaw Butte, Westbrook swung the diminutive

Schweizer in a wide, counterclockwise arc over the desert and took a bearing for home on distant Pine Mountain to the northwest. Asking his passenger if there was anything else he wanted to see before heading back, Westbrook quickly checked his fuel status. The gauge showed he had approximately one and a half hours of fuel remaining. More than enough to check out other sites if his customer so desired.

Indicating he had seen, mapped out and photographed everything he needed, Johnny Clark told Westbrook he could head on back to Bend.

Scanning the landscape around him, the technician noticed something unusual off to their right-hand side. Something looked strange to him on the desert floor southeast of Fox Butte. Clark asked Westbrook if he wouldn't mind coming back around and dropping a little lower so he could take a closer look. Trent Westbrook was only too happy to oblige. The longer they stayed in the air, the bigger the tab to the cellular company.

Dropping down to approximately five hundred feet off the ground and reducing the helicopter's speed to forty miles per hour gave the two a clear view of what Clark had only caught a glimpse of before. There, spread out before them on the arid landscape was a large herd of mule deer. A not-so-out-of-the-ordinary sight in the high desert except for one thing. They were all dead.

"What the hell?" Johnny Clark said into the voice-activated headset. "Do you see that?"

"I see it, but I don't believe it," Trent Westbrook replied. "This is not right. This many and all together. It's not right. This can't be a natural occurrence!"

Westbrook circled the helicopter around the group of downed animals looking for what might have befallen them. He saw nothing, nothing at all. No wounds, no blood, no predators, no nothing.

"Should we land and check this out?" Clark asked.

"No. I think not," Westbrook said rather emphatically. "These animals might be diseased or contaminated in some way. I think we should hustle back to the airport and report this to the authorities."

With that comment, Westbrook wheeled the S-300 back around to the northwest and headed as fast as he could back toward Bend's municipal airport. During the thirty-minute flight back, Westbrook switched to the discreet frequency Orion Air used exclusively for "ship-to-ship" or "ship-to-shop" communications. He asked Becky Irwin to contact the local State Police office and inform them of what they found.

In Oregon, fish and wildlife law enforcement was managed by the state police, comprised of specialized patrol officers trained as full-fledged game wardens. These accredited troopers were not only tasked with upholding the state's hunting, fishing, and environmental protection laws, they could also pull someone over on any highway or road and write a traffic ticket, if necessary. They were well trained, respected, extremely professional and had a candidate waiting list that went on forever.

Becky got on the phone and relayed the information on what the two flyers had discovered out in the desert to the OSP dispatch person. That person conferred with the senior trooper on duty, and they mutually decided this could be, indeed, something serious that needed immediate investigation. The dispatcher asked Becky when the pair would return to the airport, if they could sit tight until a trooper got there and interview them, and most of all, would Orion Air be able to fly someone back out to that spot if necessary?

All of this was happening while Trent Westbrook and the technician were approximately halfway back to the airport. By coincidence, Chance Barclay and his first set of passengers were in route back to the airport themselves at the same time. As soon as Becky got off the phone with the State Police, Chance Barclay called on the company's "ship-to-shop" radio channel informing Irwin he was inbound with an ETA of ten minutes, then asked if she could arrange to have a fuel truck stand by.

Becky made the call to the only fixed-base operator on the field and said their 500 would be landing shortly and needed Jet A before the next flight. The FBO was the local full-service flight center that offered everything from flight lessons to aircraft rentals, from mechanic services to charters, from pilot supplies to three types of aircraft fuel. It also managed flight operations at the small airport.

Chance Barclay was on his final approach to one of Orion's helipads when his next set of passengers walked through the front door of the company's office shortly after noon. Becky Irwin prided herself on being on top of things and could multi-task with the best of them. She had talked to the State Police, ordered fuel, and had the paperwork ready for the next set of tourists to review and sign before Barclay even touched down. To Becky, this Saturday was nothing out of the ordinary. She was just doing her job.

Excusing herself and momentarily leaving her new customers to watch a safety video, Becky slipped on a pair of noise-cancelling ear protectors and safety glasses then walked out to the flight line in time to assist with the unloading of the three passengers Barclay had taken for the ultimate mountain tour. Becky waited until Chance had spooled down the helicopter to "ground idle" and gave her the thumbs up signal before approaching the still-whirling machine. As she was helping the last passenger out of the aircraft, the fuel truck arrived and took up station on a side taxiway approximately 150 feet away from the helipads.

Irwin walked her returning passengers to the safety zone next to the hanger then went back to the front of the helicopter and indicated to Barclay, through standard hand signals, the fuel truck was waiting for him. Chance acknowledged with another thumbs up signal and a wink in appreciation for her help. A smiling Becky returned to her three tourists and escorted them, all excited and happy after their exhilarating flight, back inside to the office area then prepared the new arrivals for their upcoming adventure.

Chance Barclay waited until Irwin and the three sightseers were back inside before spooling the 500 back up to full power. Once he performed the standard systems checks, he gingerly lifted the machine up into a stationary hover over the helipad before slowly turning it around and maneuvering it toward the waiting fuel truck. Setting the helicopter down approximately twenty-five feet away from the truck, Barclay once again spooled down the engine to idle, locked down the controls then indicated to the operator he was ready to take on fuel.

Holding up four fingers told the operator he wanted only forty gallons. Because his next tour was scheduled for sixty minutes, forty gallons would give him a little over one and a half hours of flight time.

It was standard operating procedure, or "SOP," for all aircraft, especially helicopters, to only take on enough fuel, plus a reserve amount, to complete the task at hand. Fuel was heavy it was best to go with only what was required. Less weight not only improved the machine's performance, but it also allowed for more weight to be carried in other areas, like larger passengers.

The young man operating the fuel truck that day smiled back at Barclay and held up four fingers in confirmation. In return, Barclay gave him a thumbs up signal indicating the acknowledgement and that he was ready to take on the Jet A-grade fuel.

The attendant quickly unreeled the long grounding wire line, then connected it to the special contact point on one of the helicopter's skids. This was quickly followed by unreeling the bulky fuel hose. Unscrewing the cap of the recessed fuel tank, the operator stuck the nozzle into the receptacle then returned to the fuel truck to start the pumping sequence. Chance took the opportunity to fill out his logbooks while fuel was being pumped into the whirling helicopter.

Because of the quick turnaround between flights and the need to carry the minimum amount of fuel necessary for each flight, Barclay performed a standard "hot fueling" routine. This meant the helicopter was not shut down and allowed to cool off between fueling operations but was kept running at idle. This was done not only for expediency, but also to reduce wear and tear put on a turbine engine by constantly restarting, or "cycling," it.

Turbine engines were expensive to overhaul and even restarting a semi-cooled engine posed its own set of problems. Since Jet A was basically refined kerosene with a high flash point, the danger of fire was minimal, if not non-existent. A hot fueling operation, if performed correctly and with a good, aviation-rated fire extinguisher close at hand, could be done safely and efficiently.

Not so with Orion's piston powered Schweizer 300C. Its engine required a fuel with an extremely low flash point. The preferred fuel was 100 octane, low lead Avgas. This fuel was the fraternal twin to the gasoline used in automobiles. Let it come in contact with a hot surface or an open flame and a minor explosion usually resulted, with accompanying fire. Hot fueling a 300 was a catastrophe in the making. Virtually no pilot or operator hot fueled a piston-powered aircraft of any type.

Once the 500 was fueled, the operator shut off the pump, disconnected the nozzle, reeled in the hose, and wound it back up onto the truck's spool. After removing the grounding clip from the helicopter and re-winding it as well, he walked back out in front of the 500's pointed nose and gave Barclay the thumbs up signal, indicating everything was secure and he was clear to hover-taxi the short distance back to Orion's helipad. Chance acknowledged with a smile and a thumbs up signal of his own and spooled the engine back up to its maximum RPM.

The hot refueling went off without incident, enabling Barclay to transition back to the helipad in time to load and brief his 12:30 passengers. The Nebraska couple, on their way home from Hawaii, were on a short stopover on their way back across the country. They had heard of Bend and the unique beauty of the central Oregon area and wanted to see all they could on their last day of vacation. Orion Air gave them the opportunity to experience what they normally would not see by just driving around.

Chance Barclay had them loaded, buckled in and was in the process of explaining their flight plan when Trent Westbrook and his cellular technician made their approach to the company's second helipad. For the Nebraska couple, it was exciting to see a helicopter landing right next to them, especially since they were sitting in one themselves awaiting takeoff.

After touching down, Trent switched his radio over from the "common" airport frequency to the discreet, "ship-to-shop/ship-to-ship" frequency used by Orion Air. He wanted to check in with Chance as well as Becky.

"Three-two-six Charlie Bravo, three-two-five Tango Charlie," Trent said into his headset's boom microphone as he depressed the "push-to-talk" button on his control handle. Using the standard airman's phonetic alphabet, Trent was identifying who he wanted to talk to and who he was.

When they started the business, Trent and Charlie Westbrook applied for, and got, the "325 TC" designation for the Schweizer 300C. Three-two-five represented the date they were married, March 25th, and TC was for Trent and Charlie. When they acquired the MD 500E, they applied for, and received, the new designation of "326 CB" to represent their second helicopter with Chance Barclay's initials. Which probably explained one of the reasons why the 500 was Chance's favorite helicopter to fly. His name was on it.

"Tango Charlie, go ahead," Barclay replied to Westbrook, sitting a short sixty feet away from his aircraft on the second helipad. For any onlookers, it must have been quite a sight to see these two helicopters sitting side-by-side with their rotors spinning at idle with all the accompanying noise.

Trent Westbrook, normally jovial and casual when talking to Chance on the radio, sounded serious and professional, in case anyone was listening in. "Chance, we just saw something strange out in the desert. As soon as I shut down and unload my customer, I'll be talking to a game warden and possibly taking him back out to the location. Mind cleaning up the 500 by yourself if I don't make it back by late afternoon?"

Barclay told his friend and partner that would not be a problem and, true to his nature, asked if there was anything he could do.

"Negative," Westbrook responded. "Enjoy your tour with our guests from the Mid-west. Show them the usual time of their lives and I'll brief you when you get back, over."

"Roger," Barclay replied. "See you later alligator."

Chance checked his watch, which read 12:36 p.m., approximately six minutes behind schedule, which Barclay thought wasn't too bad, all things considered. Chance switched the radio channel over to the airport's common traffic frequency and announced he was departing from Orion's helipad on the south end and heading west. Then he took a quick reading of his engine instruments and slowly ran the turbine engine up to its maximum RPM. Once all his engine gauges had stabilized in their respective green arcs, he checked the helipad area for any safety concerns then looked over at the middle-aged couple from Nebraska and smiled.

"Let's go have an adventure, shall we?"

CHAPTER 6

Central Oregon Regional Medical Center
Saturday, Early Afternoon

The three doctors stood utterly transfixed.

Without talking and without touching the corpse of the old man, they just stared at him. He was slowly decomposing into nothing before their very eyes.

"I can't believe what I'm seeing!" Chief pathologist Virginia Thompson finally said, breaking the awkward silence. "We need to quarantine this room immediately and take blood and tissue samples while we still have something to work with!"

ER doctor Miles Emerson agreed and ran to the supplies locker to get what they needed. Dr. Thompson would inform the hospital's supervising doctor of the situation, the first step to implement a quarantine. All three agreed this should immediately be put into effect. County coroner Michael Clark stayed with the body, only taking his eyes off it long enough to do an occasional time check. As quickly as the old man was decomposing, Clark was afraid that by the time they could take samples or relocate the body to the morgue for a thorough clinical examination it would be nothing more than a mummified pile of bones.

Emerson returned to the room within two minutes with a collection of syringes and tissue sample kits. Virginia Thompson grabbed a couple of the syringes and started drawing off blood and other fluids wherever she could find them, including a sample of the vitreous humor from one of the eyes and a trace of urine taken directly from the bladder. Doctors Emerson and Clark each took several tissue sample kits and went to work. Michael Clark, following standard forensic pathology protocols, directed Emerson to take separate swabs of the mouth, nose/sinus area, and rectal opening. Next, they took postage stamp-sized skin samples from three separate areas as well as a hair sample complete with roots.

While Emerson and Thompson collected their samples, Clark opened up the old man's chest with a scalpel. What he saw was not pretty. Virtually all of the dead man's internal organs had become putrid, shrunken, and discolored. Their appearance reminded him of a pile of rotting meat, including the recently released smell.

Clark tried his best to breathe through his mouth as he sliced off small samples of the heart, liver, kidney, and pancreas. He totally removed one of the adrenal glands, or what was left of it.

It was a fast and crude autopsy by forensic standards. The three worked quickly and furiously trying to salvage what they could for further analysis. After approximately fifteen minutes of work, they had enough samples and turned their attention to what to do next.

Dr. Robert Parks, the fifty-one-year-old chief of staff and daytime supervisor for the weekend, strode into the examination room just as they finished. Virginia Thompson suggested he grab a set of gloves, a mask, and a pair of protective glasses before coming any closer. Parks, appreciating the professional gesture, went back outside, outfitted himself and then re-entered the room.

"I just wanted to check on you three and see for myself what the emergency was … just in case I needed to call the State and the CDC," Parks remarked, as he walked up to the three doctors.

Robert Parks was referring to the Oregon State Medical Examiner's Office and the national Center for Disease Control and Prevention. The OSME not only managed all aspects of the state's medical examiner program, but it also provided technical support to the thirty-six county coroners throughout Oregon. It was the top authority in dealing with suspicious deaths, homicides, and related incidents. The agency's Death Investigation Program was considered to be top notch.

The CDC, in addition to tracking and investigating public health trends, fielded special rapid-response teams to investigate and control the spread of epidemic diseases. Headquartered in Atlanta, it was a federal agency under the U.S. Department of Health and Human Services. The CDC was the country's final authority on infectious diseases, food and water-borne pathogens and environmental health and safety.

By alerting these two agencies, Parks would set a variety of wheels into motion, including an all-out investigation that would also include his hospital and its doctors. He wanted to make absolutely sure of what was involved with their mystery man before sounding the alarm. A premature overreaction was not in anyone's best interests.

The county coroner, Michael Clark, spoke up first. "Doctor Parks, we have been examining and taking samples from this elderly man," gesturing toward the body on the table, "who initially appeared to be aging and decomposing at an extremely accelerated rate. We're at a loss to explain this phenomenon until we can analyze the samples we've taken. Until we know what we're up against, we want to quarantine this room and this body immediately!"

Parks quickly looked at the three doctors then at the form on the exam table. What he saw distressed him. The body looked like the filleted remains of some dried-up animal. His professional curiosity compelled him to do a quick, cursory examination of his own before speaking.

"How long ago did this man expire?" He finally asked, trying to keep an open mind. Miles Emerson checked his watch, as well as the oversized 24-hour clock on the wall. His watch said the current time was now 1:14 p.m. The wall clock said 1313, PDST.

"According to Jack Winters, the senior EMT on the LifeAir flight, this man expired at approximately 10:30 this morning while in route back to the hospital," Emerson said. "I first examined him at approximately 10:55."

"Are you telling me this ... 'person' has only been dead for somewhere around three hours?" Parks frowned, somewhat dismayed. "And this is all that remains of him?"

"That ... is why I called you, Dr. Parks," Virginia Thompson broke in. "All things considered, I believed an immediate quarantine and forensic samples needed to be taken before the body decomposes any further."

"You mean disintegrates," chimed in Michael Clark.

Thompson raised an eyebrow at him. She always thought coroners had a somewhat warped sense of humor. Probably due to the nature of their work or from inhaling too much formaldehyde. Clark's comment confirmed her suspicions.

Dr. Robert Parks, a former ER doctor himself and a specialist in geriatric medicine, was having a tough time trying to understand, or even comprehend, how something like this could have happened so quickly and to such an extent. Even if the old man had died alone out in the desert and had been lying there, exposed to the elements for a week, he would not look like this. A person who had been dead for only three hours would still look fairly normal and alive. To all four doctors, this was not only medically impossible, but extremely disturbing.

After a quick minute of silent reflection, Parks finally acknowledged this was, indeed, beyond the realm of their collective knowledge. He asked Miles Emerson to institute the recommended quarantine procedures for the exam room and immediate vicinity. Then he turned to Coroner Clark and asked him if he could obtain a biohazard body bag and secure what was left of the victim in the hospital's morgue. Without being told, Virginia Thompson took custody of all the biological samples and secured them in an airtight container for transport up to the lab.

Before leaving the exam room, Parks asked all three to not say a word about this to anyone. He also asked the trio to join him in the small upstairs conference room at 2:30. He wanted a frank, professional discussion, and a concise, detailed report before deciding if he should call the state medical examiner's office and the CDC. As an afterthought, he asked Miles Emerson to see if the attending flight EMT could join them. Parks was thinking the technician might be able to shed some light on what happened in the desert, as well as on the flight back to the hospital.

As fate would have it, and as if Parks didn't have enough on his mind, the wall phone next to the door buzzed just as he was about to leave the exam room. The distracted doctor picked up the phone and punched the flashing red button.

"Parks."

"Dr. Parks," announced the hospital's main receptionist, "there is a sheriff's deputy from Christmas Valley on line #3 wanting some information about the patient LifeAir brought in this morning."

Shit, Parks thought to himself. *This is all I need right now!*

"Okay, thank you," was his perfunctory response, then he punched the clear button for line #3. "Dr. Parks here. How may I be of assistance deputy?"

"Dr. Parks, this is Deputy Mark Spenser of the Lake County Sheriff's Department. I'm calling regarding the condition and possible identity of the elderly man LifeAir picked up this morning out by the Lost Forest. Can you help me with this? I will need some information to file my report on the incident."

Robert Parks looked over at the decaying body and the three individuals standing around it for a few seconds before responding. "As you may know Deputy, the victim was found naked and without any identification. He also expired in route back to the hospital before he could provide any information about himself. Wish I could be of more help." Parks was being careful with what he said and how he said it, not wanting to raise any suspicions about their "mystery man,"

"That's sad and unfortunate. Where is the body now?" The deputy asked.

"We are placing it in our morgue for the time being as a 'John Doe.'" As an afterthought, he added, "have you, by any chance, received any reports of a missing person within the last twenty-four to forty-eight hours? We also need to establish identity so we can notify the next of kin."

"Nope, nothing yet," replied Deputy Spenser. "But I'll get back to you if anything turns up. Can you give me a call if anything surfaces on your end as well?"

"No problem, Deputy. Thanks for the inquiry." Parks ended the conversation by abruptly hanging up the phone, slowly exhaled through puffed-out cheeks, then looked at the sullen faces of the other three.

Without saying another word, a now very-concerned Robert Parks strode out of the room and took the closest elevator back up to his office. He wanted to consult his medical textbooks and journals.

Doctors Emerson and Thompson returned to take another look at the body on the exam table while Michael Clark phoned the ER reception desk from the wall phone and asked if someone could locate a red bio-hazard body bag and bring it to them. The receptionist passed along the request to one of the orderlies who immediately went down to the hospital's basement morgue, retrieved one and made his way back up to the exam room.

By this time, the body had gone through all three principal stages of putrefaction: skin slippage, bloat, and organ decay. The sixty-ish man who arrived at Central Oregon Regional three hours earlier was now in the "post decay" stage. The body had been reduced to dried and leathery organs, cartilage, and skin. There was no soft tissue or bodily fluids left. The distinctive odor of rotting flesh was also beginning to subside.

"Damn it!" Michael Clark exclaimed, making the other two doctors flinch in surprise. "We didn't take any pictures!"

A photographic record of each stage of an autopsy was standard procedure among all forensic pathologists, as well as an on-going narrative recording and pertinent x-rays. None of which had been done in this case, things just happened too fast, and the three doctors were hard-pressed to keep up with the rapid deterioration of the body.

"I guess we blew that one," Virginia Thompson remarked. "Is there even a camera or a recorder of some type in this department?" She asked Miles Emerson.

"I suppose we have something... just in case we need evidence if something we did, or didn't do, winds up in court," Emerson replied. "Should I go see if I can find one?"

"Any pictures taken now would be worthless with respect to what we have witnessed," Clark shrugged. "Still...we should have some type of photographic evidence of what remains to show the authorities. Yeah, Miles, would you mind seeing if you could rustle up something?"

Miles Emerson quickly slipped out of the room and hustled back to the department's reception desk where he asked if they had a camera stashed somewhere. The senior receptionist smiled at the serious-looking ER doctor, reached into her desk, and produced a small, disposable Instamatic camera still in its wrapper. "We like to keep a couple of these on hand ... just in case." She said with a smile as she handed the package to Emerson.

As the doctor made his way back to the exam room, he almost ran over the orderly with the special red body bag as he stepped out of the elevator. The orderly followed Emerson back into the exam room and stopped short when he saw the look on the faces of Ginny Thompson and Michael Clark.

"You're too late," Virginia Thompson flatly stated, looking first at the orderly then at Emerson.

"What do you mean, too late?" asked a perplexed Emerson.

"Look for yourself," Thompson replied, pointing toward the body on the exam table.

Miles Emerson, a seven-year veteran of emergency room situations, thought he had seen everything. He was not prepared for anything like this.

CHAPTER 7

Schriever Air Force Base, Colorado
Saturday, Early Afternoon

Immediately after concluding his conversation with Lt. Davis, Rutledge made two quick calls.

The first was to the base commander, Colonel David R. Kelly, informing him of the situation. Col. Kelly, in turn, wanted a detailed update after Rutledge finished his meeting with Lt. Davis. The second call was to Schriever's head of base security, Major Colby Jefferson.

The colonel wanted Jefferson in on the briefing with the lieutenant for a variety of reasons. Foremost among them, the major had a reputation for having innovative approaches to dealing with situations regarding investigative work. This wasn't the first time some "issue" had popped up with their highly classified project in the Northwest. Hopefully, the well-regarded Maj. Jefferson could help. He had a knack of being able to cut through the bullshit to find out what was really going on.

Although Rutledge did not yet know the extent of the "problem" itself, as Lt. Davis put it, he wanted to cover his butt nevertheless if things went sideways. The military can be extremely unforgiving if something goes wrong without a thorough follow-up. Rutledge was already on somewhat of a hot seat because his project was over budget, behind schedule, and had a history of internal issues. That being the case, the colonel saw Jefferson as something of a personal "insurance" policy.

Maj. Jefferson, to his credit, was more than just someone who oversaw security for a classified Air Force installation. Jefferson had a top-notch investigative mind and was a "by-the-book" perfectionist. The celebrated major, who held a law degree from Stanford with a minor in criminology, joined the military while still in college, courtesy of the Air Force's ROTC program. Graduating with honors, Jefferson went straight into security and intelligence work after successfully completing Officer's Candidate School (OCS). In short order, he rose through the ranks, establishing himself as a smart, unconventional problem solver. Little escaped his eagle eye or his calculating mind.

Colby Jefferson, with his "Top Secret" security clearance, was already on both the FBI and CIA's watch list for recruitment when his current enlistment ended, some two years in the future. Rutledge knew if something were amiss with his "Oregon Project," Jefferson was the perfect choice for someone who could find out what happened and fix it.

Lt. Davis and the major both arrived outside of Rutledge's closed office door at approximately the same time. Davis was surprised to see Jefferson, even though he suspected there might be others in attendance. He just didn't expect it would be the head of base security. Jefferson was aware of who the lieutenant was and knew beforehand he was going to be a part of this briefing.

Upon their knock on the colonel's door, Rutledge told the two officers to enter the office. Following standard military protocol, the major entered first, followed by the lieutenant. Both stood at attention in front of Col. Rutledge's desk and waited for the ranking officer to address them.

"At ease, men." The colonel put both hands on his desk and rose to his feet, grabbing an oversized mug of hot coffee. He did not bother to offer any to the other two officers. "Let's make ourselves comfortable over at the conference table." He nodded in the table's direction. As one of the ranking officers on the base, Rutledge enjoyed the prestige and comforts of an oversized office, complete with a large desk, leather chairs, a TV, a small conference table, and a hutch with a coffee maker.

As the trio sat down, Davis and Jefferson on one side and the colonel on the opposite side, Rutledge wasted little time. He introduced the two officers to one another then got directly to the point, something the serious-minded Colby Jefferson always appreciated.

"Lieutenant Davis here," Rutledge began, gesturing towards the junior officer while looking at the major, "is my assistant and aide-de-camp with respect to a special project we have out in Oregon." Changing his gaze to the lieutenant while he gestured toward Jefferson, Rutledge continued, "the major is here, not only in his capacity as head of base security, but also because we need someone with his background to help us determine what's going on with regards to our project." Turning his attention back to Maj. Jefferson, Rutledge added, "your involvement was requested by me and approved by Colonel Kelly. Consider yourself temporarily reassigned to me as a special investigator. Your primary duties here at Schriever will be reassigned to your subordinate."

Lt. Davis and Maj. Jefferson glanced at each other; this was obviously unexpected news to both of them.

Colonel Rutledge continued, looking directly at Jefferson. "Major, what do you know of our 'Oregon Project'... as we call it?"

"I'm aware of it, sir. But only of its existence," Jefferson replied, sitting up straighter. "I'm not privy to any specifics. However, as I understand it, this is a highly classified program and strictly on a 'need to know' basis."

"That says a lot about our security around here, especially when the head of security doesn't even know anything about this program," said a somewhat bemused Rutledge. "My compliments on keeping this base so squared away, Major."

"Thank you, sir," Jefferson said. "I appreciate the notation, but it's more of a team effort than an individual one."

T.J. Rutledge was momentarily at a loss for words. He fully expected the major, like so many of the officers he had dealt with over the years, to let his ego rake in most of the credit and return the favor. Jefferson was not the type of person to play any games of mutual admiration, however, it was simply not in his nature.

"Nevertheless," continued the colonel, "your leadership, professionalism and ... humility are duly noted."

Jefferson didn't appreciate the little barb but kept his cool, his displeasure safely tucked away behind a world-class poker face. He nodded respectfully to the colonel, not giving Rutledge the satisfaction of knowing his comment had even registered.

"You may not know anything about our Oregon Project," Rutledge continued, "but I bet you know something about the Pentagon's 'Star Wars' program."

"I do," reflected Jefferson. "President Ronald Regan initially proposed it back in 1983 as the Strategic Defense Initiative. It was a military-based, scientific program designed to develop special lasers, particle beam weapons and assorted other high-tech devices that could intercept and destroy enemy bombers, missiles, and spy satellites. I believe DARPA was doing most of the heavy lifting on the program. I remember hearing the R&D costs were initially estimated to be several billion dollars, prompting Senator Ted Kennedy to sarcastically call the proposal 'Star Wars.' I know the program was officially terminated by President Clinton in 1993, but I don't know what became of any experimentation or equipment under development, or what was actually being tested."

Colby Jefferson, with his "Top Secret" clearance and security-based connections, was no stranger to many of the research projects being conducted by the Defense Advanced Research Projects Agency. DARPA was the Pentagon's primary R&D agency responsible for the development of emerging technologies for use by the military. Jefferson remembered it had a monster budget and at least twenty-five to fifty projects in the works at any given time. Most of these were highly classified, with some even being farmed out to various universities and the private sector via research grants and hefty contracts.

An awkward moment of silence followed Jefferson's last remark concerning his lack of knowledge on what was under development. Colonel Rutledge and Lt. Davis traded a quick, almost guilty-looking glance at each other. Nor did the fact escape the sharp-eyed major that Davis immediately lowered his eyes and gripped the folder he was holding on the table even tighter.

Jefferson quickly interrupted the brief interlude himself when he asked the obvious question: "So…with all due respect, sir, what does 'Star Wars' have to do with what's going on with your 'Oregon Project'… and my role in it"? The major was always one to come directly to the point.

"Perhaps it would help to give you a little background info first," Rutledge finally said, after taking another sideways glance at the

lieutenant.

"Okay," Colby Jefferson said in reply, inviting Rutledge to say what he wanted to say.

"In the period between 1986 and 1988," the colonel began, "the Pentagon had three classified military installations constructed in the central Oregon area ... the region just east of the Cascade Range. The sites, because they were not close to any populated areas of note and because the area is fairly remote, were deemed to be ideal locations to support, shall we say ... specialized facilities."

After a short pause to take a sip of coffee, Rutledge continued. "The first one was built in 1986-87, approximately four miles east of the small community of Redmond, Oregon. The second one, identical to the Redmond complex, was constructed in 1987-88 nine miles southeast of the larger city of Bend. Exactly fifteen miles separate the two, lined up on a perfect north-south axis. They were connected electronically by dedicated fiber optic land lines and a burst-microwave transmission system. Both installations are in fairly remote desert terrain and are surrounded by property controlled by the Federal Bureau of Land Management. These two sites, for all intent and purposes, were identified as special 'Army projects' for the benefit of the public and the news media. The third facility was an Air Force radar site."

Major Jefferson listened intently, not taking any notes or interrupting in any way. He wanted the colonel to continue with his briefing, unabated. Like any good lawyer, Jefferson wanted Rutledge to voluntarily speak his mind. Hopefully, getting carried away and giving out more information than he probably intended to.

"That third and final facility, the Air Force one, was built way out in the boondocks ... in the middle of a desert. It was constructed roughly sixteen miles northeast of the little farming community called, of all things, Christmas Valley." A grin flashed across his face, as if he unconsciously responded to some private joke. "That site, the largest of the three, was built between 1985 and 1988. It was started before the other two sites and was completed approximately a year after them. The total cost of the three installations is classified ... I doubt if anyone actually knows how much, given the labyrinth of the Pentagon's budgetary process. Best guess puts the tab somewhere above three hundred million dollars, possibly even as high as half a billion."

Rutledge took a deep breath, exhaled slowly and again, glanced over at Lt. Davis before continuing.

"That third site, which took the longest to build, was also the costliest. It was initially constructed as a new-technology, over-the-horizon radar complex for detecting enemy bombers and missiles while they were out over the middle of the Pacific Ocean."

Giving the colonel a chance to collect his thoughts and take another sip of coffee, Jefferson asked his second question of the briefing. "What were the names of these three installations?"

"The Redmond complex was called the Central Oregon Unit Evaluation Facility, or COUEF. It was referred to as 'Brett Hall' and was publicized as a testing facility for the evaluation of the Army's next generation of night vision goggles. The Bend site was simply referred to as COTEF, or the Central Oregon Training and Education Facility...where training on the use of the new night vision equipment supposedly took place. The third site, the one out in the middle of nowhere, was simply and officially identified as the Christmas Valley OTH-B Air Defense Radar Installation."

"What does the OTH signify?" Jefferson asked.

"Over-The-Horizon ... the type of radar system the complex was originally built to incorporate."

"And the 'B' designator?"

"That would be for its assumed name ... Backskatter."

CHAPTER 8

Bend Municipal Airport
Saturday, Early Afternoon

At the same time as the drama unfolded at Central Oregon Regional, Oregon State Police Trooper/Game Warden Matt Shields walked into Orion Air's office, introduced himself to Becky Irwin, presented his credentials, then asked to speak to Trent and his passenger.

Although Shields was not wearing the standard, deep-blue uniform of an Oregon state police officer, he still cut an impressive, authoritative figure in his kaki-style game warden outfit. His black utility belt with the 9mm Heckler & Koch handgun was a definite attention getter.

Out on the helipad, Trent Westbrook was supervising the refueling of the S-300 when Becky Irwin walked out with the trooper and the cell phone technician. Westbrook was expecting the game warden and had asked Johnny Clark, the technician, to hang around after landing so they could explain what they saw out in the desert.

After introductions, Trooper Shields asked Westbrook and Clark if there was somewhere more private, and less noisy, where they could talk. Trent led the group back into the office area, through the lobby and into the small, back conference room. An area which also served as a classroom for Chance Barclay's student pilots.

As the trio settled in around the small conference table, Barclay was on final approach to the airport with the Nebraska couple, having completed a whirlwind, sixty-five-minute tour of the best sights Central Oregon had to offer. As the MD-500 slowly descended into a stable hover just above the empty helipad, Becky Irwin walked out of the hanger wearing her bright, orange-colored hearing protectors and tinted safety glasses. Just as soon as Barclay landed and spooled down the helicopter to ground idle, she would help the passengers out of the whirling machine and escort them back into the office.

While the engine was cooling down, Chance radioed the FBO and requested the fuel truck. By the time it arrived, he had shut down the engine and was filling out the aircraft's logbook. He was extremely happy with the tour, what everyone in the business referred to as "flightseeing." The middle-aged couple from the Mid-west were nothing short of ecstatic about their extraordinary adventure. So much so, they gave their pilot/tour guide a fifty-dollar tip to show their appreciation. Barclay later slipped the large denomination bill into Becky's tip jar when she wasn't looking.

As Chance Barclay dealt with the after-flight paperwork and refueling of the 500, Trent Westbrook and Johnny Clark were telling Trooper Shields about their unorthodox discovery earlier that day. Shields asked a substantial number of questions, most of which neither Westbrook nor Clark could answer. After the twenty-six-minute interview, the game warden asked Westbrook if he could fly him back out to the spot for a closer look. Trent said that wouldn't be a problem since they had no more flying commitments for the rest of the day and started filling out the necessary paperwork. Shields thanked Clark for his time, asked him to keep this information confidential for the time being and gave him a business card before he left just in case he thought of something else.

"Would it be possible to land at the site once we get there?" Shields asked Westbrook as they walked out to the helipad area ten minutes later.

"No ... no problem at all," Trent replied. "Just as long as we have a suitable spot and permission from the BLM to land there." Trent was referring to the Bureau of Land Management, the federal agency responsible for almost all of Oregon's desert region which was not privately owned. Landing without proper authorization on government-controlled property would be in violation of several laws.

Matt Shields chuckled. If they got busted, not only would the BLM issue a violation ticket, but the infraction would also be reported to the FAA, which would not be good for the little helicopter flight service. "Not to worry, Trent. I have the authority to give you permission to land wherever you want in the State of Oregon ... except for maybe the Reservation." Shields was referring to the Warm Springs Indian Reservation which occupied a sizable area to the north.

All Indian reservations within the United States were considered semi-autonomous nations and are granted certain rights and privileges which were federally protected. The concept of tribal sovereignty was established in the 1800s and granted Indigenous tribes the right to govern themselves under certain conditions. Landing a helicopter on tribal lands without prior authorization would be a violation of that sovereignty and be reported to the Bureau of Indian Affairs, who in turn would report it to the FBI and the FAA. None of which would turn out well for the transgressor, unless of course, the landing was the result of a *bona fide* emergency.

"Okay, then," Westbrook replied with an enthusiastic nod. "We can land wherever you want, my man. Just as long as we're good with Uncle Sam."

While Westbrook briefed both his partner and their office girl of what was in the works, Matt Shields returned to his truck and retrieved a field pack. After double checking the paperwork, the pair quickly made their way back out to Orion Air's helipads. Westbrook helped Shields climb into the right seat of the S-300, showed him how to fasten the four-point harness and how the headset worked, then gave him an abbreviated safety briefing. Walking around the nose of the little helicopter to the left-hand side, Trent climbed into the pilot's seat and fastened himself in. After checking out his flight controls and the surrounding area for any safety hazards, he fired up the engine and engaged the rotors.

The trip back out to the desert took a little over half an hour in the agile little helicopter. For both pilot and passenger, the time passed quickly as the two engaged in idle conversation and got to know one another. Trent was curious why and how Shields became a game warden for the state police. Shields, in turn, wanted to know more about Orion Air and how the small helicopter operation came to be. In the back of his mind, he thought of how useful this service might be for his line of work, especially on short notice. The two men took an instant liking to one another.

Matt Shields had served with distinction in the Marine Corps and was honorably discharged after serving two tours in Iraq. He joined the military fresh out of high school with the intent of getting a college education on the GI Bill upon his completion of service. He graduated from Western Oregon State College with a degree in criminology and was accepted into the Oregon State Police training academy immediately thereafter. Smart, personable, and extremely professional, Shields excelled in his role as a representative of the Oregon State Police. He was also the consummate game warden.

Trent approached the area from the northwest, slowly descended, then circled the herd of dead animals in a clockwise fashion. He did this so Shields would have an unobstructed view of the deer from his right-hand side door, which had been removed prior to departure for better viewing. The game warden asked Trent to make a couple of slow passes as he took a 35 mm SLR Canon out of his pack. He wanted to take a variety of pictures from the air at different angles.

An ugly scene stretched out before them. What once was a small group of around twenty healthy, wild animals was now nothing more than buzzard bait.

The bodies were strewn about, laying all over the place in various positions and at odd angles. They did not appear to have been shot and most were starting to bloat. Shields told Trent to go ahead and land, but not too close. He didn't want the downwash from the rotors kicking up dust or debris around the animals. He was not only thinking in terms of preserving any forensic evidence in case this turned out to be a crime scene, but also about the accidental spreading of any type of contagious diseases.

Westbrook set the 300 down on a flat, dried-up catch basin approximately forty-five yards from the herd and immediately spooled down the helicopter's engine and rotors to idle. Trooper Shields removed his headset, unfastened his four-point harness, then carefully climbed out of the aircraft. Retrieving the canvas pack he brought along, Shields removed from it a couple of protective face masks, two pairs of slip-on "booties" to cover their shoes, two pairs of latex gloves, and a half-dozen Petri-style dishes for collecting tissue samples.

After shutting down the helicopter and securing it, Westbrook joined the game warden. Both donned the protective gear before advancing toward the fallen herd. The trained eye of the trooper constantly scanned the ground for any telltale signs of foul play as they cautiously approached the first animal. Shields instructed Trent not to touch any of them or otherwise disturb anything until he could take pictures. The trooper was initially treating this as a crime scene.

The pair took perhaps ten or so minutes walking among the downed deer. All the while, Shields took photos and made mental notes. Trent Westbrook could only stare at the carnage surrounding them.

The game warden swept his hand out and was the first to speak. "Notice anything unusual about this scene?"

"Yeah, a couple of things, actually," Westbrook replied. "For openers, when the cell phone technician and I first saw these guys, they looked like they'd just died. Now, they look like they've been dead for at least a couple of days. They weren't bloated like this when we saw them a couple of hours ago."

"Really? That's interesting. Anything else?" Shields inquired, looking down at the animal he was standing next to with renewed curiosity.

"Usually, it doesn't take too long for scavengers to locate and start feasting on something that has died out here. A free meal is a free meal, especially in the desert."

"You have a good eye, my friend." Shields squinted as he surveyed the fallen animals. "There are no signs of any scavenging whatsoever. No coyotes, cougars, ravens, or buzzards … nothing. Doesn't that strike you as strange?"

"Weird, would be a better word," Westbrook replied. "So, what do we do now?"

"I need to check out a couple of these animals and take tissue samples. Mind giving me a hand?"

Matt Shields knew his wildlife anatomy. Dropping down to his knees, the first thing he did was pry open the mouth of a male deer with his knife and look at the teeth to determine its age. What he saw made him stop for a moment, sit back on his heels, and think. Taking out a small flashlight, he leaned back down and peered into the glazed-over open eye of the dead animal. After looking at the head, Shields moved toward the rear of the animal, checking its hide, legs, hooves and then its bung.

The game warden slowly rose to his feet. He surveyed the field of death with a new sense of concern, and urgency.

Shields quietly moved from one deer to another, and then another. Within the span of about twenty-five minutes, the seasoned game warden had examined almost a dozen animals. Trent Westbrook followed along without saying a word. Shields was on to something, and he didn't want to break the trooper's concentration or impede what he was doing.

"I don't understand how this could be possible," Shields finally said, sounding a little lost while scratching his head. "These animals weren't killed by any predators or poachers that I can see ... and it doesn't appear as if they were poisoned or diseased in any way. If I didn't know better, I'd say these animals suddenly died of old age. The only question is ... why would they all be gnawing at their own hides?"

CHAPTER 9

Central Oregon Regional Medical Center
Saturday, Early Afternoon

There wasn't enough left of the body to put into a large box, let alone a body bag.

Miles Emerson just stood there, mouth agape, dumbfounded. Virginia Thompson and Michael Clark both looked pale and sullen, like they had seen a ghost. What was a warm, breathing, human being earlier that morning was nothing more than a shriveled-up pile of mummified, skeletal remains. The mess barely resembled a person, especially one who recently died. This was not only medically impossible, but also downright frightening.

As the group stood in shocked silence, Virginia Thompson cleared her throat. "I need to go to the bathroom," she matter-of-factly said. "I think I'm going to be sick!" With that remark, the chief pathologist at Central Oregon Regional headed for the door. Emerson and Clark followed her out with their gazes, then quizzically looked at one another.

"This ...," Emerson gestured toward the remains while trying to find the right words to convey his exasperation, "this ... can't be happening! I don't know of anything that could cause such rapid cellular instability and degradation, except perhaps a mix of certain chemicals and acids, which could do anything like this, especially this fast! This is totally ... totally ... inconceivable!"

"I think the term you're looking for is ... this is totally fucked up," responded the coroner. Michael Clark was not one for mincing his words. His penchant for unfiltered, glib remarks sometimes did not sit well with his listeners. Miles Emerson did not take offense to the comment. Quite the contrary, he embraced it.

"I was looking for the right expression," the good doctor replied. "You just beat me to it."

Both men involuntarily chuckled at the remark. It momentarily lifted the apprehension and anxiety both felt.

"So ...," Emerson regained his composure while trying to initiate a more productive dialog. "Any thoughts from a forensic perspective? Given your experience in dealing with all manner of death-related situations Dr. Clark, how would you call this one?" Emerson put a slight emphasis on "doctor," hoping Clark would take the hint and offer some professional, after-death insight.

Michael Clark momentarily dropped his gaze, lost in thought. After a short, reflective period, he once again looked over at the withering body before speaking.

"I've had to deal with all sorts of ugly, mind-numbing cases over the course of my career. I've autopsied burned-beyond-recognition bodies, mangled teenagers from horrific car wrecks, people who have been submerged underwater for long periods, stabbing and gunshot victims, and even a partially eaten hiker some mountain lion ambushed. I have looked at a number of elderly people who died alone and weren't discovered for days or weeks. All were senseless deaths. No one should have to die alone ... suicide probably being the only exception."

To Miles Emerson, if only for a moment, Clark had revealed something about himself. Was it empathy? Sorrow? Misgivings about his chosen profession? Whatever it was, it was uncharacteristic for the wise-cracking coroner to be so serious and reflective. Clark's last remark and doleful expression showed something deep inside had been brought to the surface.

After a short pause to collect his thoughts, Clark continued. "Death ... regardless of the cause or circumstances, is always a sad time ... for someone. Sometimes, it is expected, straightforward, and clean. Other times, just the opposite. Either way, if there are no relatives or friends to comfort the dying, grieve the loss or celebrate their life, it's as if the dead never existed at all ... and that's the real tragedy. All lives have value. It makes one reflect on our own mortality and what the end will be like. I think as we age, we tend to think more and more about death and how it will personally come about. As we lose our ability to do the things we enjoy, how will it affect our mental and physical state? Will we suffer from any one of a hundred age-related, debilitating conditions? Will we die suddenly and unexpectedly? We all know death is inevitable ... the time will come for all of us. I cannot help but think about this man ... who he was ... what he was doing to suddenly bring him to this state. I wonder if he knew he was going to die, and if this is what would become of him."

The coroner's profound remarks hung in the air like a dense fog. They also did not answer Emerson's original question. He was hoping Clark had at least a theory or two as to how something like this could have happened to their mysterious victim. He did not expect a philosophical perspective on death from, of all people, a coroner. Before Emerson had a chance to re-engage Clark on the subject, Ginny Thompson strode back into the room.

"Sorry about that, guys," was her somewhat embarrassed greeting. "My experience in working with the dead has been ... shall I say, comfortably limited. My pathology background primarily consists of looking at tissue samples to determine cause and effect. I can establish, in short order, what type of cell malignancy is present and to what extend it has spread. This case has me baffled, and it's extremely upsetting to witness what's become of this man. I'll admit, I'm somewhat overwhelmed by all of this."

"No apology necessary Doctor," Emerson said, conveying both understanding and reassurance of her professional status at the same time. "Michael and I share the same sentiment. We are at a loss as to how to explain this or how to deal with it. This defies conventional science and known medicine."

"Wait ... what did you just say, Miles?" Clark asked. "Something about conventional science and known medicine?"

"Yes, that's correct. This situation is totally 'off the reservation,' as you would say." Emerson said, half-teasing Clark. "We've encountered something here that cannot be explained by the science and the medicine we know. I think we need to look at anything and everything possible that could do something like this, even if we consider science fiction alternatives."

"You can't possibly mean alien encounters or radically-mutated new diseases ...can you?" Ginny Thompson interjected, picking up on Emerson's line of thinking.

"All I'm saying … is we have to consider what we would normally regard as impossible, improbable, or outlandish. We have to think 'outside the box' on this, because there is no known explanation for what is happening."

Michael Clark mulled over Emerson's words for a few seconds before speaking up. "So, we take a non-traditional approach to this, and everything is fair game?"

"Everything is fair game," Emerson echoed. "Let your imaginations run wild."

After a brief reflective moment, true to form, Clark came back with an offhand remark. "So, what we have here is our very own Dorian Gray scenario."

"Dorian Gray?" Ginny Thompson asked.

"Yeah, you remember. The story about this guy who sold his soul to stay young while a portrait of him aged instead," Clark answered.

"I remember that story!" Miles Emerson announced. "It was one of those freaky stories written during the Victorian era … like *Frankenstein, Dracula, Jekyll and Hyde*. When the young *Dorian Gray* finally gazed upon the old, dusty portrait, he immediately began to age accordingly while the portrait transformed back into his younger self … they switched places. The transformation killed poor Dorian. He went from a handsome young man in his thirties to someone over a hundred in a matter of minutes. I remember reading it in an English Lit class at college."

"Very interesting, but probably not germane to what's going on here. That's just a little too far 'out there' for this situation," Thompson added. "You both realize, of course, none of us were trained to deal with speculation like this and we're unquestionably in over our heads."

Both the Deschutes County Coroner and the ER doctor nodded in acknowledgement. All knew this was unchartered territory for them. They had to disregard, to a certain point, what they knew about the aging process, death, and its aftermath. To some extent, they had to disregard their medical and scientific training. They also knew time was of the essence. If an unknown killer were out there, they would need answers and fast.

"Okay, where do we start?" Michael Clark prompted.

"Let's start with what we know," Miles Emerson said, crossing his arms. "The deceased was a middle-aged, Caucasian male. He was found naked, without any identification, out in the middle of the desert. We don't know how he got there, except for the fact he was exposed to the elements and on foot for some time, given his overall condition when he was found. Other than the fact he suffered from three cardiac arrests while being transported here, that about covers it. Did I miss anything?"

"I think we have definite gaps in our known facts," Thompson interjected. "For example: have there been any missing person reports filed in the tri-county area within the past few days? What additional information can we glean from the two flight EMTs? And, probably most important, we have yet to delve into the tissue samples taken earlier. Perhaps there are some relevant clues they can provide... if they haven't dissolved into nothing themselves."

"Christ," Emerson smacked his forehead. "Why didn't we jump on that earlier? Like right after we took the samples. That's where our attention should have been! Instead, we've wasted valuable time watching the body to see what would happen to it next!"

Dr. Miles Emerson was right, and the other two knew it. Each, in their own mind, knew whatever they found in the tissue samples would be valuable information they could relay in their upcoming meeting with Dr. Parks. Now, all feared they would have nothing to show for their earlier efforts. Worse yet, the first question Dr. Parks would probably ask is what the samples showed and whether he needed to contact the authorities. They were on the hot seat and everyone in the group knew it.

Virginia Thompson felt compelled to take charge of the situation. "Miles, would you mind securing the samples in a biohazard container and bring them up to my lab? Michael and I will meet you there. We have less than forty-five minutes before our meeting with Dr. Parks, and I sincerely hope we have something informative to tell him."

All glanced up at the oversized wall clock. It read 1:49 p.m.

CHAPTER 10

Schriever Air Force Base, Colorado
Saturday, Early Afternoon

"Backskatter?" responded Maj. Jefferson. "Sounds ominous. I've never heard of it. How big was this radar station?"

Rutledge let out a heavy sigh, "Backskatter is actually the technical name for the radar system itself. It has a unique way of bouncing its signals off the ionosphere. That's why it has a range as far north as the Bering Sea, as far south as the Galapagos Islands and as far west as Midway. It can cover a tremendous amount of the Pacific sector."

The colonel couldn't tell by the expression on Jefferson's face if he was impressed by the system's capabilities or not, so he continued, answering the major's question.

"The total area of the Christmas Valley site is a little more than twenty-six hundred acres. The actual installation, with all its buildings and equipment, takes up only about a third of that ... somewhere around 460 acres. There are three large radar arrays, a variety of support buildings, living quarters, a mess hall, recreational facilities, two mobile trailers, helipads, an assortment of oversized satellite dishes, a microwave communication tower, and a large substation on the property... all surrounded by a nine-foot-high security fence."

"That's quite the complex," Jefferson said. "You said this was 'originally' built as a radar site? What is it being used for now?"

Rutledge swallowed hard, took a sip of the now-cold coffee along with another sideways glance toward Davis then continued, intentionally sidestepping the major's question for the time being.

"Actually, the Backskatter site in Oregon was only half the package. It was the principal West Coast transmission site. The receiving site, which is almost identical, was located at Tule Lake, California … outside of Alturas, just across the border. Again, in a remote desert location and on a true north-south line with the Backskatter site. Both installations were linked through a secure satellite communication system."

Colby Jefferson tried to fit the pieces together, but thanks to the colonel's little tap dance, he still lacked segments of vital information to get the total picture. He kept his poker face intact and patiently let Rutledge continue talking. Lt. Davis shifted uncomfortably in his chair.

"Both radar sites were mothballed, officially put in 'warm storage' two years ago … in 1997," Rutledge said. "The Christmas Valley site was re-activated the following year for … experimental purposes."

That revelation hit Maj. Jefferson right between the eyes. He now needed to fill in some serious gaps. He started asking Rutledge simple, direct questions. Much like what a trial attorney would do. He started with what he considered a related line of questioning, slowly building his way up to what he needed to know. "Colonel, what were 'Brett Hall' and … COTEF originally built and used for?"

Rutledge took a deep breath and exhaled slowly before answering. "I'm glad you have a 'Top Secret' clearance, Major, because what I'm about to tell you is pretty much on a 'need to know basis.' Having said that, I'm of the opinion you should have the full picture so you can appreciate our 'little' project … as well as to help us out with the problem that appears to have cropped up." The colonel looked directly at Lieutenant Davis, who now seemed to be sweating.

Jefferson nodded in acknowledgement and waited for Rutledge to continue.

"Essentially," Rutledge spoke slowly, as if to pick his words carefully, "the two, smaller central Oregon sites were actually operating in a clandestine capacity. They were performing a task critical to national security … not night vision testing or training as the public was led to believe."

"Which was…?" Jefferson clasped his hands on top of the table while leaning slightly forward toward Rutledge.

The colonel pursed his lips, almost as if he didn't want to answer. "Command and control for the Pentagon's surveillance satellites operating in the Pacific sector. The Redmond site served as the transmission site; the Bend site was the receiving one."

"They did the same duty we do here … at Schriever?" Jefferson asked.

"Yes, but those two Oregon sites were 'the' major players back in the day. When it was suspected their cover had been compromised, they were pared down and everything was transferred here to Schriever. The transition began in 1990, approximately nine years ago and the process was completed in 1997, the same time Backskatter was put into warm storage."

"I assume both of those sites were then mothballed as well … like the radar installation at Christmas Valley?"

"To a point, yes. Over the years, two of the three sites were kept at the ready and maintained by a small staff of security personnel … just in case."

"What two sites?"

"The Bend COTEF facility and the Christmas Valley radar complex," Rutledge said. "The Redmond site was turned over to the Oregon National Guard late in 1990 after everything was initially moved from there to COTEF, and then from COTEF to Schriever in 1997."

"The surviving two sites were kept at the ready 'just in case' of what, exactly?"

"Oh, an unforeseen national emergency of some kind. All three sites were pretty much self-contained, secure, had large helipads as well as hardened bunkers beneath the main buildings."

In the back of his mind, Colby Jefferson faintly remembered a rumor he'd heard years ago about the Pentagon establishing several emergency bomb shelters across the country for high-ranking government officials, but never thought anything of it at the time. "I assume, Colonel, the reason you're giving me all of this background information is because the Backskatter installation and the Bend site have something to do with your so-called Oregon Project?"

"That is correct, Major Jefferson."

"Let me further assume, Colonel, those two sites were re-activated at the same time, for the same reason: to accommodate the 'experimental purposes' you alluded to earlier?"

"That would also be correct, Major. You are very perceptive."

"But now, something has gone wrong, and you would like me to investigate what happened?"

"As I said, you're very perceptive. I need someone of your caliber to go out there, determine what went south and see what it would take to fix it. Do you think you can do that, Major?"

"Possibly. But with all due respect, sir, I'd like to know up front what is currently going on at the Bend and Christmas Valley sites before I can answer that."

Rutledge looked across the table at Davis, who had been silently sweating for the last twenty minutes while the colonel gave his history lesson to Maj. Jefferson. "You're up, Lieutenant," said the colonel. "Tell the major what he wants to know."

A nervous-looking Lt. Davis opened the folder marked "Classified: Top Secret," which he had held in a death grip ever since they arrived for the meeting. Davis quickly looked at both officers then down at his folder, slowly exhaled and started talking.

"Both of the currently active sites, which the colonel just mentioned, were re-commissioned by an Executive Order issued by President Clinton almost two years ago. As everyone knows, the president was facing possible impeachment proceedings at the time. It was also common knowledge he has never been on the best of terms with our military. To sidestep the impeachment issue, as well as bolster his relationship with the Pentagon and the Republicans, Clinton issued a special order reinstating certain parts of Reagan's 'Star Wars' program ... namely the portion that has to do with disabling incoming missiles and bombers. The initial development of the system was done at the Air Force Weapons Laboratory at Kirtland Air Force Base in New Mexico. The Christmas Valley complex, because of its location and specialized equipment, was chosen as the main test site once a working model was built. The test site is supported by the COTEF facility outside of Bend."

"This base was put in charge of this project?" Jefferson pointed down. "How did that come about?"

"The answer to that is fairly complex sir," replied the lieutenant, taking a nervous glance toward Colonel Rutledge. "As you know, all

of the units at Schriever are a part of the Air Force Space Command
... which originally had varied research roles in SDI when it was
headquartered at Wright Patterson Air Force Base in Ohio. When
parts of SDI were re-instated by Clinton, the R&D that DARPA
was previously involved in at Wright Patterson was transferred to
Kirtland. The R&D team at Kirtland was successful at developing a
prototype capable of disabling satellites, missiles, and aircraft. When
it came time to field test this system, the Backskatter site in Oregon
was deemed the perfect location because of its remoteness and
capabilities."

"I appreciate the background brief, Lieutenant ... but you still
haven't answered my original question. Why was Schriever put in
charge of this project?"

"Sorry sir. When this base was expanded, re-tasked and renamed
last year ... in addition to our primary mission, we were assigned
the additional duty of managing the Oregon Project. I assumed it
was because we are the closest classified installation of our type to
Oregon. Other than that, I really don't know why we were given this
project."

"Colonel?" Jefferson extended his hand, palm up, toward
Rutledge. Hoping he would provide the answer.

"It's called orders, Major," came the straightforward reply.
"We were assigned a special task, given the resources to do it, and
followed orders."

"I see," Jefferson, realized now was probably not the time to
press the issue. "So, can you tell me more about this 'special task'
you mentioned?"

Colonel Rutledge cleared his throat. "We were tasked to field
test and evaluate a particular type of new technology. Essentially, we
were assigned to determine its combat viability."

"Sorry to interrupt Colonel, but can you explain how a radar
system is capable of disabling an incoming missile or aircraft?"
Jefferson was not yet sure what the program was all about.

"The technology currently under testing ... is a type of pulsating,
high-energy laser emitted by a cannon-type apparatus. Because of
its extended range and other capabilities, the original OTH-B radar
array was slated to be used as the target acquisition and tracking
system. The shots, or laser bursts, are guided by part of the original

radar system ... which has been highly modified. How it does this is extremely complicated and technical ... I don't fully understand it myself."

"This system is currently being tested ... now? How?"

At this point, Colonel Rutledge decided he had probably said enough and told Jefferson the answer to that question awaited him in Oregon. Then he asked Lt. Davis to "cut to the chase" regarding the current situation. The colonel was not of a mind at this point to give away any more information on their project than they already had. Rutledge was also eager to know what had happened at Christmas Valley earlier that morning. He was hoping for something relatively minor, like a security breach with one of the scientists or a minor equipment issue like the last time.

"At approximately 0800 hours this morning, Pacific Time ...," Davis cleared his throat and again looked down at his report. "A group of Air Force technicians and civilian engineers conducted a fifty percent output test of the COIL laser. COIL stands for Chemical Oxygen-Iodine Laser ... the chemicals are the primary component for producing the laser shots. Except for the higher concentration of chemicals and energy levels involved, it was a routine test."

"And something went wrong?" interjected Jefferson, taking a quick glance at the colonel. Rutledge sat still, listening intently, waiting to see how serious the problem was.

"Yes, but we don't know exactly what," Davis replied. "Our people had been prepping for this exercise for the better part of two weeks." The young lieutenant started to tremble, and his voice was beginning to crack. "Apparently ... during the course of the test ... something went wrong, and the apparatus had a runaway and self-destructed."

"What!" Rutledge suddenly bolted upright in his chair. "There was an explosion?"

"I'm sorry, sir," responded an embarrassed Lt. Davis. "We don't have a lot of details yet, only this initial report ... which we received a little over an hour and a half ago."

"Jesus, Lieutenant. Why the hell didn't you tell me this when you called?" Rutledge demanded, his face flushing a bright red color.

"We were on an unsecured line, sir. Just like you pointed out," replied Davis.

By his reaction, Colby Jefferson gleaned this was news to the colonel. He could also see the anger quickly building in Rutledge.

"Just what in the hell do you know, Lieutenant?" The colonel, evidentially hearing all of this for the first time, looked concerned, frustrated, and obviously embarrassed.

Trying to quell the anxiety, and anger, suddenly building in the room, Colby Jefferson matter-of-factly encouraged the sullen aide to tell them what he knew about the mishap.

"That's part of the mystery," Davis said, trying to regain his composure. "There was a fairly contained explosion ... all things considered. The laser, from what we can best determine ... had an accelerated runaway, then accidentally fired several uncontrolled shots before it self-destructed. According to the initial report, it seems to have simply disintegrated ... apparently destroying the building that contains the lab, the laser itself and all of the control equipment."

"Lieutenant Davis did this information come directly from the people at the Backskatter complex?" Jefferson asked calmly.

"No, sir. It was relayed from the Christmas Valley radar site to the Bend COTEF site. COTEF generated the report and sent it to us ... which was encrypted."

"So, you're confident all of this has been kept under wraps so far?" Jefferson asked, trying to keep Rutledge at bay for the time being so he could cool off. "You're sure nothing has leaked out either internally or externally, especially in Oregon?"

"That is correct, Major." Davis nervously glanced over at Colonel Rutledge. "This has been kept totally quiet."

"That helps," Jefferson said. "When and how did the people at the COTEF site learn there had been a problem?"

"When all communication was suddenly lost between the two sites during the test and a link could not be re-established. The experiment was being simultaneously monitored at the COTEF facility."

"And then ...?"

"The commander at the Bend site immediately sent out an eight-man security team in a couple of Humvees to find out why no test results were relayed and why all communication links were suddenly severed without warning. That would be SOP, to immediately send out a team when communication is lost for some unknown reason."

"How long did it take the COTEF group to reach the radar site once they were dispatched?"

"It took the team a approximately seventy-five minutes from when they left COTEF until they reached the Backskatter complex, sir. Considering the distance they had to travel as well as some of the back roads they had to take, I'm sure they broke a few overland speed records along the way."

At this point in the conversation, Colonel Rutledge could not hold his tongue any longer and broke in. "What'd they find once they got there, Lieutenant?"

"Not much, sir," replied the harried Lt. Davis. "According to the initial report, the main gate was ajar and there weren't any security personnel around. The place looked deserted, like a ghost town. Just to be on the safe side, the team took radiation readings before entering the complex itself … which were inconclusive."

"What happened next?"

"The team methodically checked all the remaining buildings, starting with the admin building and the staff quarters. The report stated the damage was rather extensive."

"What about the staff? Our people and the scientists?"

"According to the report, and this is what really concerns me, none of the on-site personnel could be found. All the buildings they checked were empty."

"Did they check the bunker?" Rutledge demanded.

"Yes, sir," Lt. Davis replied, "but apparently the main entry was sealed off by the accident as well. If there are survivors, I assume they're trapped inside or headed to either Christmas Valley or Bend to seek medical attention."

"You said it appeared as if the equipment self-destructed," Maj. Jefferson interjected. "How is that possible?"

"We don't know," confessed the lieutenant. "The initial report given to the COTEF site from their field team was sketchy. All they said was what I've already told you."

"Did they take any pictures or videos?" asked Jefferson.

"Yes, sir, they did … but we don't have access to those yet, they're still with the on-site field team at Christmas Valley... who are currently standing down, awaiting further orders."

For a moment or two, an eerie silence fell over the room. Each one of the three officers present silently contemplated the ramifications of an accident of this size. Finally, Colby Jefferson spoke up.

"Colonel, I suspect what happened at your 'Oregon Project' is a Class A accident. That being the case, it will require the involvement of an official USAF Accident Investigation Board. Which means my participation would be a moot point."

"Major Jefferson, so far, the knowledge of this ... 'mishap'... has been confined to Oregon and to the three of us. I still want you, and Lieutenant Davis here to go out there immediately and conduct ... an 'initial' accident investigation. What you discover will determine whether a formal Air Force or Department of Defense investigation is required or not. Will that work for you?"

After a moment of concentrated thought, Jefferson nodded. "It will."

"Good. Now ... is there anything else in your report, Lieutenant?" Rutledge shifted his attention back to his aide.

"Just one thing, sir. The COTEF team reported that approximately at the same time they got to the Backskatter site, they saw an air ambulance helicopter land then take off somewhere to the north of their position."

CHAPTER 11

The High Desert & Christmas Valley
Saturday, Mid-Afternoon

"Old age?" Trent Westbrook asked. "How on earth could a whole stinking herd of deer suddenly die of old age? Don't you think that's slightly impossible?"

"By conventional standards ...yes," replied the game warden. "This is unconventional ... very strange, and very ... suspicious. Trent, let's finish up here and check out the surrounding area. Feel like hopping over to Christmas Valley? I'd like to check in with the deputy sheriff there to see if anything else like this has popped up."

"Okay by me ... we've got enough fuel and lots of daylight left. I can radio ahead to see if someone can meet us at the airport."

After Shields had made a detailed drawing of the herd and plotted their location on his map, it didn't take long for the pair to pack up their stuff and reboard the helicopter. Both were anxious to leave the field of death with its rotting animals behind. Apprehensive about the situation, neither confessed to the other how he felt about the carnage they just surveyed.

Once airborne, Trent took a southeastern heading toward the small town of Christmas Valley, some twenty-three miles away. Cruising at a speed of 70 MPH at an altitude of 1,500 feet above the ground level, they made the short, cross-country trip in less than twenty minutes.

Along their route of travel, they could clearly see some of the area's celebrated landmarks: Green Mountain then the monolithic Fort Rock off to their righthand side, Crack in the Ground just beneath them, the Four Craters Lava Beds on their left. Neither one took note, appreciated nor talked about the volcanic oddities that represented the mysterious and violent ways in which nature had shaped the land. This was not a "flightseeing" trip for tourists. They were on a mission. All things considered; the ride was subdued.

Matt Shields was deep in thought for most of the way, scanning the desert around them for any signs of more dead animals. Trent radioed ahead to the little airport's FBO. He asked the woman who responded if she would contact the deputy sheriff's office and have someone meet them when they landed. Then he asked for a standard landing advisory … which consisted of wind speed and direction, altimeter setting, known traffic, and where the operator wanted them to set down so they wouldn't affect any fixed-wing aircraft.

Located approximately 110 miles southeast of Bend in northern Lake County, Christmas Valley, although situated practically in the middle of nowhere, was originally a planned community for retirees. The remote and rural small town never did live up to its intended purpose but managed, nevertheless, to be quaint and quiet. With a fluctuating population of around 1,300 people, the community still had everything the local residents, farmers and ranchers could want. Namely, a post office, two grocery stores, three restaurants, a gas station, a small golf course, rodeo grounds, a community hall, a variety store, a multi-grade school, a medical clinic, a hardware store, a small RV park, a volunteer fire department, an airport, and, most important to many of the locals, two taverns. The median age of the townsfolk, including the area's cattle ranchers and alfalfa farmers, was fifty-four.

Deputy Mark Spenser arrived at the airport approximately ten minutes after Westbrook and Shields set down. Trent locked down the controls, spooled down the engine, waited for the engine gauges to stabilize at the bottom of the green arcs, then shut down the machine. The two had exited the helicopter and were walking toward the little airport's office when the deputy drove up.

Introductions were quickly made then Deputy Spenser asked the two visitors if they wanted to go to his office or visit where they were. Trooper Shields suggested they make themselves comfortable at a nearby picnic table, a place fairly secluded out of anyone's ear range. He wanted to keep the conversation short, professional, and private.

"Deputy," Shields began. "We are following up on a lead regarding the killing of a number of deer out in the desert. Have you had any recent reports of poaching or problems with migrating herds of deer?" Matt Shields was not going to release any more information on their discovery than necessary. He did not want to start any unfounded rumors or create a sense of panic.

"Funny you should ask," Spenser replied. "A couple of ranchers on the northern edge of the valley called in earlier today saying they just lost several head of cattle under mysterious circumstances."

"Mysterious circumstances?" Trent Westbrook asked, inserting himself into the conversation.

"Yeah, a few years back we had an incident where half a dozen cattle were slaughtered and mutilated. Everyone speculated it was done by aliens. We sometimes see a lot of strange lights in the night sky out here. Never did get to the bottom of that one. Made the locals pretty jumpy for a while. Now, it seems like whatever happened before might be making a comeback."

"The downed animals reported today, were they mutilated like the ones from before?" asked Shields.

"Nope, strange thing ... they seem to have just up and died for no apparent reason. They were found scattered about in their pastures. I sent our local vet out earlier to see what he could make of it. Haven't heard back from him yet. Were the deer you found out in the desert mutilated or butchered in some way?"

"No ... no, they weren't. Seems they died spontaneously themselves ... just like your cattle," Shields responded. He was hoping the deputy would not pursue his present line of questioning any further. He didn't want to lie to a fellow law-enforcement officer if he could help it. Especially if he was asked how many deer had perished, where they were located and what condition they were in. "Can you show us on a map where these ranches are? I'd like to take a look for myself to see if there's any connection."

"Sure, no problem," Deputy Spenser shrugged.

Trent took the cue and hustled back to the 300, fetched an FAA Sectional Chart from the map pocket in the helicopter's cockpit, and trotted back. Shields and the deputy were exchanging business cards when Trent reached them. He quickly unfolded the map and spread it out on the table in front of them.

The Klamath Falls Sectional, which Trent had on hand, covered the bottom half of Oregon and the northern part of California. A total of fifty-four sectional charts covered the entire United States. They are the primary navigational reference for pilots flying by visual flight rules or VFR. Sectional Charts were extremely detailed and showed everything from topographic and elevation information to compass headings. If the deputy could reasonably pinpoint on this two-sided map where those ranches were, Westbrook and Shields would be able to fly directly to those spots using nothing more than visual references.

After making a couple of small circles on Trent's Sectional Chart, Deputy Spencer looked up at the pair. "I would appreciate being kept 'in the loop' on this." He removed his hat, scratched his head then put the hat back on. "Ya know, this is just one more thing to add to an already strange and busy Saturday."

As the trio got up from the table, Trent took the opportunity to casually ask the deputy what he meant by the remark. Matt Shields, although seemingly preoccupied, was paying close attention.

"Well … early this morning, I got a call about some naked old guy found out in the Lost Forest. I sent out a couple of my volunteer search and rescue people to check it out. I also called in LifeAir. I guess the man died on the flight back to Bend. I phoned the hospital later and talked to the doctor in charge, but only got a couple of details about the death. The man had no ID so they're keeping him in the hospital's morgue as a 'John Doe' for the time being."

"That must have been the LifeAir flight that went over the airport this morning," Westbrook said. "Since it came in from the east, we wondered if it was a traffic accident on Highway 20 or something like that. Anything else you can talk about Deputy?'

"Oh, just a couple of calls about some overdue hunters and the usual complaints about all the noise coming from that old Air Force radar site out east."

CHAPTER 12

Central Oregon Regional Medical Center
Saturday, Mid-Afternoon

While the three doctors were downstairs conferring in Exam Room #19, Dr. Robert Parks was in his office on the second floor hitting the books.

Although his area of specialty was geriatrics, Parks was baffled by what he had witnessed and what he knew about the aging process. His practical understanding of the subject told him premature aging could be the result of a variety of things: over-exposure to certain forms of radiation, including too much time in the sun; acute and unchecked inflammation; prolonged use of various drugs and alcohol; inherited genealogy; contracted disease; genomic instability; and cellular senescence, the cessation of cellular division/reproduction. There were literally hundreds of articles, theories, and books on the subject, not to mention on-going research. Even with all that, the aging process remained somewhat of a mystery. No one knew why some people aged differently than others or how to control it.

Parks remembered an observation one of his med school professors passed on to his students. "The real 'Fountain of Youth' lies in the discovery of how the aging process actually works," the professor was fond of saying. "It is not found in cosmetic surgery." The anti-aging industry in America was big business and getting bigger by the day. It seemed everyone was trying to get in on the action. The FDA was swamped with applications and supporting test data for a variety of new drugs, cosmetics, and procedures. Looking young and healthy, apparently at any cost, was on everyone's wish list these days.

Parks recalled seeing a Robin Williams movie a few years back about a young boy whose body grew into adulthood at an accelerated rate while his mind was still that of a child. *Jack* was the name of the movie if he remembered correctly. The boy's mother gave birth to him after an unusually short gestation period. The baby grew then physically aged at a rapid rate. When the boy finally graduated from high school at the normal age of eighteen, physically he was an old man in his 70s. In the movie, the cause of his affliction was determined to be an extremely aggressive case of Werner Syndrome, aging the boy four times faster than normal.

Premature aging syndromes, also known as progeria, included a variety of rare and serious conditions. Foremost among these were Hutchinson-Gilford Syndrome, Bloom Syndrome and Werner Syndrome. Although many scientists disagreed if these syndromes were inherited or not, all agreed they were genetically caused, even if they didn't know exactly how this happened.

Premature aging was only part of the puzzle. Rapid decomposition of a body was another.

Several external and internal factors could accelerate the process: elevated environmental temperatures coupled with increased humidity. Exposure to fire, disease … especially those associated with hemorrhagic viruses, drug addiction, obesity, and advanced diabetes, among others. Even if all these factors were present, a human body would not reach the level of decomposition their victim did within a matter of hours.

After an hour of research, the exasperated doctor finally put away his textbooks and logged onto his computer. Perhaps something on the internet could provide a clue to the cause of this mysterious affliction.

～

Dr. Virginia Thompson parked her reading glasses on top of her head and peered into the double eyepiece of the Olympus BX-40 microscope.

The twenty-seven pound, four-thousand-dollar, precision instrument could magnify a human cell large enough to clearly see its various components, right down to its nucleus. The large binocular microscope, with a magnification range of 20x – 600x was perfect for pathological analysis, especially since it provided its viewer with somewhat of a three-dimensional resolution.What Thompson saw was distressing. The fast-acting degradation of the body had a similar effect on the tissue samples the three doctors had taken earlier. From what she could tell, it appeared as if the cells she examined had simply withered into a caramelized substance.

Dr. Miles Emerson busied himself running standard chemical analyses on a few tissue samples while Dr. Michael Clark scanned various slides through a separate microscope. He was using was a Zeiss Axio Imager, a polarizing light microscope typically used in the identification of tissue samples. Simply referred to as the PLM by its users, the highly technical instrument could provide key information on the morphological, optical, chemical, and physical properties of a tissue sample.

After scrutinizing four slides, Clark discovered something unusual. Perhaps it was because of his forensic training, or because he automatically looked for things out of place, or things others would typically ignore. Clark identified a phenomenon not ordinarily found in a decomposing human body.

"Hey Miles, Ginny, come take a look at this." Clark said, waving them over.

The other two doctors looked up from their work, glanced at each other, got off their lab stools and crossed the lab to Clark's station.

"Find something?" Thompson asked.

"Not sure." The coroner's frowned. "Just out of curiosity, and because I couldn't see anything I could readily identify in these samples, I set the PLM to scan for anything unusual that might be present.

"What'd you find?" Miles Emerson asked.

"I think our mystery man was the victim of some radical genomic or cellular instability… possibly triggered by some type of chemical and/or radiological combination. It almost looks like this man's cells were thoroughly irradiated in some way. Which, I might add, is something I've never seen nor heard of before." Clark shrugged. "Remember Miles suggested we need to consider any possibility ... to think outside the box? So, I came up with this theory after I identified radical DNA and RNA mutation in several of these samples."

All three doctors were aware of the consequences involving issues within a living organism's DNA or its RNA. The two complemented one another and were considered to be the single most important molecules in cellular biology. They were responsible for the storage, transfer and reading of all genetic material. Which, if not passed on during normal cell division, will result in a variety of life-ending afflictions.

"DNA mutation?" Virginia Thompson asked.

"RNA mutation as well?" Miles Emerson added.

∼

Flight EMT Jack Winters was already in Dr. Park's office when the ER doctor, hospital pathologist, and the coroner filed in at 2:35 p.m.

"Talk to me ... what have we got?" Parks asked, coming right to the point. Given the diminutive size of the office and the reason for the meeting, no one in the group felt inclined to sit and discuss the issue in a comfortable fashion.

All were solemn, serious, and somewhat at a loss for any real answers. All knew the gravity of the situation and that time was of the essence. The group stood in a loose semi-circle in the center of the office. Virginia Thompson, as the de facto leader of the lab group, spoke first.

"Just like our victim, the tissue samples we obtained earlier deteriorated at an accelerated rate." Thompson's voice displayed obvious frustration. "We can only speculate as to the cause, based upon what remained of the samples we examined."

"So ... no concrete diagnosis?" Parks asked.

"No, nothing conclusive. As I said, only speculation" Thompson said in reply, crossing her arms. "As you know, our victim experienced a somewhat atypical death, followed by an unprecedented rate of decomposition which led to a rapid and total cellular degradation ... all within a period of five hours. We 'scoped' as many of the samples as fast as possible but didn't see anything we could readily identify as to what might have caused this."

"Where you able to determine if this could have been caused by some new, as yet unidentified disease?"

"No … no we didn't, but given our collective knowledge and experience in dealing with all manner of pathogens, the samples showed no viral or bacterial signatures. There were also no signs of any malignancy. Whatever caused this, we don't think it is contagious or transmittable in any way."

"In your professional opinion," Parks asked, clasping his hands together in front of his chest, "is this something we need to alert the CDC and State's Examiner's office about?"

Dr. Thompson looked down as if contemplating the gravity of her response. "No… no I don't think so. We don't know enough about our mysterious affliction to make any kind of a call on this … yet. Considering this seems to be a solitary incident and it doesn't appear to be transmittable, perhaps we should keep this 'in house' for the time being."

The remainder of the group silently nodded in agreement and looked at the floor as if not knowing what to say or do next.

"Okay," Parks continued, shifting his feet. "Since we haven't seen nor heard of anything similar like this happening anywhere else, we have to assume this is an isolated case. I agree we need to keep this quiet and not talk about it except amongst ourselves. I don't want to create any unfounded rumors or have any number of people, especially the press, crawling all over this hospital in a panic about some sort of killer zombie disease. Everyone good with this?"

The others quickly glanced around at each other and again nodded. Having made the determination of not sounding any premature alarms, Parks was anxious to proceed to the next pressing question. "Alright, then. I appreciate your cooperation and support on this. So … any theories as to what may have caused this phenomenon?"

"Just one," Virginia Thompson gingerly offered. "Michael saw something inexplicable in several of the slides. He came to the hypothesis our victim was exposed to something which appears to have caused radical DNA and RNA mutation in his cells."

After a brief, reflective moment to contemplate what he just heard, Parks looked at her. "Walk me through how this could result in accelerated aging and decomposition."

"For starters," Thompson began, "we think whatever caused this cellular mutation was some sort of energy- or chemical-based exposure, possibly both. We can't determine what yet, but if our theory is correct … this condition began by affecting the cytosine chemical base of the cells. Because the pyrimidine coding of genetic information in both DNA and RNA was radically altered, it created a cascading effect so even healthy cells were affected and no longer capable of reproducing or dividing. The speed of the reaction was so pronounced, it automatically accelerated aging and decomposition.

"In other words," the venerated coroner added, "our man was instantly poisoned … to such an extent, his entire cellular structure, including that in his bones, started collapsing like a row of dominos."

"Jesus … is such an event even possible?" Parks goggled at his team. "This theory of yours defies conventional medicine and known science. You realize you people are talking about something right out of a science-fiction movie!"

Clark, Thompson, and Emerson couldn't help but chuckle at the remark. This was exactly the type of rationalization they had struggled with earlier. EMT Winters could only stand there in utter confusion, guessing this was some private joke between the doctors he was unaware of.

"So," Parks continued, regaining his composure, "what you're telling me is aggravated and accelerated cellular senescence is our culprit. Is that the gist of it?"

"With an undetermined, super-duper kick-start of some sort," Clark added.

After an awkward moment of total silence in the room, Parks looked over at Flight EMT Winters. "Jack, anything you can add to this? Perhaps something out of the ordinary about the circumstances of the pick-up or the flight back to the hospital? Anything at all?"

Jack Winters slowly shook his head. Not only was he dumbfounded at having witnessed what happened to his patient, he was now fighting off a growing sense of dread over what he just heard.

Dr. Parks pursed his lips and looked down at the floor, deep in thought. "Okay everyone, let's call it a day and sleep on this one. If you feel so inclined, you can continue working, but I don't see what else we can do for the time being. Remember, mum's the word on this. If you discover or think of anything else, I'll be here all day tomorrow."

Everyone in attendance slowly walked out of Parks' office and headed back downstairs, all except for Jack Winters.

He couldn't shake the notion he and Emily Spooner were the last two to have any living contact with the victim. Although Virginia Thompson had stated what happened to the man was probably not contagious, Winters stood there at the doorway looking down at his hands.

He was examining them for any signs of premature aging.

CHAPTER 13

Schriever Air Force Base, Colorado
Saturday, Mid-Afternoon

To Maj. Colby Jefferson, it looked as if Lt. Colonel T. J. Rutledge was about to blow a gasket.

He was obviously not a happy man after hearing what had become of his high profile "Oregon Project." The astute major could only imagine what a disaster like this could mean for the colonel's military career. Jefferson surmised no matter how things turned out, Rutledge would never see the eagle of a "full bird" colonel on his uniform, let alone a general's star.

Lieutenant Logan Davis wasn't faring much better. As the bearer of disastrous news to his immediate supervisor, the young officer looked like someone who had just been summarily fired. Jefferson could not help but feel sorry for the junior officer This would probably derail, if not end, his Air Force career before it really got started. The glamorous appeal of working on a "Top Secret" military project became an ugly albatross hanging around the lieutenant's neck.

Jefferson and Davis unconsciously flinched when Rutledge slammed his fist down hard on top of the table.

"God damnit!" the colonel blurted out, spittle clinging to one corner of his mouth. "I need answers ... and I need them ASAP! I want you two to in Oregon by nightfall. I'll arrange to have a plane from Peterson shuttle you out there as fast as possible and have the commanding officer at the Bend COTEF site arrange pickup and billeting. Go pack, tell your people that you're on a special TDY assignment but not where you're going, and report back to me in one hour for further instructions. Any questions?"

"Just one, sir," Jefferson quickly inserted. He still had a few gaps of information he needed to fill in while he had the opportunity. "In order for me to do my job … to do both you and this 'initial' investigation justice, I need to know who the players are. What does the chain of command look like for your Oregon Project?"

Rutledge stiffened, then quickly glanced over at his aide. Davis, in turn, dropped his gaze to the floor. To Jefferson, it was obvious the two were not sure if they should be forthcoming with this level of information. At this point, the colonel was probably in no mood for additional dialog either. The man didn't want conversation. He wanted action.

"What you're asking, Major, is strictly on a 'need to know' basis … for reasons of national security and project integrity. It is also above your pay grade. I'm sure you can understand and appreciate that."

"Yes sir, I can," replied Jefferson, not accepting the brush-off. "However, to accomplish what you have tasked me to do, I need to know who's who in this program. With all due respect, sir, I'm sure you can understand and appreciate that as well."

Rutledge winced at Jefferson's comeback. It wasn't an outright rebuke of a superior officer to Jefferson's way of thinking. He simply needed to know how the command and accountability structure worked. He wanted a clear picture of the operational side of the project. To any lawyer worth his salt, he was simply doing his due diligence.

After Jefferson's last remark, the room became deathly silent once again. Rutledge just stared at the chief of base security with a clenched jaw and pulsating temple. He wasn't of a mind to tell the major any more than he already had. Jefferson also concluded that, given the circumstances, the colonel was quickly reaching his limit of tolerance.

Jefferson's request was fair and reasonable. He sensed Rutledge knew it as well. Lieutenant Davis, to his credit, just sat there and said nothing, but was notably unnerved by the colonel's demeanor. The ensuing body language from the two men was unmistakable. Jefferson suspected there was more to this project than anyone was willing to talk about.

Rutledge took a deep breath and blew it out his nose, flaring his nostrils. "As you already know … Major," Rutledge finally said, somewhat regaining his composure, "this program was created by an Executive Order … which means the top brass and civilian leaders at the Pentagon are in on the game. After that, the 'org chart' starts with the Air Force's chief scientist at DARPA. Because we're part of Space Command, Schriever was put in charge of this one project … unfortunately, I am not privy to what other components are in the works, nor who is involved … period."

Maj. Jefferson suspected the colonel's answer was another attempt to dodge his original question. Like any good attorney, he let it ride and refocused his approach while trying to rein in Rutledge's temper. "Does this mean you, as the manager of this individual project, are the top person insofar as accountability goes?"

"Not exactly, Major," Rutledge answered curtly. "Although the two majors who are on-site at COTEF and Backskatter report directly to me, and I have autonomous oversight, I still have to follow the chain of command right on up to the two-star who's in charge of this region."

"Does this CoC also include our base commander, Colonel Kelly?"

"It does," replied Rutledge. "He's my boss and aware of all aspects of what's going on out in Oregon, but I don't exactly know where it goes from there. I'm sure you're well aware of how secret projects work in the military."

After a brief, contemplative moment to absorb what he had just been told, Jefferson decided he probably had pushed the issue about as far as he dared for the time being. He had enough basic information to start putting the pieces together and he could see the colonel's stress meter was close to being topped out.

"I am. I appreciate your candor on this matter Colonel and what information you have provided. Now it's time for me to go to work."

"Good. Now … are there any other questions … from either of you?"

The two officers stood in unison, simultaneously replying, "Sir, no sir!" "Good … you are dismissed," snarled Rutledge.

~

Tom Wangler

As soon as the pair left his office, Lt. Colonel T.J. Rutledge settled into his comfortable leather desk chair and reached for the bottle of antacids he kept in a bottom desk drawer. The revelation of what had happened earlier in Oregon and the exchange he had with Colby Jefferson quickly turned the coffee in his stomach into a percolating acid. He needed to calm himself, as well as his stomach, before he did anything else.

After a ten-minute reflective period, he picked up his phone.

His first call went to his boss, Colonel David R. Kelly, the commanding officer at Schriever AFB. Rutledge briefed his superior officer as to the nature of the incident with the Oregon Project and informed him of his recovery plan. Colonel Kelly was obviously distressed by the news and authorized Rutledge to do whatever he felt necessary to resolve the situation. He also requested updates as information became available, day or night. Rutledge concluded his call by asking his boss to give him seventy-two hours to figure out what was going on in Oregon before informing anyone else.

His next call went to the base's logistics officer. He needed the LO to put together all the necessary paperwork; travel orders, vouchers, credentials, and per diem money advances necessary for the pair to travel and operate outside their assigned area. Even on a Saturday, the captain who answered the call assured the colonel he would jump right on it.

Rutledge's third call went to the commanding officer at neighboring Peterson AFB to arrange for a C-140 JetStar to ferry his two officers to Oregon. The mid-sized executive jet was typically on 24-hour standby for any transport, scheduled and non-scheduled. With a maximum speed of 491 knots-per-hour (565 MPH), the JetStar could make the roughly 925-mile flight from Peterson to Bend in approximately two and a half hours. If Jefferson and Davis could leave within the next ninety minutes, they should be in Bend by 6 p.m. local time, just before sunset.

The colonel's fourth call went to Major Derick Roberts, the commanding officer at COTEF in Bend. Maj. Roberts and the on-site commanding officer at the Backskatter site had shared responsibilities for the day-to-day operations of the Oregon Project and reported directly to Rutledge. The colonel wanted to know if the major had any current information, which he did not.

Roberts did inform Rutledge he had dispatched all available personnel to the Backskatter site, along with a bevy of support material and supplies. Maj. Roberts wanted to take every precaution to contain the situation and maintain project security. He was also in search and rescue mode to find his missing people. They were key in determining what had gone wrong.

Rutledge appreciated the speedy response and thanked the major for his efforts. Then he briefed Roberts on what was in the works from his end. He also made the necessary arrangements to have his people taken care of while on temporary duty (TDY). Maj. Roberts assured Colonel Rutledge of his full cooperation in the matter.

Having done all that, Rutledge once again reached into his bottom desk drawer. His objective was not the oversized bottle of colorful antacids; this time he reached for his hidden bottle of Jack Daniels.

CHAPTER 14

Christmas Valley
Saturday, Late Afternoon

The flight from the little Christmas Valley airport to the north in "three-two-five Tango Charlie" was quick and straightforward.

Based upon the information provided by Deputy Spenser, Westbrook and Shields had no trouble finding the ranch they were looking for. Located approximately fifteen miles northeast of the airport in the area known as Peter's Creek Sink, the pair flew directly to the field containing the fallen cattle.

The exact location was easy to spot from the air. Dead animals were strewn all over the place.

On the northwestern corner of the field, Trooper Shields spotted three pickup trucks parked next to two of the downed animals with several people gathered around. Shields guessed the group contained the local veterinarian and several ranchers.

Trent slowly circled the area looking for an appropriate place to set down that wasn't on private property. To land in the field where the others were would be an FAA violation since he didn't have the landowner's permission to do so. He saw an unpaved county road just to the west of the field and told Shields where he intended to land.

The group of four men in the field watched the little helicopter make a slow, descending turn over them then settle onto the road a scant sixty yards away. Two people from the group walked towards the aircraft as Trent began spooling down the rotors. The pair waited on the field side of the barbwire fence while Westbrook powered down the machine to an idle. Trent asked Shields if he would check with the pair of onlookers to see if he could relocate the helicopter from the road to the field. The two ranchers were obviously surprised when a state game warden climbed out of the aircraft, grabbed a field pack, and started walking toward them.

From his view in the cockpit, Westbrook could clearly see Shields introduce himself and explain to the two men the need to move the helicopter off the road. A thumbs up signal from the game warden was all Westbrook needed. He spooled up the engine and rotors to maximum RPM, then gently lifted the helicopter back into the air. Holding an altitude of only twenty feet above the ground, Westbrook slowly air-taxied the machine over to the field and set down halfway between the fence and where the main group was assembled.

Matt Shields was already in a conversation with the two men who greeted him as they walked past the idling helicopter to where the others were standing. As soon as the rotors had spooled down and the engine temperatures had stabilized, Trent shut down the aircraft. He quickly removed his headset, unbuckled himself, climbed out of the helicopter, then started walking toward the group stationed around two dead cows. To Westbrook, the scene was eerily reminiscent of what they had seen earlier in the desert.

"Trent," Matt Shields said as Westbrook approached the group. "This is Dr. Mike McCary, the veterinarian Deputy Spenser told us about. These gentlemen are the ranchers who have lost a number of cattle within the last twenty-four hours. This is Steve White, Mike Williams, and Ronald Gilliam."

"Nice to meet you all," Westbrook shook hands with the four individuals. "I wish this could have been under better circumstances."

After the introductions, Shields turned his attention to the veterinarian as the pair moved away from the group and stood over one of the dead animals. "Dr. McCary, how many head of cattle are there like this one?"

"So far ... it looks like about a dozen," McCary said, clenching his jaw. The vet seemed genuinely distressed about the number.

"Any ideas as to what may have caused this?"

"From what I've been able to determine, all the cattle I've examined so far seem to have died fairly quickly and all from the same set of circumstances."

"Which was …?"

McCary cleared his throat and glanced at the three ranchers standing off to the side before lowering his voice. "Natural causes … old age."

"Let me get this straight. All of these cattle died at approximately the same time from the same thing … and that was old age? How can that be?" Shields was being careful not to let on he was already aware of a similar occurrence.

"That's my initial diagnosis until I can get some tissue and blood samples to the diagnostic lab at OSU."

Oregon State University, home of both a well-known agricultural-science college and the only veterinary school in the state, had a top-notch lab capable of diagnosing any one of a thousand animal diseases or conditions. "Have you already taken your samples?" Shields asked as Trent Westbrook joined them.

"Just finished … but noticed something peculiar about the condition of these animals just before you two arrived. According to these ranchers, their cattle all collapsed and died earlier this morning. By the time I arrived, they'd already started to bloat and now all of them are in the initial stages of decomposition. All of which is highly unusual for a recently-deceased animal, except for maybe in tropical climates," McCary shrugged. "I'm also at a loss to explain why they all seemed to have been chewing at themselves, like they were trying to get at something under their hides."

Shields and Westbrook looked at one another, instantly reaching the same conclusion: whatever killed the deer must have also killed the cattle. The three ranchers murmured amongst themselves after hearing McCary's last remark,

"Have you ever seen or heard of anything like this before?" Shields asked.

"No," responded the exasperated veterinarian. "This is something I can't explain …so many cattle … the same condition … and all at the same time."

"I'm sure there's some rational explanation for all this," Shields said, trying not to create undue alarm. He wanted to control the situation and not let things get out of hand.

"So, what killed them?" blurted out one of the ranchers, walking up to the three men. He seemed annoyed with the quiet discussion going on between them.

"Don't know yet." McCary said, "Hopefully, OSU can give us some answers after I get these samples to them."

"What are we supposed to do in the meantime?" One of the other ranchers asked, also joining the group. "We all have livestock roaming about. Are they in any danger?"

"No, I don't think so," McCary said. "I don't see any evidence of poisoning or anything like that. This looks like a singular, isolated incident. Again, maybe OSU can provide us with some answers. Until then, keep an eye on your livestock and let me know if anything else happens."

Dr. McCary was trying his best to reassure the ranchers their cattle were not in imminent danger, and that he would get to the bottom of what happened to them. The veterinarian could see the men were gravely concerned about their herds and, like Shields, didn't want to give them cause for panic.

McCary and Shields both knew that rumors and speculation regarding this incident would spread like wildfire through the small, tight-knit community. This could seriously complicate matters and impede their work. Before things went any further and got out of hand, Shields took the initiative and did what came naturally for a law enforcement officer.

"I'll need to get a statement and some additional information from the three of you and Dr. McCary so I can start an official investigation and file a report." Matt Shields announced as he retrieved a small, handheld tape recorder from his pack. He said he needed to interview each member of the group separately. Matt Shields wanted to get the facts, not initiate a group discussion based on wild assumptions.

While the trooper conducted his interviews, Westbrook made his way back to the Schweizer and prepped the little helicopter for flight. He went through his checklists, started the engine, and engaged the rotors as Shields was finishing up with the ranchers and the veterinarian.

Climbing back on board, the officer strapped himself in, then donned the voice-activated headset and looked over at Westbrook. "Okay, Trent. I think we've done enough damage out here for one day. Let's head back to Bend."

~

Only sixteen minutes into their flight back, Shields saw something that didn't look quite right to him.

Just to the north of Aspen Butte, he spotted a beat-up, white pickup truck pulled off to the side of a dirt road with both its doors wide open. Shields asked Westbrook to fly lower and circle the vehicle so he could take a closer look. Although it was hunting season and not out of the ordinary for a pair of hunters to abruptly pull off the road and jump out of their rig to take a quick shot, something about this picture didn't look right to the seasoned game warden. The truck appeared to be totally abandoned.

The pickup, an older model Ford, was parked at an odd angle, ready to plunge off a small embankment. Both doors had been left open as if someone were in a big hurry to get out. Shields asked Trent to slowly circle the rig so he could take pictures and record the license plate number. After a few minutes of orbiting the area, Shields had what he needed and told Westbrook he could head back to Bend.

"What do you think all that was about?" Westbrook asked.

"Remember that comment Deputy Spenser made about some overdue hunters?" Shields replied. "You never know … that could be their rig. I'll check out the license number when we land and get back to the deputy."

"Always on the job, eh?" Trent remarked.

"It comes with the badge," came the somewhat candid reply.

CHAPTER 15

Schriever Air Force Base, Colorado
Saturday, Late Afternoon

Maj. Colby Jefferson and Lt. Logan Davis met the timeline for their departure to Oregon with time to spare.

After leaving Lt. Colonel Rutledge's office, both hustled back to their quarters, packed, informed their respective workmates they were on TDY for an undetermined period but not where, then reported back to Rutledge.

Everything was ready for them. They were given their travel orders, a new set of credentials, per diem money and the latest update from Oregon. Maj. Jefferson was also issued a special American Express credit card with a ten- thousand-dollar limit.

A ride had been arranged to Peterson Air Force Base, a quick thirteen mile drive to the west. After checking in at the dispatch desk, a Master Sergeant on the flight line verified their identities, credentials, and documentation before letting them board the C-140 JetStar.

The sleek, white executive jet was "wheels up" at 1610 hours, 4:10 p.m., Mountain Daylight Savings Time.

Like any good investigator, Jefferson wasted little time in turning the two and a half hour flight to Oregon into a work session. He started by engaging the hapless Lt. Davis in idle conversation, hoping to reduce his stress level as well as glean additional information about the project.

"Tell me Lieutenant, how long have you been in the Air Force?"

"Six years, sir. Four years in ROTC at Texas A&M, and two years at Wright-Patterson."

"Texas A&M? That's a fairly prestigious school in the eyes of the Air Force. What was your degree in?"

"My major was in aeronautical science. I minored in political science."

"Sounds like an interesting combination," Jefferson, was attempting to establish a more cordial working relationship with the young officer. "Did you get good grades?"

"I was in the top ten percent of my class, sir."

"Excellent … and please, Lieutenant, call me Colby when there's just the two of us. May I call you Logan?"

Lt. Davis was both surprised and happy with the comment. His entire exposure to the Air Force, even during his ROTC days, was one of military formality and customs. This was especially true in his brief time with Lt. Colonel Rutledge, who insisted on always being saluted and addressed formally, sometimes to excess.

"I … I guess that would be okay sir. Just as long as it's between the two of us."

"Of course. Where is home for you and how did you wind up in Texas?

"I'm originally from Las Vegas, A&M offered me a scholarship. I was also impressed with their ROTC program."

"What made you want to join the 'Boys in Blue'?"

"Our home in Vegas was just a stone's throw away from Nellis Air Force Base. Every day, I watched those big, bad beautiful jets come and go… they were absolutely amazing. Whenever the base had an open house, I always talked my parents into taking me there. I guess I was in love with the Air Force long before I decided to join."

"So … how did you come to be a 'ground pounder' instead of a pilot?"

"I couldn't pass the vision exam for a fighter pilot and flying something else didn't appeal to me, so I went into administrative work."

"Sounds like you made a good choice despite your initial disappointment," Jefferson said. "Your story sounds similar to mine. I couldn't pass the eye exam either. Oh, how I would have loved to be at the controls of an F-15 or a Falcon. With my background, it came down to either security work or being a JAG officer. Since being a lawyer for the Air Force didn't seem as exciting as security work, well … here I am."

"Sounds as if you made a good decision as well, sir."

Now that an initial level of mutual respect and rapport had been built between the two, Jefferson decided this was as good a time to set some ground rules.

"Logan, I want you to know up front that I appreciate your helping me out on this and I will not betray anything of a confidential nature you share with me. I consider your participation in this investigation as being vitally important. I regard you as an equal and a valuable member of this team. We'll need to work together and support one another to find out what happened to your project and why. That being said … I also need to know I can trust you, unconditionally, on what develops from here on out. I don't like being second-guessed, thrown under the bus, or ratted out … especially to the likes of someone like T. J. Rutledge. Do you think you can do that?"

The major's words were like music to the young lieutenant's ears. In his brief time working for Rutledge, he came to regard his superior officer not as an officer and a gentleman, but as an egomaniacal asshole who had little regard for subordinates. Now, here was an officer who knew how to treat his men … with dignity and respect. Davis took an instant liking to the major.

"Yes, sir," enthusiastically replied the lieutenant, "it will be my privilege to work with you, sir."

For the remainder of the trip, Jefferson tapped into the young officer's knowledge concerning everything he knew about the Oregon Project. For starters, he learned Rutledge was not the first choice to head it up. Davis didn't know who was originally slated as the manager, nor how the colonel ended up with the job. The major also learned Rutledge suffered from PTSD, probably a result of his time in Iraq. He was also considered to be somewhat "unstable" by several of the officers at Schriever, an opinion shared by Davis as well.

Jefferson learned the project was extremely well-funded and deemed of "highest importance" by the Air Force and Joint Chiefs. It was one of the top projects on DARPA's list per President Clinton's Executive Order. How the likes of T.J. Rutledge ever became the manager of such an important project was a mystery to Jefferson.

That was a question he hoped to answer during the course of his investigation.

Although Lt. Davis tried his best to explain some of the technical and operational details of the project, most of it was still way over Jefferson' head. He did manage to comprehend the basic principles of how the COIL laser worked. It was a complicated, dangerous process. One which lent itself to all manner of unforeseen problems.

Chemical-based lasers, Jefferson learned, had been under development since the 70s, long before Ronald Reagan instituted his "Star Wars" program. Their unique ability to store extremely high levels of energy while readily disposing of waste heat provided the perfect combination for a new generation of defensive weapons. The ability to shoot down incoming ICBM missiles, bombers and the like while still over an ocean was considered a distinct advantage in the event of war.

Theoretically, creating a high-powered laser blast capable of shooting down something traveling at a high rate of speed seemed to be doable. The engineering challenge lay in the ability to safely control the chain reaction that generated the excited molecules of oxygen and iodine, channeling them through an optical resonator, then firing the weapon. The resulting pulsating blasts were similar to bullets being fired from a machine gun; except they were "bullets" of highly concentrated light with almost infinite range. Jefferson had to admit the extent of his knowledge regarding lasers was limited to the lights at rock concerts and cat teasers. He made a mental note to learn all he could about this innovative technology while in Oregon.

Davis explained there was more to it than just creating a high-powered laser shot. Target identification, acquisition, tracking, and engagement was a straightforward affair. That technology had been around for two decades. The problem was in marrying up the two, distinctly different technologies into one functional system.

Evidently, the technicians, engineers, and scientists had found a way to successfully use the original Backskatter radar for identifying potential targets and acquiring them at long range. Developing a reliable way to track and engage the targets with a killer laser shot was still a work in progress, hence the field testing in Oregon.

To Colby Jefferson, all this definitely fell into the realm of "rocket science." It was extremely complex technology. One, which he surmised, needed a great deal of safeguards and failsafe measures.

Jefferson asked the lieutenant about the previous issues they experienced with the project. Davis started with the logistical problems they encountered in getting everything into place so work could begin. Due to the project's classified and secretive nature, all the equipment, personnel and supplies had to be acquired, then shipped piecemeal to Bend and Christmas Valley. This was done in a way that would not arouse suspicions or give the orbiting Soviet spy satellites something to photograph.

During this same period, a certain amount of remodeling and new construction work at the Backskatter site also had to take place. The building that contained the original radar equipment had to be enlarged and updated to accommodate the COIL laser system, plus the control lab. Additionally, two new buildings had to be constructed to accommodate the staff, provide office space, and create a secondary lab. The original perimeter fence had to be upgraded along with the installation of additional security measures. Large generators were brought in to handle the extra power requirements, which in turn required a total upgrade of the installation's substation and main electrical systems.

No local contractors were used during this period. All the construction workers, technicians and materials were brought in from the outside by DARPA and the Air Force. It took almost a year of planning and over a year of construction to get everything in place before any experimentation could begin. As to be expected, nothing went according to plan. The timeline called for the project to be up and running within a year. It took almost two.

"Is there anything else I should know," Jefferson asked of the boyish lieutenant. "Anything at all?"

"I have told you everything I know," Davis said. "I'm not privy to a lot of what's going on … I don't think Colonel Rutledge wants me to have the full picture. He even 'cautioned' me on what I should and should not be telling you."

"I appreciate your candor Logan … perhaps we can fill in some holes about this project together."

"Roger that, sir."

For the remaining time they were aloft, Colby Jefferson consulted one of the Air Force manuals he brought along. Aptly titled "AFI 51-503," the thick manual contained "Air Force Instruction" on the conduct of investigating mishaps, accidents, and the reporting of such. It didn't take long for the astute major to realize he would be working in an extremely thin "gray area" when it came to conducting Rutledge's "preliminary accident investigation." To his mind, if what happened in Oregon was as bad as Lt. Davis described, not only would the Air Force want to conduct a full-blown accident investigation board of its own, but so would the Department of Defense and possibly even Congress itself. Jefferson knew he had to conduct a thorough investigation into all the facts and circumstances surrounding this incident. What he came up with could either stop the probability of a long and involved inquiry or justify initiating one.

As the C-140 descended and made its approach to Bend's municipal airport, Colby Jefferson adjusted his watch to the local time. It was now 5:30 p.m. PDST. They had made the trip from Colorado to Oregon in just under two and a half hours.

Jefferson tightened his seat belt and tried to relax. His mind raced, subconsciously attempting to sort out everything he now knew about the Backskatter project. He had a thousand-and-one missing pieces of critical information and he dwelled upon what could have possibly happened to all those people who were at ground zero.

CHAPTER 16

Bend Municipal Airport
Saturday, Late Afternoon

The high-pitched whine of the inbound JetStar immediately captured the attention of both Trent Westbrook and Matt Shields.

The two had just exited the S-300 and stood talking in front of its bubble canopy while waiting for a fuel truck to arrive. The Lockheed jet was quite the sight as it made its final approach to runway "Three-Four." With its flaps and landing gear fully extended, all landing lights on, and accompanying noise level, the C-140 was one impressive airplane as it came in for a landing.

Because the threshold of "Three-Four" was on the south end of the airport and only one hundred yards away from Orion Air's helipads, Westbrook and Shields had a front row seat to the aircraft's approach and touchdown. It was unusual for a jet of its size, especially one with Air Force markings, to land at the small municipal airport.

"There's something you don't see every day," remarked Shields. "Or do you? I don't spend enough time out here to know if that happens every once in a blue moon or not."

"This is a first for me," Westbrook replied. "Typically, a jet like that would land at Redmond … Robert's Field has much longer runways and an isolated tarmac for government use. That's where the Forest Service has its tanker and smoke jumper base."

Chance Barclay, inside Orion Air's hangar, had heard when his partner and the Trooper returned from their flight to the desert. Helicopters were not quiet machines when making a landing approach. Becky Irwin had long since gone home, and Barclay was putting the finishing touches on the cleanup of the MD 500 when he heard the jet's approach. He stopped what he was doing and walked out of the closed-up hanger to the helipad, joining Westbrook and Shields.

The three watched as the pilot of the C-140 skillfully touched down just after crossing the threshold markings at the end of the runway then immediately reversed the thrust of its Pratt & Whitney engines and raised the flaps. This was a standard landing technique to "unload" or reduce the lift on the wings and transfer the aircraft's weight to the landing gear, causing a breaking action. The pilot also lightly applied his breaks, which got more robust as the end of the 3,459-foot runway rapidly approached. The high landing speed of the jet would carry it the full length of the runway.

The combination of the three actions quickly slowed the aircraft and it stopped a scant 150 feet short of the end of the runway. There was little room for error in this landing.

Once it was stopped, the pilot applied power to the twin engines on the starboard side of the fuselage and slowly turned the jet around and began "back taxiing" on the main runway to the ramp area. The jet was too large to use the airport's narrow taxiways, so it used the main runway instead. The three men watched as the aircraft turned off the runway, crossed the taxiway and came to a stop on the vacant east side of the ramp area. With its engines running at idle, the jet's stairway door popped open, and two men disembarked with their bags. They immediately crossed the tarmac to the parking lot, met by two men in uniform, got into a waiting SUV, and quickly left the airport heading south.

Having disgorged its passengers and closed back up, the C-140 pilot spooled up its engines and moved back toward the runway. Taxing once again on the main runway, it slowly worked its way to the south end of "Three-Four" then again, turned and came to a stop facing north. While "standing on the breaks," the pilot quickly ran up the four engines to an ear-piercing scream, creating a sizable dust cloud that billowed off the end of the runway behind them. When the pilot released the breaks, the jet leapt forward as if catapulted off a carrier's deck and raced down the runway. It was airborne and making a steep climb out in less than twenty seconds. The group watched the impressive takeoff from their vantage point and saw the

JetStar make a wide, right-hand climbing turn then slowly disappear to the southeast.

"Wow!" The game warden said. "This is like going to an airshow! Have you ever seen anything like that at this airport?"

"Nope ... never." Trent Westbrook was in as much awe as Shields. "I wonder what all that was about."

"That ... gentlemen ... was a C-140 JetStar," offered Chance Barclay. "It's typically used for transporting high-ranking military and civilian officials around the country. What it's doing here and with those two Air Force boys is anybody's guess."

"Matt, I'd like you to meet my partner, Chance Barclay. Chance, this is Officer Shields of the Oregon State Police."

Just as Westbrook was introducing the state trooper to Barclay, the fuel truck arrived. Westbrook excused himself from the group and walked over to where the truck was holding station. Trent instructed the operator on how much fuel he wanted in the Schweizer, then walked back over to Shields and Barclay. All three casually walked back toward Orion's hanger.

Walking through the hanger and past the now spotless 500, the group made their way to the office area. Once inside, Westbrook asked the game warden if they could share what they had discovered out in the desert with Barclay. Shields said that would be okay but requested the two not talk of the matter to anyone else. He emphasized he was conducting an official investigation into the afternoon's events which required confidentiality. Both pilots readily agreed.

Shields pulled out a notebook and the small tape recorder from his pack as all three sat down at the small conference table. The game warden had been taking a great deal of notes and recorded statements during the day. He wanted to add anything else Barclay and Westbrook could think of while visiting.

Shields began the conversation by again, cautioning the two on the sensitive nature of what they were about to discuss, then he reviewed everything that had happened out in the desert and at Christmas Valley. Understandably, Chance Barclay had a few questions, none of which either Shields or Westbrook had answers for.

To all three men, this was a bona fide mystery. Something out in the desert had systematically killed a number of wildlife and cattle without provocation or cause. Although the locals may want to believe extraterrestrials were involved, it was an opinion not altogether shared by the three men. Shields was at a loss to explain how so many animals could just suddenly up and die of old age at approximately the same time and in the same general area.

Then Matt Shields suddenly remembered the marooned truck and the overdue hunters.

The game warden asked if he could use a phone to call his office. He needed to find out who owned the truck as well as to check back in with Deputy Spenser. It only took a minute for the person on the other end of the call to verify ownership and address for the vehicle. It was registered to a man from Christmas Valley.

Shields checked his watch. It was now 5:59 p.m. He quickly called Deputy Spencer and relayed the news. Spencer confirmed that the truck did indeed belong to one of the overdue hunters, who went out early that morning with a friend, someone also reported overdue. Because the location of the truck was just across the county line and now in Deschutes County, Spencer asked the trooper if he could notify the local sheriff's department of the situation.

Although the deputy said he planned to send out a couple of his own search and rescue volunteers, Deschutes County had a much larger and better equipped volunteer group, and they would probably want to send out a team of their own. Daylight was now a key factor. Sunset would occur in twenty minutes, at 6:20, with nightfall happening approximately fifty minutes after that. Any search and rescue teams sent out now would probably be searching in the dark, not a good set of circumstances for anyone.

With only one and a half hours of daylight remaining, Westbrook and Barclay decided on the spot they would be willing to assist with their helicopters. Following that offer, Shields made two quick calls. One to the dispatcher at his office, and the second to the Deschutes County Sheriff's office. Both parties understood the urgency of the situation and authorized Shields and Orion Air to immediately begin an air search. Shields gave the boys a thumbs up while still talking to the dispatcher at the sheriff's office.

Trent Westbrook and Chance Barclay hustled back out into the hanger. They did quick preflight checks on "three-two-six Charlie

Bravo" then pulled it out of the hanger. Both agreed the MD-500 would be best for the job, considering its speed and ability to carry more people than the 300. It was also fully fueled.

The initial plan was to put Barclay at the controls with Shields sitting in the front along with him. The rear passenger seats would be occupied by Westbrook on one side and a Deschutes County Search and Rescue observer on the other. The four sets of eyes, instead of two, gave them the best chance of locating the missing hunters before nightfall.

By the time they were ready to go, a pickup truck screamed up to the hanger and a volunteer searcher climbed out. After a quick round of introductions and safety briefings, Westbrook helped the trooper and the volunteer into the helicopter, got them strapped in, then gave them instructions on how to use the voice-activated headsets. Chance Barclay had already started the aircraft's engine and was going through his run-up checks when the three got onboard.

Once all of his engine instruments settled into their green arcs, Barclay wasted little time in getting the helicopter airborne and headed southeast. He took note of the time, 6:32 p.m. He estimated a flight time of approximately fifteen-to-twenty minutes to reach the site of the abandoned truck. They would have approximately one hour of twilight to search before it got completely dark.

CHAPTER 17

COTEF & The High Desert
Saturday, Early Evening

Two security guards met Colby Jefferson and Logan Davis at the airport.

The two men introduced themselves and asked their visitors for their identification. Quickly verified, the four men got into the black SUV and sped out of the airport's parking lot heading south on Powell Butte Highway. At the intersection of U.S. Highway 20, the driver took a left turn and headed east toward the desert. At the nine-mile marker, the driver turned east onto Dodds Road and proceeded approximately one-quarter mile to the unmarked entrance to the COTEF facility. The two guards in the front kept silent for the entire trip. Maj. Jefferson and Lt. Davis were just as quiet. Both were checking out the high desert landscape as the miles sped by.

The SUV stopped at a checkpoint gate one-third of the way down the 300-yard-long driveway where credentials were shown and authenticated before the group was allowed to continue to the parking area.

What they saw upon exiting their ride impressed both Jefferson and Davis. Before them stood a massive, nondescript two-story building. The steel-framed, concrete-walled facility was what one would expect of a classified military installation.

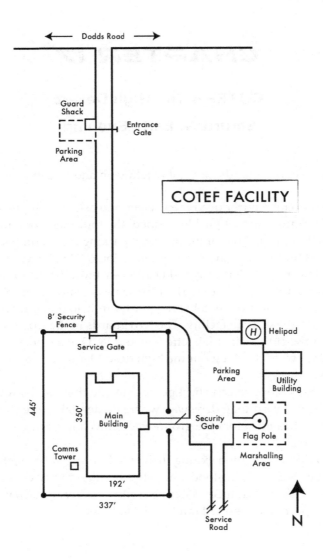

Surrounded and partially hidden from the highway by a forest of Juniper trees, the structure looked impenetrable. Oriented on a north-south axis, the immense drab-colored building was surrounded by a formidable chain link fence topped with razor wire and security cameras. A tall tower, complete with several microwave communications dishes loomed above the structure on its southwest corner. Except for the main entrance area on the structure's east side, the building was windowless.

The parking area where they exited the SUV was bordered on the east side by an equally impressive equipment storage shed and garage. To the south was a landscaped marshalling area complete with a flagpole, lawn, and picnic tables. To the north was an empty, cordoned off helipad.

Their two greeters quickly walked them inside after stopping at the main gate of the building's perimeter fence. Maj. Derick Roberts, COTEF's on-site commander, waited for the pair as they entered the front lobby area. After introductions, the major and his two guests went directly to the facility's conference room. Two enlisted airmen took charge of their bags and quickly disappeared down a long hallway.

Four people waited for them in the conference room. Jefferson looked at the sullen faces. One man was not in uniform; the other two men and a woman all wore Air Force uniforms. To Jefferson, the atmosphere in the room was what one would expect at a funeral, as if everyone were still in a state of shock.

A visibly shaken Maj. Roberts introduced himself and the others to Jefferson and Davis. The uniformed people all sat next to one another, two wearing the rank insignia of captain, the third and only woman in the group was wearing the bars of a 1st Lieutenant.

Jefferson guessed the remaining individual, a middle-aged man dressed in civilian attire, was someone in the intelligence community. Maj. Roberts simply introduced him as a "project advisor."

Once seated around the oversized, oval-shaped conference table, Colby Jefferson came right to the point. His and Davis' reason for being there was to conduct a preliminary accident investigation. They were sent to determine the extent of the damage, what went wrong, account for their missing people, and learn what it would take to get the project back on course. Based on their findings, a more comprehensive investigation may or may not be done by an official accident investigation board. Colonel Rutledge would be making that call depending on what he and Lt. Davis discovered on this trip. Col. Rutledge expected a detailed report, and time was of the essence. They had seventy-two hours, three days, to come up with their preliminary findings.

Jefferson asked for the current situation was the radar site. Maj. Roberts stated he had dispatched all available personnel to Christmas Valley, along with a bevy of support equipment, just before noon. A caravan of two Humvees, a communications/command vehicle, a field medical unit, and a utility truck loaded with provisions reached the site around 1300 hours (1 p.m.). Including what was left of the original group sent out, the number of people on site at the Backskatter complex totaled twenty-one people. Two had returned to COTEF shortly before the larger group was sent out. One of those individuals was the captain in charge of the first responders, now sitting across the table from Jefferson.

Maj. Roberts explained that his priority, when it appeared the test had gone sideways, was to immediately get a detail to the site, secure it, determine the status of the staff, then report on the extent of the damage. After receiving the initial report from the field, his second priority was to notify Colonel Rutledge and dispatch the larger contingent. He wanted to fortify the first group and expand the search and rescue efforts. Roberts hoped that by sending out all those vehicles into the desert they didn't attract too much attention. There were already one too many conspiracy theories floating around regarding COTEF.

Jefferson listened to Maj. Roberts' briefing without interruption. He wanted the major to continue, unabated, hoping to pick up on any tidbits of select information of which he was unaware. Roberts did not provide any. He did however, occasionally glance at the civilian sitting at the far end of the table, as did the other three officers. Lt. Davis also noticed that but said nothing.

"Any word on the staff?" Jefferson finally asked.

"No … not as of an hour ago," replied Roberts. "We are in constant communication with the on-site teams, but they have not found anyone. Only scattered articles of clothing and other debris."

"Are they digging through the rubble?

"They have managed to search all of the buildings left standing and the remains of those destroyed. The field team is now in the process of clearing the entrance to the bunker."

"Major, how long can someone survive down there?"

Roberts took a deep breath and glanced around the room. "If the life-support equipment is functioning properly, they could conceivably survive down there for up to six months."

"If the equipment fails?"

Roberts grimaced. "Twenty-four hours ... max."

Jefferson checked the time on his watch before speaking, "I think getting into that bunker and checking to see if any people are in there ... hopefully alive and well ...should be our first priority now."

Everyone in the room nodded in agreement, including the "project advisor" sitting by himself at the end of the table.

After concluding his briefing, Roberts asked Jefferson what he and Lt. Davis would like to do next.

To proceed with the investigation, Jefferson said he needed to first, interview everyone at COTEF who were directly involved with the project. He also needed to visit with every member of the on-site team who first responded to the accident, as well as their relief people. He wanted to start immediately, within the hour, and continue late into the night if need be.

Jefferson asked Maj. Roberts if he could arrange for a helicopter to fly him and Davis out to the Backskatter site first thing in the morning. He concluded his remarks to the group by expressing his gratitude for their hospitality as well for their help and support. He stressed they were all on the same team and it was in everyone's best interest to help him find out exactly what happened. In doing so, he had tacitly set the expectation he would accept nothing less than total cooperation from everyone at COTEF. Colby Jefferson left no doubt in anyone's mind he was in charge of this investigation. He also left the distinct impression he was someone not to be taken lightly.

Jefferson asked if he and Lt. Davis could be shown their quarters, where they could get something to eat and where he could make a call. He declined the typical courtesy tour of the facility, at least for the time being. He needed to report back to Colonel Rutledge and let him know they were at the COTEF facility and had started their inquiry. Before being escorted out of the room, Jefferson also asked Maj. Roberts if he would set up an interview schedule beginning with the Air Force people present. He asked for one-hour blocks of time starting in sixty minutes, 1900 hours, 7:00 p.m. He planned on working late.

~

Chance Barclay pushed the MD 500 to its limit, wanting to get out to the desert as fast as possible while they still had light. He didn't waste time gaining altitude after takeoff. Keeping the helicopter speeding along at a scant 1,000 feet off the ground, he gave his passengers a thrilling twilight ride.

Next to him in the front sat Trooper Shields, on the aircraft's right side. In the back seat on the left side, directly behind Barclay, was the Deschutes County Sheriff's SAR volunteer. On the right side, behind Shields, sat Trent Westbrook.

Both Shields and the SAR volunteer had special hand-held radios so they could stay in contact with their respective agencies. Shields was talking to the dispatcher at Bend's State Police office while the volunteer spoke to both his dispatcher and the deputy sheriff at Christmas Valley. That deputy, in turn, was in communication with the two groups of search and rescue volunteers he sent out earlier.

As Barclay crossed Highway 20 and the large Central Oregon Irrigation Canal at milepost 7, he could clearly see the red warning beacon atop COTEF's communication tower off to his eleven o'clock position. Like many Central Oregonians, he wondered what was really going on at this secretive military facility. Conspiracy theories of all kinds had been circulating ever since COTEF and its sister complex in Redmond were built. *Perhaps we'll never know,* he mused as he flew on.

With a top speed of 175 MPH, the MD 500 made the thirty-six-mile trip from Bend to the site of the abandoned truck in less than fifteen minutes. The flyers arrived on site looking for any signs of the missing hunters by 6:50 p.m. Barclay and company had approximately one hour before it got completely dark. At least now that the sun had set, they wouldn't have to worry about missing something hidden in the shadows. There weren't any.

Starting with the truck directly beneath them, Chance Barclay started a clockwise search pattern. With each circle he made, they got farther out from the truck. Barclay kept his airspeed at an even thirty-five knots, approximately forty MPH, in an effort to keep the helicopter as level as possible, thus giving all three of his observers ample opportunity to scan the area on both sides of the aircraft.

After twelve minutes of flying in ever-widening circles, Trent Westbrook spotted something off to their right-hand side and asked Barclay to orbit the area at a lower altitude. There, on a patch of open ground, everyone on board could clearly see what Westbrook had observed.

"What the hell?" Trent Westbrook said into the voice-activated headset.

"Looks like clothing … hunting clothing. See the orange vests?" Shields pointed.

"I see rifles and packs over on this side," added the volunteer searcher sitting behind Barclay.

"But no hunters?" Barclay asked. "Anyone see anything that remotely resembles a man?"

"Nope, nothing here," Westbrook replied, straining his eyes in the fading light.

"Nothing here either," added the volunteer.

"It's getting harder to see the ground," Shields said. I wish I'd brought a spotlight or something."

"CB, turn on the landing light." Westbrook suggested to his partner. "That should give us enough light to check things out."

Barclay tapped one of the little side buttons on the cyclic control handle. A wide beam of bright white light suddenly illuminated a large oblong-shaped patch of ground in front of them. Swinging the aircraft around and holding it in a hover about 200 feet off the ground, all could now clearly see the scattered clothing below. The collection of articles included hats, hunting vests, guns, packs, and to everyone's surprise … boots.

"Do you see what I see?" Barclay asked over his headset.

"This is really strange," Matt Shields said. "I've never heard of a hunter stripping down and then abandoning everything, including his gun if he's lost. Something else is going on here!"

"Pretty hard to get lost out here," Westbrook added. "There are lots of landmarks, and if these are the two missing hunters from Christmas Valley, they should know their way around this country even in the dark."

"I'm going to call this in," remarked the volunteer observer. "Hopefully, the ground team sent out from Christmas Valley is somewhere in the vicinity and can check this out."

"Chance, can we land somewhere around here?" Shields asked. "I think we need to take a closer look before calling in the calvary."

Westbrook answered. "It's almost dark, and I don't believe anyone brought a flashlight. I think we should mark this spot on our GPS, pass the information along to the ground search teams, and head back."

"Trent's right guys," Barclay said, "If I land close enough to keep the 'copter's landing light on this spot everything will get blown all over the place ... along with any clues as to what may have happened here."

"You're probably right," Shields admitted. "Let's report this and head back. I can work with both sheriff's departments tomorrow if the ground teams come up empty tonight."

Chance Barclay punched the locater key on his dash-mounted GPS, marking the latitude and longitude coordinates of the spot. Then he wheeled the helicopter around in a climbing turn back toward the northwest. Both the game warden and the SAR volunteer quickly contacted their people on their handheld radios to let them know what they had discovered and where.

As they climbed skyward and the distant lights of Bend illuminated the horizon, a nagging thought kept crossing the mind of Matt Shields. He couldn't imagine why someone would strip off all their clothes ... especially their boots, then leave them out in the middle of nowhere.

CHAPTER 18

Bend & COTEF

Saturday Evening

For a Saturday night, Central Oregon Regional Medical Center was unusually quiet. They did not have the usual number of inpatients to care for, nor were there any emergencies or the typical number of weekend calls at the ER. All things considered; it was almost too quiet.

Although Doctors Thompson, Emerson, and Clark had long since called it a day, and Jack Winters' ten-hour shift had ended over two hours ago, Dr. Robert Parks was still on the job. Even though Virginia Thompson and the others had assured him they didn't consider what happened to their mystery man to be contagious, Parks was still very much concerned. He had something that resembled the remains of a recently deceased, elderly man down in the morgue without any real explanation as to what happened to him. Parks couldn't shake the sinking feeling he hadn't seen the last of this.

After additional research and pouring back over his notes, he too decided it was time to go home. Parks checked out with the night security officer then strolled through the ER on his way out to the employee's parking lot, saying goodnight to any staff member he encountered. Passing through the lobby of the ER, he took note of the time on the large wall clock next to the reception desk, it read 7:08 p.m. Thanks to the puzzling affliction his staff had to confront, Parks had just put in an exceptionally long twelve-hour day.

~

The security guard stationed outside of the conference room escorted Colby Jefferson and Logan Davis to their quarters.

He led them down one hallway, turned at an intersection and went down another. To the two officers, this place was a maze of connecting hallways, offices, workstations and sleeping quarters. Along the way, their escort pointed out the officer's latrine where they could "utilize," shower and clean up. They were also shown where the "DFAC," or dining facility, was located if they wanted to get something to eat.

Jefferson's sharp eye caught a separate, elevated section with thick steel doors sealing it off from the rest of the facility. It was basically a building within a building. The heavy steel doors were all closed, posted with "Authorized Personnel Only" signs along with a keypad entry system. Two armed guards patrolled the area. Jefferson could only guess what was going on behind those closed doors and wondered why so much extra security.

The two officers were assigned a single oversized room that had two beds, with one nightstand between with a lamp, two small desks, and two standing lockers. All drab, military-issued equipment. Lt. Davis remarked the place reminded him of his first year's dorm room at Texas A&M. Their ever-present escort seemed unamused by the comment.

Once the pair had unpacked, which took all of ten minutes, Jefferson asked where he could use a phone, preferably one with a secure line. Their escort showed Jefferson to a small office next to their quarters that had been specifically set aside for their use. The small room had a standard-issue metal desk, a desk lamp, desk chair, two side chairs, a phone, computer, and a small corner workstation with a typewriter.

Jefferson was given the keys to their quarters and the office, then was instructed on how to use the facility's phone system. Their escort excused himself then shut the door behind him. The major immediately placed a call to Lt. Colonel Rutledge at Schriever and updated him as to their status as well as the current situation at Backskatter. Once that little chore was completed, Jefferson joined Davis in the DFAC for a meager meal of soup and salad, leftovers from the staff dinner served earlier that evening. After they finished, the same security guard escorted them back to the conference room.

Jefferson planned to ask Maj. Roberts if a chaperone would be the norm for their entire time at COTEF. He was not used to being "shadowed" like this while at a military installation.

Maj. Roberts waited for the pair outside the conference room. Roberts asked his guests if their accommodations were all right, if they had the opportunity to check in with their boss, and if they got something to eat. Jefferson again thanked the major for his hospitality, assuring him everything was fine. Then he asked Roberts about their escort and if he had acquired a helicopter for the following morning.

~

Chance Barclay gingerly set down the MD-500 on Orion's #1 helipad, turned off its bright landing light, locked down the controls, then spooled down the aircraft's turbine engine.

Once the rotors had slowed and the engine had cooled off enough, Barclay shut down the machine. Though the rotors were still turning, all four individuals removed their headsets, unbuckled themselves then climbed out of the helicopter. The Deschutes County Sheriff's SAR volunteer and Matt Shields both commented that climbing down from the 500 was a challenge, especially since both missed the booster step getting out. Trent Westbrook couldn't help but chuckle. The deputy and the trooper were not the first passengers to experience the challenge of getting in and out of the 500, especially since it sat almost three feet off the ground because of its tall skids.

While Westbrook and the two law enforcement officers visited a safe distance away from the slowing rotors of the helicopter, Barclay stood next to the machine filling out the aircraft's logbook using the floorboard of the pilot's station as a desk. He took note of the time, now 7:55 p.m. Their flight to and from the desert, plus their search time, accounted for approximately one hour and twenty-three minutes. With almost thirty minutes for travel time, their search time was calculated to be fifty-one minutes.

By comparison, Barclay guessed it would take the two groups of volunteers from Christmas Valley almost an hour of driving just to get to the abandoned truck, let alone conduct any type of search.

Both Shields and the volunteer searcher commented to that same fact when Barclay mentioned what they had accomplished in less than ninety minutes with the aid of a helicopter. True to his subtle nature, Barclay never passed up the opportunity to promote their business.

It was too late in the day to order fuel for the helicopter, so instead of standing around waiting for a fuel truck, the group continued their discussion inside Orion's hanger.

"So ... what happens now?" Westbrook casually asked the state trooper as they walked inside.

"I've got a lot of paperwork to do," Shields said, "but first, I think I need to visit with Deputy Spencer out in Christmas Valley as well as help our volunteer here brief the local sheriff's search and rescue people. I also need to get the tissue samples we took off to the state crime lab ... looks like I'm going to have a busy week."

"Do you think you'll be needing our services again in the next couple of days?"

"Hard to say. That depends on what the Christmas Valley boys find tonight and what my supervisor wants to do next."

"Well ... if you need us, we're here," added Chance Barclay joining the group. "This has been quite the day, and we've enjoyed working with you and our volunteer here."

Matt Shields returned the gesture. With a handshake to both Westbrook and Barclay, he walked out of the hanger toward the parking lot with the sheriff's SAR volunteer in tow.

"Damn ... if this just don't beat all," remarked Barclay as the two partners strolled back out to the helipad. "Who would've thought that a quiet Saturday of flying would turn into something like this?"

"CB, I've got a feeling we haven't seen the last of Trooper Shields or heard the last of what's going on out in that desert." Westbrook replied in a serious tone. "We have an unexplainable situation here and I think we need to honor the trooper's request to keep quiet about it."

"I'm with you on that, partner. Want to help me bring the 500 inside and put her to bed?"

"No problem, ace. Before I leave, I should probably check to see if we have any work for tomorrow. After today, it'd be nice to have a day off. You know ... we could sneak up to lake, do a little fishing and drink some beer."

"That sounds like an awesome idea … you bring the beer."

They tucked-in the 500 then Chance headed home. After reviewing the day's flights in both helicopter's logbooks, Westbrook checked the following week's schedule. It was depressingly light. With nothing else needing to be done, he decided it was time to go home and unwind. As he walked through the front part of the office, the blinking amber light on Becky's desk phone caught his eye.

He assumed the waiting message was from Charlie. She was undoubtedly worried that he and Chance had been called out to do a special night flight on behalf of the state police. Trent felt guilty for not calling her as soon as they landed.

Surprisingly, the call was not from the Mrs. but from a Maj. Derick Roberts of the United States Air Force. Trent only half-listened to the message as he vainly tried to scribble it down on a notepad. He had to replay it two more times before he got all the information written down.

The major was interested in their capabilities and availability. He didn't ask about cost. The major explained he needed to shuttle people back and forth between the COTEF facility and the Air Force radar site at Christmas Valley. This would be an open-ended, special-services contract for up to a week in length and he needed a dedicated helicopter capable of carrying anywhere from two to four passengers at a time. The major also stressed such work would be highly confidential in nature and that Orion Air would be required to sign several, non-disclosure documents and provide personal information on all pilots and staff members. If all of this were acceptable, the major asked to be called back as soon as possible so arrangements could be made for the following day. The callback number was a local listing.

"Wow!" Trent said after listening to the message for the third time. Something like this would be a financial boost to the little company and could lead to bigger and better things. Namely, more government-type work. He tried to contain his excitement as he punched the auto-dial button for Chance Barclay's home.

Barclay picked up on the third ring, answering with his typical "CB's Bar and Grill" response.

"Chance my man, you're not going believe this!"

CHAPTER 19

COTEF

Saturday Evening

Colby Jefferson took Maj. Roberts aside before the three officers entered the conference room. Jefferson needed answers to a couple of questions, and he wanted to keep the conversation as discreet as possible.

He didn't buy the major's explanation regarding their "escort" but kept his opinion to himself. The notion of having a babysitter to constantly show them around or help them out when needed did not sit well. Jefferson reasoned the constant presence of their "personal attendant" was to keep tabs on them and make sure they didn't wander into any restricted parts of the building. The major also suspected both he and Davis were under constant surveillance. Once again, Jefferson guessed there was more going on here than anyone was willing to talk about. Maj. Roberts was adamant their escort would stay in place. "Standard project protocol" was his only explanation.

When asked about a helicopter to ferry them out to Christmas Valley whenever needed, Robert's explained the Oregon National Guard would be willing to release a OH-58 Kiowa Jet Ranger with crew. Provided, of course, upon availability and if the Air Force was willing to provide specific mission details and reimbursement. Conditions which were unacceptable to the security, as well as the secrecy, of the program. This was one more "red flag" Jefferson added to his growing list of suspicions and concerns.

"Not to worry, Major," Roberts added seeing the disappointment in Jefferson's face. "I have contacted a local company who are more than willing to take on the job."

"Really? How about confidentiality and vetting?" Jefferson responded, not sure if he was comfortable with the idea of using civilian contractors for such sensitive military work.

"I have someone working on that as we speak. We will have strict, non-disclosure agreements for them to sign and I have people checking out the company's employees. The FAA has already responded to my request for information and assures me their record is clean, their FAR Part 135 Operating Certificate is in order, and all licenses are current. One of their pilots is also ex-Army with an old security clearance."

"What else can you tell me about them?"

"The name of the company is Orion Air. It went into operation a couple of years ago at the Bend airport. The company is owned by its two pilots ... one is a former warrant officer who flew in Desert Storm, and the other one served with the Peace Corps in Central America. They have two helicopters. One is a five-place McDonnell-Douglas 500 and the other is a three-place Schweizer 300. Besides the principals, there are only two other employees of record. One is the wife of one of the pilots and the other is a young office girl just out of high school."

"No mechanics or line personnel?"

"They appear to have all of their maintenance needs either done by the local operator at Bend's airport or by companies over in the Willamette Valley. I don't think they're big enough to have their own mechanics or line personnel. All things considered, I see them as hungry for business and since they only have a few employees, easy to monitor and control."

"Can they be here at 0800 tomorrow morning with the larger helicopter? I'd like to visit with the pilots and check out their machine before committing to them."

"They can. We can also use the opportunity to sign the paperwork if they pass muster. We should have all the background checks completed by then as well."

"Okay Major, go ahead and make the call," concluded Jefferson. "Now, if you please, Lieutenant Davis and I would like to go inside and start our interviews."

"Am I to assume, that all of these interviews you will be

conducting exclude me?"

"That would be correct. This investigation is under the authority of the commanding officer at Schriever, Colonel Kelly and the project manager, Lt. Colonel Rutledge. My instructions are to conduct a thorough examination of the events and people involved in this incident. As such, I need to interview all the players separately and in private to corroborate and establish the facts. My initial task is to determine what went wrong and why. This also includes the possibility the project may have been compromised in some way."

One of the main items Jefferson needed to determine as quickly as possible was whether gross negligence or sabotage were factors. He chose not to share this point with Roberts since it could directly impact his career. To Jefferson's way of thinking, somewhere is this crowd there might even be a scapegoat in the making.

"I understand all that," replied the exasperated Maj. Roberts. "What I don't understand is why I, as commander of this base, am to be excluded from the process."

"As the commanding officer at COTEF and a partner in what's going on at the Backskatter site, I understand you must feel a responsibility for what happened, as well as an obligation to be an active participant in this inquiry. Rest assured, you will be interviewed just like everyone else, as well as being consulted. However, I'm sure you can understand why we must conduct our investigation this way. The Air Force will be looking for a complete and impartial report. Your participation in the interviews could be construed as interference or subterfuge. I don't think you want to unintentionally compromise the integrity of the process. That wouldn't look good for anybody."

Maj. Roberts had just been "butt burned" and everyone present knew it. Jefferson wanted to give everyone ample opportunity to speak openly and freely. If Maj. Roberts were to be present during the interviews, that would probably not be the case. Jefferson also requested that any security cameras in the conference room be turned off. He wanted complete privacy and strict confidentiality while he visited with COTEF's staff.

After an uncomfortable period of silence, Roberts tacitly acknowledged Maj. Jefferson's explanation on how things needed to proceed, said the cameras would be turned off, then excused himself.

Lt. Davis stood dumbfounded by the exchange. He felt sorry for
Maj. Roberts, but knew standard investigative protocols had to be
followed. Shaking his head in sympathetic understanding, Davis
followed Maj. Jefferson into the conference room. The time was now
1910 hours, 7:10 p.m. PDST. Jennifer Blackstone, the young first
lieutenant, waited inside for them.

Jefferson and Davis spent almost an hour with the twenty-
four-year old junior officer. Her job primarily consisted of being
Maj. Roberts' administrative assistant. In addition to typical clerical
duties, she was responsible for whatever the major tasked her to do.
She was in an advantageous position to know more about what was
going on with the project than most.

Jefferson's interrogative strategy was to initially ask everyone
the same line of questions. First, he wanted to know about their
specific roles and responsibilities in the Backskatter project. Next,
he dove into their backgrounds and areas of expertise. Finally, he
asked a variety of questions regarding the fatal experiment that
happened earlier that day. He would be looking for any new pieces
of information as well as any inconsistencies in each person's story.
He needed to fill in several gaps. He encouraged everyone he
interviewed to know they were free to speak their minds. Hopefully,
such an approach could provide valuable insights as to what could
have caused this catastrophe.

After hearing about the lieutenant's job and background,
Jefferson asked Blackstone about the on-site staff at Backskatter. To
his surprise, it wasn't as large as expected. It usually consisted of
only twenty-five individuals. Four DARPA engineers and scientists,
four Air Force technicians, three lab assistants, two cooks, one
maintenance person, a ten-person security detachment, and the
onsite commander, Major Seth Michaels.

All stayed on site, and most rotated out every eighty-four hours,
or three and a half days, being replaced by a similar group from
COTEF. Once each group returned to Bend, they spent a half day
in debrief then each was given a two-day pass. All personnel and
their rotations were tightly controlled. Jefferson asked the young
lieutenant if any extra personnel were sent to Christmas Valley to
assist with the test that morning. To Blackstone's knowledge, there
weren't any. When they learned of the severity of the accident from

the first responders, most of the technical staff was sent out to the Backskatter site along with the second group of responders.

Finally, the major asked the young woman if she would care to share any rumors, thoughts, or personal insights. Shifting nervously in her chair, Blackstone mentioned everyone was under a great deal of pressure to meet the project's timelines, something not out of the ordinary for a Top Secret government project. Other than that, nothing else came to mind. To both Jefferson and Davis, she seemed rather uneasy and tight-lipped during the entire hour.

Their second interview of the evening was one of the two Air Force captains. Captain Devon Mitchell was responsible for base security at both sites and was in charge of the detail which initially responded to the accident. He described how his group had been alerted, briefed, and dispatched to the radar site. Jefferson was impressed by how fast and professionally the response was pulled off; almost as if they had done this exercise a time or two beforehand.

The captain went on to say what they found when they first got to the facility, all of which was included in the initial report Lt. Davis presented at Schriever. Then the three watched the thirty-two-minute video taken when the response team first arrived at the Backskatter site. It wasn't pretty.

The person operating the camera began rolling footage just as the two Humvees came upon the facility. The video was in color, shaky at times, and was narrated by the airman operating the camera. All manner of noise, talking and yelling could be heard in the background. Under the circumstances, it wasn't a bad job of film making.

It also showed exactly what had been described in the initial report: the main entrance gate was open and partially off its hinges, the facility looked totally deserted, the doors to all the surviving buildings were wide open, and the level of destruction was painfully obvious. The main building was nothing more than a smoking pile of rubble. The equipment room where the COIL laser and microwave generators were housed was completely gone.

Papers, debris, and articles of clothing were scattered all over the place. The place looked like a war zone, but without any bodies. Other than the uniformed security, rescue responders and engineers sent from COTEF, there were no other people about. None. The initial report sent to Lt. Davis didn't do justice to the level of destruction all now saw on the oversized monitor.

When the video finished playing, the room remained somber and quiet for a minute. Capt. Mitchell, seeing the complete video for the first time, looked as if he had just lost his best friend. Lt. Davis was pale and obviously shaken. Jefferson was deep in thought.

The video clearly demonstrated the seriousness of the accident. It was brutally obvious something major had occurred. It comprised probable loss of life with at least several million dollars in damages. To Jefferson, this was definitely a "Class A" accident, per USAF definition. This meant a formal accident investigation board would be required. His next thought was of his own role in the matter. Was he sent to buy time for Rutledge under the guise of doing a preliminary investigation or was there another reason?

Jefferson finally broke the silence when he asked the captain about the status of the on-site staff. Twenty-five people, including the site's commander, had suddenly and without a trace, vanished from the face of the earth.

CHAPTER 20

Bend's Oregon State Police Office
Saturday Night

Matt Shields was in deep thought. He had just concluded a lengthy phone conversation with Deputy Sheriff Mark Spencer in Christmas Valley.

Shields sat at his desk inside the State Police's new office located on the northern end of Bend. Their conversation raised more concerns than Shields could rationally sort out.

For starters, the two Christmas Valley search and rescue teams the deputy had dispatched came up empty. Other than clothing and gear, no trace of the missing hunters was found. Over three hours of searching in the dark by four volunteers resulted in nothing but what the absent hunters had left behind.

Spencer asked about the status of any searchers being sent out by the Deschutes County Sheriff's office. Shields said they had people on standby pending what Spencer's group found. The deputy planned to send more volunteers back out at first light and said he would contact the Deschutes County Sheriff's office for help if needed. Although the deputy had the highest regard for the capabilities of his counterparts to the north, he hoped to keep this a localized affair.

Secondly, and perhaps the most disturbing to the game warden, was the revelation of what became of the cattle he and Westbrook looked at earlier.

According to Deputy Spencer, all the affected ranchers had called earlier and reported when they went back out to their fields later that day to render their dead animals all had withered into nothing but skin and bones. The deputy knew this was highly irregular for an animal that had died within the past twenty-four hours. He had never heard of such rapid decomposition in livestock. Not wanting to reveal what he knew; Shields concluded the conversation with the deputy by promising to stay in touch.

Shields decided he needed to go back out to the desert to check on the remains of the deer he and Westbrook had surveyed earlier, and perhaps pay a second visit to the deputy and the local vet as well. Something was terribly wrong here, and if the deer were in the same condition as the cattle, his little investigation was on the verge of becoming far more serious than he originally imagined.

The game warden checked in with his supervisor for authorization to continue with this investigation full time and to re-engage the services of Orion Air. After hearing all the details of what had transpired that day, the senior trooper gave Shields the go-ahead.

He immediately looked up the home number for Trent Westbrook but dialing, checked the time. It was now 9:26. Shields decided it wasn't too late to be calling someone on a Saturday night and started dialing. Charlie Westbrook picked up after the second ring. After identifying himself, the game warden asked if he could speak with her husband.

Trent Westbrook wasn't surprised to hear from Shields.

"Hello, Matt. Long time no see. Any news on our missing hunters?"

"Negative. The only thing the SAR teams could find were the items we spotted from the air. You don't sound all that surprised to be hearing from me."

"Actually, I was hoping to hear from you tonight. I was thinking I should check in with you before tomorrow morning just in case."

"Just in case ...?"

"Yep. We got a call from the Air Force to shuttle a couple of folks from the old Army COTEF site out to the equally old radar site out at Christmas Valley in the morning."

"Now there's a coincidence for you. I was hoping you could fly me out to Christmas Valley as well. I'd like to take another look at that herd of deer we found, as well as check in with Deputy Spencer about a couple of things."

"I'm guessing you want to follow up on those missing hunters and possibly the dead cattle as well."

"You are very perceptive my friend. That's exactly what I'd like to do. I've been given authorization to utilize your services to the extent I deem necessary. Can you squeeze me into your schedule?"

"Absolutely. Chance is taking the 500 out for this little Air Force job. I only have to be at their COTEF facility to be checked out and sign some papers. Then I'm free, along with the 300, for the rest of the day."

"You didn't have any other plans?"

"Chance and I were thinking about going up to the lake for a little fishing was all. Going flying and making some money in the process sounds more appealing. Besides, I haven't hooked a fish in years."

"Yet you still have a valid fishing license, right? Sorry … professional habit."

Trent laughed. "Yes, I do. I justify that little expense as doing my civic duty for the Oregon Department of Fish and Wildlife. Someone's got to make up for the cheaters."

"Well thank you for supporting my department. I, for one, appreciate your patronage, spirit, and … honesty. What time should I meet you at the hanger?"

"We're scheduled to be at COTEF at eight o'clock. I'll drive out there so I can come back to the airport after they're through with me. I'm thinking I should be back at the hanger no later than 9:30. Will that work for you?"

"Absolutely. See you at 9:30 and have a good rest of your evening."

CHAPTER 21

COTEF

Saturday Night

Capt. Devon Mitchell couldn't add anything more about the missing staff. Nothing other than what he already told them. The follow-up report from the second response team pretty much summed up the grim situation regarding the fate of twenty-five people.

In the back of his mind, Colby Jefferson knew the key to ultimately finding out what happened lay with anyone who might have survived the accident. If there were no survivors, it would make it extraordinarily difficult to recreate what happened. There would not be a definitive conclusion as to what had transpired that morning out in the desert.

For a few minutes Jefferson thought about what he had seen on the video, then looked across the table. "Captain Mitchell, was the building that housed the personal quarters for the staff destroyed?"

"No, sir, it was not. That was one of the buildings left intact."

"Did your people check out this building for survivors or anything out of the ordinary?"

"Yes, sir, we did. That was one of the first buildings we searched. Nothing was amiss. The rooms, sleeping quarters, latrines ... the DEFAC, and even the recreational area looked squared-away and normal."

"That being the case, Captain, can you guess as to why clothing was scattered about ... as in ... outside of the buildings?"

Capt. Mitchell sat upright in his chair, as if a light bulb suddenly went off in his head. He had subconsciously disregarded the scattered clothing just like he had with the papers and debris floating around the complex. Then a quizzical look crossed his face as he thought of something else.

"Major Jefferson, we found more than just clothing. There was also ... shirts, pants, berets, lab coats and ... shoes. It looked as if the staff ... all of them ... stripped off everything they were wearing and just left them lying about."

Colby Jefferson and Logan Davis sat back in their chairs and looked at one another. They both knew this was an important clue. A vital piece of information which could lead them to discover what happened as well as the fate of the staff. Something unknown had caused twenty-five people to suddenly strip off all their clothes then up and disappear without a trace.

Jefferson, suddenly remembering something he learned during the briefing at Schriever, asked a crucial question, "Captain, it's my understanding that the Backskatter site has a hardened bomb shelter beneath one of its buildings. Is that correct?"

"Yes ... yes, there is! It's beneath the main building. The one which was destroyed."

"I think we need to get inside that bunker ASAP," Jefferson said. "It's extremely important we rescue anyone who could be trapped in there. Captain Mitchell ... can I impose upon you to contact the field team right away to see if they've made any progress regarding that?"

"You bet! I can make the call just as soon as you're finished with me. Is there anything else you'll be needing from me tonight?"

"Just one more question Captain," Jefferson added, "you said in your initial report your team saw a medevac helicopter make a landing somewhere to the north of your position. Has anyone followed up on the possibility that might have been for one or more of the survivors?"

Lt. Davis quickly looked at Jefferson then at Mitchell. He had totally forgotten about that little tidbit of information. His appreciation for Jefferson's keen mind went up another notch. He wondered why no one at COTEF had thought of that possibility.

Colby Jefferson thanked the captain for his first-responder efforts and for being so forthcoming with what he knew. Then he excused Mitchell so he could contact the field team at Backskatter for any new developments.

At exactly 2100 hours, 9:00 p.m., Capt. Mark Webster knocked on the conference room door. He was let into the room by the departing Capt. Mitchell. The two exchanged nods and proceeded in opposite directions at the doorway.

After introductions were made and all three were seated, Jefferson asked his standard line of questions. Capt. Webster was a thirty-something graduate of the Air Force Academy in Colorado Springs. For most of his career he was stationed in Washington D.C. and worked at the Pentagon doing a variety of jobs, most of which, were with DARPA. Over the course of the last four years, he had been a low-level supervisor on two semi-secret weapons projects. The "Oregon Project," because of its Presidential priority, was viewed by the ambitious captain as a "fast track" to grander things. Jefferson, always a quick and accurate judge of character, quickly decided that the captain was more politician than military officer.

Capt. Webster's job with the Backskatter project was to coordinate and facilitate the efforts of the engineers and technicians at COTEF and their counterparts at Christmas Valley. His primary responsibilities were to make sure everyone was on the same page, on the same schedule, and quickly take care of any problems. He conducted all briefings between the two groups who regularly rotated between COTEF and Backskatter. Jefferson ascertained the captain was somewhat of a control freak and probably held the key to the whole operation.

Other than apprise Jefferson and Davis of his status, Capt. Webster wasn't volunteering any added information and seemed guarded with his answers. Jefferson was convinced he knew more than he was telling but was unable to trip up the young captain. Webster was one cool character. He was also clever, smart, and seemed to regard Jefferson not as a fellow officer or as an accident investigator, but more of an adversary.

Capt. Webster's time in the conference room with Jefferson and Davis was the shortest of the group, a mere forty minutes. As soon as the door shut behind the departing officer, Colby Jefferson turned to his young assistant.

"I think that's enough for tonight. We'll resume our interviews tomorrow."

"Yes, sir … it's been a long day," came the agreeable response from Davis.

"I need to stretch my legs before we call it a night. Want to take a walk with me, Lieutenant?"

"Yes, sir ... I'd like that. Do we have to take our escort in tow?"

"Let me see what I can do about that. Now, if you would, please ... take our stuff back to our room while I go visit with Major Roberts. Plan on meeting me in the front lobby in ten minutes."

"Roger that, sir ... ten minutes."

Jefferson had serious reservations about the actual mission of the Oregon Project and what was going on at the COTEF site. It was obvious to him after interviewing the first three people, that two had been coached on what to say, what not to say, and how to say it. He had more "red flags" waving around in his head at this point than Red Square in Moscow. With the exception of Lt. Davis, he wasn't sure who he could trust.

Jefferson found Maj. Roberts in his well-appointed office just off the front lobby. The major appreciated hearing his guests were finished for the night. He was in no mood to hang around any longer than he had to. It had been a long, frustrating, and stressful day for everyone. He was anxious to go home, rest, and get out to the Backskatter site as early as possible the next morning.

He understood Jefferson's desire to go for a walk and unwind but requested, for security reasons, that he stay close to the facility. He said a walking path on the inside of the security fence surrounding the main building was available. To walk completely around it, he said, was probably somewhere around 2,000 feet, approximately four-tenths of a mile. Roberts said if that's what they wanted to do, he would have the roving guard dogs put back in their kennels to accommodate them. He also said the security guard at the building's front entrance could buzz them out as well as back in, and their assigned escort would wait for them in the lobby.

Once again, Jefferson thanked the major for his hospitality and cooperation. He also said he and Davis would probably only make one lap before calling it a night themselves. Almost as an afterthought, Roberts informed Jefferson that Orion Air had been contacted and would be arriving at 0800 the following morning.

Upon leaving Roberts' office, the two majors were almost run over by Lt. Davis hustling down the hallway to meet

Jefferson on time. The security guard "buzzed" the three men out the front door. They walked the forty-five feet together to the gate at the building's security fence. Using his key card, Roberts opened the gate, bade his guests a goodnight, waved at the security camera atop the fence, closed the gate with a loud click, and then walked across the parking lot to his car.

Jefferson and Davis stood at the gate for a minute watching Roberts cross the parking area, get into his government-issued ride, and drive away. "Is it me Lieutenant, or does it feel like we're somewhat incarcerated here?"

CHAPTER 22

COTEF & Schriever Air Force Base
Saturday Night

Lt. Logan Davis chuckled at Jefferson's remark.

"This place does have a penal type of ambiance to it. I wouldn't be a bit surprised if it isn't turned into a maximum-security jail after the Air Force gets through with it."

Jefferson found Davis' comeback equally amusing. "Okay buddy let's get some air and see where this little walk takes us."

From the main gate, located midway on the east side of the security fence, the two walked north for about 255 feet before reaching the northeast corner of the fence, which also held a security camera. There, they took a turned left and followed the fence heading west. A large parking area filled the north side between the fence and the building. The north end of the structure also contained an oversized loading dock and several sealed containers. The subdued up-lighting along the building's exterior walls gave it a sinister look in the darkness.

"This place gives me the creeps." Davis broke the eerie silence in a low voice. "It doesn't look at all like what I'm used to in a military setting."

"No doubt it's different," Jefferson said. "It does have a strange look to it compared to what we have at Schriever. Now that's what a military facility should look like."

"Is it my imagination Major, or does it seem like all these security cameras we keep seeing are following us?"

"They're probably motion-activated and will move with us until we're out of range and another camera can pick us up. We have the same type of system at Schriever."

The pair reached the northwest corner of the fence, complete with another security camera, then turned south along the fence's long axis on the west side. The barking and snarling of several dogs interrupted the silence, obviously unhappy about being in a kennel as opposed to roaming about doing their job.

"How about those free-ranging guard dogs? We don't have those at home, do we?" Davis asked.

"No ... no we don't. I'm not entirely sure if that conforms to established security SOPs or not. I've never seen nor heard of dogs being used like this before ... except for maybe in a department store or mall."

"Boy, I sure hope their handlers have them secured. The last thing I want to do tonight is go to a hospital with a dog bite. Those critters have a reputation for being fairly vicious."

"If those dogs come after you, it will be as a pack, and you won't have to worry about going to any hospital."

"How reassuring ... you really know how to make someone feel comfortable with their situation, Major."

"I try," came the bemused reply.

The two compared notes and perspectives regarding the project and the environment at COTEF for the remainder of their walk between the northwest corner and the southwest corner. The 475-foot stretch along the western side of the perimeter fence provided a good opportunity for the pair to visit privately.

Both agreed something more was going on with this program than what they were originally led to believe. Lt. Davis was becoming increasingly unhappy with the notion of being lied to or otherwise kept in the dark about the inner workings of the program. The pair came to the realization they needed to proceed with caution and cover each other's backs.

From the southwest corner, the two walked along the southern section of the fence until they reached the southeast corner and turned northward. After five minutes of walking the eastern side of the fence, they came back to their original starting point at the entrance gate. Their "lap" around the inside of the fence made a perfect rectangle. During their walk, they also took note of the building's dimensions and features. It was also rectangular and by their estimates, slightly larger than a football field.

The security guard at the building's main entrance buzzed them back in, where they were welcomed by their replacement escort. Jefferson checked in with Capt. Devon Mitchell as soon as they reached their assigned office. After their interview with the first responder, Jefferson had asked the captain to check if there had been any progress in opening the bunker beneath the destroyed main building.

Although most of the rubble had been cleared away from the entrance, Mitchell informed them, the second unit response team had yet to get through the main blast door and into the bomb shelter itself. The door was designed to be impenetrable, and if either the entrance or exit controls were damaged, could only be opened with the aid of a high temperature cutting torch.

After banging on the doors with a sledgehammer for a half hour without a response from the inside, the team acquired acetylene welding equipment from one of the site's service buildings and were in the process of cutting through the bolts that locked the six-inch-thick, hardened steel door in place.

The second response team commander believed they were making progress, planned to work through the night, and hoped to be able to break through sometime the following morning. That being the case, there was a good chance they could gain access close to the twenty-four-hour mark.

Colby Jefferson thanked the captain for the update then joined Davis in their sleeping quarters. After visiting the latrine, the two officers finally crawled into their bunks at 2305 hours, 11:05 p.m., and welcomed some well-deserved sleep.

～

Lt. Colonel T.J. Rutledge woke with a start when the cell phone on his nightstand buzzed. The luminescent dial on his watch read 2400 hours, 12:00 midnight, MDST. Half awake, he grabbed his Nokia 7110 and slipped out of the bedroom. He didn't want to wake his wife.

Once in the hallway, he flipped open the phone and sleepily answered with his customary response. "Rutledge."

"Sorry to disturb you so late, Colonel, but you said you wanted to be kept apprised of the latest developments here." The familiar voice on the other end of the line sounded distant and somewhat tinny.

"What's new?"

"Your two boys have been busy. They have already started interviewing key members of the staff. As far as I can tell, without learning anything significant. Major Jefferson has requested all surveillance cameras be turned off in the conference room during his interviews, so I don't have any information as to what was being said or done in there."

"What about the time they spent out of the conference room?"

"They've been under constant surveillance since their arrival, including in their quarters and during the little stroll they took around the outside of the building."

"They walked around the outside of the facility … without an escort?"

"Yes, but inside the perimeter fence where they could be contained and monitored the entire time."

"Any audio?"

"Only a word here and there. Nothing substantial. It was hard to follow their conversation because of the barking dogs and road noise from the highway."

"What are they doing now?"

"Sleeping, I assume. They've been in their quarters for almost an hour. The video feed from their room is dark which means they're probably 'down for the count.' I'll check on them after we finish talking."

"What are their plans for tomorrow?"

"A local helicopter company has been retained to ferry them out to the Backskatter site."

"A local company? Have they been checked out and cleared?"

"Yes, they have. They're clean and have a solid record. One of the pilots is ex-Army with an old security clearance."

"Anything else?"

"Still no sign of survivors at Backskatter. The second response unit is in the process of trying to breach the door on the bunker. They hope to have it open sometime tomorrow morning."

"Have you had a chance to check out the civilian medevac helicopter … the one that landed to the north of the site early this morning?"

"No, not yet. I was planning to do that first thing tomorrow when everyone heads to Christmas Valley."

"Check back in with me as soon as you learn anything or something new develops."

"Will do. 'Night Colonel."

DAY 2

Sunday, October 17, 1999

CHAPTER 23

Bend Municipal Airport & COTEF
Sunday Morning

Chance Barclay picked up his friend and business partner shortly before 7 a.m. It was the convenient thing to do since both lived in the same part of town. From Barclay's home in the Ladera subdivision to Westbrook's home in the Tanglewood subdivision was a short seven-minute drive. By a twist of fate, the two wound up living only two miles apart in the southeastern corner of Bend.

From Westbrook's place to the airport was pretty much a straight shot: a seven-mile, fifteen-minute drive with only one stop light to slow them down.

Both had gotten up early, looking forward to what this day brought them. Barclay was excited to be able to do something "military" and Westbrook was looking forward to working with Oregon State Game Warden Matt Shields again.

The two were dressed in their standard company attire of black tennis shoes, light gray cargo pants and matching black polo shirts with Orion Air's logo on the front left side. They wanted to make a good impression on their first encounter with the Air Force. The two partners also anticipated a profitable month so were understandably in a chatty mood on their drive. Their eagerness to get rolling made the trip out to the airport seem faster than normal.

Upon arriving at their hanger, Barclay called the airport's FBO and ordered fuel for the 500. Westbrook already had the 300 fully topped off. He did this upon returning from the desert with Trooper Shields the previous day. By the time the pair had moved their machines out of the hanger and positioned them on their respective helipads, the truck carrying Jet A aviation fuel arrived and went directly to the larger helicopter.

While "Three-Two-Six Charlie Bravo" was being attended to, Barclay and Westbrook performed the standard pre-flight inspections on their machines. At 7:34, Barclay climbed into the sleek MD-500, went through his cockpit checklist then fired up the Allison 250-C20 turbine engine. By prior arrangement, and while Barclay was going through his startup procedures, Westbrook locked up the hanger and headed back out to CB's truck.

Chance Barclay knew exactly where the COTEF site was located. He didn't have to resort to either a Sectional Chart or his GPS locator to find his way out to the semi-hidden complex. From an altitude of 1,500 feet, Barclay approached the facility from the northwest. He could easily see where Dodds Road branched off U.S. Highway 20; approximately a quarter mile down that road lay the unmarked entrance to COTEF.

The driveway leading to the facility appeared to be several hundred yards long with a barricade gate and guard shack about one-third of the way down. Barclay could see two guards standing at the gate watching him as he slowed the helicopter and started his descent.

Chance made a wide, descending counterclockwise circle around the facility to determine wind direction and the best approach for landing. He took note of the complex's layout as he did so. The large rectangular main building was oriented on a north-south line, surrounded by a high security fence. On the east side was a large parking area and just to the east side of that stood another large building, oriented east to west. Located on the north side of the parking area, close to the second building was the oversized helipad. The entire complex was situated in the middle of nowhere, surrounded by Juniper trees, sagebrush, and desert.

Chance took note of the wind direction from the flag on the flagpole and made his final approach coming in from the eastern side. With the morning sun at his back, he slowly descended with the nose of the helicopter pointing west into the light breeze. As was his habit, he made a perfect landing right on top of the helipad's painted "H."

Even with a head start of ten minutes, Westbrook still could not beat his partner out to the COTEF facility. Barclay's Toyota Tundra was no match for the speedy McDonnel Douglas helicopter. By the time Westbrook pulled up to the main security gate, Barclay had already set down on the helipad and was in the process of spooling down the engine to "ground idle," a standard procedure to cool the turbine prior to shutting down.

After checking his ID, a security guard in a Humvee escorted Westbrook from the driveway checkpoint to the main parking lot just as Barclay was finishing up. Standing clear of the helipad and off to the side was the welcoming committee of Majors Jefferson and Roberts, Capt. Webster, Lt. Davis, and a security guard. All except for Davis were wearing camo airman battle uniforms. Lt. Davis was dressed in the standard USAF service uniform.

The soldier in the Humvee indicated to Westbrook where he should park, then parked next to him and personally escorted Trent over to the group. True to his nature for precision, Chance Barclay had landed, shut down his helicopter, removed his headset and seatbelt harness, then hopped down onto COTEF's concrete helipad at exactly 0800 hours, 8:00 a.m., PDST.

After introductions were made, the group made their way across the parking area to the entrance checkpoint at the security fence. One of the accompanying security guards buzzed them through the gate as well as the building's main entrance. Barclay and Westbrook needed to show the guard manning the lobby picture IDs. Both were signed in and issued special visitor passes, then all proceeded to the conference room.

Once seated around the large, oval-shaped table, the two pilots were briefed as to the nature and conditions of the job.

Their mission would consist of transporting various people back and forth between COTEF and the Christmas Valley radar complex. Maj. Roberts explained that at least the 500, and possibly the smaller 300 would be needed for perhaps up to a week. They would be on twenty-four-hour standby for this entire period, expected to be available to fly on a moment's notice.

Westbrook said that shouldn't be a problem. The only thing they had on their schedule was for Trent to fly a game warden out to Christmas Valley for the day, and he'd be using the 300 for that little job. Chance Barclay and the 500 were completely open for the entire week. Nothing else was scheduled until the following weekend.

Trent also mentioned this type of arrangement would not only result in their standard hourly rate for flying the two helicopters but would also include a "standby" rate for being on 24/7 call-out status. When Trent gave them an estimated cost of what all this could entail, none of the Air Force people even flinched.

Maj. Roberts went on to explain the necessity for their services. The two pilots were told the Backskatter site was re-commissioned to evaluate an experimental laser-guided, radar tracking system. If the experiments panned out, all U.S.-based radar sites around the world would be upgraded with the new technology. The result would be the instantaneous recognition and tracking of approaching aircraft from extreme distances. Hence the requirement for a high degree of project security. Roberts' demeanor and delivery never once indicated what he was telling Westbrook and Barclay wasn't entirely accurate or true.

Unfortunately, the major continued, the main generator for the laser had self-destructed during a "high output test." In short, Orion Air was being hired to support an official Air Force inquiry into this accident. Maj. Roberts emphasized they would be providing a valuable service to their country,

Westbrook and Barclay were told the penalties for disclosing any of this could be extreme, which also pertained to any of their employees. They were also given a "cover story" to share with anyone who asked about the work they were doing, then presented with a pile of paperwork to review and sign. Major Roberts concluded his briefing by asking the pair if they had any questions.

Westbrook only had one. He wanted to know if there were any serious hazards, such as radiation leaks, they could be exposed to. Roberts assured the two pilots there were none.

To the surprise of the Air Force people, Westbrook presented paperwork of his own for them to sign. This consisted of two forms: a declaration they had received a pre-flight safety briefing per Orion Air's FAA Part 135 requirements, and a waiver of liability. Maj. Roberts signed on behalf of all military personnel who would be flying with them.

Once finished with the thirty-five-minute meeting, the group headed back outside. The two majors, along with Captains Webster and Mitchell would be flying out to the Backskatter site immediately with Barkley.

Maj. Roberts, as the commander of COTEF with shared responsibility for the Oregon side of the project, wanted to see the extent of the damage first-hand and take control of the recovery work. Capt. Mitchell, as the commander of the first responder group, wanted to check in with his replacement and be on-site when the bunker was opened. Captain Webster, as the coordinator between COTEF and Backskatter, was interested in the status and security of the highly secretive equipment. As the lead investigator for the accident, Maj. Jefferson would be looking for answers to any one of a hundred questions.

Lt. Davis, who would not be flying out with the group on this trip, had the assignment of following up on the civilian medevac helicopter spotted the previous morning north of the Backskatter site. Jefferson also asked the young lieutenant to "snoop around" a bit to see if he could glean any undisclosed information about either the project or the accident.

Trent Westbrook simply climbed back into Barclay's truck, was escorted off the property by a security guard leading the way in a Humvee and headed back to the Bend airport.

CHAPTER 24

Central Oregon Regional Medical Center
Sunday Morning

As the weekend duty supervisor at Central Oregon Regional, Dr. Robert Parks was not particularly looking forward to working on this Sunday. Putting in a long and somewhat stressful Saturday, coupled with a fitful sleep, tempted the doctor to stay home or at least sleep in a bit. Parks was not one to shirk his responsibilities however, and after enjoying a leisurely breakfast with his wife, arrived at the hospital shortly after 9:30 a.m.

When the employee's parking lot was relocated behind the building's northwest side, Parks made a habit of entering and leaving the hospital through the ER station. This route gave him a feel for what was going on, emergency-wise, and he always enjoyed greeting the staff members on duty and personally thanking them for their service.

As was his custom, he made a point of stopping at the reception podium at the main entrance and asked the attendant if anything noteworthy happened during the night. The middle-aged man behind the counter informed him it was an unusually quiet night for a Saturday then nodded towards a young man in an Air Force uniform waiting for him.

Parks thanked the man and strode over to where his visitor was sitting and introduced himself.

"Dr. Robert Parks," he said, extending his hand. "How may I help you?"

"Lieutenant Logan Davis, sir," Davis stood up and shook the offered hand. "I wish this were a courtesy call, but I'm afraid I'm here on official Air Force business. Is there someplace we can talk in private?"

The young lieutenant wore the standard dark blue, service dress uniform with a light blue dress shirt and dark blue tie. With his nameplate on the right breast of his jacket, his service ribbons and specialty badges on the left and his rank insignia on his shoulder boards, he cut an impressive figure. He also drew several stares and a few admiring glances, mainly from the female staffers on duty.

"Yes," came the delayed response. Parks took a couple of seconds to think what the Air Force could possibly want with him or his hospital before answering. "We can either visit up in the cafeteria over a cup of coffee, or we can go to my office. What's your pleasure?"

"I would prefer your office, if you don't mind, sir."

"Okay if we take a short detour so I can get a cup of coffee? My treat if you'd like one."

"Thank you, sir. I would appreciate that."

After stopping off at the cafeteria and picking up two large coffees, the pair proceeded up to Parks' second floor office. Once comfortably seated around a small meeting table, Davis came right to the point.

"Dr. Parks, I understand your emergency-response helicopter made a pick-up yesterday morning northeast of Christmas Valley. As you may know, we have a classified radar installation located in that same general vicinity. Early yesterday morning we had an accident at this site and several of our people are now unaccounted for. My purpose in coming here is to determine if your helicopter might have picked up one or more of our technicians and if so, what condition they might be in."

Robert Parks shifted uncomfortably in his chair and took a sip of coffee before answering. "Your information is correct about LifeAir's mission to the desert, Lieutenant. Unfortunately, the sole patient they picked up expired from cardiac arrest during the flight back. The flight EMTs could not revive him. Since he had no identification on him, and no one has reported a missing person, we have him in our morgue for the time being as a 'John Doe.'"

"Would it be possible for me to see the body?"

"I'm sorry Lieutenant, but hospital policy and privacy laws

prevent me from letting you do that … unless you can establish some type of relationship with this person." Parks was of no mind to let anyone see what was left of this man until he had more answers as to what happened to him.

"Can you at least give me a description of him?"

"Yes, I can do that. Male, Caucasian, about five feet six, approximately one-hundred sixty pounds, partially bald, somewhere around early-sixties in age. Any of that sound like one of your missing people?"

"No, not really," came the disappointed reply. "The oldest person we had working for us was in his mid-forties." After a contemplative moment to take a sip of his own coffee, Davis thought of something else to ask the doctor. "Dr. Parks, you said this person didn't have any identification on him and since I can't see him … can you at least describe what he was wearing when he was found?"

Parks wasn't sure if he should answer the question or not, then decided to anyway, just in case it brought something to mind. "Unfortunately, he wasn't wearing anything. He was found naked and alone by a couple of hikers."

"Naked?"

"Yes, hence the reason for no ID. The man wasn't even wearing any jewelry." Then Parks thought of something that could be a possible game changer. "Lieutenant, would you happen to have any dental records for your missing people?"

Lt. Davis thought of the personnel files kept at COTEF. Thanks to military thoroughness, they had records on everyone who worked at the facility as well as the Backskatter site. He didn't know offhand if these records contained any dental information or not, but he could easily find out.

"Possibly. I will need to do some checking and get back to you on that. Is there anything else you can share without violating your policies?"

"Sorry Lieutenant, I can't think of anything. How can I reach you if I need to?"

Taking a pad of paper and a pen from his briefcase, Davis wrote down his name and the main phone number at COTEF then handed it to Parks. In return, the doctor gave Lt. Davis a business card and said he would be on duty for the entire day.

Thanking the doctor for his time and help, Davis shook hands with Parks and asked his host if he wouldn't mind showing him the way back to the visitor's parking lot.

After walking the lieutenant out, Parks took his time getting back to his office. He was lost in thought, subconsciously reviewing the discussion he had with Lt. Davis.

If the lieutenant could provide dental records for his missing people, and if there was a match with the "John Doe" in the hospital's morgue, then perhaps, just perhaps, the Air Force could shed some light on what happened to their mystery man. That being so, Parks was optimistic they would have answers to all their questions and be able to put this improbable episode behind them.

The next issue to resolve, once they identified their "J.D." was what to do with the body itself, or what remained of it. He reasoned he couldn't turn it over to the military or family looking as gruesome as it did. That might open up a whole new set of problems. Problems he didn't even want to think about.

Parks decided on the only course of action he could think of. When he got back to his office, he would make a call to Michael Clark and see if the coroner, with his experience in identifying dead people, could help with the dental forensics, as well as recommend a good cremation service.

~

During the drive back out to the COTEF facility, Davis kept replaying in his mind everything Dr. Parks had told him about the hospital's unidentified victim.

Except for the age factor, the dead man could be any one of about a dozen people working at Backskatter at the time of the accident. He could understand the hospital's position in not letting him check out the body, not that he really wanted to do something like that anyway. Identifying a dead body, especially one in questionable condition, was not on his "A" list of things to do on a Sunday morning.

The one thing that kept coming back to him was the condition the man was found in: "naked and alone" was the phrase. "Naked and alone." Somewhere in the back of his mind, this piece of information rattled around. He couldn't quite put his finger on what this meant but knew there was a connection somewhere. Whatever it was would surface at the right time. He turned his thoughts instead to the dental records.

Davis hoped the personnel records kept on file at COTEF might help. It would be easy to separate those persons who were at the radar site at the time of the accident from those working at COTEF. Eliminating those who were female or non-Caucasian should narrow down the list to a handful of people. From that point he could provide the dental records, if they had any, of those individuals to Dr. Parks for comparison.

He estimated he could possibly accomplish all this by mid-afternoon. Davis thought it would be a good thing to have some relevant news, however the identification process turned out, when Major Jefferson returned from the desert.

CHAPTER 25

Bend Municipal Airport & Christmas Valley
Sunday Morning

"Good morning Mr. Trent," was the cheerful greeting from Matt Shields as Westbrook climbed out of the borrowed truck. The game warden was early for their rendezvous.

"Good morning, Officer Shields," Trent Westbrook said in equally cheerful response as the two walked toward Orion Air's hanger. "Ready for another day of mystery, suspense, and low-level flying?"

"Can't wait. I'm hoping to get some answers today to a lot of nagging questions, most of which kept me up for part of the night. I appreciate your help on this investigation and hope this trip won't be a waste of time."

"Flying, no matter what the reason, is never a waste of time, my friend. Especially when one is getting paid to do it."

Matt Shields chuckled and shook his head at the remark. Often, he felt exactly the same about his job. He got paid to spend time in the great outdoors and do the things he naturally loved to do.

The pair entered the hanger through the front office door. Out of habit, Westbrook checked the big weekly status board on the wall behind Becky Irwin's desk. He shook his head in dismay that nothing had changed since he last looked at it the previous night. Trent grabbed a marker and made a notation that both helicopters would be out for the day, then checked the weather for the second time that morning.

There were no changes. The high this day was expected to be in the low 70s with light winds, no clouds and unlimited visibility.

"Severe clear" in pilot lingo.

Westbrook amended the paperwork Shields signed the day before, to include this day and possibly the next one as well. Complete and accurate records were an FAA requirement for their business, and if not correct, could cost them their operating certificate. Matt Shields understood the reasoning for this; his job with the State Police required much the same.

After locking up, the pair left the hanger by the back door and headed for the S-300 parked on the #2 helipad. Once on board and situated, Westbrook went through his checklist then fired up the 190-horsepower Lycoming engine. When the engine temperature gauge had stabilized in the green arc, he engaged the rotors. After a five-minute warm-up period and safety checks, Westbrook carefully raised the helicopter off the pad and air-taxied over to an adjoining taxiway.

With a final safety check of the surrounding area and a radio announcement "in the blind" to any aircraft in the vicinity, Westbrook rotated the hovering 300 to point southeast then slowly raised the collective in his left hand while simultaneously pushing the cyclic in his right hand slightly forward. The sensation Matt Shields felt as the helicopter picked up speed and the ground suddenly melted away beneath them remined him of a carnival ride at the county fair. A takeoff in a helicopter, any helicopter, was definitely a rush.

～

Chance Barclay loaded his passengers then instructed them on the use of the four-point seat belt harness and voice-activated headsets. Then he climbed into the cockpit himself, strapped in and went through his startup checklist before firing up the turbine engine.

Because rank has its privileges, Majors Jefferson and Roberts sat in the front with Barclay. Captains Mitchell and Webster occupied the back seats. By coincidence, the weight distribution pretty much balanced out. "Weight and balance" were crucial factors in flying aircraft, especially helicopters.

When the 500 was ready, Barclay performed a "maximum

performance" takeoff, going almost straight up, to safely clear the parking area and the surrounding trees before transitioning to horizontal flight. The sensation was like going up in a high-speed elevator, which caught the back seat passengers by surprise even though Barclay had informed them of his intentions.

The roughly sixty-seven statute miles from COTEF to the Backskatter site was a relatively quick trip in the agile 500. Traveling in a straight line and at a low altitude, Barclay not only gave his passengers a smooth and scenic ride but also managed to get them to their destination in only twenty-six minutes. Something which impressed his passengers.

The trip itself was quiet and uneventful. Conversation stayed to a minimum, primarily consisting of Barclay answering questions about the 500 and his military background. Because everyone on board could hear when someone spoke, thanks to the voice-activated intercom system, none of the Air Force people talked about either the project or the accident. They didn't want Barclay knowing any more than what he'd already been told or what was necessary.

Barclay flew directly to the radar site by visual references alone. He didn't need the coordinates he previously entered into his GPS unit. Overflying Horse Ridge and keeping Pine Mountain off to his left, Chance took a southeasterly heading toward the sand dunes he could see off in the distance. From an average altitude of 5,500 feet mean sea level, or approximately 2,000 above the ground, he had an expansive view of the desert before him. The 11,000 acres of the off-white sand dunes just to the north of the Backskatter site stood out like a beacon.

As was his habit, Barclay slowed his helicopter as he started a gentle descent when he was approximately three miles out from his intended landing site. His approach mirrored what he did upon arriving at COTEF earlier. He circled the complex in a counterclockwise fashion while reducing his speed and altitude. This enabled him to visually check things out from his vantage point in the pilot's left-hand seat. What he saw below was impressive.

Three separate, massive radar arrays were arranged in a flared "U" shape. One of the behemoths faced northwest, the center one faced due west, and the third faced southwest. Each array consisted of fourteen towers stretched out in a row and interconnected by a lattice of metal. Attached to each tower on the western facing, front sides were smaller rotating arrays. Barclay estimated each array must be anywhere from seventy-five to eight-five feet in height and around three hundred feet in length. Each array looked like a giant erector set and something straight out of a 1950s science fiction movie.

Set behind the arrays, were two large buildings, what was left of a third building, several container or trailer-type structures, a large water storage tank, two service-type buildings, an electrical substation, a tall communications tower, two over-sized satellite dishes and possibly what remained of a third. Two helipads lay just to the east side of a large parking area, which was also on the east side of the group of buildings.

The complex was huge and formidable and surrounded by a tall chain-link security fence. The sheer size and appearance of the Backskatter complex was intimidating and ominous at the same time.

Tom Wangler

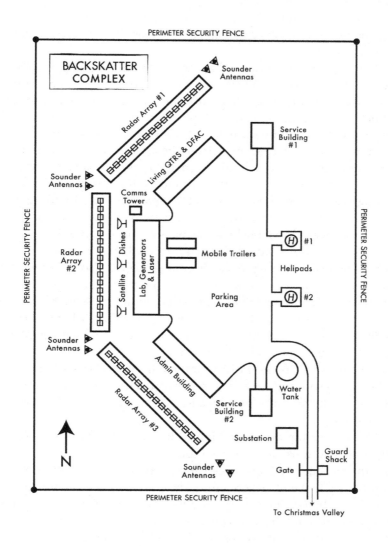

151

From their elevated vantage point, Barclay and his passengers could readily see the extent of the damage the accident had created. Maj. Jefferson thought the ground level video he and Lt. Davis viewed the night before didn't do justice to what he now saw firsthand from the air. A large number of people moved about all over the place. To Chance Barclay, they looked like an army of ants foraging for food.

Barclay made a gentle landing on one of the helipads, directly over the "H" marker. While Barclay spooled down the engine and rotors, the four Air Force officers managed to remove their headsets, unbuckle themselves and climb down from the helicopter unaided. They patiently stood by the machine until their pilot gave them the thumbs up to proceed away from the aircraft. Waiting to greet them were the captain currently in charge of the on-site response and recovery team and two security guards. The group piled into a waiting Humvee and headed off in the direction of the buildings.

As a condition of their contract with the Air Force, Chance and Trent were not to leave the helipads while at Backskatter. It would not only be a serious security breach for a civilian to be wandering around the highly classified site, but the Air Force also didn't want any outsiders to see or know anything more than they were told. Considering the circumstances surrounding the accident, there were also the issues of safety and liability, something Chance could readily understand. The nearby security guard armed with an M-16 was also a stark reminder of those conditions.

The first thing Barclay did after the four officers hustled away was to finish shutting down and securing his helicopter. Climbing down from the machine, he took a long stretch and surveyed his surroundings.

The three radar arrays dominated his view. They were massive structures and were much more impressive on the ground than from the air. Equally impressive were the two remaining satellite dishes. They looked like something straight out of a sci-fi movie as well. Other than the cluster of buildings and miscellaneous support structures, the only thing he could see was a large pile of rubble in the center of it all with a lot of people working around it.

Chance didn't know how long he would be marooned on the helipad, so he planned to spend the morning filling out the 500's logbooks and tending to his helicopter. He also thought about contacting Westbrook to see how he and the state trooper were doing. After their meeting at COTEF but before they went their separate ways, the two agreed to stay in touch throughout the day, just in case.

Turning on the King KR 87 VHF radio was a straight-forward process in the 500. All he had to do was flip on the battery switch, flip on the avionics power switch, toggle to the preset frequency for their "ship-to-ship/ship-to-shop" communication, put on his headset then make the call. He didn't even have to start up the helicopter. He could also talk to Westbrook while both machines were sitting on the ground.

He decided to wait on making any call until he knew something more or when his passengers got ready to depart the radar site. After attending to his paperwork and his aircraft, Chance decided his next course of action would be to do the only reasonable thing anyone would do in a similar situation. He planned to take a nap.

He never got the opportunity.

CHAPTER 26

Christmas Valley & Bend
Sunday Morning

The trip back out to the desert for Westbrook and Shields was not as quick as Chance Barclay's. Still, it was uneventful flight, if not outright pleasant given the beauty of the high desert in the fall.

The game warden spent the time updating Trent on what he had learned since their last visit. It came as a surprise to Westbrook to learn the fate of the dead cattle and the news their missing hunters were nowhere to be found. Both men shared the same concerns. They had a real mystery on their hands and speculated these two incidents, along with what had happened to the herd of deer, might somehow be related.

To add another item to the strange series of events, Shields also brought up something he remembered Deputy Spencer saying to them at the Christmas Valley airport. He recounted the LifeAir mission the deputy had summoned to pick up a suffering old man at the Lost Forest. Shields wondered if this were yet another element to their mystery and decided he would ask the deputy about it.

As an afterthought, Shields asked Westbrook how his meeting with the Air Force went.

"It went okay," Westbrook replied. "Not quite what I expected, but then you never know about these things. At any rate, we got the job."

"Anything you can talk about?" Shields silently wondered if there was any connection with the arrival of the two Air Force officers the previous day and their growing mystery.

"No, not really. We had to sign a non-disclosure agreement not to discuss what we'll be doing for them and why. I really do wish I could tell you more, but I can't. I hope you understand."

"Not to worry. I appreciate the fact you aren't one to betray a confidence. I've asked the same of you. I understand the position you're in and wouldn't ask you to compromise your integrity."

"Thanks. I knew you'd understand."

"Just the same, I thought it was highly unusual that in the midst of all these strange events, the 'Boys in Blue' suddenly show up out of nowhere and immediately hire the only helicopter service around."

The comment raised a little alarm bell inside Westbrook's head. *What if there is a connection?*

~

Deputy Sheriff Mark Spencer and local veterinarian Mike McCary were waiting for them when they arrived at the airport. Matt Shields had called the deputy prior to leaving Bend with a request to have them join him for a follow-up meeting and provided an estimated time of arrival. The sixty-five-mile trip had taken the pair a respectable fifty-two minutes in the diminutive S-300. An envious Trent enviously thought they could have made the trip in half the time if he were flying the 500.

All sat at the same picnic table as before and wasted little time in updating one another. Deputy Spencer started off by briefing the others regarding the status of the search for the missing hunters. Other than finding the abandoned truck and the scattered articles of clothing and hunting gear, the two search teams had come up empty. Not much to show for a six-hour effort on Saturday night and an early start on Sunday morning. Deputy Spencer asked Westbrook and Shields if they wouldn't mind taking extra time on their way back to Bend to scout the area between Quartz Butte and Pine Mountain, an area the ground search teams had yet to cover. The two said that wouldn't be a problem since they would be in the vicinity anyway.

Matt Shields asked Dr. McCary about the condition of the cattle. The perplexed veterinarian confessed he was at a loss to explain how recently deceased animals could decompose so radically in so little time. Westbrook and Shields exchanged a quick glance yet said nothing about the dead deer they surveyed the previous day. McCary went on to describe, in grisly detail, what the animals looked like when he went back out to the ranches late Saturday afternoon and again earlier that morning.

The cattle were all dried up, almost mummified. Once cut open, their insides resembled burnt bacon crumbles and their bones were chalky and yellow. All things considered, stated the veterinarian, the animals looked like they had been dead for at least one-two years, not twenty-four hours. As improbable as all of this sounded, Westbrook and Shields wondered if the insides of the deer would be in similar shape.

All agreed this was something beyond their collective knowledge. As professionals dealing with all manner of animals, Dr. McCary and Trooper Shields were especially distressed. Westbrook and Deputy Spencer were plain worried. No one in the group had ever witnessed or heard of anything like this happening before.

"Deputy … yesterday you said something about LifeAir picking up an old man out in the Lost Forest. Is that correct?" Shields asked.

"Yep. Strangest thing. I followed up on that later in the day by calling Central Oregon Regional. I needed to find out how things turned out so I could finish my report on the matter."

"Strange in what way?"

"Well, seems the old man died on the trip back to the hospital. Since he was found naked and without any identification, we didn't have a clue as to who he was or where he came from. The hospital's keeping him on ice in their morgue under a 'John Doe' for the time being. The doctor in charge said if anything further develops, he'd give me a call and asked me to do the same."

"You haven't heard anything since? No missing persons reports. Nothing at all?"

"Nope. Just the one about our missing hunters is all. Why do you ask?"

Matt Shields, as a professional law enforcement officer, was not one to believe in coincidences.

"Doesn't it strike you as a little odd that all of these unexplained incidents … the naked old guy, the dead cattle, the missing hunters … all happened on the same day, and all in close proximity to one another? Doesn't that make you wonder if they're not somehow connected?"

~

Upon arriving at COTEF, Logan Davis went to see Maj. Roberts' administrative assistant, Lt. Jennifer Blackstone, the attractive young woman they interviewed the previous night.

Davis asked the lieutenant if the personnel files they had on everyone included dental records. To her knowledge, they did. Davis asked her if she could pull all the files for the staff present at Backskatter for the test on Saturday, all twenty-five people.

Blackstone initially expressed hesitancy at the request, saying she should get Maj. Roberts' approval before releasing the records. Davis reminded the lieutenant this was an official, independent Air Force-sanctioned investigation, and her cooperation would be "highly" appreciated. After a moment or two to think it over, the young woman complied with Davis' request.

Sitting alone in the conference room, Davis took his time going through each file. First, he eliminated all the women. Next, he eliminated everyone who was not Caucasian. He was left with a stack of seventeen files. More than he would have thought.

Unfortunately, the dental records were not as complete as he had hoped, some were even non-existent. *Shit*, Davis thought to himself. *This is not going to be as easy or as straightforward as I'd hoped.*

Although disappointed, he still thought there might be enough to hand over to Dr. Parks for comparison. Perhaps, just perhaps, the good doctor and his people could find a match. If not, by the process of elimination, they could at least narrow the number down to a few candidates. Davis was hoping lady luck would be shining on him today.

He put the dental records for each of the seventeen people into separate manila folders and labeled them with a special code of his own design. He didn't want to provide any names, ranks or other designations to Parks, nor to anyone else, until he was sure of a positive ID. To keep track of who was who, Davis made a list for himself identifying each person by their ID number and their job on the project. Finally, he bound all the folders together with a thick rubber band and slipped the package into his briefcase.

Having accomplished all this, he returned the files to Lt. Blackstone, thanked her for her help and informed her he was going back into Bend. He also told her he didn't know when he would be returning.

CHAPTER 27

The Backskatter Site
Sunday Morning

Chance Barclay, from his distant vantage point, suddenly heard all manner of yelling and commotion coming from the direction of the buildings. Everyone was running toward the pile of rubble where the central building once stood.

All he could do was watch the flurry of activity and guess as to what was going on. There was also something about the destroyed building that seemed odd to Barclay. Something he couldn't quite put his finger on. Whatever it was, things didn't look right to him.

He remembered seeing from the air two large buildings and what remained of a third. The three, separate structures were laid out in a similar pattern as the massive radar arrays, a flared "U" shape. Each one located directly behind an array.

Suddenly, Chance realized what didn't look right. Having been to war and seeing firsthand the destruction created by a bombed-out building, he now recognized the structure had been demolished by an implosion, not an explosion. No building debris was strewn outward. There were no scattered structural components, pieces of concrete, furniture, or anything of the sort. Only papers, office supplies, and clothing lay about. He wondered what could have possibly caused an entire building to collapse and crumble inward like this.

Then Barclay remembered the set of binoculars he had on board the 500. Scrambling into the helicopter's cockpit, he retrieved the high-powered optical instrument and sat down in the pilot's seat. From this vantage point, Barclay could scout out the complex unseen.

Except for the guard patrolling the parking area and keeping an eye on him, two men guarded the main entry gate while a half-dozen others patrolled and searched the area surrounding the buildings. From what he could determine, the remaining responders clustered around the southern end of the destroyed building. Included in this group were the two majors and the two captains he had flown in earlier.

Although he was a good two hundred feet away from the ruins, if Barclay shifted to his right, into one of the front passenger seats, he had a good line of sight and could clearly see what was going on. A ramp on the southeast corner of the rubble had been cleared away, exposing a subterranean entrance of some sort. Chance could see an assortment of equipment and several men feverishly working around the entrance. Then everyone started yelling.

~

It took the second unit response team approximately fourteen hours to cut through the twelve, hardened steel bolts that secured the main blast door to its frame. Each side had four two-inch thick cylindrical bolts. The top and bottom of the door each had two bolts. Because the team had only one cutting torch, and every bolt took approximately a half hour to cut through, it took the group all night to breech the door. Additional hours were consumed by equipment setup, changing out the acetylene tanks and by rotating the people doing the cutting. With more torches, the group could have breached the door in half the time.

Colby Jefferson stood next to Capt. Devon Mitchell at the top of the ramp leading down to the door. Maj. Derick Roberts and Capt. Mark Webster stood off to the side. The four men did not want to impede the work in any way. Capt. Mitchell checked his watch. It read 10:25. The 24-hour limit had expired at approximately 8:00 that morning. He was hoping the two and a half-hour difference wouldn't be a life-or-death factor.

Although the oversized door was now free of the locking bolts securing it, getting it open posed a set of new challenges for the recovery team. Four massive, spring-loaded hinges on the backside allowed the door to swing open inwards, toward the inside of the bunker. If any one of these hinges was damaged in any way, it would make getting the door open extremely difficult.

It took all of two minutes for the team to discover that crowbars and prybars couldn't open the door any farther than a foot. Something more substantial was needed. Devon Mitchell came up with the idea of using the hydraulic jacks off the Humvees.

By strategically placing four jacks between the frame and the door and using long pieces of pipe for better leverage on the handles, four of the largest men in the group were able to squeak the door open inch by agonizing inch. After twenty minutes of demanding work, the team managed to open the one and a half-ton steel door far enough for someone to slip through. Maj. Roberts limited the number going inside for safety reasons. Four of the responders, two of whom were certified field medics, carefully scooted inside with flashlights.

The interior of the bunker was dark and musty smelling. All electricity, including standby generation, had been severed. The musty odor told them the ventilation system wasn't working, which meant the oxygen levels could be either low or non-existent. The conditions did not give the team members a great deal of confidence in finding anyone alive.

From the massive blast door to the first interior room of the bunker was all of twenty feet. It wasn't much of a room, more like a pseudo-airlock of sorts. The sliding door opened easily, revealing a large room with open wall lockers, or stalls, on each side. Each stall contained protective clothing, a gas mask, portable breathing equipment, a hard hat, work gloves, and protective eyewear. None of this gear was missing from any of the twelve stalls. To the members of the search team this was another bad sign.

The leader of the four, the captain in charge of the second response unit, tried to make a call to the outside on his walkie-talkie. He wanted to give constant status reports as they progressed through the underground bunker. When he couldn't make contact, he realized why: it was standard procedure in all new military bomb shelters to line the walls with lead. This was done to impede radioactivity from reaching the inside. The unintended consequence was it prevented any two-way radio communication between the inside and outside. A dedicated telephone line went upstairs, but the system had been destroyed when the building imploded. At this point, the captain instructed his men to leave all doors open to provide as much fresh air as possible to enter the interior of the bunker.

The door on the far end of the room slid open easily revealing a short hallway leading to a larger room. The four responders, sweeping their flashlight beams around the room, saw numerous workstations and desks. Most were adorned with either computers, communication gear, or large monitors. Due to the lack of power, none of these was active. This room must be the main command room for the bunker and the backup control room for the original Backskatter radar system.

Two opposing hallways led out of this room on the far end. The captain instructed two of his men, which included one of the medics, to take the hallway to the left. He and the other medic went on to check the hallway to the right. Each hallway was a short four feet in length but looked longer because of the workbenches sticking out from walls in front of them.

The hallway to the right emptied into a large area that contained two latrines and a separate sleeping area with bunkbeds and lockers. The hallway to the left opened up into a large kitchen/dining room area. The entire underground bunker had a layout resembling a large capital "T." The captain thought there must be more than one way in and out of this bunker. There had to be a "back door" somewhere.

CHAPTER 28

Christmas Valley & Bend
Sunday Noon

After their conversation with the deputy and vet, Westbrook and
Shields headed north to look at the herd of dead deer.

There wasn't much to see. All the animals looked dried up and
withered. Nothing was left except mottled hide, protruding bones,
and antlers. They decided there was no reason to land, so Westbrook
made a couple of lazy orbits around the scene while Shields took a
few pictures.

Neither could think of a rational explanation for what happened
to both the deer and cattle. The notion of a possible alien encounter
never came up.

The sixteen miles from Squaw Butte to the area south of Pine
Mountain took the 300 only fourteen minutes of flight time. They
had promised Deputy Spencer they would check out the area
and get back to him. At an average altitude of 1,500 feet above the
ground, Westbrook crisscrossed the area following a north-to-south
grid pattern, working their way from east to west. They saw nothing
but an expansive desert. No missing hunters, no search parties, no
people out exploring, and no wildlife.

They would have stayed out longer and expanded their search,
but the little helicopter was getting low on fuel. They'd been flying
for almost three hours this morning and the endurance of the little
helicopter was limited to approximately three-and-three quarter
hours of flight time. Westbrook estimated they could safely make
it back to the airport if they left within the next five minutes. Trent
didn't like cutting things any closer than need be.

After landing, Westbrook went through his normal shutdown procedures then asked Shields what he would like to do next. The game warden said he didn't think he would be needing the services of Orion Air for the rest of the day and thanked Westbrook for his help. He also asked about availability for the following day.

"Unfortunately, both Chance and I are on 24/7 standby with both our helicopters ... including the rest of the day for me. That's a result of our contract with the Air Force," Trent confessed. "We'll be that way for the rest of the week as well, I'm afraid. Sorry."

"Not to worry," Shields replied. "I doubt there will be a need to revisit the desert anytime soon."

"Going to take the rest of the day off then?"

"Nope. Think I'll go pay a visit to Central Oregon Regional."

~

Dr. Robert Parks met the coroner, Dr. Michael Clark, at the Pilot Butte Drive-In for a late lunch. He felt inclined to treat the doctor for his help on Saturday, and to engage his services in helping him identify their John Doe.

Parks ordered his usual, a robust Rueben sandwich with a Pepsi. Clark was hungry for a big, fat, greasy, bacon cheeseburger. Watching Clark eat the cholesterol-laden behemoth made Parks wonder how much longer the coroner could eat like this before he wound up in a morgue himself.

After the usual, perfunctory small talk, Parks came right to the point. He wanted to personally thank the pathologist for his contribution of the previous day. Then he asked Clark if he would be willing to help identify what remained of their mystery man through dental records. Parks also wanted to hear the coroner's thoughts on cremating what was left of the body.

Dr. Clark enthusiastically agreed to helping with the identification. This was not only his forte, but he was also curious to see who this person was and to hopefully, find out how such a horrible thing could have happened to him. True to his nature of believing in full disclosure, Parks also told his guest about his encounter with Lt. Davis.

Dr. Parks explained why the Air Force was interested in the

LifeAir pickup and thus the reason for providing dental records. Michael Clark could readily see the possibility of a connection. If their decimated victim were indeed one of the unaccounted-for Air Force people from the mysterious radar site, that would be a big step in determining what happened to him.

Dr. Clark stopped eating and set his burger down. "Robert, there's something going on here that's very wrong. For starters, we know what happened to our John Doe is medically inexplicable. We don't have a clue how something like this could have happened. Now this ... with the Air Force having an interest in him as well. Somehow, some way, my gut tells me this may be related ... and not in a good way."

Dr. Robert Parks suddenly lost his appetite and set his sandwich down as well.

~

It was early afternoon when Logan Davis walked through the main entrance at Central Oregon Regional, re-introduced himself to the man standing behind the reception podium and again asked to see Dr. Parks.

The cordial receptionist politely informed the lieutenant that Dr. Parks went out for a late lunch and wasn't expected to return for another hour or so. Davis asked if he could drop off some folders for the doctor, telling the well-dressed man that Dr. Parks would be expecting them. The attendant assured Davis he would personally see to it the doctor got the folders and asked the Air Force officer if he would like to leave a note with them. Davis scribbled something on a notepad, folded it, then slid it under the rubber band holding the stack of folders together. Handing the package to the receptionist, Davis thanked him for his help and strode out of the hospital.

Although Davis was initially planning to go straight back to the COTEF facility, he decided to take a short detour to the Bend airport instead. It wasn't far out of his way and with all the signage, was easy to find. He also vaguely remembered the route from being picked up there the previous day.

He really didn't have a good reason for doing this except to do a little background checking on Orion Air and its owners.

What he found out was entirely positive. From talking to some of the local airport people, Davis determined Orion Air had a stellar safety and customer satisfaction record. It seemed everyone at the airport was thrilled to have a helicopter service on site, and all held Westbrook and Barclay in high regard. He assumed Maj. Jefferson would be happy with this news.

~

Unbeknownst to either Logan Davis or Matt Shields, the two passed each other about two miles from the airport. Lt. Davis was on his way to check out the helicopter service they'd hired, and Trooper Shields was on his way to the hospital to determine who LifeAir might have picked up Saturday morning.

Like Davis, Shields parked in the visitor's parking lot and entered the hospital through the main entrance on the east side. Also like the lieutenant, he was greeted by the same attendant at the reception podium.

"Good afternoon," the man greeted Shields with a cordial smile. "How may I help you, Officer?

Matt Shields was dressed in his standard blue, military-style, game warden uniform with his badge and name plate prominently displayed on the front. His web utility belt with his 9 mm Hecker & Koch nicely complemented the outfit. There was no denying he was an authentic Oregon State Police Officer.

"I would like to speak to someone about the LifeAir mission to Christmas Valley yesterday. Would that be possible?"

"Let me check with the supervisor on duty, sir. He just got back from lunch and I'm sure he can help you." The receptionist plucked the white phone off the wall behind him and punched in the three-digit extension for Parks' office. Parks and Clark had cut their lunch short to return to the hospital and were in the process of sorting through the thick stack of manila folders left by Lt. Davis when the phone rang. Parks picked up the annoying intrusion on the second ring.

In a calm, professional voice, the receptionist said an officer from the state police was waiting in the lobby to talk to him. Parks said he'd be right down, hung up, and told Clark he'd be right back.

For the entire three-and-one-half minutes it took Parks to organize the folders he was working on, leave his office, walk down the hallway to the elevator and make his way down to the lobby, he wondered why someone from the state police would want to speak to him on a Sunday. He hoped it wasn't anything serious or something to do with one of his staff. That was all he needed right now.

Parks was somewhat relieved when he reached the lobby and saw the officer waiting for him was a game warden, not a patrol officer or detective. After introducing himself and shaking hands with Shields, he asked his visitor how he could be of service.

"Dr. Parks, I'm investigating a series of unexplained events which happened around the Christmas Valley area yesterday. It's my understanding LifeAir picked up a man at the Lost Forest early yesterday morning ... is that correct, sir?"

For a brief moment, Parks thought his heart and stomach had traded places. The Ruben was suddenly coming back to haunt him.

"Yes ... that is correct," Parks said, trying to control his apprehensions. "Did they violate any laws in the process, Officer?"

"No, nothing like that. I was informed by the deputy sheriff at Christmas Valley he had requested a pickup of a man found alone in the desert who was in mortal danger. What can you tell me about this?"

"Excuse me ... Officer Shields, I'm somewhat at a loss understanding what's going on here. You're asking me about the same things as everyone else lately."

Shields narrowed his eyes. "Everyone else? Who else has been talking to you about this incident?"

"For openers, my staff and the county coroner are involved ... then there's the deputy from Christmas Valley, and earlier today, an officer from the United States Air Force."

CHAPTER 29

Schriever Air Force Base
Sunday Afternoon

Lt. Colonel T.J. Rutledge had just popped open his second beer. As was his Sunday habit, he was comfortably seated in his favorite chair watching a football game, one he had been looking forward to all week. The Denver Broncos were in the process of kicking the snot out of the Green Bay Packers when his cell phone buzzed.

"Talk to me," Rutledge demanded, muting the sound on the television set. "Did you follow up on the medevac helicopter?"

"Yes and no," came the distant reply. "Lieutenant Davis got to the hospital before I did. I didn't want to repeat his steps for fear of compromising my position."

"So, what can you tell me?"

"Davis spent approximately an hour at the local hospital, came back to COTEF, and started digging through the personnel files."

"The personnel files?"

"Yes. Evidently, he separated out the files for everyone who was at Backskatter the morning of the accident, then removed their dental records."

"Why did he do that?"

"Apparently, the hospital couldn't identify the person they picked up. Thinking it might be one of our people, Davis provided them with the dental records to see if there was a match."

"Clever. Was there?"

"Don't know. Seems it will take time to determine if it is or not. Davis also took a side trip to the airport after dropping off the dental records at the hospital."

"The airport? Do you know why?"

"My guess is he was checking out the helicopter service Major Roberts hired. I don't know if he did this on his own, or if Jefferson instructed him to do it."

"Interesting. Anything from the Backskatter site?"

"Haven't heard of anything, Colonel. Orion Air, the helicopter service Roberts commissioned, shuttled Majors Jefferson and Roberts, along with Captains Mitchell and Webster, out to the site at 9:15 this morning. They wanted to be there when the bunker was opened."

"I know Roberts and Jefferson ... remind me again who Mitchell and Webster are," Rutledge demanded, rubbing the bridge of his nose.

"Captain Mark Webster is responsible for the on-site coordination of activities between COTEF and Backskatter. He's that Academy zoomie we got from DARPA. I believe Major Roberts updated you not too long ago on his background and duties. Captain Devon Mitchell is regular Air Force. He's responsible for security at both sites and oversaw the first responder group following the accident."

"Are either aware of our ... 'agenda'?"

"Webster is, but not Mitchell. He's only sanctioned to work as head of security and has been kept out of the loop."

"That helps. The fewer who are in the know, the better."

"Which reminds me, Colonel," the voice on the other end took on a more serious tone. "Exactly what do Major Jefferson and Lieutenant Davis know?"

After a brief pause, Rutledge answered. "Neither one has the full picture. Jefferson, as head of base security at Schriever, was tasked by me to find out what the hell happened out there and write a preliminary accident report. I'm hoping this will satisfy the powers that be, or at least buy us some time to clean this up. Major Jefferson, as a project outsider, will hopefully provide them with a benign, impartial report. One that absolves us of any culpability while keeping our plans a secret. Lieutenant Davis, as my administrative assistant on this project, is nothing more than a glorified clerk and 'go-fer.' He keeps me up to speed on the day-to-day goings-on in Oregon. Does that answer your question?"

"Pretty much. I still think I need to keep a close eye on those two. Anything else, Colonel?"

"Just stay on top of this. We need to keep this situation absolutely under control and contained … at all costs. I don't think I need to remind you of what's at stake here. If this thing gets away from us, I shudder to think what the implications could be for some of us."

"Relax, sir, I've got this. I've delt with situations like this before. If you can do what needs to be done on your end, leave me to deal with the Oregon side of things."

"Just be careful … and don't go off half-cocked on some wild notion without checking in with me first. Got it?"

"You're the boss."

"Before you sign off, is there any news yet about possible survivors?"

"Nope … nothing yet. I occasionally check in at the communications room thinking something might be coming in anytime. The bunker should've been opened by now. Is there anything else you think I should be doing?"

"Just check back in as soon as you've got something new."

"Will do, Colonel."

After a moment of silence, the line abruptly went dead. Rutledge set his cell phone down and took a sip of beer. Then he turned off the TV and told his wife he needed to take care of something back at his office.

CHAPTER 30

COTEF
Sunday Afternoon

Logan Davis made it back to COTEF shortly after 2 p.m.
Somewhat at a loss as what to do next, he checked in with Maj. Roberts' administrative assistant, Lt. Blackstone. He was curious about any updates from the Backskatter site. He was excited to hear the bunker beneath the destroyed main building had finally been opened and a search and rescue team had entered. Blackstone and several others were hanging out in the communications room, anxiously awaiting news on possible survivors. Other than that, nothing else was happening. No calls from Dr. Parks at the hospital or from Col. Rutledge in Colorado.

Since there didn't seem to be any "escort" around to shadow him, Davis decided now was a good a time as any to do a little snooping, per Maj. Jefferson's suggestion. But first, he headed down to the DEFAC to grab something to eat.

The two civilian cooks were somewhat surprised to see the young officer in a dress uniform walk into their dining area. Although accustomed to seeing various military and non-military people come and go since the project was initiated, they sensed something different about the well-dressed, mild-mannered young man who asked about getting a late lunch.

To his delight, the pair of middle-aged ladies were only too happy to put together a quick meal. Thanking the pair for accommodating him, Davis took the tray containing an impressive-looking BLT sandwich, an individual bag of potato chips, apple slices and can of Pepsi to the nearest table. He had consumed half of the sandwich when a middle-aged, male technician in a lab coat walked into the area, glanced around then headed straight for the coffee urn.

Davis saw this chance encounter as a golden opportunity to engage with someone "in the know" about the project without interference. As the technician walked back out with his fresh mug of coffee, Davis blurted out the first thing that came to mind.

"The coffee in the lab must be pretty bad for you to sneak in here for the good stuff."

"You have no idea," came the serious sounding reply.

Logan Davis chuckled at the remark and shook his head. "Oh, trust me. I've had my share of nasty shit over the years. That's why I've given up on military Joe, especially when it's made by enlisted pukes. I've always suspected they either spit in it or piss in it."

Davis' remark brought a genuine belly-laugh from the man as he casually strolled over to the lieutenant. "You got that right, my friend. I'm seriously thinking about converting to tea while working here. You must be one of our visitors from Colorado."

"Yep. Lt. Logan Davis." The officer said, noticing the name on the man's ID tag. "I'm here with Major Colby Jefferson ... Brian. Colonel T.J. Rutledge sent us here from Schriever to investigate yesterday's accident."

The technician lowered his gaze and shook his head. "That should never have happened. I warned them it was too soon to change the laser medium and ramp up the power of the microwave generator without adequate testing and safeguards."

After an awkward moment of silence, the man introduced himself as Brian Reynolds. Davis casually asked the man about his job at COTEF and learned the technician was actually one of the project's principal engineers.

Davis played along with the man's obvious frustration as if he knew what the engineer was talking about. "The colonel shared with me some concerns about that as well. He thought the target power level of 1,000 kilowatts was a little on the high side."

Reynolds scoffed. "Rutledge is either badly mis-informed, utterly confused or full of shit about the power setting we're trying to reach."

Davis quickly recognized he was talking with a disgruntled

worker and could quite possibly glean key inside information from him. He had to be careful and not come across as too pushy or eager. He had to play it cool.

"According to my knowledge of the project," Davis went on while casually taking another bite of his sandwich. "I was of the understanding 'we' were trying to reach one million watts of output. Isn't that one thousand kilowatts?"

"Your math is correct, Lieutenant. However, the latest directive wants us to up the ante by a factor of ten."

Davis raised his eyebrows. "To ten million watts? Ten thousand kilowatts?"

"Yep, you got it. First it was fifty kilowatts, which was a piece of cake. Then came one hundred fifty kilowatts, five times more powerful than anything we've previously done. Then came a thousand kilowatts, and now ... now we're going for almost a gigawatt."

"Is that even possible?"

The laser engineer pursed his lips tightly and subtly shook his head. "It should be, given the right combination of mediums, magnetron power and pulse settings. Unfortunately, now we may never know."

Davis steered the conversation away from the accident itself, quickly re-engaging the man with a technical question. "I assume a power setting of that magnitude can only be possible with shorter duration bursts. Is that right?"

"You know your physics my friend," Reynolds replied, who seemed happy to abandon his negative thoughts. "The original 'shots' were pulsed at one second intervals. With the increased power levels, we had to go with shorter duration bursts ... which we got down to one-half second. Imagine firing laser 'bullets' at a rate of one hundred twenty a minute at a range of up to a thousand miles."

"So ... with the addition of higher power levels, the duration of the shots had to get shorter. I'm assuming that was necessary to prevent dangerously high levels of heat build-up."

"You're absolutely correct, Lieutenant. Our experiments and calculations told us we need to pulse our laser blasts somewhere in the neighborhood of a thousandth of a second each. One on, one off. The rate of fire for such a machine would amount to approximately one hundred blasts a second. If you could see the shots with the naked eye, it would look like a steady stream of fire. But, since it's a highly concentrated form of light energy, you can't see or hear it."

"Well ... that should make it easier to hit an inbound ICBM or bomber."

"And then some. Sorry, but I need to get back to work. I'm trying to figure out what went wrong as well. Nice chatting with you Lieutenant."

Davis sat back in his chair as he watched the man walk out of the DFAC, lighter on his toes than when he walked in. Nothing like a good cup of coffee and getting something off your chest to elevate your mood, Davis thought.

His short conversation with the laser engineer had set his mind racing. Ten million watts of energy, 10,000 KW per laser burst. Rattled off at a rate of one hundred blasts per second, 6,000 blasts per minute, and with a range of a thousand miles. It was almost inconceivable. Davis wondered how such a feat was even possible, given the level of technology they were working with.

Then a strange thought crossed his mind. Something Reynolds said about the laser's capabilities. And then some were his exact words. "What in the world did he mean by that?" Davis said aloud to himself. It wasn't so much as what the engineer said as the way he said it. There was something almost giddy about it, something akin to bragging. Shaking off the troubling thought for the time being, Davis made a mental note to talk to Maj. Jefferson about including Brian Reynolds in their line-up of people to interview.

Davis returned to what remained of his lunch. He had barely stuck a potato chip in his mouth when Lt. Blackstone came running into the DEFAC.

"They've opened the bunker!" she shouted.

CHAPTER 31

Central Oregon Regional Medical Center
Sunday Afternoon

Matt Shields asked Dr. Parks if they could talk somewhere more private about the LifeAir pickup. Parks suggested they go to his office and include the county coroner, Dr. Michael Clark, in the discussion. As a seasoned law enforcement officer, Shields had the ability to read facial expressions and body language fairly quickly, almost to an incriminating degree. What he saw in Robert Parks told him something was amiss here.

On the walk back up to Parks' second-floor office, Shields took the opportunity to put the doctor at ease with a few "small talk" questions. He had to earn the doctor's confidence if he was going to get as much information from the man as possible. He didn't particularly like using strong arm legal tactics unless he had no other choice.

Michael Clark was surprised to see Parks walk through the office door with a State of Oregon Game Warden in tow. After introductions were made, Shields explained he was in the middle of an active investigation into the mysterious deaths of a group of deer and cattle in the Christmas Valley area. He also mentioned there was an on-going search effort for two missing hunters in the same vicinity. He was curious if there was any connection with the LifeAir pickup and these unexplained events. After what Dr. Parks had mentioned in the lobby, he was also curious about the Air Force's interest in the matter as well.

Doctors Parks and Clark were dumbfounded. Both instantly recognized the real possibility of a connection between all these occurrences and looked at each other quizzically. In a truly brief period of time, their mystery corpse was suddenly the center of an awful lot of attention.

Dr. Parks spoke up first. "Officer Shields, the Air Force is interested in our patient, who died in route to the hospital, because they have several people unaccounted for at their Christmas Valley radar installation. Something about a bad accident. A young lieutenant inquired about our pickup to see if the patient could possibly be one of their missing people."

"Has this person been identified as such?" Shields inquired.

"We don't know yet. The lieutenant provided us with dental records to see if there was a match. Doctor Clark and I were just about to go down to the morgue and perform an examination when you asked to see me."

"So, there was no identification on this man? I'm assuming it was a man?"

"Yes, yes it was. He was found naked, alone and suffering from dehydration and exposure. He was delirious and unable to speak. Because he was without any clothing or personal effects, we couldn't establish an identity. We asked about possible missing persons reports, but nothing turned up. That's why he is temporarily residing in our morgue as a John Doe. Then the Air Force showed up."

"Interesting. I'd like to see the body if I may."

"I'm not sure we can let you do that, Officer Shields. Not only would it be against our policy, but we believe the body may be infected with an undetermined disease of some sort."

"I can get a court order if that's what you require. I'm sure you have sufficient protective equipment on hand, or you and Dr. Clark wouldn't be performing an examination."

Matt Shields was not one to be dissuaded or cut off so easily. He was determined to find any link between the dead man and the events he was investigating.

Robert Parks was boxed in, and he knew it. Interfering with an active investigation by a law enforcement officer could put him and the hospital in the realm of obstruction of justice. He had no choice but to comply. Clark stood there without saying a word. He waited to see how this would play out.

"A court order won't be necessary, Officer," Parks said, clearing his throat. "But I do insist both this conversation and what you see remain extremely confidential. We're dealing with several unknowns here, and we'd like to keep this as quiet as possible. Like you, we're looking for answers. I hope you understand."

"Because this is an active investigation, everything I'm doing is highly confidential Doctor. Please, rest assured you have no worries regarding my integrity or that of the state police. As I said, this is an official investigation."

Robert Parks thanked the game warden for his professional discretion and invited Shields to join him and Clark in the morgue. On the elevator ride down, Michael Clark thought of something the officer said earlier.

"Officer Shields, you said the cattle and the deer you found all died under mysterious circumstances. Is that correct?"

"Yes. It was the strangest thing," Shields replied, unconsciously rested his hand on the butt of his gun. "They all looked like they died together and fairly quickly … then decomposed at a rapid rate."

The two doctors flinched like they'd been hit with a cattle prod. Michael Clark's spontaneous remark of "Jesus Christ!" pretty much summed up what both doctors were thinking.

CHAPTER 32

The Backskatter Site
Sunday Afternoon

The four men who entered the bunker were being careful and methodical. Searching the warren of rooms in the dark with flashlights wasn't a straightforward or easy task. It took time.

The captain in charge of the detail and his team canvassed the bunker from beginning to end looking not only for any of their missing people, but also for possible clues as to what happened. In the dining area, the second pair of responders discovered two people slumped over one of the tables.

With their heads resting on their folded arms, both looked like they were catnapping. Next to them on the table sat flashlights that were either turned off or had extinguished their batteries. The flashlights sat on top of some papers. It looked as if the pair were leaving behind notes.

The two responders were momentarily transfixed by the eerie scene their flashlights illuminated. Then one of the victims moaned.

The field medic and his partner quickly responded to the victims to check them out. Both were women, and both were semi-conscious with labored breathing and weak pulses. The medic instructed his partner to gently move the woman he was checking to the floor as he did the same, then asked his partner to go find the captain and his teammate and have someone to go fetch one of the portable breathing apparatuses.

In less than three minutes, all four members of the search team were huddled around the two women, now lying face up on the floor. The portable oxygen apparatus was administered intermittently between the two as the field medics checked out each survivor. They were alive but experiencing labored breathing. Their vital signs were weak, and they were probably dehydrated. Both medics agreed; all things considered; they weren't in that bad of shape and should be okay.

The captain instructed one of his responders to hustle outside, inform Maj. Roberts of what they found, and return with more men and two stretchers.

Once apprised of the situation, Roberts decided the next course of action would be to get the two women, along with their attending field medics, back to COTEF as quickly as possible. He didn't particularly want to take them to a hospital unless he had no other choice. Because the COTEF facility had a first-rate infirmary stocked with high-end medical equipment, the secure site would be his first option.

The major instructed one of the nearby responders to hustle out to the helipad and tell the Orion Air pilot to warm up his helicopter. This was going to be an emergency medevac. Roberts also told the airman to have Barclay radio his partner at the Bend airport and have him hustle out to Backskatter in the other helicopter. The major wanted to get back to COTEF as well. He wanted to debrief the two women before Jefferson or Davis had a chance to talk to them.

~

From his vantage point, Chance Barclay watched the flurry of activity surrounding the southern end of the destroyed building. Everyone was yelling and running around like something big just happened. He was surprised to see a young airman break away from the group of people and run across the parking lot toward him.

Wide eyed and out of breath, the soldier told Barclay they found survivors and they needed to get four people back to COTEF as fast as possible. He also said Maj. Roberts wanted the other helicopter dispatched to Backskatter immediately.

Barclay quickly climbed into the 500's cockpit and flipped on the battery switch, followed by the avionics master switch. As soon as he had power to his radios, he put in a call to Trent Westbrook via their discreet ship-to-ship/ship-to-shop frequency.

"Three-two-six Charlie Bravo to Orion Air," Chance announced. "Trent, got your ears on?"

"Orion Air up and running," came the delayed response from Westbrook.

"Hope I didn't catch you in the middle of taking a pee."

"Nope. I was on the other side of the office. What's up?"

"The Air Force wants you to get your butt out to the Backskatter site ASAP. If you left immediately, what would be your ETA?"

"Seventy-five minutes, tops. What's the rush?"

"The recovery team has found survivors. I'm taking them back to COTEF as soon as they get loaded. I'm assuming they want to start ferrying key people back there as well."

"Okay. Leaving within fifteen. Talk to you in route. Orion Air clear."

"Three-two-six clear."

As soon as he signed off, Barclay flipped off the avionics master switch but left the battery on. This was the first step in starting up the 500. He needed electrical power to spin up the compressor section of the engine before igniting the turbine section. The entire startup would amount to approximately six minutes of a series of procedures followed by safety checks. He had spooled up the helicopter to idle power and was ready for takeoff when a Humvee came screeching up to the helipad.

Maj. Roberts and Capt. Mitchell got out of the front seat and assisted the two field medics sitting in the back with the two survivors. The four men helped the women into the helicopter and, per Barclay's instructions, buckled them in. One medic climbed into the front with one of the victims while the other medic got in the back with the second one.

Yelling above the engine and rotor noise, Maj. Roberts asked Barclay if he was able to reach his partner. Chance told him Westbrook was on his way and should arrive within the hour. Roberts asked Chance if he could return as soon as he dropped off his passengers. Barclay said no problem, but he needed to fuel up before returning. Roberts gave a thumbs up and retreated a safe distance from the noisy machine.

After a quick status check of his passengers, the engine gauges, and the surrounding area, Chance slowly raised the collective and the 500 was airborne. The chronometer on the helicopter's instrument panel read 2:05 p.m.

CHAPTER 33

Central Oregon Regional Medical Center
Sunday Afternoon

The hospital's weekend supervisor, the county coroner, and the game warden huddled around a stainless steel exam table in the hospital's morgue.

Both doctors and the trooper wore biohazard suits with protective face shields and latex gloves. Not knowing exactly what they were dealing with, they didn't want to take any chances with their personal safety. On an adjacent table, spread out and labeled, lay the seventeen dental records Lt. Davis had provided earlier.

As with the dead deer and cattle, not much remained of the man's body to look at. The remains barely resembled anything human. The corpse was dried up and withered. It looked like an ancient mummy after being run over by a bulldozer. Nothing was left except mottled skin, protruding bones, and an indescribable odor. To Trooper Shields, the dead man looked exactly like the dead animals he had surveyed at Christmas Valley.

He disclosed as much to Parks and Clark, who immediately stopped what they were doing and looked at each other. The ensuing silence was palpable. The expression on the faces of the two doctors said it all: they were genuinely alarmed.

Shields broke the strained silence, suggested they concentrate on the task at hand. If this person could be identified as one of the Air Force people, the determination would go a long way in solving a major mystery. Both doctors agreed and went back to work.

Clark didn't need to surgically open the mouth to begin his examination; it was already locked wide open in a gaping, grotesque fashion. Since tooth enamel was harder than any other substance in the human body, teeth would remain intact long after all other body parts had decayed or otherwise been destroyed. Many a victim of fire or chemical destruction were identified as a result. Even if only a few teeth were available, a forensic pathologist could still make a positive identification with the help of accurate records.

The preferred method of doing this was by using X-rays. If those were unavailable, notations on a tooth chart could still be used. Lt. Davis had provided both pieces of information for his missing people. Clark was optimistic they could identify this man if he were indeed one of the missing Backskatter workers. A positive ID would be a significant step in helping them find out what happened to him.

The coroner began by first, examining the dead man's teeth while Dr. Parks took notes. Information about the number of teeth, location of missing teeth, number and location of any fillings or crowns, and any other obvious features were noted. This information would be compared against the charts and X-rays Lt. Davis provided. When a correlation was made, a more thorough, tooth-by-tooth analysis would be performed to insure a positive ID.

Although the two doctors took their time, being both careful and thorough, they had positively identified their mystery man in less than an hour. Unfortunately, and thanks to Lt. Davis' coding system, they could only refer to him as "Subject OP/BS 015." They still had no name or other information, but he was definitely one of the missing Air Force people. It was a step in the right direction.

Returning the body to the biohazard bag and placing the bag in the morgue's refrigerated locker, the trio removed their protective garb, scrubbed up and returned to Parks' office with their notes and the files. The two doctors had much to talk about, especially regarding their next steps. Both had expressed their frustration about not being able to have a name or any background information on their man. Such would have been useful in helping to determine what had happened to him as well as what they should do next. Regardless, both were still in agreement the remains needed to be cremated before turning them over to family or the Air Force. They would say this was standard procedure when the cause of death was an undetermined disease.

Matt Shields asked Dr. Parks if he would get in touch with his

Air Force contact and ask him to come back to the hospital. Shields instructed the doctor to say a positive ID had been made but didn't want to release the information over the phone. Shields wanted to talk to the young lieutenant face-to-face, and for the time being, didn't want the Air Force to know the state police were involved.

A definite connection had now been made between several mysterious incidents. Matt Shields was now hot on the trail and looking for some serious answers. His instincts told him the Air Force was the key.

CHAPTER 34

Bend Municipal Airport & COTEF
Sunday Afternoon

As soon as Trent Westbrook ended his radio conversation with his partner, he exited the hanger by the back door and half-trotted out to the helipads.

In anticipation of being called out at a moment's notice, he had the Schweizer 300 re-fueled when he and the game warden returned from the desert earlier that day. No pre-flight inspection was necessary; it had already been done prior to the first flight and after the re-fueling procedure. Nothing else needed be done. He was ready to go.

Engine start-up, rotor engagement, run-up checks, and safety scans took all of seven minutes. Trent was airborne a scant eleven minutes after talking to Barclay.

Northwest of Pine Mountain, Westbrook made a radio call to Chance using their discreet frequency. "Three-two-six Charlie Bravo, three-two-five Tango Charlie, over. How do you read CB?" Using standard pilot phraseology, Westbrook identified who he was calling and then identified himself before continuing with his call.

"Loud and clear. Charlie Bravo in route to COTEF. Five south of Pine Mountain at six-five. Trent, what's your location?"

Chance Barclay was telling Westbrook he was on his way back to Bend, flying in a northwesterly direction. His location was five miles south of the predominant landmark of Pine Mountain and he was flying at an altitude of six-thousand, five-hundred feet above sea level, approximately twenty-five hundred feet above the ground.

Trent Westbrook responded he was just north of the same

landmark, flying in a southeasterly direction at an altimeter reading of five-thousand, five hundred feet. Essentially, the two helicopters were on a collision course except for the fact that Barclay was flying a thousand feet higher than Westbrook.

The FAA established this transit scheme back in the late 1940s, after the end of World War II. Aircraft flying by visual flight rules and traveling in a westerly direction, with a magnetic compass heading between 180-359 degrees, were required to fly at even altitudes plus five hundred feet. Aircraft flying in the opposite direction were to fly at odd altitudes plus five hundred feet. The thousand-foot separation had kept many an aircraft from potentially disastrous encounters.

"Tango Charlie is ten miles north at five-five," responded Westbrook. "Backskatter ETA fifty minutes. Are you coming back out?"

"Roger that, Tango Charlie. After COTEF drop off will refuel then head back to the radar site. Stay in touch."

"Roger that, Charlie Bravo. Have a safe flight."

Within two minutes time, both pilots saw each other as the 500 passed over the 300 heading in the opposite direction. As designed, Westbrook was a thousand feet lower than his partner. There was also about a half-mile horizontal separation between the two. Although it was normally hard to see a fast-moving passing aircraft, the flashing strobe lights on the underbelly of both helicopters made each easily recognizable from a distance. Both pilots gently rocked their machines as they passed one another. This was a pilot's standard way of saying "hello" and "I see you" when flying in close proximity to another aircraft.

~

At the same time Barclay finished loading up his passengers at Backskatter and Westbrook left the Bend airport, Lt. Davis and Lt. Blackstone paced outside the door of COTEF's communications room. They had heard earlier two survivors had been found in the bunker and were being airlifted back to COTEF for evaluation and treatment. Both were anxious to hear how things were going and if the survivors were okay.

The "Comm Room" served a dual purpose at COTEF. Not only was this the location where all classified and non-classified military and project communications took place, it also served as the main switchboard for receiving all external calls to the facility. The lone operator had the responsibility of screening any incoming calls from the outside before routing them to the appropriate department or person. At the most, this only happened maybe once or twice a day. All "official" telephone traffic was automatically routed through COTEF's secure telecommunication system.

The young airman sitting at the console was surprised to see the #1 outside line light up as he took a sip of coffee. He couldn't imagine who would be calling the facility on Sunday, of all days. After answering, he turned to the two young officers standing in the doorway and said the call was from a Dr. Parks at the local hospital who needed to speak to a Lt. Logan Davis.

Davis immediately identified himself to the operator and asked if he could take the call in private somewhere. Jennifer Blackstone said he could use the phone in her office, a short distance down the hallway, right next to Maj. Roberts' office. Davis thanked her for the offer and hustled down the corridor.

The door was propped open. Upon entering, Davis noted how much the young woman's office reminded him of his own back at Schriever. The only exception was she had newer, nicer furniture and had a separate, inside door that connected her office directly to the major's. Davis made a mental note that, once he got back to his home base, he was going to talk to his boss about a few upgrades.

The young officer pushed the flashing button on the console and said into the handset, "Lieutenant Davis here."

"Good afternoon, Lieutenant. This is Dr. Parks from Central Oregon Regional Medical Center. We have positively identified our John Doe as one of your missing people."

Davis' heart jumped in his chest. "I wish I could say this was good news. Thank you, nevertheless, Doctor. I will need to make some recovery arrangements on behalf of the Air Force. What is the identification number for the victim?'

"I'm sorry, Lieutenant. I can't give you that information over the phone ... you will need to come back to the hospital. We have a lot of paperwork to fill out, which will require your signature, and we will need the full name and some other information for our records … as well as for the death certificate. Releasing the body is a separate matter. Please understand, we have legal requirements that need to be satisfied."

Logan Davis suddenly remembered he was dealing with a civilian entity with its own set of rules. He was not working with military people or with military protocols. He was operating outside his sphere of influence. He decided he needed to check with Maj. Jefferson before going any further.

"Dr. Parks, let me check with my superior officer first. I need clearance on how he would like to proceed with this. Can I get back to you later today?"

"Of course, Lieutenant. I will be here until five this afternoon."

"Thank you once again, Doctor. I appreciate your help on this."

After hanging up, Davis sat down then rocked back in the comfortable chair, exhaled, and quietly said to himself, "So, what the fuck do I do now?"

CHAPTER 35

COTEF

Sunday Afternoon

Chance Barclay and his passengers were approximately ten minutes from landing when he thought to ask the medics if they wanted to return to Backskatter after unloading their survivors.

The one riding up front with Barclay, obviously the senior of the two, said he would. The second one, riding in the back seat, said he would stay with the two women at COTEF. Chance informed the senior medic after their drop off he would need to go to the airport, refuel and then they could head directly back to the desert. The medic gave Barclay a thumbs up.

Chance Barclay, flying the faster MD 500, was the first to land at his destination. He had set down on the helipad at COTEF and was spooling down his machine when Westbrook was still nineteen minutes away from the Backskatter complex.

Waiting for Barclay and his passengers were several members of the COTEF staff. All were eager to help unload the survivors and get them inside for further examination. The two field medics were the first to disembark from the helicopter and, with the help of others, gently assisted the two women out of the whirling machine and into a waiting golf cart. The senior medic climbed back into the front seat, strapped himself in, re-donned the headset then gave Barclay a thumbs up signal saying he was ready to go.

At approximately the same time, Trent Westbrook approached the radar site from the northwest. As he descended, Trent could clearly see the layout of the massive complex in the distance. He was duly impressed. He could also see the helipads and made a descending, counterclockwise circle around the area before gently setting down on the same helipad his partner had used. Waiting for him at a safe distance was Maj. Roberts.

Once Trent had spooled down the rotors and locked down his controls, he motioned for the major to approach the helicopter from the front and climb in on the right-hand side. Although Roberts didn't have the opportunity to look over the second Orion Air helicopter earlier that morning, he was surprised to discover the front seat of the little 300 was almost as large and comfortable as that of the 500. A third person, however, would have made things a bit crowded.

All things considered; it was a quick turnaround for Westbrook. Once he had the major loaded, strapped in and briefed, he was airborne within six minutes of landing. The ensuing fifty-five-minute trip back to COTEF was a quiet ride for the pair. Roberts seemed to be either deep in thought, or lost in thought, for almost the entire trip. Unbeknownst to Westbrook, the major was anxious to get back to COTEF and check up on the status of the two survivors. He also wanted to talk to them before either Jefferson or Davis could interview them.

Westbrook, as a condition of their agreement, decided he shouldn't ask any questions about how things were going. Instead, he just answered a few questions from Roberts regarding their ETA and if he had heard anything from his partner in the other helicopter.

~

Before making his approach to the COTEF site, Chance Barclay had radioed ahead to the FBO at the Bend Airport requesting fuel. He also requested a hot fueling procedure and informed the dispatcher this was going to be a fast turnaround. The dispatcher said a truck would be waiting for him at Orion Air when he arrived.

Chance made a standard approach and landing on the company's #1 helipad. After spooling down the engine and rotors, he locked down the controls and indicated to the waiting fuel truck he was ready to tank up. The attendant quickly moved the truck into position and initiated the hot fueling procedure. Everything went off like clockwork.

Out of habit, Barclay checked his wristwatch for the time. It was now 2:35 in the afternoon. They had made the trip from the Backskatter site back to COTEF, unloaded their passengers and were almost ready for a turnaround flight back to the desert in less than an hour.

Within fifteen minutes, the 500 was fully fueled, the fuel truck had left the area, and Barclay was in the process of spooling the helicopter back up to maximum RPM. After a check of his engine gauges and the surrounding area for any safety issues, Chance unlocked his controls and slowly raised the collective. Barclay and his passenger were instantly airborne and headed southeast.

As agreed, once clear of the airport's five-mile controlled traffic area, Chance switched frequencies and made a radio call to Westbrook in the 300.

"Three-two-five Tango Charlie, Three-two-six Charlie Bravo. Trent, got your ears on?"

"Tango Charlie up and running Charlie Bravo. What's your twenty?"

"Charlie Bravo clear of S-Zero-Seven. In route to Backskatter. ETA around three chimes. Over"

Barclay told his partner he had just left Bend airport's control zone, was heading back to the radar site, and his estimated time of arrival was 3:00 p.m. S07 was the FAA designator for the Bend airport, which has the standard five-mile control zone which extended in all directions from the center of the field.

"Charlie Bravo ... Tango Charlie is ten southeast of Pine Mountain at four-five. Will make drop at COTEF then RTB Bend, refuel and await further instructions. Over"

Westbrook told his partner he was approximately halfway back to the COTEF site, flying at four thousand-five hundred feet indicated altitude, approximately fifteen hundred feet off the ground. He was flying low and fast trying to get his passenger back to COTEF as quickly as possible. After dropping off Maj. Roberts, he would "return to base" at Orion Air for fuel and wait to hear where to go next.

"Tango Charlie ... Charlie Bravo approaching Pine Mountain now. We're at five-five and have you at our eleven o'clock. Will call when back at COTEF... over."

"Roger that, Charlie Bravo. Have a safe flight."

Although approximately ten miles separated the two helicopters at this point, almost too far to see one another with the naked eye, the powerful flashing strobe lights on the underside of both aircraft made their position easily visible from a distance.

The two pilots passed each other just to the west side of Pine Mountain. Both were obviously in a hurry and pushing their helicopters to the limits. Time was of the essence at this point and neither one wanted to disappoint their clients.

It took Trent Westbrook sixteen minutes to reach COTEF after passing his partner going the opposite direction. It would take Chance Barclay approximately twenty-two minutes to travel more than twice the distance to Backskatter. Both would land at their respective destinations within fifteen minutes of each other.

Waiting for Chance Barclay and the 500 on the tarmac at Backskatter were Maj. Colby Jefferson, Capt. Mark Webster, and an unidentified third person in fatigues. None of the three looked as if he were having a good day.

CHAPTER 36

COTEF & Backskatter Site
Sunday Mid-Afternoon

Lt. Logan Davis was having a hard time trying to sort everything out, all of which seemed to be happening at the same time.

His anxiety regarding what was now going on with their "Oregon Project" was starting to wear on him. He instinctively felt a sense of foreboding regarding the recent turn of events.

One of their missing people from Backskatter had been positively identified as the man picked up by a medevac helicopter the previous morning. Unfortunately, he arrived at the local hospital as a DOA patient. Not only would he and Maj. Jefferson be unable to glean any information about the accident from him, now it seemed they would also have issues recovering the body. The fact he was found naked out in the middle of nowhere remained a nagging, unanswered question. Naked … no clothes. That perplexing thought rose again. Was there a possible connection between this and all the clothing scattered about the Backskatter complex? Logan Davis couldn't help but wonder.

He also thought about the two survivors. He recounted watching the larger Orion Air helicopter disgorge two responders and a pair of survivors after landing. All of whom, except for one of the responders, climbed into two golf carts along with COTEF personnel and disappeared toward the northern end of the facility. He assumed they were headed towards the loading dock. As soon as the golf carts were a safe distance from the helicopter, the responder who stayed behind climbed back on board and it immediately took off, heading west. He reasoned they were headed back to the airport, probably to refuel. Since one of the responders was on board, he figured they would undoubtedly be going back out to the Backskatter site afterwards.

Davis desperately wanted to see how the survivors were doing and to talk to them but was told the facility's infirmary was off limits to non-essential personnel. Once again, he felt like an outsider and intentionally being kept in the dark.

It also came as a surprise to hear Maj. Derick Roberts, COTEF's commanding officer, was inbound from the desert in the smaller helicopter and would be landing shortly. Roberts, along with Capt. Mark Webster, the on-site project coordinator, and Maj. Jefferson had all left earlier that morning for the Backskatter site. He assumed the three officers would be there all day, and possibly into the night. He did not expect anyone to return to COTEF this early. Roberts must be anxious to debrief the two survivors, before he and Maj. Jefferson could visit with them.

Then there was the subtle revelation from the engineer he encountered in the DEFAC earlier that day. The laser system under development was ten times more powerful than what he had been told, and it apparently had more capabilities as well. This tidbit of information all but confirmed to him something more was going on here than met the eye.

While Davis pondered all of this at his workstation in their assigned office, he was informed by one of the communications people to expect the arrival of Maj. Jefferson, along with Capt. Webster and a third person, within the hour. To the young lieutenant, the return of these three, especially hot on the heels of COTEF's commanding officer, was yet another indication something important might be up.

Logan Davis anxiously looked forward to seeing Maj. Jefferson. He not only wanted to know what was going on, he also needed to get the major's input on how to deal with the hospital and what they should do regarding the now-identified remains of the Backskatter accident victim. The two investigators had a lot to talk about.

~

Once again, Trent Westbrook, flying the Schweizer 300, and Chance Barclay, flying the MD 500, passed each other going in opposite directions.

Trent Westbrook was on his way back to COTEF to drop off Maj. Roberts while Barclay and his passenger were on their way out to the desert radar site. While in route, they stayed in touch and updated each other on what they were doing.

Westbrook, after dropping off the major, planned on going back to the airport to refuel and await further instructions. Barclay would drop off his medic/responder and pick up Maj. Jefferson, Capt. Webster and a third person then return to COTEF as well. The two pilots and their helicopters were doing more flying on this Sunday than they would normally be doing in a week. Both expected this to be a profitable month for their young company.

Both pilots landed at their respective destinations within fifteen minutes of one another. It was 3:46 p.m. when Barclay set down at the radar site. Westbrook landed at COTEF shortly after 4:00 p.m.

Barclay's third passenger turned out to be the commander of the second response unit, the one who replaced Capt. Devon Mitchell, of the first unit on Saturday. Although Capt. Mitchell was part of the original group Barclay had flown out to Backskatter earlier that morning, Mitchell decided to remain at the site. He wanted to relieve the overnight shift commander.

It was evident to Chance that everyone at the radar site seemed tired, frustrated, and basically, wrung out. As industrial accidents go, Barclay thought this one must have topped out at a ten in the Air Force's book.

Once Chance spooled down the helicopter to ground idle and locked his controls, he told his departing passenger he could exit the aircraft toward the front. Then he motioned for his three waiting passengers to climb aboard. After everyone had strapped in and donned their headsets, Chance gave them an abbreviated safety briefing. Then he casually announced since this was going to be a relatively quick flight, the customary inflight drinks and snacks would not be served. It was a classic Chance Barclay comment, one which generated a few chuckles from the group. It was also a welcome relief for the three men who seemed to be under a great deal of stress.

~

Trent Westbrook set down 325 Tango Charlie on COTEF's helipad at 4:06 p.m., unloaded Maj. Roberts and immediately took off for the airport.

Prior to landing, Trent informed the major he needed to re-fuel and would remain at the airport for the next call-out unless Roberts wanted him to return to COTEF. Maj. Roberts said that would work but reminded Trent that he and Barclay were still on 24/7 standby status per their agreement. Westbrook anticipated as much and told the major he'd be ready when called.

Chance Barclay, flying the much faster MD 500, landed at COTEF only twenty-one minutes after Westbrook had left the highly classified complex for the airport. It took Barclay slightly longer to unload the three passengers than the single rider Trent ferried. After the three men were a safe distance away from the helipad, Chance spooled his aircraft back up to maximum RPM, made an almost vertical high-performance takeoff, and headed northwest toward the airport.

At approximately 4:46 p.m. Barclay set down 326 Charlie Bravo on Orion Air's #1 helipad, right next to 325 Tango Charlie on #2 helipad and initiated his shut down sequence. Because none of the Air Force people had requested a quick turnaround or another flight in the immediate future, Chance looked forward to a break and getting something to eat. He was also anxious to exchange notes with his partner on their day of flying.

CHAPTER 37

COTEF & Central Oregon Regional Medical Center
Sunday Mid-Afternoon

Lt. Logan Davis was on the tarmac when "three-two-six Charlie Bravo" touched down at 4:31 p.m. He had been anxious to talk with Maj. Jefferson all afternoon.

As soon as the three Air Force officers had climbed out of the helicopter and moved a safe distance away, Chance Barclay spooled his machine back up to full power and took off. His passengers, Lt. Davis and any other COTEF personnel outside at the time watched the impressive max performance takeoff and the machine's speedy departure to the west.

With a quick salute, followed by a handshake, Davis expressed his appreciation in having the major back on site. They had a great deal of catching up to do.

"Welcome back boss," Davis said with genuine regard. "How was your flight? Probably more important ... how was your day?"

"Lieutenant Davis." Jefferson replied with a slight grin. "Thank you for coming out to greet me. The flight was good, thank you. I trust your day was more productive than mine."

"Oh, you have no idea, Major. We have a lot to talk about!"

The two investigators held back from the others while walking toward the building and stopped short of going inside with the others once they were through the security gate.

"Major, mind if we visit out here for a few minutes before going inside?" Davis asked, looking around to see if anyone was within earshot.

"No, not at all. What's on your mind?"

"Major, I strongly suspect we are under constant surveillance and that everywhere inside this place is bugged … including our quarters. I don't think anything we do or say will be private once we go in. Also, I don't think we can trust anyone here. I think there's more going on with this project then we've been led to believe."

The tone of Lt. Davis' voice and the anxious look on his face said he was dead serious.

"Okay, Lieutenant, what do you suggest?"

"Since we need to go into Bend to visit with the 'top doc' at the local hospital, I can fill you in on everything that's happened on the ride in. Unless the car I've been using all day is bugged, we'll be able to have a private, confidential conversation the entire time we're away from COTEF."

"Sounds like a good plan. Do we need to do anything before we head out?"

"I need to gather my notes and make a quick call to the doctor in charge to let him know we're on our way. He said he'd only be there until 5:00 p.m. Hopefully, he'll wait for us."

"Okay … let's check in, do what you need to do, and we'll rendezvous back at the front desk in ten minutes. I need to hit the latrine then the DEFAC. Hopefully, I can grab something to go."

The two officers were buzzed into the building by the security guard at the front desk. They signed in then immediately went their separate ways.

～

State Trooper and Game Warden Matt Shields had been hanging out at Central Oregon Regional all afternoon.

After his visit with Dr. Parks and Coroner Clark, he stayed at the hospital in case the Air Force showed up unexpectedly. He was in the cafeteria enjoying a cup of coffee while going over his notes when Michael Clark strolled into the facility.

"Hello Doctor," Shields greeted the coroner with a warm smile. "Care to join me? I'd like to pick your brain on a few things if I may."

"I'm not sure I have much of a brain left after this weekend," quipped Clark as he sat on the opposite side of the table. "This 'mystery affliction' we all seem to be dealing with has me at wit's end. I'm concerned we may have something here that has the potential to get really ugly … real fast."

"I couldn't agree with you more, Doctor. Tell me, please, everything you know or have discovered about the death of this man. I'm trying to fill in some holes here."

Clark took a good fifteen seconds of deep thought before answering the game warden. He started by recounting everything from the beginning. Everything from the time he received the original call to come to the hospital the day before and everything that had transpired right up to this point. With an occasional interruption to clarify something or answer a specific question from Shields, the coroner talked for almost twenty-five minutes.

Matt Shields could readily see a connection between the dead deer in the desert, the dead cattle at Christmas Valley, and the dead man residing in the hospital's morgue. It was undeniable. The deer, the cattle and the mummified corpse had all been exposed to the same thing. Exactly what it was and how it could do something so insidious so quickly was the big question. All his investigative instincts told Shields the Air Force was involved. But how? More importantly, why?

A shudder went down his spine as he suddenly thought of the two missing hunters. What if they were exposed to the same thing that killed the deer, the cattle, and their mystery man? If they had been, where were they and in what condition? Possibly, there were others they didn't know about yet.

Shields tried to shake off the troubling thoughts when Dr. Robert Parks strode into the cafeteria.

"I thought I might find you two here," said the doctor. "The Air Force just called. They're on their way in."

CHAPTER 38

Bend Municipal Airport & Central Oregon Regional Medical Center

Sunday Mid-Afternoon

"Boy, you two sure have been busy today," remarked the attendant as he climbed down from the idling fuel truck.

Chance Barclay had already shut down his helicopter and was walking toward the truck to inform the young man how much Jet-A he wanted when the attendant greeted him.

"You got that right," Barclay answered, stretching his arms, and flexing his fingers. "I would bet our day isn't over yet either. Mind putting in a full sixty-four gallons?"

The twenty-year-old operator smiled and gave Barclay an enthusiastic thumbs up then climbed back into his truck to head out to the #1 helipad where the 500 was still cooling down.

Trent Westbrook had been waiting by the back door of Orion Air's hanger ever since he heard Barclay's radio call saying he was in bound with an ETA of five minutes. Westbrook watched the typical "spot on" landing Barclay was famous for and waited until his partner had visited with the fuel truck operator before approaching him.

"Welcome home, partner," Westbrook cheerfully said. "How was your day? Tired of flying yet?"

"Hardly," Barclay chuckled. "You know I could do this all day … day in and day out. I just wish we were doing this under better circumstances."

"Yeah, I'm with you there. What's going on out in the desert is pretty grim. What's the latest?"

"Nothing more than the responders found two survivors at Backskatter. Speaking of which … I think I set a new record in getting them loaded and back to COTEF for evaluation and treatment."

"Seems like everyone you took out to Backskatter, and then some, have now been shuttled back to Bend. Any idea what's going on?"

"Not a clue. This is sure a tight-lipped group. However, my military background tells me something is really wrong here. I wouldn't be surprised if we don't get called out again today. What's the latest with your game warden?"

"Officer Shields is convinced the Air Force has something to do with all the strange animal deaths out at Christmas Valley. When he left here, he was headed for Central Oregon Regional to see if there was a possible connection between the dead deer and cattle, and the man LifeAir picked up yesterday morning."

"You haven't heard anything from him?"

"Nope. Don't really expect to unless he finds out something he thinks I should know about. Want to get something to eat?"

"Man, you know how to read my mind like an open book! I'll fly if you buy … pardon the pun. I think one of us needs to stay here just in case the Air Force comes a-callin'."

Westbrook took a twenty-dollar bill out of his wallet and handed it to Barclay. They agreed a couple of big, fat, juicy hamburgers with all the trimmings were in order. Barclay gladly took the twenty, grabbed his truck keys and headed for the parking lot.

"See you later alligator," Westbrook called out. "Remember … you're now driving a truck, not flying a high-performance helicopter!"

~

On the drive to the hospital, Davis filled in Maj. Jefferson on everything that had transpired during his absence.

He began with the story behind the identification and complications surrounding the recovery of the dead Backskatter victim. He went on to talk about the disgruntled engineer he met in the DEFAC then finished with his suspicions regarding the project.

Jefferson asked the usual number of questions to make sure he had a clear picture of things then thanked the lieutenant for his hard work and initiative.

The twenty-one-minute drive from COTEF to Central Oregon Regional went fast. Davis barely covered everything he wanted to brief the major on by the time they pulled into the parking lot. They continued talking all the way from their parked car to the front entrance, where a different greeter/attendant met them.

The man had been briefed beforehand to expect the junior Air Force officer and said Dr. Parks was expecting them. Davis asked if he and Maj. Jefferson needed to be escorted to the doctor's office or if they could make their own way up. The attendant said that wouldn't be a problem, gave them directions then dialed Parks' office to let the doctor know the military had arrived and were on their way up.

Dr. Robert Parks was waiting for the pair when they emerged from the second-floor elevator, introduced himself to Colby Jefferson, then escorted the pair down the winding corridor to his office.

The two Air Force investigators were genuinely surprised when they entered the room to find another man in a lab coat and a uniformed law enforcement officer. They weren't expecting to deal with anyone other than the hospital administrator. Jefferson quickly surmised recovering the remains of their missing accident victim was not going to be as straightforward as he originally thought.

Parks introduced the coroner and the game warden to his two visitors then explained the Oregon State Police had an active investigation in progress which might include the now-identified body they had in the hospital's morgue. The two Air Force officers glanced at each other.

Matt Shields took the cue and stepped forward. "Gentlemen, yesterday morning, approximately at the same time your man was air lifted from the Christmas Valley area, a herd of dead deer was discovered in the same vicinity. A report was also filed with the deputy sheriff in the local township regarding a number of cattle that had suddenly up and died under mysterious circumstances in the same area as well. Additionally, there are two missing hunters whose abandoned truck was also found in the same general location."

Shields paused momentarily to let his lead-in register with

the two officers before continuing. "If I were to plot all of these separate incidents on a map, they would all line up on a northwest to southeast line ... which also includes your radar site."

Jefferson pursed his lips and clenched his jaw at the revelation. Davis dropped his gaze to the floor in thought. The look on their faces told Shields the two officers were unaware of these other happenings. Both were now trying to come to terms with the notion the Backskatter accident might have had something to do with these other incidents.

After a moment of contemplative silence, Colby Jefferson regained his composure and spoke up. "Officer Shields, with all due respect, Lieutenant Davis and I were sent here to investigate an accident which happened early yesterday morning at that radar site. Neither one of us has any knowledge of what you are talking about."

"It is my belief, Major, that your investigation has now crossed paths with my investigation. I don't know yet whether a crime has been committed, but I need to follow through with any leads ... including what happened to your worker."

Colby Jefferson had no recourse. His authority ended at COTEF and Backskatter. He was in civilian territory, and now the local authorities were involved. He needed time to think, to rationalize how all this could be related.

"From what you've just said, Officer Shields, you're implying the Backskatter accident may have something to do with these other occurrences. I don't understand how this could be remotely feasible. On what basis can you assume there is a connection?"

Jefferson was not trying to be confrontational or intimidating, he simply wanted to know how something like this could be connected, or even possible.

"That's an easy one to answer," chimed in Michael Clark. "Why don't we all just take a little stroll down to the morgue?"

CHAPTER 39

Schriever Air Force Base
Late Sunday Afternoon

Lt. Colonel T.J. Rutledge sat at his desk in the admin building at Schriever enjoying his second drink of Jack Daniels when his cell phone buzzed.

"Jefferson and Davis are at the hospital," said the distant voice on the phone. "The person who was air lifted from the desert yesterday has been positively identified as a worker from Backskatter."

"Who was it?" Rutledge asked.

"Don't know yet. Davis gave the hospital all the dental records we had on the Backscatter crew without attaching any names to them. Davis used a coding system of his own design to keep the victim's name a secret."

"Clever. So only Davis knows the man's identity?"

"That would be my guess. I'm assuming once the hospital released the code number to him, Davis pulled the complete file on the worker and headed straight for the hospital along with Major Jefferson."

"Well, if Davis pulled the man's file, it should be easy to identify who it was by simply checking the roster for what file is missing."

"I'm afraid the lieutenant is smarter than we gave him credit for. After he and Jefferson left COTEF, I went into the 'vault' and checked to see whose file was missing. Apparently, Davis left the facility with the files of everyone working at Backskatter the morning of the accident."

"Shit! I seriously underestimated those two. Here I was hoping for a simple, straightforward, clean investigation to get the brass off my ass so we can pick up where we left off and now things are getting out of hand."

"Any ideas on what we should do next, Colonel?"

"Just stay on top of this and watch your butt. If Jefferson and Davis are half as smart as they appear to be, they'll figure out what's actually going on with this project and what part you play in it."

"Can we afford to let that happen?"

"Listen. I know what you're thinking and how you people operate. As I said before, don't do anything that will arouse any undue suspicion. Be smart. Be careful. Call back as soon as you have anything new."

With that remark, Rutledge abruptly hung up on his caller and reached for his drink.

CHAPTER 40

Central Oregon Regional Medical Center
Late Sunday Afternoon

The service elevator from the hospital's second floor down to the basement-level morgue easily accommodated the group of Dr. Parks, Coroner Clark, OSP Officer Shields, USAF Maj. Jefferson and Lt. Davis.

On the ride down, Michael Clark took it upon himself to subtly ask the two Air Force officers if either one had been to a morgue or seen a dead body before. His intention was to prepare them for what lay ahead.

Both admitted they had not been to a morgue but yes, had been exposed to dead people. Jefferson said the last time for him was when he was put in charge of a suicide recovery detail. He helped remove a young airman from a base where he was stationed at the time. It wasn't a clean death nor a pleasant task. Davis recounted how traumatized he'd been upon seeing his favorite uncle, the victim of a bad car accident, lying in a casket at a funeral home.

Clark respectfully acknowledged both instances. He was of no mind to question or challenge how either man felt about their experience. He informed them what they were about to see was completely different. The deceased, as Clark described him, was a victim of some unknown malady which radically aged him then broke down his body at an accelerated rate. He pulled no punches in painting a gruesome picture of the victim's condition. Clark didn't want to shock or surprise the two officers when he uncovered what was left of the dead man.

Exiting the elevator, Dr. Parks led the group down a wide

hallway to the double entry doors leading to the morgue. The first set of doors they went through opened into a changing room. Dr. Parks opened a large storage locker and handed each man a disposable bio-hazard suit, complete with a face shield and latex gloves. He informed the two Air Force officers this was standard procedure when dealing with an undetermined cause of death. Colby Jefferson and Logan Davis exchanged anxious glances and started changing. Both had now developed the same sense of dread regarding what the "Oregon Project" might actually be producing.

Once everyone was ready, Michael Clark led the group through a second set of double doors into the main portion of the morgue. The mixed smell of formaldehyde and isopropyl alcohol greeted the group. Matt Shields and the two Air Force investigators scrunched up their noses at the strong odor. The two doctors, accustomed to the smell, barely noticed it.

Clark proceeded to the stainless-steel wall of refrigerated drawers and opened one up. He beckoned the others to come over as he slid out the tray containing the body. As was the case with any cadaver suspected of having an undiagnosed disease or one covered in blood when found, the man's remains were enclosed in a red biohazard body bag.

Michael Clark waited until everyone had assembled around the tray before he completely unzipped the sack. A distinct acrid stench billowed out. Then he peeled back a plastic sheet covering the remains.

Colby Jefferson couldn't believe what he saw. To him, the deceased man looked like roadkill. Something that had been dead for a long time and had been run over multiple times. The corpse had withered to such an extent it was only half the size it should have been. Jefferson's mind reeled. This man had died a mere thirty-one hours ago, yet this was all that remained of him. A tremor shot down the major's spine and he unconsciously dropped his gaze to the floor.

Logan Davis turned white as snow and said he needed to use the bathroom, then quickly left the room. Jefferson turned away from the body and stood in stunned silence as Clark covered the man back up, zipped shut the special bag and slid the tray back inside the compartment. He closed the insulated steel door with a loud, foreboding click.

After a minute of silence to regain control of his emotions and to think, Jefferson turned to Matt Shields. "Did the deer and cattle you examined at Christmas Valley look like this?"

"Right down to the toenails," came the solemn response from Shields. "Now you understand why I say there is a connection between these unexplained deaths, disappearances, and your radar site. I don't believe any of this is coincidental, Major. I believe the accident which happened yesterday morning at your secret complex is somehow responsible for this ... all of this. These are unnatural and senseless deaths. That's why I'm asking you for your help in determining just what the hell happened out there yesterday. We need to stop this before..."

Colby Jefferson paused for a few moments to consider what the implications would be if he cooperated with the Trooper and fully disclosed what he knew. He was at a crossroads and knew it. National Security, he finally thought, will just have to take a back seat on this one. Jefferson decided to confide in Shields and the doctors, sharing information and resources was in everyone's best interests. It was the right thing to do.

As the three men left the main room and entered the dressing area, a somewhat embarrassed Lt. Davis joined them. Each man slowly and carefully removed his face shield, protective biohazard suit, and gloves, then disposed of them in a special container. Even though none, except for Michael Clark, had touched anything, they all still scrubbed up before they left the morgue.

On the elevator ride back up to the second floor, Jefferson informed Trooper Shields and the two doctors of his intentions. But before disclosing any classified information, he asked for unilateral and unconditional confidentiality. He explained why he needed this. He still had to draft an official report on the accident. Shields, Parks, and Clark readily understood the situation and agreed. The trio asked as much from the two Air Force officers. They had paperwork of their own to do as well. Additionally, no one in the group wanted to be responsible for creating a panic if word of this got out.

Instead of going back to Parks' office, the doctor led the group to a small conference room located on the same floor. Once seated around an oblong table, Dr. Parks began by recounting everything that had happened since the victim was picked up by LifeAir. He made a point of saying the hospital had managed to keep a tight lid on the whole affair. He deferred to Michael Clark to talk about the degradation of the body and what the lab team had come up with.

Michael Clark said the lab group, whom he identified, had determined the victim had received a lethal combination of some type of radiation. He went on to explain how the group thought this combination somehow mutated the DNA and RNA structure of the man's cells, changing them to such an extent it caused ultra-fast aging as well as pronounced decomposition after death. Colby Jefferson, Logan Davis, and Matt Shields listened intently and only interrupted the two doctors to clarify a few facts.

Shields spoke next, explaining the situation with the herd of dead deer and the fallen cattle. Clark asked if any tissue samples had been taken of the dead animals. Shields said yes, there had been, but neither he nor the vet at Christmas Valley expected to receive a report for several days. Clark said he'd wager a month's salary the samples would show the same toxicology results as the dead man from the desert.

Shields finished by talking about the two missing hunters and what they found in the desert.

"You found only their clothes?" queried Colby Jefferson, suddenly realizing another connection.

Shields only nodded in affirmation.

"That's exactly what we found at Backskatter ... just a bunch of clothes strewn about!"

"The man LifeAir picked up in the desert yesterday was without any clothing as well," added Michael Clark.

The five men all looked at one another as if they'd just been told the secret whereabouts of the Holy Grail.

"Son of a bitch," the Air Force major quietly said.

CHAPTER 41

COTEF Facility
Sunday Evening

Maj. Derick Roberts was anxious for Colby Jefferson and Logan Davis to return to the facility. He wanted to know the identity of the dead Backskatter worker and what was being done to recover the body. He also wanted a detailed briefing on what the two investigators had come up with so far.

In the interim, Roberts had debriefed the two survivors. The pair couldn't shed much light on the accident itself. Both women, cooks at the facility, were taking inventory of the emergency provisions in the bunker when an alarm went off and the main door automatically closed and locked, trapping them inside. Neither was aware of what had happened or what was going on outside.

Roberts sent a fresh crew out to the radar site to relieve the second set of responders. He didn't want anyone to get burned out working the accident. Site security, finding the missing staff members and determining what happened were the priorities. Cleaning up the mess would come later, when they had the workforce and proper equipment to do it safely. The major thought a twelve-hour rotation for each group was long enough. He kept hoping against hope the situation could be contained and one of the field teams would find more survivors.

Once he had a chance to visit with Jefferson and Davis, Roberts looked forward to calling it a day and going home for a little R&R. Most of the technical and support staff, those on shift this Sunday, had already left the facility by late afternoon. Except for the nighttime security detail and the two Backskatter survivors, only four others remained: the medic who was monitoring the condition of the two survivors, Lt. Blackstone, the secretive civilian "advisor," and one lab technician, Brian Reynolds, the man Lt. Davis had spoken with earlier in the DEFAC while having lunch.

The fifty-one-year-old engineer was working overtime trying to determine what went wrong as well. As part of the technical side of the project, Reynolds felt compelled to figure out exactly what happened and why. He also felt a sense of responsibility to find out what became of his missing coworkers and the remainder of the Backskatter staff.

Reynolds, being non-military, felt somewhat like an outsider at COTEF. This feeling wasn't a result of anything said or done by the Air Force people, it was just a case of personal paranoia. He always felt like everything he did was being scrutinized.

Brian Reynolds began his professional life after graduating from MIT with a degree in mechanical and chemical engineering. He accepted an internship at Oak Ridge National Laboratory in their neutron science department. After five years of demanding work with few promotions, the young engineer found himself yearning for other opportunities and challenges. He took a position at DARPA to work on advanced radar systems, where he developed an interest in laser technology. Over the years, he moved through various DARPA projects, eventually landing a position at the Air Force's Weapons Laboratory at Kirtland Air Force Base. When the experimental COIL laser was disassembled and shipped to Oregon for field testing, he was part of the transition crew.

Although highly professional with regard to his work ethic, Reynolds was often at odds with the Air Force and their secretive way of doing things. He also felt slighted about being passed over for promotion on numerous occasions. He was of the opinion this was because he wasn't "politically connected," as they say. To everyone at COTEF, Brian Reynolds came across as aloof, somewhat of a loner, yet brilliant. He fit the typical stereotype of a driven, resolute scientist.

By the luck of the draw, he was stuck at COTEF on the morning of the accident instead of the radar site. His job during the test was simply to monitor the various power readings of the equipment at Backskatter. Initially, he felt slighted for not being part of the on-site team for the "big" test. He attributed his displacement to the fact he had voiced his concern, on several occasions, about the inadequate number of safeguards for a test using dangerous gases and extreme power levels. As it turned out, he was right.

Perhaps it was a case of survivor's guilt, or because he felt challenged to determine exactly what went wrong before someone else did. Whatever the reason, the accident had a profound effect on him. More than ever before, he was a driven man.

CHAPTER 42

Central Oregon Regional Medical Center
Sunday Evening

The little conference room on the second floor of Central Oregon Regional suddenly became smaller and slightly uncomfortable for the two doctors, the two Air Force officers, and the Oregon state game warden.

They had just hit upon an important clue that apparently, tied everything together. The common element was the lack of clothing in all cases. Matt Shields let out a deep sigh and added the observation on how the dead deer and cattle appeared to be chewing at their own hides at the time of their death.

"Almost like they were trying to take their 'clothes' off as well," remarked Michael Clark. The wily coroner was always quick at connecting the dots.

"What would make a bunch of people suddenly remove their clothing and make a variety of animals try to chew off their own hides?" Logan Davis asked, his voice rising with apprehension.

"The only logical explanation I can think of," Robert Parks said, "would be if they all felt something got underneath their skins or something was burning them."

"Like their skin was on fire," Michael Clark said.

Everyone quickly glanced at the coroner, thinking the same thing. He possibly just hit the nail on the head. If someone felt like they were burning up, the natural reaction would be to remove all clothing. Or, as in the case of the animals, gnaw at their own hides.

With this latest revelation, Matt Shields desperately wanted to visit the Backskatter site and expressed his desire to Colby Jefferson.

As the military's lead investigator for the accident, and given the growing number of unexplained connections, Jefferson could understand the game warden's interest. He explained why this would not be possible at this time. Not only was Backskatter a classified military installation, and therefore closed to civilians, but it was also the scene of a serious accident under investigation. Jefferson did promise however, in accordance with their mutual trust agreement, to share any new information he came up with. Shields was obviously disappointed but conceded this was the way things had to be … for the time being at least.

Almost as an afterthought, Lt. Davis gripped the edge of the table and reminded them all they still needed to identify the dead Backskatter worker. He asked Dr. Parks for the coded identification number as well as for the return of all the dental records. Parks told the group he'd be right back, left the room and trotted down the hallway to his office. Quickly returning with the stack of manilla folders and his notes, Parks handed the folders to Davis then sat back down. Taking his reading glasses out of his lab coat pocket and adjusting them on his face, Parks checked his notes then read the number aloud.

"We have positively matched one of the dental records you provided to the victim," Parks said. "You have him coded as 'Subject OP/BS 015'… out of curiosity, what does all that mean?"

Davis looked down at his notes as well then let out a heavy sigh. "OP stands for Oregon Project. BS stands for Backskatter staff. The 015 identifies him as the fifteenth person I pulled files on. His name is … Aaron Thomas … and apparently, he was one of the top engineers responsible for the experimentation going on at Backskatter."

"How old was he?" Parks asked.

"His DOB was May 7, 1954," Davis said, looking down at the file.

"Jesus. That would have made him only forty-five years old!" Michael Clark said. "Everyone associated with his case swore he was in his sixties when he was picked up and brought to the hospital … and he continued to age even after death. This just keeps getting more absurd by the minute."

A heavy silence fell over the group as each man weighed

the seriousness of how something like this was even possible. All thought pretty much the same thing: how could a relatively young man radically age, die, and be reduced to a mummy-like state in such a brief period of time?

Robert Parks broke the somber moment by saying he needed to borrow the man's file for a few minutes to complete the death certificate and to finish the hospital's paperwork on the matter. A pale-looking Logan Davis slowly handed the man's dossier over to the doctor, then shifted his gaze to the stack of folders sitting on the table. He thought about the twenty-two still unaccounted for staff members.

Parks took the file, looked at it momentarily as if considering the enormity of what they had just learned, then walked out of the room. In the ten minutes he was gone, the remaining group of four sat in relative silence. Michael Clark, as a seasoned pathologist, still pondered how fast the victim had aged and decomposed. Matt Shields' thoughts were about the two missing hunters, fearing the worst and the fact they may never be found. Colby Jefferson reflected on what he now knew as fact and what he still needed to find out. How he was going to include all of this in his official report was yet another vexing issue. Logan Davis was stuck on the notion something other than what they had been told was going on at the secret radar site. What he had just learned deeply troubled him.

Parks returned to the conference room, paperwork in hand, and sat opposite Colby Jefferson. "Major." He began, sliding the file and other papers toward Jefferson. "Here is your file on this individual ... and here is the official, signed Certificate of Death with accompanying paperwork. Per local health department requirements and our standard practice of dealing with an individual who died from an undiagnosed disease ... we will have the body cremated before turning over the remains to the military or to the victim's family. That last form is a disclosure and acceptance form which states that you, as a representative of the United States Air Force, understand why we are doing this and that you agree to it."

Jefferson took the pen offered by Parks, quickly read the document then signed both copies. One for the hospital, one for the Air Force.

With the official paperwork completed, the five men concluded their meeting with a handshake and an agreement to get back together the following day. Same place. Same time.

~

On the drive back to COTEF, Jefferson asked Davis to take a side trip to the airport, since it was more or less on the way. The major wanted to visit Orion Air and talk with its two pilots. He wanted to make arrangements to fly back out to the desert the following morning. There was still a lot of unfinished work to do. A considerable number of questions remained unanswered. Considering the number of people he assumed would want to do the same, he figured they'd need the services of both helicopters.

The stopover did not take long. Both Trent Westbrook and Chance Barclay were happy to be flying another day and thanked the major for the visit. Jefferson told the two pilots they were done for the day but to be at COTEF with their helicopters at 0730 hours the following morning. He further informed the pair to expect a fair amount of flying throughout the day. After the customary handshakes, the two officers climbed back into their motor pool car and left, heading south.

Chance Barclay noticed the two officers seemed to be preoccupied, as if something were troubling them. He mentioned as such to his partner, who also said they looked more serious than earlier … if that was even possible.

The remainder of the ride back to COTEF was consumed by a review of everything the two officers had seen and talked about at the hospital. Both agreed with Dr. Parks and company; cremation of the body would probably be in the best interests of everyone. The condition of the dead man would, most likely, create a whole new set of problems if viewed by others. Especially, if the relatives of the mummified man decided to sue or go public and disclose what the Air Force had done to their loved one.

As they turned east off U.S. Hwy 20 onto Dodds Road, Davis asked his partner if he wanted to do more interviews this evening. Jefferson said he did, starting with the two survivors and anyone else Davis thought they should see.

"Just one," the Lieutenant replied. "If he's still here … a lab technician … an engineer by the name of Brian Reynolds."

CHAPTER 43

COTEF Facility
Sunday Night

Maj. Colby Jefferson and Lt. Logan Davis checked in at the entrance gate to COTEF shortly after 6:45 p.m. Once cleared, they drove to the parking lot and parked. They were similarly vetted to enter the compound through the fenced security gate. The final hurdle for entry was at the main entrance door where the security guard manning the front lobby buzzed them through.

Upon their entry, the guard informed them Maj. Roberts was waiting to see them in his office.

Both were surprised to see the major's young assistant still working at her desk. The newly minted first lieutenant was of the belief that advancement and choice assignments were the product of working longer hours than the boss. So far, this attitude and corresponding work ethic had paid off for her.

Roberts was not in the best of moods. The on-site commander for the "Oregon Project" was tired, frustrated, and obviously distressed. He was not only worried about the future of the project and the unaccounted for Backskatter workers, but also his future with the Air Force itself. He was of the opinion whatever Jefferson and Davis discovered about the accident and what they wrote in their report would be the key to his fate.

Roberts' first asked about their visit to the local hospital.

Colby Jefferson announced, thanks to the initiative of Lt. Davis, the dead man at Central Oregon Regional had been positively identified as a member of Saturday's Backskatter staff. Jefferson explained the hospital's policy and state guidelines for dealing with a death of this nature. The body, once cremated, would be turned over to the Air Force. Jefferson then presented the death certificate and the disclosure paperwork to Roberts.

The identity of the dead man came as somewhat of a surprise to the major. He considered Aaron Thomas to be one of the project's top people, as well as someone he professionally befriended. He did not ask about the condition of the body.

Neither Jefferson nor Davis said anything about the group conversation at the hospital, nor who attended. Per their agreement with the doctors and game warden, the two investigators wanted to uphold their end of the deal and keep what they had learned confidential. Roberts' second question concerned the status of the investigation itself.

Jefferson said nothing conclusive had been discovered at the scene of the accident, but he planned to revisit the site again first thing in the morning. He went on to say he would appreciate the opportunity to visit with the two survivors as well as anyone at COTEF actively working on the project.

Roberts pondered this request for a fast second or two then said he'd like to wait until morning to discuss this further. The two investigators could tell the major was in no mood to be either cordial or accommodating. All three of them were tired and needed a break. Jefferson informed the major he and Davis were going to get something to eat and call it an early night. It had been a long day for everyone.

As a parting gesture, Jefferson asked Roberts if he wanted to go back out to the Backskatter site in the morning with them. Roberts said he would and asked who else would be going. Jefferson said probably the leaders from the first or second response teams in addition to any other staff members who wanted to make the trip. Jefferson said he had arraigned for both helicopters to be at COTEF by 0730 hours. There would be room for extra passengers.

Maj. Derick Roberts slowly got up from his chair, stretched and said he would ask his assistant to spread the word. He grabbed his cap and car keys, bade his visitors a good night, and then strode out of his office without saying another word.

~

By sheer, dumb luck, Brian Reynolds walked into the DEFAC to get a cup of good coffee when Colby Jefferson and Logan Davis were there visiting with one of the cooks. Having missed the evening staff meal, the pair still hoped they could get something to eat.

Reynolds spotted the friendly Air Force lieutenant from Colorado and waved from across the room. Davis waved back and beckoned him to come over to where the two investigators were pleading their case for food. The obliging cook took pity on the pair and said she'd be right out with something. Davis introduced Jefferson to the middle-aged engineer and asked him to join them while they waited for their meal.

The three men sat together at the end of one of the long cafeteria-style tables to visit. After the cordial "nice to meet you" and "what do you do here" exchanges, Davis took the initiative to ask Reynolds why he was working so late on a Sunday.

Reynolds explained he was on a quest to determine what went wrong with Saturday's experiment. Both investigators instantly realized this man could, conceivably, solve the mystery of what happened and why. The two men also knew they had to be somewhat coy in their approach or risk blowing a golden opportunity.

Davis innocently asked Reynolds if he could explain, in simple terms, exactly how a COIL laser worked. Colby Jefferson inwardly smiled because he knew his young assistant was doing the same type of "warm up" questioning before getting to what he really wanted to know. The young lieutenant was a quick study.

Before the engineer could answer, however, a cook brought them out a tray of sandwiches and two cups of beef barley soup. She gave the pair of servicemen a warm smile as they expressed their grateful appreciation, then retreated to the kitchen area.

"Well," responded Reynolds, helping himself to half a sandwich. "First you need to realize lasers are nothing more than a highly concentrated form of light. Like all sources of energy, light waves come in a variety of frequencies. Think of a very bright, highly focused flashlight, one that temporarily blinds you. A light source of this strength has a higher frequency than say, an ordinary sixty-watt light bulb would."

Brian Reynolds was giving the two investigators a basic lesson

in physics and clearly enjoying being the center of attention. He also
was enjoying the sandwich he helped himself to. As the two Air
Force officers ate themselves, the engineer kept talking.

"Understand, if you will, that light is nothing more than a form
of moving energy. To be considered a true laser, the apparatus needs
to produce its light by stimulating the release of photons, or light
particles. Depending on the medium used and other factors, a laser
can produce a variety of wavelengths ... actually, anywhere from the
infrared range to the ultraviolet range."

"So," asked Colby Jefferson, interrupting the engineer's roll.
"How does one actually create an instrument like this ... one that can
be used for military purposes?"

"Good question, Major. A laser of this size needs five basic parts
to do what it does. First, there's the medium ... the source of atoms
that get excited and emit light of a specific wavelength. The COIL
laser uses a combination of liquid gases for its medium. Then there's
the energy source, which jacks up the atoms to an extremely excited
state. We use high frequency microwaves for this. Next comes the
undulator ... a system of magnets that force the electrons to oscillate
back and forth, condensing them. This is followed by a chamber of
mirrors and special lenses, called the optical resonator, which further
concentrates the light beam. Last, but not least, the whole shebang
must have an exhaust system to eliminate the instantaneous build-
up of heat. By the way, did you know that laser actually stands for
'light amplification by stimulated emission of radiation'?"

The two officers looked at each other in bemused amazement,
shaking their heads. Logan Davis went back to his original question
regarding how the COIL laser was able to produce its enhanced
shots.

"Well, in non-technical terms, the oxygen-iodine laser is
classified as a 'excimer laser'... which means it uses a combination
of reactive and inert gases as its lasing medium," began Reynolds.
"For our laser, we use hydrogen peroxide to produce singlet oxygen
as the medium ... which excites a mixture of helium and iodine
downstream. The instantaneous reaction creates super-excited
photons which are channeled through the undulator and optical
resonator."

"The final product is an instantaneous burst of concentrated energy. The strength of which, by the way, is measured in kilowatts because it is a form of light energy. The rate at which the chemicals are injected, combined, and stimulated determines the rate of fire and the strength of the laser pulses. Does any of this make sense to either of you?"

"To a point … yes," confessed Logan Davis. "I was actually briefed in detail on the basics while working for Colonel Rutledge at Schriever."

"You lost me at 'light amplification by stimulated emission of radiation'," chuckled Colby Jefferson, trying to keep things fairly light for the time being as he casually took another bite of his sandwich.

"It is kind of 'rocket science' to some degree, I suppose," Reynolds said, taking a sip of the freshly brewed coffee. "Oh, I almost forgot … and this is a critical component of the laser … it must have a serious computer. One capable of managing everything from start to finish … from controlling the valves and pumps that inject the chemicals to the waste gates that eliminate the heat build-up."

"So, what, exactly, is used to stimulate this concoction of gases?" asked Davis.

"As I said before, we use high frequency microwaves," the engineer said. "The more electrical energy we put into the magnetron, the faster the reaction occurs. This also directly contributes to the strength of the laser itself … again, the timing and sequence is computer controlled."

"You mentioned earlier you had experimented with a power setting that produced laser blasts of 10,000 kilowatts emitted at a rate of one hundred shots per second. Is that correct?" Davis said, mostly to bring Jefferson up to speed on the conversation he had earlier with Reynolds.

"Right you are, my young friend. We originally experimented with a Deuterium Fluoride laser system because it was easy to construct and control. We shit-canned that idea because the system didn't provide the power required to disable a missile or aircraft at extreme distances. That's when we went to the COIL solid state laser system. The beams are more intense but must be fired in pulses to keep the system from overheating. You figured that part out on your own when we last talked."

Colby Jefferson wanted to get a clearer picture of how effective this weapon system actually was. "Can you explain to me how a laser beam like this works in shooting down enemy bombers, missiles, and satellites?"

Reynolds smiled, trying to appease the major. "Ever put an egg or something metal into a microwave and turn it on high?"

"Once, when I was a youngster," came the embarrassed reply. "It took me an hour to clean up the mess the egg made before we could use the microwave again. We couldn't get rid of the smell for over a week. I also tried re-heating a burrito once, wrapped in tinfoil. In short order, my lunch became an electrical fire and fried the microwave. That was really scary."

Reynolds chuckled. "Put a combination of certain chemicals into a metal container and do the same. You can turn your countertop microwave into a bomb that will take out the whole kitchen. But to answer your question … when the high-energy laser pulses repeatedly strike an object, they create instantaneous heat buildup internally, similar to what a microwave does. Hit the target continually, and it simply fries the internal electronics of an aircraft or missile. Without a functioning guidance or electrical system, the offending weapon will simply stop working, explode, or fall into the sea."

Brian Reynolds' last remark sparked a troubling thought in Jefferson's mind.

"What would happen if a person, like the pilot in a bomber, were to get hit by one or more of these blasts?"

CHAPTER 44

COTEF Facility
Sunday Night

"Good question, Major," Reynolds ruefully replied as he took another bite of his sandwich. "Without actually seeing what the COIL laser can do to a human being, I can only speculate."

The engineer's comment registered with both investigators. The two Air Force officers lowered their gazes. Both thought of the body they had viewed earlier at the hospital.

"I would venture to guess the unfortunate victim would cook from the inside out in some fashion. Unlike your microwaved egg, which has a harder, denser surface area allowing rapid internal heat buildup, a human being would not simply explode. Human skin, which is softer and more porous, would basically absorb the laser blasts. This would probably melt the underlying layer of adipose tissue first … that layer of fat beneath the skin. As the body gets hit with repeated blasts, the cellular structure of the internal organs would probably also start to change. They might even get cooked themselves to some degree. Ever watch a piece of bacon frying? Pretty much the same thing. The fat melts before the meat cooks. The end result would be a toasted pilot who can't fly an incoming bomber."

Logan Davis suddenly lost his appetite and gingerly set his sandwich down.

"What would happen if these high energy laser blasts were directed at, say, an advancing enemy tank or soldiers?"

"I'm sure it would pretty much be the same story," Reynolds shrugged. "A tank could easily be disabled just like an aircraft.

It's occupants, and anyone exposed to direct, or even indirect, laser blasts would probably either be cooked or have their cellular structure changed. Once the process is complete, the unfortunate victim would probably resemble something like an oversized piece of jerky."

The two Air Force Officers looked at each other in shocked silence. The forthright project engineer painted a gruesome picture of what would become of someone exposed to a COIL laser blast ... exactly like the mummified body they viewed at the hospital, and exactly like the game warden's description of the dead animals at Christmas Valley.

Shaking off that disturbing vision, Jefferson changed the subject. "What kind of power levels would a laser of this size need?" The major was starting to appreciate the complexities of creating and operating such a machine, intrigued with the technology it required.

"Everything is electrically-driven. The chemical actuators, pumps, valves, injectors, magnetron, exhaust system, undulator, optical resonator, the computerized control system, the acquisition and targeting system ... everything. We draw power directly from the Bonneville Power Administration's 500 kilovolt transmission line just to the west of us ... which is convenient because the BPA is a government agency. Since we have our own substation, no one outside of the government knows anything about the amount of power we're using. If need be, we can supplement what we get from the BPA with the three 500-kilowatt generators we have on site at Backskatter. Between the two sources, we easily have enough power to enable the laser to hit the 10,000 KW mark."

"Sorry, I'm not an electrical engineer," quipped Jefferson. "Are you talking about a lot of electricity?"

"Enough to light up a third of San Francisco."

"Wow, that is a lot of power!" Jefferson whistled. "What about the range of the laser blasts themselves?"

"On our last, big trial run which we ran at twenty percent capacity, we were able to hit a target on top of Pine Mountain ... some forty-seven miles to the northwest. Although we were right on the money with repeated laser blasts, they weren't strong enough to punch a hole in the one-inch-thick metal target. But they did leave an interesting discoloration on the back side of the metal itself ...

which means it could have done some serious internal damage to an aircraft or missile. The test that went sideways yesterday was supposed to be at fifty percent capacity. I wouldn't be a bit surprised if seventy-five to one hundred percent weren't achieved in the uncontrolled runaway."

"Is that what you meant when you said this system was capable of so much more?" Logan Davis asked.

"I'm not exactly sure what you two have been told about the ultimate capabilities of this laser system are." Reynolds set down the remainder of his sandwich, leaned back in his chair and lowering his voice. "All I know is, once perfected, you could park this baby on the side of some mountain in South Korea and take out the whole leadership of North Korea while they watched a parade. The laser shots themselves can't be seen or heard, so no one would be the wiser. With high-input and highly controlled reactions, a direct line of sight, and ideal atmospheric conditions, this laser can kill 'whatever' at an estimated distance of between 500 and 1,000 miles."

"Jesus Christ!" Colby Jefferson paled.

"You're not suggesting this laser will be used as a long-range offensive weapon … capable of a first strike or for political assassination of foreign leaders … are you?"

"All I'm saying is this: this weapon has almost unlimited potential. If the long-range COIL laser system can be fully developed before another country can do it, we could tip the balance of military power in our favor for years."

The three men talked for over an hour in the pleasant and solitary surroundings of the DEFAC. Not only did Brian Reynolds give the two investigating Air Force officers a layman's description of how lasers worked, but also gave them some insight on the depth and scope of the weapons system. The conversation ended with the disgruntled engineer explaining how he thought the accident happened.

"Lack of adequate safeguards and control measures. Probably a result of pressures to meet timelines," he surmised. The man was obviously bitter about the way things had turned out.

Jefferson asked Reynolds if he would like to join them for a trip out to Backskatter in the morning. The major explained that a trained eye like his might be able to determine, beyond some reasonable doubt, exactly how the accident unfolded. Jefferson hoped the engineer could provide answers to a great many unanswered questions.

Reynolds jumped at the invitation. He had tried on his own, without success, to re-create the circumstances leading up to the accident. By visiting the site and rummaging through what was left of the equipment, he was sure he could fit the pieces together and come up with a solid theory.

Jefferson said he would make the arrangements, told the engineer what time the helicopters would be at COTEF, and thanked him for the science lesson and his cooperation.

As the three prepared to part ways and leave the eating area, a security guard entered and asked the major if he and the lieutenant planned to take another walk around the compound before calling it a night. The guard wanted to know if he should have the dogs put into their kennels or left out. Jefferson looked at Davis, who nodded and then said yes, they would like to stretch their legs. But first, Jefferson said he needed to make his nightly check-in with Colonel. Rutledge at Schriever.

Reynolds said if they would let them know when they were ready, he would walk out with them.

CHAPTER 45

Schriever Air Force Base
Late Sunday Night

Lt. Colonel T.J. Rutledge abruptly woke from a fitful, alcohol-induced sleep when the cell phone on his nightstand buzzed. Half asleep, he clumsily reached for his Nokia 7110, knocking it onto the floor. Grabbing blindly for it in the dark, before it woke his wife, almost made him fall out of bed.

"What?" He said curtly into the little phone as he got to his feet and padded out of the bedroom.

"Sorry to disturb you at this hour, Colonel ... we may have a problem." The familiar voice on the other end of the line sounded serious and cryptic.

"What time is it?" was the colonel's groggy response.

"It's now 2230 hours, 10:30 out here in Oregon. That would make it 11:30 your time, sir."

"This had better be good, damnit. What's going on?"

"Jefferson and Davis took a trip to the hospital this afternoon. The person the medevac helicopter picked up in the desert yesterday was positively identified as one of the lead scientists at Backskatter."

"Yes, I know. Jefferson called earlier to update me."

"Did you know the man?"

"Yes, I knew him. Aaron Thomas. He was one of the lead engineers on this project from the beginning. He'll be hard to replace. Did you get a chance to work with him?"

"I met him on a couple of occasions when he came to COTEF to confer with the engineering group here. Other than that, I can't say I really worked with the man."

"Jefferson didn't say anything about the disposition of the body. What do you know about that?"

"It's my understanding the body is still at the hospital. It won't be released until it's cremated … something about an undetermined disease."

"What do you mean … undetermined disease?"

"Evidently, the doctors at the local hospital could not identify what exactly killed Thomas, so they're not taking any chances with his remains."

"Interesting … does Roberts know about this?"

"He does. He finished visiting with Jefferson and Davis about thirty minutes ago."

"What's going on with Roberts?"

"The major is on top of things. He's been rotating security and work crews out to Backskatter on a regular basis. It looks like it may take a week, or longer, before everything is cleaned up."

"What's the status of the two survivors?"

"They seem to be doing okay. Major Roberts has already debriefed them, but not Jefferson or Davis. Roberts won't let your boys near them until he's ready."

"That's good. What's going on tomorrow?"

"Jefferson has arranged for both the helicopters to ferry people out to the site. Roberts will be going, along with Jefferson and Davis and the commanders of the first two response units. There will also be a couple of others, but I don't know who yet."

"You said something about a problem … explain."

"Jefferson and Davis had a chance encounter with one of the engineers monitoring yesterday's test from COTEF. The three had a nice, long chat in the DEFAC while your guys got something to eat."

"Which engineer?"

"Brian Reynolds. Know him?"

"Shit. Yeah, I know the little bastard. He has caused problems for me and this project before. Do you know anything about their conversation?"

"Plenty. I have most of it on tape. Reynolds spilled the beans about everything. Jefferson and Davis not only know the key technical aspects of the laser, but they also know it's being developed for possible offensive as well as defensive purposes …

among other things."

"Sonofabitch! If those two write all of this up in their report … not only is the Air Force in trouble … so, are we. Once the real purpose of this project is fully disclosed to the top brass and the congressional oversight committee, the next posting for many of us will be Leavenworth! Where are those two now?"

"They're taking a walk outside, just like they did last night. I'm assuming they're suspicious that everywhere inside the building is bugged, so they go outside to talk in private."

"Great … just great. I'm beginning to regret sending those two out there. I was hoping for a quick, clean investigation. I should have sent people with lower IQs."

"Colonel, I have an idea on how to stop this investigation. We can still salvage this operation."

"Listen, I don't want to hear about anything you plan to do. Just take care of it. Understand?"

"Is that an authorization, Colonel?"

"All I'm saying is that this needs to be fixed … got it?"

"Rest assured Colonel … in forty-eight hours all of this will be behind us."

CHAPTER 46

COTEF Facility
Sunday Night

Colby Jefferson and Logan Davis were deeply concerned.

The pair had just said goodnight to Brian Reynolds at the security gate and started their counterclockwise walk around the inside of the security fence. They summed up what they knew at this point, and it all added up to the creation of a dangerous weapon and a cover-up to disguise its actual purpose. They weren't sure who they could trust anymore. They also agreed they should share what they just learned, to some extent, with the two doctors and the game warden.

The two investigators were in the process of walking along the long western side of the fence when the barking security dogs drowned out their conversation.

"Those dogs sound really pissed. Must be because they're locked up and we're out here," Logan Davis remarked, looking toward the noise nervously.

"Yeah, I'm sure they're pretty upset. Probably not used to being in a kennel at night ... especially when there are strangers roaming the grounds," replied Jefferson.

"By the amount of noise they're making, it sounds like a fair number of them too. I wonder what breed they are."

"At Schriever we use German shepherds ... but Belgian Malinois are gaining popularity. Some units also use Dobermans, pit bulls and Rottweilers. I would venture to guess there are anywhere from four to six dogs patrolling this fenced off area ... probably free roaming. Which means no handlers."

"Major, you said something last night during our walk about not needing to go to a hospital if they ever got to someone. Were you serious about that?"

"Ever see pictures or a video of what these types of dogs are capable of?"

"Nope. Not sure I want to. Have you?"

"Yep. When I was going through my initial security supervisor's training, we watched a video of two Rhodesian Ridgebacks taking out a lion. Even after they killed the animal, the dogs kept tearing at it. It wasn't a pretty sight. But the point was made … unleashed and unsupervised security dogs could pretty much do the same thing to a human intruder if given enough time."

"Jesus … two dogs killed a lion?" Davis said, his voice noticeably cracking.

"Logan, are you okay? You seem extremely concerned about these dogs."

"Profoundly paranoid would be a better term … with good reason. When I was a little boy delivering papers, a neighbor's pit bull came after me. He knocked me off my bike and was biting me as I tried to fight him off. The owner came storming out of his house when he heard me screaming, grabbed a baseball bat and smacked the dog in the head a couple of times until he let go of me. Then he proceeded to beat the stunned animal to death right in front of me. I don't know what traumatized me more, the dog attack or that man wielding a bloody baseball bat. At any rate, it took about a dozen stiches to close the wounds on my arms and legs. I still have nightmares about it."

"That must have been terrifying … I can't imagine what it must have been like. Something like that should never happen to a little kid. Did you have any dogs later … while growing up?

"Are you kidding? Every time a large dog even came close to me, I'd tremble and scream … sometimes even wet my pants. We had plenty of cats though. I like cats. I don't like dogs."

"I think we've walked far enough for tonight. What say we turn around and go back? It's time to call it a day, partner."

"Thanks, Major."

Jefferson patted the lieutenant on the shoulder and nodded.

DAY 3

Monday, October 18, 1999

CHAPTER 47

Bend Municipal Airport, COTF & The Backskatter Site
Monday Morning

Trent Westbrook picked up Chance Barclay at exactly 6:25 a.m. on Monday morning.

The eighteen-minute drive from Barclay's home to Orion Air's hanger at the south end of the airport was filled with all manner of talk about the previous day of flying. Both pilots were understandably excited to be doing another full day of defying gravity in service to their country.

The two had again dressed in their standard company attire of light gray cargo pants and matching polo shirts emblazoned with the company's logo. Unlike the black shirts they wore on Sunday, today's choice was a white polo with a gray collar that matched their pants. Both men believed professional dress went a long way in making nervous passengers more at ease when flying in a machine that screwed itself into the air.

The pair arrived at the airport at approximately 6:45 and immediately moved their helicopters out of the hanger and performed the standard pre-flight inspections. At the completion of their flying the previous day, and as was their standard practice, both aircraft were fueled, serviced, and made ready for the following day.

A quick check of the weather revealed pretty much the same as for Saturday except for a slightly higher temperature in the afternoon. The two pilots determined density altitude would not be a limiting factor in today's flying.

"Density altitude" referred to the unique combination of temperature, humidity, and altitude. With dryer, warmer air, and high elevations, the thinner the air becomes. With fewer air molecules to work with, engines, propellers, and rotor blades became less efficient. This phenomenon effected helicopter performance and reliability more so than it did to standard aircraft. On a hot day at Bend's elevation of 3,456 feet above sea level, Orion Air's Schweizer 300C with is piston-powered engine and three rotor blades would struggle to get into the air with just one person on board.

After checking the weather, Trent called COTEF and asked to speak to Maj. Roberts. He wanted to know how many passengers there would be for the day, as well as their names and weights. He and Chance would do a quick "weight and balance" calculation to determine who would be riding in what helicopter, as well as what the seating arrangement would be.

By 7:16 both helicopters were in the air and headed southeast toward the COTEF facility. In anticipation of accommodating the landing of two helicopters instead of one, Colby Jefferson had arranged to have the parking area in front of the large utility building cleared of all vehicles.

Chance Barclay, flying the larger and faster MD 500, was the first to set his helicopter down on the site's main helipad landing toward the west. Trent Westbrook, flying the smaller and slower 300, followed Barclay in and landed in the cleared parking lot, also facing west. Both pilots spooled down their machines to ground idle, locked down their controls and prepared to board their passengers.

Waiting for them at a safe distance was a group consisting of Maj. Colby Jefferson, Lt. Logan Davis, Brian Reynolds, Maj. Derick Roberts, and Captains Devon Mitchell and Mark Webster. Dressed in Air Force camo ABUs, they looked like a bunch of G.I. Joes ready for battle.

This would be Logan Davis' first trip out to the Backskatter site, and he eagerly looked forward to it. As did Brian Reynolds, who wanted to see the damage firsthand, hopefully to determine what caused the accident. Derick Roberts was present to fulfill his role and responsibilities as the commanding officer at COTEF and hoped to find out what became of the remaining Backskatter staff. Devon

Mitchell, as the person in charge of COTEF security and Saturday's first response unit, wanted to follow up on the status of site security as well as the recovery operation itself. Mark Webster, whose primary responsibility was to coordinate the R&D efforts between the two sites, was more interested in keeping an eye on the two investigators than doing any real work himself.

The participation of the egocentric Capt. Webster concerned Jefferson the most. Webster had little to say in Saturday night's interviews and had exhibited a disdainful attitude about being questioned by strangers. Jefferson's instincts once again told him the young captain was someone to keep an eye on.

By prior arrangement, and because of the weight and balance considerations, the two Majors, Roberts and Jefferson climbed into the front seat of the 500 while the two captains, Mitchell, and Webster, climbed into the back. While those four were being boarded, the smaller Lt. Davis and Brian Reynolds climbed into the 300.

Once everyone was strapped in and outfitted with a headset, each pilot gave their passengers a quick safety briefing then spooled up their machines to maximum RPM. Because it was a Monday and a regular workday, the COTEF facility was fully staffed, a sizable number of whom were drawn outside because of the activity and noise level involved with a pair of helicopters preparing for takeoff.

Chance Barclay lifted off first, executing his favorite departure of an almost straight up, maximum performance takeoff. Trent Westbrook followed, taking a less aggressive and more stomach-friendly shallower departure. Turning to the southeast as they climbed out, both helicopters quickly disappeared from view, leaving the group of spectators with nothing more to do but go back to work.

Per their prearranged flight plan, the two pilots flew low and slow. With an indicated altitude of 5,500 feet mean sea level, the two helicopters could not only take advantage of the denser air 2,000 feet above the ground, but they could also make better time without having to climb to a higher altitude. The two also flew in "fingertip formation" with Barclay in the lead and Westbrook slightly behind him off to the right. Their horizontal separation was a comfortable five hundred feet. Barclay flew the faster 500 at an indicated airspeed of only sixty-one knots (70 MPH) so Westbrook could keep up with him in the slower 300.

Although both helicopters were equipped with voice-activated intercoms for internal communication, both pilots previously set their radios to "ISO" status. This feature isolated any ship-to-ship conversation they might have from their passengers. The system allowed for a private communication without any of their guests listening in. As was their habit, Barclay and Westbrook stayed in constant communication during the fifty-minute trip out to the radar site.

The two aircraft made a coordinated approach to the Backskatter helipads. Both helicopters approached from the northwest and circled the complex in a counterclockwise maneuver as before. Barclay landed the 500 on the northern #1 helipad at the same time Westbrook landed the 300 on the southern #2 helipad. It was a picture-perfect formation landing for the pair. They had performed this maneuver many times when flying both machines for tour groups. It was, understandably, an impressive sight for those watching from the ground.

Once the two pilots had locked down their controls and spooled their machines down to ground idle, they let their passengers disembark. The group gathered in the parking area between the two helicopters and visited for a few minutes while Barclay and Westbrook shut down their aircraft. The group of five Air Force officers and lone civilian walked toward the center of the complex while the two pilots finished their after-landing procedures.

Colby Jefferson, Derick Roberts, and Devon Mitchell sought out the current on-site incident commander while Logan Davis and Brian Reynolds headed directly to what was left of the central building. Mark Webster hung back, keeping to himself while he watched the others and surveyed the damage from a safe distance.

Once they had secured their aircraft, Barclay and Westbrook convened between the two helipads to watch the on-going activity in the center of the complex. Both remarked how they would love the opportunity to walk around and check things out for themselves, but they had to abide by their agreement not to leave the helipads.

Davis and Reynolds stopped short of the area previously occupied by the main lab and laser. The technician tried to picture, based upon the level, and spread of destruction, how things must have played out. Davis simply stood by, dumbfounded by the extent of the damage. Although he had read and re-read the initial report and viewed the video taken by the first responders, seeing the devastation up close for the first time had a profound effect on him. Not only did he wonder how anyone could have possibly survived this, but also wondered how they were going to rebuild and restart further experimentation.

Breaking the silence, Reynolds finally spoke up. "It's true," he bluntly said through clenched teeth, trying to control his bitterness.

"What's true?" asked the wide-eyed Logan Davis.

"What Einstein said about technology and what mankind does with it."

"How's that?"

"'Two things are infinite,' Albert Einstein once said. 'The universe and human stupidity … and I'm not sure about the universe.'"

CHAPTER 48

Backskatter Site
Monday Mid-Morning

"Find anything?"

Logan Davis flinched at the question. He did not hear Colby Jefferson walk up behind him. He was totally focused on what Brian Reynolds was doing. The engineer was walking around the debris where the laser cannon and the northern end of the central building once stood. Davis secretly hoped Reynolds didn't turn up any charred or mummified bodies in the process. The lieutenant was, understandably, a little on edge.

"Jesus Major," Davis intoned as he spun around to face his partner. "It would be nice if somehow you announced your presence before scaring the shit out of someone."

Jefferson chuckled, momentarily setting aside the seriousness of their situation. "Sorry 'bout that. Do you need to change your shorts?"

"Very funny ... and no, I don't need to change my shorts."

Jefferson decided he should probably leave well enough alone and changed the subject. "What are you two up to? Have you found anything significant yet?"

"Nope ... sorry to say," replied the exasperated young lieutenant. "Has anyone else come up with anything?

"Sadly ... yes," came the solemn reply. "Yesterday evening, while a small team checked the perimeter fencing, ten bodies were discovered at various locations. According to the team's report, it looks as if all tried to get away. Apparently, they were also found in the same condition as the man we saw in the hospital's morgue.

They were also found without any clothing."

"Ten bodies ... and they were found naked?"

"Yeah. That pretty much confirms the theory about what happened and how they were killed."

"Where are their remains?"

"They were all placed in body bags, packed in ice, and are temporarily being stored in the north service building under guard. Want to take a look?"

"Are you kidding? No ... no way. Seeing one person in that condition was enough for me, thank you. Are you planning to check them out?"

"Have to ... just to verify they all died like our man in the morgue. I think we need to get an Air Force forensic team out here to identify the bodies and take charge of the remains. I don't want to get the locals any more involved than they already are."

Logan Davis nodded his head in agreement, momentarily at a loss for words, sickened by the tragic news. Then he thought of Brian Reynolds and asked Jefferson if the engineer should see the bodies.

"I'm not sure that would be a good idea right now." Jefferson pressed his lips together. "I'd like to keep our man focused on what he's doing. Hopefully, he'll come up with something definitive. We'll save the ugly stuff for later ... if at all."

The two investigators stood facing each other for a few moments. Each had dropped his gaze and stared at the ground, lost in his own thoughts. Finally, Colby Jefferson reached out and patted his junior partner on the forearm, then turned away to walk toward the #1 service building.

Logan Davis silently watched the major cross the parking lot, then turned his attention back to Reynolds and his scrounging.

~

Chance Barclay and Trent Westbrook were still locked in conversation between the two helipads when the senior Air Force officer broke off from the main group to walk over to his partner. Both pilots witnessed the exchange between the two investigators but couldn't hear the conversation. When Jefferson reached out to his young apprentice then walked off, the gesture was unmistakably profound. Something significant and somber had happened.

The two pilots looked at each other then watched Jefferson cross the parking area and enter the service building just to the north of them.

"I wonder what that was all about?" Westbrook asked.

"It looked like the major was delivering some bad news," Barclay replied.

"I wish we could be more 'in the loop' of what's going on here."

"Me too. I guess the only way we'll find out is if they tell us. Since that's not likely to happen, all we can do is follow the rules and provide the service they're paying us to do. Come on, Trent, let's give our birds a thorough service check. We can only do what we can do."

~

Brian Reynolds carefully and methodically checked out the area around the epicenter of the accident. From his first observations of the scene with Lt. Davis, he had determined the laser cannon had discharged several blasts toward the northwest before self-destructing. The faint scorch marks on the #2 radar array told the story. The distinguishable pattern of discoloration on the metal of the array's support structure was somewhat invisible to the untrained eye. But to the highly astute engineer, it was obvious the laser cannon became, in non-scientific terms, literally a "loose cannon."

Reynolds figured the uncontrolled laser blasts went out in a ten-degree arc on the south side of the intended target on Pine Mountain, at various elevations. He couldn't tell how long this runaway had been going on before the weapon self-destructed. Knowing the capabilities of this machine, he had hoped the equipment failed and self-destructed without discharging any laser shots. He was distraught to learn this was not the case. A series of unaimed and potent oxygen-iodine laser blasts had indiscriminately sprayed the desert to the northwest.

~

Colby Jefferson was having a tough time keeping his breakfast in his stomach.

The remains of the ten workers looked exactly like what he saw at the hospital. There was no denying it now. The destroyed COIL laser was responsible for a great deal of carnage.

Jefferson thought about the remaining twelve, unaccounted for, staff members working at Backskatter the morning of the accident. Although the major still hoped they would turn up safe and sound, he was becoming increasingly pessimistic about their chances of survival.

Trying to fit all these pieces together, a separate thought suddenly struck him: how did the game warden, the one he met at the hospital yesterday, learn of the herds of dead deer and cattle ... and who else was in the picture?

Thanking the guard on duty for his service, Jefferson ambled out of the service building. He tried to process what he now knew and what he still needed to find out. Then he noticed the two helicopter pilots working on the MD 500 at the north helipad. *I wonder ...* the major thought to himself.

"You boys tired of flying yet?" Jefferson asked casually, walking up to the pair. Westbrook was in the process of cleaning the helicopter's bubble canopy while Barclay was entering something into a logbook.

"Are you kidding?" Westbrook grinned. "Flying helicopters is what we live for. How are things going, Major ... need a ride back to COTEF?"

"No ... no ride right now, thanks, but I do have a question for you boys."

"What's that?" Chance Barclay asked, setting down his paperwork and stepping over to where Jefferson and Westbrook stood.

"By any chance, did either one of you do any flying out to the desert yesterday with a game warden?"

CHAPTER 49

Backskatter Site
Monday Mid-Morning

Chance Barclay and Trent Westbrook froze then looked at each other. Their body language and the expression on their faces told Colby Jefferson what he wanted to know.

"Why yes, we both made trips out to this area yesterday with a game warden ... why?" Trent Westbrook asked.

"Was his name Matt Shields?"

Again, the two pilots looked at each other before Chance Barclay spoke up. "How do you know that?"

"I met Officer Shields yesterday at your local hospital. Lieutenant Davis and I went there to confirm the identity of a man picked up Saturday morning just to the north of here by a medevac helicopter. He was one of the workers here. Unfortunately, he didn't survive the flight back to Bend. Shields was at the hospital when we got there, doing follow up work on the same incident." Jefferson was careful not to disclose any more information than necessary until he knew the extent of what the two flyers knew.

"Wow," Westbrook rubbed his forehead. "I'm at a loss for words. All I can say is Officer Shields is conducting an active investigation into the mysterious deaths of some wildlife and cattle in the area. He hired us, just like you did, to shuttle him back and forth for the day. He also told us not to talk about what was going on until he concluded his investigation."

"Listen, guys ... what I'm about to tell you two is strictly off the record and not to be repeated." Jefferson looked seriously at the pilots. "Can I trust the two of you on this?"

Barclay and Westbrook nodded in agreement. Jefferson took a deep breath, glanced around, then told them the whole story of his time at Central Oregon Regional. His narrative included his suspicions regarding the connection between Saturday's accident and a number of dead people and animals.

Colby Jefferson talked for almost twenty minutes. He was only interrupted a couple of times by the two pilots who filled in details regarding their own involvement. It was now painfully obvious that prior to its own destruction, the COIL laser had caused numerous casualties. Possibly more they were yet unaware of. Everything started to come together. The cause of the mysterious deaths had been solved, and a botched military experiment was responsible.

To Jefferson, only three questions now remained unanswered: How did the machine fail, who was responsible, and why was its real purpose kept concealed? He also guessed the buck didn't stop with Colonel Rutledge ... there had to be several, higher-ranking individuals involved in this conspiracy. This last notion gave him a sudden chill. To what lengths will these people go to keep the purpose of this project a secret and moving forward?

For their own protection, Colby Jefferson did not to tell the two partners the entire story regarding the laser's capabilities. He simply told them it was a high-tech defensive weapon that could change the balance of power in the event of war. He went on to explain that by telling them this, he was putting his career in jeopardy, and if the story ever got out, he could be looking at doing hard time in a military prison.

Westbrook and Barclay assured the major of their complete cooperation and silence on the matter. Both pilots knew the stakes were high and told Jefferson he could count on them to do whatever was necessary. Jefferson thanked the pair, nodded in appreciation, and then turned and walked away.

Trent Westbrook and Chance Barclay watched as the major headed toward the remnants of the central building. "Wow," was the only thing Trent could think of to say. "This is some serious shit, man."

"You got that right, brother," Barclay's responded. "Let's get back to work and pretend, for the time being at least, our conversation with Major Jefferson never happened."

~

Brian Reynolds broke off from his probing about and walked over to Logan Davis.

"Lieutenant … would you mind getting me a medium-size box of some kind? One about so big." Roberts spread his hands apart by a couple of feet.

"Did you find something?" Davis asked.

"I think so. But I need to make a diagram and take a couple of pictures before I can retrieve anything."

"What is it?"

"I can't be sure, but it looks like various parts of the laser's inner workings."

Logan Davis emitted a soft whistle then took off in the direction of the administration building. As he started to walk away, Reynolds also asked him to check around to see if any papers or notebooks were retrieved during the initial cleanup. Davis said, "No problem-o" and headed toward the administration building.

Reynolds grabbed a clipboard with a pad of paper and his camera from the pack he brought. He started taking pictures and made a diagram of the area as he retraced his steps.

Davis returned approximately fifteen minutes later with a wooden box and a large garbage bag. The bag contained the remnants of all the papers the first response group found strewn about when they arrived at the complex after the accident.

During Davis' absence, Reynolds had tagged and diagrammed the location of the various components he previously identified. He asked Davis if he wouldn't mind following him around with the box while he picked them up. The young Air Force officer was only too happy to accommodate the engineer. Davis began to think Reynolds was on to something and was excited to be a part of it.

Colby Jefferson had made his way from the heliports to the administration building to visit with Maj. Roberts and Capt. Devon Mitchell, the current on-site incident commander. By now, he had correctly guessed both men were aware of the condition of the ten bodies now residing in the #1 service building. Neither Roberts nor Mitchell confessed they had yet to see the bodies for themselves. Their body language told Jefferson they were in no hurry to do so either. Both men did however, express their appreciation for the work Jefferson was doing and had nothing new to offer.

After concluding his visit with Roberts and Mitchell, Jefferson decided to check back in with Logan Davis and Brian Reynolds at the site of the destroyed central building.

CHAPTER 50

Backskatter Site
Late Monday Morning

Capt. Mark Webster pretended to survey the damage caused by the destroyed laser. The young captain was discreetly observing the interaction between Jefferson, Davis, and Reynolds from a safe distance. He inconspicuously watched Jefferson leave the group, cross the parking area, and go into the #1 service building.

Webster had heard rumors regarding a major discovery of some kind but did not know what the details were. He assumed Jefferson was going to the service building to check things out for himself.

From his vantage point in the center of the parking area, Webster had a clear view of the entire Backskatter complex. Looking north, he could see the #1 service building, living quarters and the DFAC for the staff, and the huge #1 radar array behind them. To the west stood two mobile trailers, what was left of the central building, several satellite dishes and the equally impressive #2 radar array. He watched Davis and Reynolds rummaging through the debris for a few minutes before shifting his gaze to the south. Standing slightly damaged by the accident was the administration building and looming behind it, the #3 radar array. Farther south stood the #2 service building and the electrical substation by the main entry gate.

He wasn't looking for anything in particular, just keeping an eye on all the activity. As he continued to survey the complex, Maj. Jefferson exited the #1 service building and walked over to the helipads. Watching the exchange between the major and the two pilots, without hearing them, Webster wondered what on earth the investigator and the two flyers could be talking about for so long.

Then he heard the voices of Logan Davis and Brian Reynolds as they came up behind him.

"Hey Captain Webster, how goes it?" Davis chirped.

"Hello Lieutenant," Webster replied, more aloof. "I was just trying to figure out what needs to be done to get us back on track. What do you two have there?" Webster pointed at the box Davis carried.

"Brian here, found some parts of the laser he wants to take back to COTEF for analysis. We were just on our way over to the helipads to see if we could catch a ride back."

"Mind if I go with you? I think the people here have a fairly good handle on things, and I need to finish some paperwork."

"Sure, the more the merrier, I always say," Davis quipped as he started walking toward the helipads.

Colby Jefferson finished his conversation with the two Orion Air pilots and walked back across the parking area where he met Davis, Webster, and Reynolds.

Logan Davis quickly explained what they had found and Reynolds' desire to get the articles back to COTEF. Mark Webster said he needed to get back to work on a report. Jefferson told his partner to tell the pilots he authorized a return trip for the group. As the three men headed for the helipads, Jefferson asked Webster to hold back for a minute. He wanted to talk to the captain privately.

Although Webster was a bit dubious regarding Jefferson's intentions, he nevertheless accommodated the major. Professional courtesy as well as curiosity had won out over any apprehensions he may have had.

Jefferson came right to the point. He had some "evidence" he wanted to show the captain. Evidence that could be considered a major part of his investigation. The fact that the lead investigator wanted to take the ambitious captain into his confidence made an instant impact. Mark Webster was all ears. He had been hoping something, anything, would turn up that would exonerate him as a major player in one of the worst accidents to befall an important Air Force project.

Colby Jefferson quickly walked Webster over to the #1 service building. After they returned the salute from the guard outside, they entered the well-lit building.

The #1 service building at Backskatter was mainly used to store spare parts, non-perishable food items, and miscellaneous supplies. For all intents and purposes, it was the primary warehouse for the complex. The #2 service building, on the southern end of the parking area, served as a shop and motor pool.

Jefferson led Webster over to the building's west wall, where a row of sacks was laid out on the floor. A second guard was dumping ice into a couple of the sacks. Webster was so anxious to see the evidence Jefferson had alluded to, he didn't realize he was looking at a row of body bags.

Jefferson asked the guard if he could brush away the ice he just poured into the first bag so the captain could take a look. The airman said, "Yes sir," complied with the major's request, then took a step back.

The thought of what the ice was for never crossed Webster's mind. He was totally focused on the sack and what evidence it might contain. Anxious with anticipation, he looked at Jefferson, hoping to see something in the major's face that would indicate something special was awaiting him. The major simply tilted his head in the direction of the open bag as if to encourage the captain to help himself.

Mark Webster knelt beside the sack, grabbed its open edges, and pulled them wide open. The abrupt action caused the bag to roll slightly toward him, spilling out the remainder of the fresh ice. There, fully exposed in the well-lit service building, the withered and decimated body of a naked man stared back up at him. Then the stench followed.

It took a second or two for the hapless captain to fully comprehend what he was looking at. When it finally registered, Webster rocked backwards, landing on his butt. His mouth, covered by a clasping hand, emitted only a low groan. His eyes were opened wide, almost bulging. He went white as a sheet and started hyperventilating.

Colby Jefferson, standing behind Webster, reached down, grabbed the captain under his armpits, and helped him back to his feet. It took a couple of seconds for Jefferson to steady the young officer. He hoped the captain wouldn't faint on the spot. Webster couldn't stop staring at the contents in the bag. Then he shifted his gaze to the nine other bags lined up next to it, audibly gasped, then raced out of the building.

"Thank you for your service, airman," Jefferson said to the guard in attendance. He took a final look at the dead staff member, respectfully lowered his head, turned, then silently walked out of the building. The serviceman stood still, caught off guard by the reaction from the young captain. Looking down at the opened bag, he slowly shook his head before picking up his bucket and headed out a side door for the DEFAC. He needed more ice.

CHAPTER 51

Backskatter Site
Late Monday Morning

"You son of a bitch!" was the only thing the deflated Mark Webster could say to Colby Jefferson when the major caught up to him in the parking area.

The young captain stood bent over with his hands on his knees. He looked like he was either trying to catch his breath or get sick.

"Is that how they taught you to address a superior officer at the academy … Captain?" Jefferson calmly replied.

"You intentionally baited me. You set me up! Why?"

Setting aside the young officer's insubordination, Jefferson faced the captain, looking him straight in the eyes. "As you are Major Roberts' right-hand man and the coordinator between the two sites, I wanted to know the extent of your knowledge regarding the damage this weapon caused before it destroyed itself. Your reaction told me you were unaware of the fact this laser had indiscriminately killed an unknown number of people, wildlife, and livestock."

"Why would I be a party to a cover-up of that magnitude?" Webster asked in between shallow breaths.

"Because … I believe you, your boss and everyone else associated with this project has intentionally kept this laser's capabilities, purpose, and intent a closely guarded secret. There is a conspiracy going on here to cover all this up … especially so with regards to this accident in general and my investigation in particular."

The ensuing silence without comment from Mark Webster further confirmed Jefferson's suspicions. The captain was at a loss for words and wouldn't meet Jefferson's gaze. The body language unmistakably said guilt.

"Well … what's the story?" Jefferson finally demanded.

"There is no story, and this conversation is finished … Major." Webster abruptly said and stormed off.

Jefferson watched the agitated captain walk off in the direction of the administration building before turning and walking back toward the helipads. Guessing Capt. Webster had changed his mind about returning to Bend, Jefferson wanted to see if Lt. Davis and Brian Reynolds were squared away and ready to head back to COTEF themselves.

Chance Barclay witnessed the exchange between the two officers from his vantage point between the helipads. Barclay and Westbrook were facing in a westerly direction, toward the parking area, making plans with Lt. Davis and Brian Reynolds to fly them back to Bend.

Barclay asked his partner if he wouldn't mind flying the lieutenant and the technician, along with what they had collected, back to COTEF in the 500. Trent Westbrook's face lit up with excitement at the prospect of flying the company's "hot rod," something he didn't get to do very often. Barclay explained he was thinking Maj. Jefferson would want to go back as well. That being the case, he wanted to fly alone with the major so he could talk privately with him. The smaller 300, with its cozy interior and open cockpit, would serve this purpose well.

When Jefferson joined the group, arrangements were quickly made to fly the three military people back per Barclay's seating suggestion. The major asked the nearby guard if he would inform Maj. Roberts of their plans, including his intention of sending the larger helicopter directly back to Backskatter once the group was dropped off at COTEF.

Reynolds, with his box of debris, overstuffed garbage bag and backpack, climbed into the back seat of the 500 while Davis climbed into the front seat along with Westbrook. Colby Jefferson climbed into the 300's right seat as Chance Barclay climbed into the left-hand pilot's seat. After strapping in and conducting the standard safety checks, both pilots fired up their helicopter's engines. Westbrook lifted off first, doing his climb-out directly between the #1 and #2 radar arrays. Chance Barclay watched his friend clear the radar arrays before performing the same departure maneuver himself.

Westbrook kept the indicated airspeed of the MD 500 below sixty-five knots (75 mph) so he wouldn't leave Barclay behind on the trip back. Although he had the urge to fly at the machine's maximum cruise speed of 135 knots (155 mph), the two pilots had agreed to fly back to Bend in the same manner as they flew out. Low and slow.

As was his plan, Chance Barclay engaged Colby Jefferson in a serious conversation on the ride back. He asked if Jefferson had more to the story than what he had told them earlier. Being no stranger to how the military worked, especially with classified information, he suspected Jefferson was being careful about what was being said in front of Westbrook.

Jefferson first asked Barclay about his military background. The major was duly impressed. So much so, he decided to take the ex-Army Warrant Officer into his confidence and told him everything.

To Chance Barclay, everything now made perfect sense ... the classified military bases, the secret Air Force laser project, the horrific accident, Orion Air's engagement, the mystery of the dead deer and cattle, the condition of the dead staff members, the involvement of the local hospital ... everything.

Jefferson explained how he envisioned the cover-up and ensuing conspiracy of silence following the accident. He went on to further explain why he was telling all this to Barclay. In short, he needed a backup plan. Jefferson also talked about his upcoming meeting at the hospital and his intention of revealing everything to the game warden and doctors as well.

As both helicopters approached the COTEF complex, Jefferson and Barclay agreed to keep what was discussed between them highly confidential ... for the time being. Colby Jefferson thought he would now have three aces as "hole cards," Chance Barclay, the state game warden, and a select group of doctors at Central Oregon Regional. If something, anything, were to change the integrity of his investigation and its outcome, the truth behind this whole disastrous affair would not be lost.

After landing and unloading their passengers, the two Orion Air pilots headed for the airport to refuel. They also agreed Trent would take the 500 back out to Backskatter while Chance returned to COTEF in the 300. Barclay wanted to be on standby for Maj. Jefferson if needed. He also thought the larger and faster 500 would be better at ferrying people back to COTEF from the secret desert complex. Westbrook was only too happy to have the opportunity to put in more flying time in the speedy 500.

Before they went their separate ways, they synchronized their watches. It was now 1:31 p.m., PDST.

CHAPTER 52

Schriever Air Force Base
Monday Afternoon

Lt. Colonel T.J. Rutledge nervously paced in his office. He was having difficulty concentrating. The growing pile of paperwork on his desk would just have to wait.

Rutledge desperately wanted to dip into his stashed bottle of Jack Daniels but knew better. Getting caught drinking while on duty, or even having a bottle in the office, was bad for one's professional military career. Instead, he opted to switch from coffee to a sixteen-ounce can of a high-caffeine energy drink. As a result, the colonel could not sit still. He was unable to focus on much of anything except his worries.

When his cell phone buzzed, Rutledge stopped pacing and looked at his watch. It read 2:05 p.m., MDST. He stared at the annoying instrument sitting on his desk for a moment before picking it up.

"Rutledge."

"Afternoon, Colonel," came the distant reply. "Just thought I'd update you on this morning's activities. Can you talk?"

"Yes ... you're calling later than I expected."

"I was waiting to see who returned from Backskatter before calling."

"So ... what do you have to report?"

"A group consisting of Majors Roberts and Jefferson, Captains Mitchell, and Webster, along with Lieutenant Davis and Brian Reynolds flew out this morning at 0745 hours ... local time. Major Jefferson, Lieutenant Davis, and Reynolds returned about thirty minutes ago, approximately 12:40 our time. Reynolds had a large box filled with debris he collected from the wrecked laser."

"Where are they now?"

"Jefferson and Davis are in the DEFAC getting a late lunch. Reynolds is holed up in the lab ... probably studying what he brought back from the desert."

"If anyone can figure out what happened, it would be Brian Reynolds. He was a major player in the design and construction of the COIL laser. Did anyone say anything to you when they got back?"

"Major Jefferson said ten bodies had been recovered, but nothing about their condition. He also said he was going to contact you about getting a forensics team out here to transport the bodies back to Schriever ... including the one at the local hospital."

"Curious ... he hasn't contacted me yet. Probably waiting until after eating lunch or until he makes his nightly call-in. Anything else?"

"Major Jefferson sent the larger of the two helicopters back to the radar site and is keeping the smaller one here on standby for the time being."

"Did he say why?"

"No, sir ... only that he wanted one here in case anyone needed to go back out to the desert on short notice."

"Listen ... I want you keep a sharp eye on Jefferson and Davis, and especially Reynolds. What he finds out, and what he conveys to the other two will determine our next move. Once we know what caused this accident, we can start over ... hopefully, with minimal interference from above. What the major and my young assistant find out will also determine what needs to be done with regards to their involvement. It is vitally important we keep the purpose of this project 'sub rosa'."

"Don't worry Colonel, as I said before ... I'm on top of this and have a plan to keep ourselves safe and clean."

"And, like I said before ... I don't want to know about any of your 'plans.' Just make sure by the end of the week we're in the clear, everyone's happy, and we can resurrect this project."

"Yes, sir ... I'll check back in at the end of the day when everyone is back on site from Backskatter."

"I'll be looking forward to some positive, productive news." Rutledge said, abruptly ending the call.

The veteran Air Force Officer took a few minutes to reflect on the conversation with his "mole" at COTEF. His apprehensions and anxieties surrounding what the next forty-eight hours would bring drove him to return to his desk … and to its hidden fifth of whiskey.

"Fuck it," the colonel said to himself as he reached for a glass and the forbidden bottle of brown liquid.

CHAPTER 53

COTEF Facility
Monday Mid-Afternoon

Brian Reynolds was working like a man possessed. For over two and a half hours, he had been organizing and studying everything he brought back from the desert without a break. He didn't even take the time to grab a quick lunch or a cup of good coffee.

The laser engineer had turned a one corner of COTEF's oversized laboratory into a forensic workspace. He had set up two large folding picnic tables and had laid out on them everything he collected at Backskatter. Next to the tables, on a wall adorned with several oversized bulletin boards and a six-foot-long white board, he had pinned or taped up a variety of the salvaged Backskatter papers along with various engineering diagrams.

Between his intimate knowledge of the laser's workings, his recollection on how it was set up at Backscatter, the notes and diagrams he made while at the scene of the accident, the mangled parts he scrounged up, and what he could glean from the assortment of papers he brought back, Reynolds was hopeful he could piece together exactly what happened to the laser.

As he made notations on the white board, Maj. Roberts' administrative assistant strolled into the lab. The serious-minded Lt. Blackstone asked Roberts if he required anything or was planning to go back out to the desert. The young woman was, simply "minding the store" until her boss returned from the radar site. The busy engineer said he wouldn't mind something to eat and a cup of fresh coffee from the DEFAC and yes, he would like to go back out to the radar site to do some more looking. Blackstone said she would ask one of the cooks to bring him a lunch tray and would make the arrangements to have him fly back out to Backskatter. After quickly looking over the engineer's work area, the young woman shook her head in astonishment and left the lab without further comment.

By 3:30 p.m. Reynolds had a fairly good idea of what went wrong but definitely needed a return trip to the radar site to verify his theory. Leaving his work as it was, the engineer grabbed his backpack, a camera, and notebook, then left the lab and headed for the lobby, via the DEFAC. He needed one more hit of caffeine.

In the dining facility, Reynolds once again ran into Maj. Jefferson and Lt. Davis. Having finished their own lunch, the pair were going over notes of their own when the engineer strolled in.

"Why is it I always run into you guys here?" Reynolds said, greeting them as he walked in.

Both officers chuckled at the remark before Jefferson answered him. "We like this place better than the conference room or our closet-sized office. We can spread things out, visit mostly in private, and have the cooks at our beck and call."

Reynolds chuckled as well, "Yep, the snacks and coffee ain't bad either."

"How goes your research?" Davis asked, in-between bites of a potato chip.

"So far, so good. I think I know what went wrong but I need to go back out to the site to follow up on a few things. Want to go with me?"

"I wouldn't mind, Major ... if it's okay with you." Davis crumpled up his now-empty bag of chips.

"I don't think you'd be back in time for our 5:30 meeting at the hospital, Lieutenant. Brian here can make the trip by himself and spend as much time as he wants at the site," Jefferson replied.

"Hospital?" Reynolds raised his eyebrows.

"Yep ... unfortunately, we've run into a bit of a snag getting the body we identified yesterday released." Jefferson did not want to disclose any more than he had to for the time being.

"What body?" Pressed Reynolds.

"The person picked up north of Backskatter Saturday morning by a medevac helicopter. Lieutenant Davis spent most of yesterday tracking down where he went and was instrumental in identifying the person as a worker at Backskatter."

"No shit," replied the surprised engineer. "I didn't hear about that. Who was it?"

"Aaron Thomas. Did you know him?"

"Aaron? Hell yes! We worked together at Kirtland when this project was originally put together. What happened to him?"

"He was found naked, alone and suffering from exposure at a place called the Lost Forest. A medical transport helicopter was dispatched from the local hospital to pick him up, but he died on the return trip. Since he had no clothing or any form of identification on him, the hospital put him in their morgue as a 'John Doe' until Davis figured out a way to ID him. They won't release the body until they're finished with the autopsy." Jefferson hoped the engineer wouldn't press for more information. He had lied about the autopsy but figured it would appease any further questions Reynolds might have for the time being.

"Aaron Thomas ... my god." Reynolds rubbed his chin. "He was one of the lead scientists on this project. If I can find some of his notes either here or at Backskatter, they may shed further light on how all this came about."

Colby Jefferson suggested they all walk out to the helipad and get Reynolds squared away to immediately fly out to the desert. He wanted to ask the Orion Air pilot if he would standby at Backskatter to fly Reynolds back when he was finished.

As expected, Chance Barclay told the group it wouldn't be a problem and loaded Reynolds into the 300. After the standard start up, warm up, and takeoff, Barclay took a shallower climb out to keep his airspeed up as he headed southeast.

The trip out to Backskatter was faster than usual for the pair. Not only did Barclay fly low and push the little helicopter as fast as he could, but he was also helped along by a light tailwind coming out of the northwest. From takeoff to landing, the ex-Army CWO managed to get his passenger to the radar site in forty-eight minutes.

Although the flight time in the Schweizer 300 for this trip was somewhat faster than the usual fifty-five minutes, it lagged far behind the MD 500 with its typical flight time of twenty-eight minutes. Still, Barclay's solitary passenger never complained, he thoroughly enjoyed the ride with the wide-open view from the bubble canopy and the always-entertaining Chance Barclay for a pilot.

Trent Westbrook was genuinely surprised to see "Three-Two-Five Tango Charlie" approach over the top of radar array #2 and make a shallow, descending turn over the southern end of the complex then gently set down on the helipad next to him. Westbrook took a quick look at his watch as Barclay locked down his controls and spooled down the machine. It was 4:43 p.m.

CHAPTER 54

Central Oregon Regional Medical Center
Monday Late Afternoon

Maj. Colby Jefferson and Lt. Logan Davis strolled into Central
Oregon Regional at exactly 5:15 p.m. and checked in at the reception
desk. They were immediately signed in then headed directly for the
elevators. Alerted by the greeter at the reception desk, Dr. Robert
Parks was waiting for them when the elevator doors slid open on the
second floor.

Exchanging in the usual small talk, the trio headed directly for
the little conference room where they met before. Already present
were coroner Michael Clark and Oregon State Trooper/Game
Warden Matt Shields. By prior arraignment, all had agreed to meet
at 5:30 on this day following Jefferson and Davis' excursion to the
accident site.

Dr. Parks began by informing the group the body of their
recently identified John Doe had been taken to a local crematorium
that morning and would be ready for pick up the following
afternoon. Maj. Jefferson thanked Parks on behalf of the Air Force for
making the arrangements and said the hospital would be reimbursed
for any expenses.

Trooper Shields spoke next, asking the two Air Force officers
what they had discovered since the conclusion of their meeting
the previous day. Colby Jefferson began by relating what Lt. Davis
and he had learned about the COIL laser and what it could do to a
human being or animal. He was careful not to disclose any classified
information to the group, especially with regard to the weapon's
ultimate capabilities and his suspicions surrounding the use of

it. Jefferson also recounted details of their trip to the Backskatter site, including the fact that ten more missing staff members had been found ... all in the same condition as the body sent to the crematorium and the animals Shields had surveyed around Christmas Valley.

Doctors Parks and Clark, along with Shields, instantly recognized how something like a misguided laser blast of this type and strength could produce the gruesome results it did. For them, the cause of death to their John Doe and the resultant aftermath was now readily apparent. The description Jefferson gave of the ten bodies he viewed at Backskatter was further confirmation. The mystery surrounding the death and rapid decomposition of the dead had now been solved.

Matt Shields, however, still needed to know how something like this had gotten away from the Air Force in the first place, and more importantly, what was being done to prevent similar occurrences. He still needed to conclude his investigation and write a report of his own. Colby Jefferson told Shields and the rest of the group they were closing in on the cause of the accident and assured them, once a determination had been made, he would pass along the information.

Jefferson once again thanked the two doctors and the trooper for their cooperation and discretion regarding this matter. He emphasized, that in his opinion, it would be in everyone's best interests if this entire episode, from a civilian standpoint, was never mentioned publicly. Knowing how the media worked, all readily agreed and promised to keep the entire incident under wraps.

Shields was also curious what would happen next. Jefferson said he was going to request an Air Force forensic team come out and take charge of the bodies and the cremated remains. He and Lt. Davis would probably be flying back to Colorado in the next day or two, where he would write up his official report and present it to his superior officer.

"Is that where it ends?" the game warden asked.

"Hardly," Jefferson snorted. "Actually, it's probably just the beginning of what's to come next."

"What would that be?" Shields alternated his gaze between the two officers.

"There will probably be an internal board of inquiry. The Air

Force will be looking to pin this on someone ... most likely someone or some group who are way above my pay grade. Given the severity and cost of this accident, I'm sure it will go all the way to the top ... and eventually involve some congressional oversight committee."

"What about the Backskatter site and the future of the laser itself?"

"Based upon my findings and recommendations, I'm sure the Air Force will clean up and 'sanitize' the site. Everything will be taken back to the Weapons Laboratory at Kirtland Air Force Base and development will continue on the COIL laser there. I'm assuming it will be a while before the system will be at a point for further testing."

"I sincerely hope the Air Force isn't going to be testing it here anymore," Michael Clark said.

"Highly doubtful Dr. Clark," Jefferson said. "I'd like to think that any further testing will be done in New Mexico ... where, in my opinion, it should have been done in the first place."

Dr. Parks had been quietly sitting through this exchange waiting for an opportunity to ask a key question. Something that had been weighing heavily on his mind since the beginning.

"Major Jefferson," the doctor finally said, picking his words carefully. "What this laser can do to people is nothing short of ... insidious, if not inhumane. I'm afraid once this laser is fully developed and deployed, the temptation will be to use it as a weapon of mass destruction ... to prematurely age and wipe out entire armies or terrorist groups."

"Doctor Parks," Jefferson respectfully replied, "on that point I'd have to agree with you. Conversely, this weapon is no more insidious than being burned alive by napalm. It is no more inhumane than to have one's legs blown off by a land mine. Given its capabilities, it can't even compare with what a nuclear weapon can do. There is nothing fair or just, or humane, when it comes to war. Now, given all that ... this laser ... if properly used, can prevent a nuclear-tipped missile or a bomber from attacking our country and wiping out millions of innocent people. Personally ... and professionally ... I support the development of this system as a strategic defensive weapon. I share your concerns about the possibility for its misuse and will make special note of such in my report and any testimony I may be required to give."

"Point taken Major."

Following Parks' solemn response, the room fell silent. All the meeting's participants sat there, sorting out in their own minds what the pros and cons would be for the future of a system like the COIL laser.

Finally breaking the silence, Matt Shields looked across the table at Colby Jefferson and Logan Davis, then asked an unassuming question. "Major, when you finish this job and submit your report ... what will happen to the two of you?"

CHAPTER 55

Backskatter Site
Late Monday Afternoon

Brian Reynolds wasted little time once the 300 landed. He removed his headset and unbuckled his four-point harness before Barclay had a chance to fully spool down the engine and lock the controls. Reynolds was on a mission, and time was of the essence.

As soon as Chance Barclay gave him the thumbs up, Reynolds grabbed his backpack, climbed out of the helicopter, and strode off in the direction of the administration building. The first thing he planned to do was to scour the place in search of any notes the deceased Aaron Thomas may have left behind. Once he checked out the admin building, he planned to continue his search of the shattered central building and the surrounding area. Reynolds had a solid theory of what caused the runaway and destruction, but he needed conclusive proof. He just hoped it wouldn't take him a month of Sundays to find what he was looking for.

Once Barclay had shut down and secured his helicopter, he walked over to the second helipad where the 500 was parked. He wasn't at all surprised to find his partner trying to take a cat nap in the right-hand passenger seat. He would have done the same thing if he could. Being on indefinite standby was boring stuff.

"Hey, partner." Barclay patted Westbrook on the leg. "Time to rise and shine and look like we're on the job."

"I am on the job," replied a groggy Trent Westbrook as he struggled to sit upright. "I'm just resting my eyes in anticipation of a quick departure."

"Nice comeback. Looks like I woke you none too soon then.

Major Roberts, along with Captains Mitchell and Webster are headed this way. Time to put on your game face, sleepy head."

As the three Air Force Officers approached the two pilots, Westbrook climbed out of the 500 and stood next to his partner. Mark Webster matter-of-factly asked what Brian Reynolds was doing back at the site. Barclay told him Maj. Jefferson wanted the engineer flown back to Backskatter so he could do a little follow-up work.

Before Webster could ask another question, Maj. Roberts asked about Maj. Jefferson and Lt. Davis. He obviously wanted to know why the pair had not accompanied Reynolds and what they were up to. Barclay confessed he didn't know what was going on with the two investigators. When he left COTEF with Reynolds, to his knowledge both Jefferson and Davis were still there.

Chance Barclay instinctively sensed something was up, especially by the tone of the questioning and by the way Roberts and Webster exchanged concerned glances. Maj. Roberts stole a quick look back at the central building before asking Barclay if he could fly them back to COTEF immediately. Obviously, he was concerned about something.

Barclay gestured toward Westbrook and told the three officers Trent would fly them back in the 500 since he was on standby to ferry Reynolds back as soon as he was finished. Roberts gnawed on his lower lip for a moment before nodding his approval then started climbing into the 500's right front passenger seat. Captains Mitchell and Webster climbed into the back seats. There was no dialog between the three Air Force people, which Barclay thought was rather odd.

Westbrook asked his partner if he should come back to the radar site or stay at COTEF once he dropped his passengers off. Barclay suggested he check with Maj. Roberts and watch his fuel status just in case. He also asked Westbrook to monitor their "ship-to-ship" frequency in the event something came up. Trent Westbrook gave his friend a thumbs up and climbed into the 500's pilot's seat. He was only too happy to be flying "Three-Two-Six Charlie Bravo" again.

From a safe distance, Barclay watched his partner go through his pre-startup checklist then fire off the 500's turboshaft engine. When everything was ready, Westbrook gave the standard thumbs up signal to Barclay, unlocked the controls, then raised the collective handle. The powerful 500 gently lifted straight up before transitioning to a climb out, flying directly over the top of the remains of the central building then between the #1 and #2 radar arrays. The nimble McDonnel Douglas 500E disappeared toward the northwest in a matter of seconds.

Once Westbrook was gone with his passengers, Barclay decided to give the 300 a thorough post-flight check while waiting for Brian Reynolds. He would have loved to stroll over to the ruined central building and give the engineer a hand but needed to abide by the conditions of their employment to stay on the helipad.

∽

Brian Reynolds had already collected a ream of notes from the admin building and was once again rummaging through the devastated central building. He concentrated his efforts in the section of the building that housed the liquid gas tanks and the microwave exciter. After an hour of digging through the rubble, Reynolds found what he was looking for, packed up his things and headed back out to the helipads.

"Ready to head back?" Chance Barclay asked as Reynolds approached the helicopter.

"Yep. Found what I was looking for. If we leave right away, what time do you think we'll be getting back to COTEF?"

Barclay looked at his watch. The time was now 5:58 p.m. Sunset would occur in about 20 minutes. Doing some quick calculations in his head, the pilot said startup to takeoff would take approximately six minutes. Add to that, another fifty minutes or so of flight time and they should be back in Bend around 7:00. They would be arriving after dark.

"Will that work for you?" Barclay asked.

"Absolutely … let's hit the road, Chance my boy."

After getting loaded, Barclay wasted little time in getting the little helicopter started and engaged its rotors. While waiting for the engine gauges to stabilize "in the green," he switched on the avionics power and made a radio call to Trent Westbrook. There was no immediate reply, so Barclay spooled up the engine, unlocked his controls and made a shallow departure towards the northwest, right between radar arrays #1 and #2.

On the fifty-minute flight back to the COTEF facility, Reynolds tried to study the notes he picked up at Backskatter in the fading light while Barclay made repeated attempts to raise his partner. At approximately the mid-point, he finally made contact and informed Westbrook they were on their way back with an ETA of around 7:00. Trent said he was still on standby at COTEF and would make sure the auxiliary landing site was free and clear for them, then signed off.

As the 300 skirted the southern edge of Pine Mountain, Chance Barclay nonchalantly asked Reynolds if he had determined the cause of the accident. The engineer was hesitant to answer at first, but he liked Barclay, so out of respect, he answered his question.

"To me, it looks like the computer-controlled actuators that inject the gases into the combustion system failed."

"Okay." Chance Barclay gave a quick smile. "I'm not sure I understand what all of that means, but as long as you do I guess that solves the mystery."

"To a point, yes." The engineer shook the notes in his hand. "Somewhere in this mess there are still several unanswered questions … and a responsible party. Someone didn't do what they were supposed to do … and it destroyed a multi-million-dollar piece of equipment and killed twenty-three or more people."

CHAPTER 56

COTEF Facility
Early Monday Evening

Trent Westbrook and his three passengers arrived back at COTEF at approximately 5:45 p.m. after a quick twenty-five-minute flight. Westbrook flew low and fast across the desert, relishing the speed and capabilities of the 500. Whenever he got to fly the McDonnel Douglas product, it was hard for him to go back to flying the smaller, piston-powered 300. He was perpetually envious of his partner for how much flying he got to do in the sleek, turbine-powered machine.

During the flight, Westbrook managed to ask the sullen Maj. Roberts if he wanted the helicopter on standby at the facility for the evening. Roberts said yes, he would, and asked Westbrook if he needed to refuel at the airport. Trent said he had enough for one more round-trip and would remain at COTEF until released for the evening.

Upon landing on the facility's main helipad, Westbrook quickly spooled the helicopter down to ground idle and locked the controls. His three passengers had already removed their headsets and seat harnesses and were waiting for Westbrook to give them permission to disembark. When Trent gave them the thumbs up signal, the three officers carefully exited the machine and headed for the main building's security gate.

Westbrook took his time cooling down the Allison turbine before completely shutting down. Although he loved flying the 500, it had been a long day and he was tired. He hoped his next flight would be to Orion's home base at the airport.

~

The drive back to COTEF for Jefferson and Davis was occupied by an exchange of thoughts and opinions regarding the COIL laser and the events of the past two days.

The pair had just turned onto Dodds Road when Logan Davis asked a question that had been on his mind since they finished their meeting at the hospital.

"Major ... you really didn't answer Trooper Shields' question about what's next for us. Your 'I expect we'll either be reassigned or go back to what we were doing' response was pretty ... vanilla. You don't really believe that will happen ... do you?"

"Logan ... I don't really know what's in store for either of us after this is over," Colby Jefferson lamented. "I rather suspect when 'the shit hits the fan' after I've filed my report ... our previous jobs at Schriever will change. I honestly don't know what will happen. I appreciate being asked the question, though. Shields and everyone else will undoubtedly go back to life as usual. For us, who knows? I would like to think ... I'd like to think we won't get caught up in the fallout from this mess."

"Hopefully," replied Davis, ever the optimist. "You and I will walk away from this unscathed with at least one meritorious award. That would be good for both our careers ... don't you think?"

"Yep, that would be nice." Jefferson didn't want Davis to get caught up in the negative possibilities. He wanted to keep things on a positive note with the young lieutenant and keep him focused on finishing the job.

The two officers checked in at the first security gate and proceeded to the parking area where they parked their motor pool car in the designated space. Not in any big hurry to go inside the COTEF facility, the two continued talking in the car for almost twenty minutes. They wanted to finish their conversation without the possibility of any eavesdropping.

Ironically, Jefferson and Davis were just getting out of their car when Barclay made his final approach to the alternate helipad in the 300. Although the sun had set almost forty-five minutes ago, it was still light enough outside for visual references. The approaching helicopter, with its navigation lights, strobe, beacon and landing light on, looked like it could have been a UFO coming at them in the darkening sky. The duo stopped short and watched the little white helicopter make a perfect landing right on top of the painted "H."

"Wow, what timing!" Logan Davis said, obviously excited to see Brian Reynolds back from the desert. Even in the fading light, he noticed a somber-looking Maj. Roberts and an equally serious Capt. Webster exit the main security gate and head toward the helipad. Davis quickly looked at his partner as if to say, do we need to intercept them before they talk to Reynolds?

As the four Air Force officers descended on the now-idling Schweizer 300, Trent Westbrook climbed down out of the parked 500 and moved in that direction as well. Chance Barclay noticed their arrival had gained an awful lot of attention. He mentioned as such into the boom microphone of his headset. The helicopter's voice-activated intercom system instantly transmitted what was said into the headset Reynolds was wearing. The engineer simply responded, "I don't like the looks of this."

Chance Barclay spooled down the helicopter's engine and rotors to ground idle and turned off the bright landing light while surveying his surroundings. Off to his right, Trent Westbrook waited between the two machines to visit with him. Approaching from his 10 o'clock position in front were Maj. Roberts and Capt. Webster. From his left side, Maj. Jefferson and Lt. Davis were also walking towards him. For a brief second, and just for spite, he considered spooling the 300 back up to maximum RPM and taking off for the airport.

When the helicopter's engine gauges had stabilized in the lower end of their green arcs, Barclay switched off the avionics power switch then shut down the engine before turning off the aircraft's navigation and running lights. The after-landing shut down procedure took all of six minutes. Barclay could see the people surrounding him were getting impatient.

Barclay and Reynolds removed their headsets and unbuckled their seatbelt harnesses then stole a quick glance at each other.

"I wasn't expecting a welcoming committee," came the solemn comment from Brian Reynolds.

"Me neither," Barclay replied. "What do you suppose this is all about?"

"Looks like everyone is curious what I found at Backskatter."

"Are you going to show them what you found and explain what you came up with?"

"Hell no ... I need to do more research in the lab before I can make a conclusive determination."

"So, what are you going to tell them?"

CHAPTER 57

COTEF Facility
Monday Evening

The assembled group of five men stood in a loose semi-circle in front of the 300.

All were waiting for Barclay to give them the "all clear" sign to approach the helicopter. When he did so, the four Air Force officers converged on the righthand door where the laser engineer sat. Trent Westbrook strode over to the left-hand door where Barclay was at the pilot's station.

Brian Reynolds slowly climbed down out of the 300 and, before greeting his people, reached back inside to grab his backpack.

Maj. Roberts was the first to speak and asked the engineer if he found anything definitive.

Reynolds glanced at all four officers, if only to acknowledge their presence, then said, "No ... wasted trip ... sorry," and started to walk away.

Roberts pursed his lips and looked down, as if deep in thought. The suspicious Capt. Webster narrowed his eyes and stared at the engineer as he moved on. Jefferson and Davis looked at one another with a semblance of a smile on their faces. Both knew Reynolds was on to something and didn't want to divulge what he knew to the likes of Roberts and Webster ... not yet.

Jefferson stole a quick glance toward the two pilots then walked over to Roberts. He asked the commander of COTEF if he could release the services of Orion Air for the rest of the evening. Although by this time it was practically dark outside, Roberts had to give the matter thought before he said no ... changing his mind about keeping the 500 on site. He said he would like to have both helicopters back at the facility at 0730 hours the next morning.

Roberts informed Capt. Webster he was going home and instructed the captain to tell Lt. Blackstone as such. He also suggested to the humorless Webster he should do the same, then walked off in the direction of his car.

Logan Davis and Brian Reynolds broke off from the group at this point to make their way toward the security gate and the main building beyond. Once checked in, their first stop would be to hit the DEFAC. They had missed the evening staff meal but hoped the kitchen staff would take pity on them again.

As everyone departed the area, Colby Jefferson approached the two pilots standing next to the 300. He heard Maj. Roberts tell them they were finished for the day and for them to return to COTEF the following morning at 7:30.

"Hey guys," Jefferson said, greeting the two pilots. "Looks like your day of flying for the Air Force is finished. Guess I'll see you bright and early tomorrow."

Then, almost as an afterthought, he again thanked the pair for their service and their discretion on the conversation they had earlier at Backskatter.

Not knowing what to say, Barclay and Westbrook nodded and headed towards their respective machines. Chance Barclay fired up the still warm 300 and quickly spooled it up to takeoff status. Trent Westbrook needed a bit more time to do the same with the 500, so Barclay took off first and headed directly for the airport. Once the 500 was ready, Westbrook followed suit, hoping this wouldn't be the last time he'd have the opportunity to fly the 500 on this job.

～

Colby Jefferson, Logan Davis, and Brian Reynolds huddled at the end of a table at the far end of the DEFAC. They wanted as much privacy as possible while visiting and eating. Once again, one of the cooks provided them with a collection of food left over from the day's staff lunch and dinner.

"Nice brush-off to the major," Jefferson said as he took a sip of freshly brewed coffee. Off to his side, Logan Davis let out a little chuckle. "You know he's going to be really pissed when he finds out you lied to him, don't you?"

"Yeah ... what's he going to do?" Reynolds smirked. "Court Marshall me? Fire me? What? I've been thrown out of better places than this. I could also make better money by going into the private sector and wouldn't have to put up with all this bullshit."

The comment produced a quiet chuckle from the two officers. Following the remark from the combative engineer, there was a long pause in the conversation while all three men nibbled at their dinner.

"So, did you find anything to confirm your suspicions?" Jefferson asked.

"I did ... and it was worse than I thought. I can't believe there wasn't more damage considering how quickly things went sideways."

"How so?" Logan Davis asked.

"Remember me telling you how we initially experimented with deuterium fluoride as our principal gas medium, but switched to a combination of oxygen and iodine for greater power?"

"Yes ... what about it?" Jefferson replied, taking another bite of his meal.

"Well," Reynolds swallowed what he was eating in one gulp. "There's more to it than that. Sorry ... I didn't know the extent of your knowledge on the subject or what your level of authority was when we initially talked about this."

"Brian ... what are you trying to tell us?" Jefferson tried not to show his impatience with the engineer.

Reynolds inhaled deeply and blew it out through pursed lips before answering. "Approximately two months ago, the heat was put on us to come up with a laser shot of extremely high power. We were told we needed to hit a target located on the side of Mt. Jefferson, some 114 miles to the northwest, and show considerable damage to it. According to our calculations and experiments, this would have been possible with a change in the primary gas medium and a higher power setting on the magnetron."

"What did these changes consist of ... specifically?" Jefferson asked.

"It was proposed the laser fuel be switched from basic hydrogen peroxide, which produces the singlet oxygen for the initial reaction, to deuterated hydrogen peroxide. The DHP gas is fairly unstable when compared to hydrogen peroxide but provides greater efficiency and power ... especially when excited by an accompanying increase in microwave stimulation."

"This combination of using new gases with an increase in microwave power ... caused this accident?"

"Yes and no."

CHAPTER 58

COTEF Facility
Monday Evening

"Explain, please," Colby Jefferson prompted.

"All things considered," Reynolds said. "The addition of the DHP gas and increased microwave power settings should have worked beautifully except for one crucial factor."

"Which is?"

"The computer system that controls the entire process, start to finish, was not re-programmed to make the necessary adjustments for these changes."

"That's it? An overlooked computer program is responsible for one of the worst industrial accidents in Air Force history?"

"You have to understand, Major, to create a laser blast of this magnitude is an extremely complicated process. I tried to give you an idea of what that entails when we visited yesterday. The technical hurdles can be significant. There are actuators which control special valves, which control the proper amount of gas injected into the initial combustion chamber. At the precise moment, the magnetron delivers a specific amount of radiological energy into this chamber to excite the molecules to the optimum level. As the super-excited molecules go through the remaining processes to become a shot of pure light energy, a means to immediately release any heat buildup also needs to happen. All of this happens simultaneously and can only be coordinated and controlled by a series of sensors and a highly integrated computer program ... actually, two interlocking computers control the process. It was designed this way because everything happens instantaneously ... which means only a computer, with its microprocessors operating at the speed of light, can make it all work in unison."

"So, in other words ... somebody 'screwed the pooch' by not making the necessary changes to the computer program ... the one that controls the process? Is that the gist of it?"

"That's the primary culprit," Reynolds said. "If the program had been modified as required, along with a few mechanical adjustments to the rest of the system, the laser would have automatically shut itself down if there were any problems or abnormal readings on the optical sensors. In short, in the haste to meet the timeline and get this shot off, too many safeguards and procedures were not followed ... or were missed altogether. Changing the fuel mixture and the power settings without making the necessary modifications to the rest of the system resulted in unintended consequences. This accident was preventable ... it was the result of a major oversight."

The three men sat there in relative silence for a few moments before Logan Davis spoke up. "So, it all boils down to a simple case of human error?"

"More like gross negligence, Lieutenant."

"I don't understand how something like this could happen." Davis replied, shaking his head.

"Oh, I've seen things like this go south before. Ever since I went to work for the Pentagon, I have seen too many cases where mistakes were made in the name of urgency ... the push for results above all else. Time is money and all that other bullshit. Most project managers don't understand that developing highly technical products and weapons take time and require safeguards on top of safeguards during development. The H-Bomb wasn't built in a day you know."

"Can you explain to us how you envision what happened during the runaway?" Jefferson asked.

The laser engineer rubbed his chin for a moment, then let out a heavy sigh before answering.

"There must have been an uncontrolled chain reaction in the primary combustion chamber when the microwaves hit the gases. It was so intense it must have destroyed all control features and fail-safe systems, then kept propagating itself through all six stages of the process ... including the firing of random shots. When the ejector exhaust system failed, the instantaneous heat buildup was so immense it created an explosion ... further fueled by the gas tanks. Finally, the blast must have been so profound ... the laser, the lab, the building, and anyone in the immediate proximity would have either been vaporized or irradiated with a toxic mixture of lithium and iodine. The initial explosion must have been something resembling a large fireball, undoubtedly collapsing quickly enough to create a vacuum. The air rushing back in to fill the void must have been relatively strong ... strong enough to suck everything back into the center of detonation. That would explain why the first impression of the accident was that of an implosion."

Davis turned to look at his fellow officer and sadly proclaimed, "Major, I don't think we're going to find any more survivors ... or any more bodies."

Jefferson could only nod in agreement. The ugly reality of how the accident happened and what it did now weighed even more heavily on the minds of the two Air Force officers. Brian Reynolds suddenly lost his appetite at the thought of what the end must have been like for his fellow co-workers at Backskatter and pushed his plate away.

After several minutes of quiet reflection, Jefferson sat up a little straighter, cleared his throat and asked the engineer another question. The lead investigator suddenly thought of something mentioned earlier.

"Brian, you said this incompatible computer program was the primary culprit. What did you mean by that?"

Before answering Jefferson's question, the laser specialist quickly glanced around the room. He wanted to make sure no other eyes or ears were in the vicinity.

"Someone ... somewhere ... had to start the ball rolling," Reynolds said above a whisper. "Someone had to order the change in what fuel gases to use and to make the required magnetron changes. That 'someone' also pressed for an accelerated timeline, which resulted in the overlooked computer program and any additional safety measures. This person could not have been any of the scientists, engineers, or technicians on the project. They don't have that kind of authority."

"Jesus," was the only word to come out of Davis' mouth as he lowered his head and gently pushed his half-eaten meal away.

"Brian," Jefferson said, "Your 'someone' could be anyone from a two-star in the Pentagon down to Colonel Kelly at Schriever, or to Lt. Colonel Rutledge, or even Major Roberts. Maybe the whole chain of command is involved. Whoever did this … is directly responsible for the deaths of over twenty people … not to mention the destruction of millions of dollars of government property. Tell me, who do you think did this?"

Reynolds glanced separately at the two investigators, silently contemplating what he was about to say and how it would be received. Then the frustrated engineer cleared his throat, looking again at each officer before speaking.

"According to the notes Aaron Thomas left behind and what I've uncovered on my own, along with personal experience … it wasn't anyone in the chain of command you just mentioned. I'm fairly sure of that. If there's a weasel in this woodpile, all fingers point to none other than our very own and overly-ambitious Captain … Mark … Webster."

CHAPTER 59

COTEF Facility
Monday Night

"Can you prove any of this?" Jefferson asked.

"Circumstantially yes ... conclusively no." Reynolds shrugged. "Everything I've told you about the accident itself ... what caused it and how things came about, can be proven ... more or less. It was just a matter of collecting notes, bits and pieces of debris, remnants of the laser, and what was left on the mainframe computer. I just connected the dots."

"But you have nothing concrete on Webster ... is that it?"

"No, nothing concrete. Only speculation based on what I've picked up from others and from what Aaron Thomas had in his notes. I wish I had something to hang the little bastard with, but I don't."

Before the conversation could go any further, the ubiquitous Lt. Blackstone strode into the DEFAC and asked Jefferson if he and Lt. Davis planned to take their nightly stroll around the perimeter fence. She said the dog handlers wanted to know if they should kennel their animals or not. Jefferson looked at his watch, which read 8:05, then over at Davis, who nodded.

Colby Jefferson informed the young woman that, yes, they would like to stretch their legs and would plan to go out at 2100 hours. Blackstone said she would inform the handlers, bid the men a good night, then disappeared down a long hallway.

"Has she always been so ... so straightforward?" Logan Davis asked Reynolds, trying to choose his words carefully.

"Yep, pretty much," Brian Reynolds said in a flat voice. "That woman has illusions of grandeur and is the consummate obsessive-compulsive poster child."

The two Air Force officers laughed at Reynolds' description of the ambitious young lieutenant. Obviously, she was not the most popular person on site, probably a result of being Roberts' administrative assistant as well as his eyes and ears on the rest of the staff. Her somber demeanor and cool personality didn't help.

As the three finished their conversation, Jefferson asked Reynolds if he would care to join Davis and him on their nightly stroll. He wanted to ask the engineer a few more questions but wanted to do it outside to avoid being overheard. Reynolds was more than happy to continue their conversation in a more private setting.

Jefferson said he needed to check in with Colonel Rutledge at Schriever first and would meet the other two in the lobby in thirty minutes. The three men finished their meal and returned their trays to the kitchen before leaving the DEFAC to go their separate ways. Jefferson headed for their assigned office while Davis went back to their quarters. Brian Reynolds returned to his lab to review more of Aaron Thomas' notes.

When his call finally went through to Colonel Rutledge, Jefferson came right to the point. A probable cause for the accident had been determined. This was without question a "Class A" accident and could no longer be considered an incident or mishap. A formal DoD investigation was required. Jefferson recommended a forensic team be sent from the Dover AFB Forensic Medical Facility to recover and identify the ten bodies along with the ashes of Aaron Thomas. He further recommended a special detachment be sent from Kirtland ASAP to finish cleaning up the Backskatter site, salvage what they could, and ship everything back to New Mexico. Jefferson said this same team should also secure, remove and relocate the existing lab at COTEF back to Kirtland as well. The move would, essentially, close down the Oregon side of the project. In his opinion, all of this was a necessary move ... especially when it came to maintaining project secrecy and security. Finally, Jefferson said he would like to have Rutledge on site at COTEF the following day at 1300 hours, local time (1:00 p.m. PDST), for a detailed briefing with all on-site principals in attendance.

As expected, T.J. Rutledge was not happy. After Jefferson had given his report, the colonel said he would fly out to Oregon the following morning but would hold off on Jefferson's other recommendations and any further action until after his on-site briefing. Rutledge concluded the call by informing Jefferson he would contact COTEF's commanding officer, Maj. Roberts, regarding his ETA on Tuesday, then abruptly hung up.

The fifteen-minute phone call with his superior officer did not leave Colby Jefferson with a warm and fuzzy feeling ... quite the opposite. He was now convinced the Colonel was a part of the conspiracy to cover up the COIL laser's alternative purpose as well as the accident itself. He decided to make a second call to Colorado ... this time to an old classmate from OCS who worked at Peterson Air Force Base. After talking with his friend at Peterson, Jefferson made a third call ... one that went to the state police. For the time being at least, he decided to keep these calls on the "QT."

After finishing his calls and making a couple of notes, Jefferson left the office and walked down the hallway to the front lobby area. Logan Davis and Brian Reynolds were already standing at the main exit chatting with the security guard. When the major joined the group, the guard acknowledged their intentions and buzzed them out.

A rush of cool air greeted the three men as they passed through the second set of doors. The balmy daytime high of seventy-two degrees had turned into a chilly forty-six-degree evening. All three remarked they wished they had worn heavier jackets.

Per their routine, the two Air Force officers, with their guest in tow, started their circuit at the building's main security gate. Waving at the camera on top of one of the posts, the trio started walking north along the inside of the high fence toward the northeast corner. Once they rounded that corner and were walking in a westerly, counterclockwise direction along the fence's northern section, their amicable chatting turned into a more serious dialog.

Brian Reynolds, after once more reviewing the notes of the deceased Aaron Thomas, was now totally convinced of his original assumptions. The destroyed laser was a direct result of negligence ... promoted by a bad, unauthorized decision, made by an overzealous officer. He too, was now of the opinion that a cover-up was in the works and this whole mess could not simply be "written off" as an unfortunate incident. He also felt partially responsible for the deaths of so many of his fellow workers and the damage caused by the random firing of the laser's last moments.

Colby Jefferson tried to reassure the distressed engineer what happened was not his fault. Quite the contrary. The major reiterated that Reynold's had tried, on several occasions, to warn of inadequate safeguards and unreasonable timelines. Jefferson also told Reynolds his report would reflect that fact and if it weren't for him, the cause of the laser's destruction might never be known. Brian Reynolds felt exonerated by Jefferson's remarks and thanked him.

As the group turned south at the northwest corner of the fence, Jefferson told the other two he planned to conduct a detailed briefing the next day for all those involved … including Lt. Colonel T.J. Rutledge, who would be flying out in the morning.

Davis and Reynolds were in total agreement with the plans. They wanted to know what they could do to prepare for the briefing and asked who would be in attendance.

Before Jefferson could answer, the flood lights atop the fence's corner posts suddenly went out. "What the hell?" Jefferson said, looking around.

The distinct sound of snarling and barking came from the southern end of the building. All three men froze as the noise intensified.

"Oh shit!" shouted a terrified Logan Davis. "The dogs are loose!"

CHAPTER 60

Schriever Air Force Base
Monday Night

Colby Jefferson's phone call to his boss reached Schriever's main switchboard at approximately 9:40 p.m., MDST. The operator on duty transferred the call to Colonel Rutledge at his off-base home.

Upon hearing Jefferson's report, Rutledge let his frustrations with the whole affair get the better of him; he hung up after the major finished talking. After pouring himself a stiff drink of his favorite whiskey, he called Colonel David R. Kelly, Schriever's base commander at home to update him on the status of the investigation. He left out the part regarding Jefferson's recommendations to close down the Oregon side of the project and transfer everything back to Kirtland Air Force Base.

Col. Kelly decided he too, should attend the briefing. He instructed Rutledge to make the arrangements for them to fly out to Oregon in the morning. Rutledge was not too keen on the idea but now was not the time to question his boss.

Rutledge made a subsequent call to Schriever's logistics officer requesting a flight to Oregon for two the following morning. Due to the lateness of the hour, the LO said she could make no guarantees, but would see what she could do and promised to get back to Rutledge as soon as she had something.

Within an hour, the LO got back to him. A C-140 JetStar would be ready for departure at 1100 hours the next morning from Peterson AFB. Rutledge asked the LO if something earlier couldn't be scheduled. The officer said she'd tried, but the aircraft was already booked for an early morning flight. Rutledge asked what the ETA in

Oregon would be if they left on time.

"With the time zone difference, approximately 1230 hours sir."

Rutledge said that would work and told the LO to confirm with Peterson that he and Colonel Kelly would be there at 1030 hours and ended the call.

The thankless logistics officer made a notation on the flight manifest for the JetStar's flight crew to expect a "wing king" (base commander), and a "scrambled egg" (a derogatory term for a ranking officer), for their second flight of the morning.

Rutledge decided to check in with his "mole" at COTEF and inform his contact to expect him and Colonel Kelly for Tuesday afternoon's general briefing. He was also curious what had occurred during the day. The colonel was hungry for any updates or current information. Rutledge wanted to be well prepared for Jefferson's meeting.

After several rings with no answer, the phone on the other end switched over to an "at the sound of the tone …" voice mail message. Rutledge abruptly disconnected the call and wondered what was going on. His secret contact at COTEF was usually on the line after the first ring … if not the first to call altogether. This was highly unusual.

Rutledge poured himself a second drink and tried to sort out what he knew. Obviously, Jefferson had accomplished his two objectives: find out what went wrong, and to determine what it would take to get the coveted project back on track. He was uncomfortable with the thought his chief investigator may have discovered more than he was supposed to. Rutledge also worried about the participation of Brian Reynolds in the investigation. Reynolds had been troublesome in the past, and both Rutledge and Major Roberts considered him indirectly responsible for the project being behind schedule … and not by a small amount either.

Rutledge wondered about his secret operative at COTEF. What was the last thing said from a previous phone conversation … "in seventy-two hours all of this will be behind us"?

CHAPTER 61

COTEF Facility
Monday Night

Even in the subdued downlighting of the building's exterior lights, Colby Jefferson easily recognized the breed of the fast-approaching dogs by the sound of their aggressive snarling, their distinctive pointed ears, and their lean silhouettes.

COTEF's free roaming guard dogs were Doberman pinchers ... Jefferson counted four of them.

He had worked with this breed of dog when he was going through security training and knew their capabilities. They were fearless, lethal, and fast, especially the males. Dobermans had been clocked at a top speed of thirty miles per hour. They also had a formidable bite, averaging over 300 pounds of pressure. Their true strength however, lay in quickly delivering multiple bites and stubbornly hanging onto an object. A Doberman was capable of mutilating any animal or man, including crushing bones or ripping out a throat.

Originally developed in Germany in the late 1800s, Doberman pinchers were bred to protect tax collectors from robbers and to persuade reluctant citizens to "fork over" what they owed. Categorized as one of the large breed dogs, Dobermans could be as big as thirty inches tall and weigh up to 100 pounds. Highly intelligent, extremely loyal, and having and intimidating appearance made them a top pick for personal protection as well as for guarding property. They were the canine equivalent of a heat-seeking missile. Once trained Dobermans were locked onto a target, there was little chance of the target getting away. An unfortunate victim would be lucky to escape with their life.

The use of these dogs at COTEF confirmed to Colby Jefferson that whoever was in charge of this program was dead serious about its security and secrecy. He knew of no other military installation that employed the use of these deadly animals in this manner.

Brian Reynolds had never been more scared ... he knew what these dogs were capable of. Logan Davis was hysterical with panic. Only Jefferson remained in control of his emotions and the situation.

"Don't run!" The major whipped off his jacket and belt. "Do this!" He wrapped his jacket around one arm and waved his belt like a whip. "Back up against the fence so they can't get behind you!"

After a second or two of indecision, Reynolds imitated Jefferson. Terrified, Davis tried to bolt. Jefferson grabbed the back of his jacket collar and slammed him against the fence. The sudden, violent movement caught the dogs off guard, and they stopped where they were. For a few seconds, the animals milled at a distance, watching, but then regained their composure and pressed forward, snarling.

Jefferson surmised these Dobermans were not used to seeing prey stand their ground, or huddle in a group like this. The temporary standoff gave Jefferson time to think as well as help his partner prepare to defend himself. Although Davis was shaking uncontrollably, he managed to get his jacket off and wrap it around his left arm, then unfasten his web belt and pull it free from his pants.

All three men pressed their backs up against the fence and stood within two feet of one another. Davis stood between Jefferson, on his left, and Reynolds, on his right. They prepared to fend off their attackers, each man aware he'd be fighting for his life.

The four Dobermans spread out in a semi-circle, growling, and feigning an attack while looking for an opening to lunge at the trapped men. In the dim light, their massive white teeth gleamed as they snarled and snapped. As soon as one of the animals made a move, the rest would immediately follow. That was how a pack brought down its prey, by a coordinated attack.

"They'll charge as a group ... from different directions." Jefferson shouted. "Like a lion tamer, stick out your wrapped arm for protection then pop 'em in the face with your belt! If they grab the belt, don't let go of it! Let 'em play tug of war with you! Now, start yelling at them!"

The attack came exactly as Jefferson predicted. As soon as one dog made a move, the rest followed in unison. It was four against three. All three men were now essentially engaged in hand-to-hand combat with trained killers.

Two of the animals lunged at Logan Davis, sensing his fear. One went for Jefferson, and the other jumped at Reynolds. All four dogs leapt, becoming airborne. They were trained to go for the head and neck, or to knock a man down where they could do real damage.

To his credit, Logan Davis quelled his panic. Quite the opposite. Rage had now supplanted his fear. He was determined not to be a dog attack victim for the second time in his life. As the first dog flew towards his chest, the second dog went for his groin. Davis instinctively put his wrapped arm up to shield himself against the first animal and twisted sideways so neither dog would have a clear frontal shot at him.

The movement worked. The first dog latched onto the protected arm. When it hit, Davis was forced back into the fence as he turned. The unexpected move resulted in the second animal's bite to snap just short of his thigh. The dog latched onto nothing more than a mouthful of loose-fitting cargo pants and partially ripped away the side pocket.

With its momentum stopped, gravity came into play for the first dog while it tried to get a firmer grip on the lieutenant's forearm. Ninety-four pounds of seething Doberman crashed down onto the second animal. The bottom dog collapsed under the weight of the larger dog, releasing its bite on the cargo pants.

Davis rotated to where he could get a clear shot at both dogs while they were temporarily stunned. The animal latched onto his arm shook its head as it clamped down even harder, unconcerned about the struggling dog laying beneath him. If it weren't for the jacket, the Doberman would have easily shredded Davis' arm. The bottom dog remained on its side, trapped beneath the larger one but struggling to get free. Aided by a rush of adrenalin, Davis hauled his right foot back and delivered several quick kicks to the pinned dog on the bottom. The blows landed squarely in the animal's chest, breaking two ribs. The dog yelped in pain, struggled to get onto its feet, then limped away from the men.

With one attacker out of commission, Davis turned his attention to the animal tearing at his covered-up arm. Instead of using the belt as a whip, he shortened his grip and used it more like a flexible club. The tenacious Doberman remained locked onto his arm as Davis repeatedly snapped the buckle end of his belt into the dog's face. One of the blows opened a nasty gash on the dog's nose while another almost put the animal's eye out. The wounded Doberman let go of his arm and retreated back a couple of yards, feverishly shaking its injured head.

For a moment or two, the injured dog just stood there out of range, probably sensing he was vulnerable. Davis knew the attack wasn't over. Both dogs were down but not out. They were still highly trained and unrelenting guard dogs. The fight wasn't over, only temporarily halted.

CHAPTER 62

COTEF Facility
Monday Night

The attack on Logan Davis and his defensive actions lasted all of fourteen seconds. To the lieutenant, it seemed more like a lifetime.

The Dobermans going after Colby Jefferson and Brian Reynolds were just as vicious as the two who went for their companion. While Davis defended himself, the dog in front of Jefferson launched himself toward the major's chest. At the same time, the fourth Doberman went for Reynolds' face.

Colby Jefferson made the same initial move as Davis. He turned sideways, exposing his left side to the animal with his wrapped forearm raised up in a defensive manner. The flying Doberman latched onto the easy target, forcing Jefferson back into the fence. The animal's weight pulled the major down into a hunched-over position. Jefferson only had a few seconds before the animal shredded the jacket and went to work on the arm itself.

The major regained his footing and tried to raise his arm as high as he could while the dog still gnawed on it, hoping to get the animal's front legs off the ground where it wouldn't have any leverage. Giving it his all, Jefferson managed to do just that … but just barely. He'd have to act fast, or the dog would regain the advantage.

With the Doberman's teeth securely locked onto the wrapped forearm and its front feet off the ground, Jefferson did what came naturally. He tackled the animal, football style. The swift action drove the dog backwards onto the ground. The major landed full force, knees and elbows impacting first, on top of the struggling animal, rupturing its spleen. The internal hemorrhaging took an instant toll. The dog released its bite on Jefferson's arm and started howling in pain. Struggling to get on its feet, the animal gingerly limped off and joined the other two injured dogs. Three of the lethal guard dogs were now temporarily out of commission.

When the last Doberman hit the 174-pound engineer, it was with enough force to knock Reynold's violently back into the fence. The force of impact was so strong, Reynolds was knocked unconscious when his head bounced off the heavy metal fencepost behind him. Sensing the man was done, the dog stopped its attack and turned its attention to the next person. In the semi-darkness, a panting Logan Davis never saw the dog coming for him. He was still transfixed on the injured animals in front of him.

Having now abandoned his attack on the engineer, the Doberman lunged at Davis' exposed right leg and latched onto it just below the right hip. Davis cried out in anger as much as pain from the surprise attack, then started whacking at the dog's head with his doubled-up web belt. The Doberman stood his ground, regripped his bite and shook its head. Sensing the blows from his belt weren't detouring the animal, Davis let go of his belt, spun to his right, and trapped the animal between himself and the fence. Bracing his feet and grabbing the chain link fence with both hands, Davis squeezed the dog into the fence with all his strength. The trapped animal released its hold on the leg and tried to squirm free. Davis kept the animal pinned between his hip and the fence, straining to increase the pressure.

The dog Davis initially injured with facial wounds had now recovered enough to resume its attack. As the Doberman took aim and lunged for the back of the distracted lieutenant, Colby Jefferson took a long stride and kicked the animal squarely in its side before it could reach his partner. The force of the kick knocked the animal down but did not seriously injure it. The dog quickly regained its feet and just stood there snarling, obviously looking for another way to attack or trying to decide which of the two men it wanted to go after.

The Doberman Davis had trapped against the fence was now in a frenzy. Breathing was getting harder and harder, and it snapped at anything and everything, including the fence. Davis kept up the unrelenting pressure until the animal stopped its struggling and passed out.

The remaining Doberman made its decision and turned its attention on the man who just kicked it. Colby Jefferson squared off in front of the bleeding dog with one eye almost swollen shut and waited for it to make its move. He didn't have long to wait. The animal bolted at him like a racehorse coming out of the gate. In two strides it became airborne, going directly for Jefferson's face.

The major barely got his wrapped left arm up in time to catch the gaping mouth of the dog. The Doberman hit Jefferson hard enough to make him take a couple of staggering steps backward before losing his balance and falling to the ground. The animal firmly latched onto his arm and violently shook its head as it landed on top of its victim.

For a few seconds, man and dog thrashed around on the ground. Jefferson kept his wrapped arm in front of him the entire time, protecting his head. The Doberman was focused on trying to do considerable damage to the major. The relentless dog never sensed Logan Davis coming up fast behind him. When he got within range, Davis kicked the dog as hard as he could right between its back legs.

The unexpected blow to its groin caused the Doberman to hunch up and release its grip on Jefferson's arm. The animal howled and staggered a couple of steps before turning around to face its attacker. Relieved of the animal's grip and weight, Jefferson rolled away from the dog and got to his feet. It was now two against one. Two men and one dangerous dog in pain.

To the surprise of both men, the Doberman backed off. In obvious distress, the animal cautiously moved away, joining the other two at a distance, nursing their own injuries. The dogs were hurt and, even with their killer instincts and advanced training, sensed these humans were dangerous. The dog Davis pinned against the fence and squeezed the air out of still lay on the ground, semi-conscious.

Jefferson instructed Davis to check on Reynolds while he positioned himself between his two companions and the dogs. Brian Reynolds had a nasty bump on his head and was groggy, but otherwise okay. Davis helped the engineer to his feet then all three men slowly moved north along the fence. The three standing

Dobermans watched the men inch their way away from them. The dog Davis rendered unconscious was now on its feet, coughing and trying to catch its breath. As soon as it did, Jefferson guessed it would join the other three in a renewed attack. These dogs were trained not to give up.

Without warning, the complex's high-intensity perimeter fence lights popped on, followed by a high-pitched horn. Caught by surprise, the three men and the four dogs froze in place.

As the whole area inside and outside of the perimeter fence lit up, four men stormed out of the building.

From the southern end of the structure, two of the dog handlers rushed out. From the northern end, two security guards closed in on the group with their guns drawn. The dog handlers yelled their code word at the dogs to stand down while the remaining guards told Jefferson and his people to stay where they were and put their hands up.

All did as they were told. The dogs stopped their stalking movements and were quickly leashed up by their handlers. The Dobermans lunged and snarled at Jefferson and his companions. Although injured, they were simply showing their handlers they were still on the job and would like a second shot at the three intruders.

Jefferson identified himself and the other two. The two security guards holstered their weapons then asked the three men if any of them needed medical attention. Aside from a large welt on the back of Reynolds's head and a few assorted bumps and bruises, the only other injury suffered by the group was a bad bite to Davis' right leg.

The two guards started to escort the three men to the infirmary while the dog handlers took their animals back to the kennel area.

It had been a harrowing experience for the three men who simply wanted to take a walk and talk about a few things. None would have ever guessed they'd wind up fighting viscous guard dogs, nor how close they may have come to losing their lives.

DAY 4

Tuesday, October 19, 1999

CHAPTER 63

COTEF & Schriever Air Force Base
Tuesday Morning

Maj. Derick Roberts checked in at the front gate to COTEF at exactly 0715 hours. From there, he proceeded to the main parking area and parked in his designated spot. As he climbed out of the Air Force-issued carpool sedan, he wistfully looked over at the two empty helipads. He secretly loved having two helicopters on site and at his disposal ... even though they were civilian, not military. Their presence and availability gave him a sense of prestige and power. He looked forward to seeing the two machines come in for their standard formation landing at 7:30.

From the parking area, Roberts walked up to the main security gate at the fence leading to the building's entrance, punched in his special code, and waved at the camera on top of one of the posts as the gate clicked open. He was being watched by the person monitoring all COTEF's security cameras.

To enter the building itself, Roberts had to swipe his security/identification card to release the door's mag lock entry system. Walking through the lobby, he acknowledged the security guard standing at attention behind the reception desk before heading to his office. Lt. Blackstone was waiting for him in the hallway. She had some bad news regarding the previous night's events.

To the major's dismay, he learned the free-roaming guard dogs were not secured in their kennels when Maj. Jefferson, Lt. Davis and Brian Reynolds took a late walk around the inside of the perimeter fence. His first question was why Reynolds was with the two investigators. His second question was if anyone had been injured.

Blackstone couldn't answer the first question but informed the major that Lt. Davis had sustained a nasty bite wound to his right hip, Jefferson had a collection of cuts and bruises, and Brian Reynolds had received a minor concussion. Roberts was surprised to hear that all the dogs had been injured in the encounter, two of them seriously. Blackstone went on to report one of the handlers took both animals into town for treatment at a 24-hour emergency vet clinic. Both were operated on, with only one surviving.

"Jesus Christ! How in the hell did this happen?" Roberts demanded.

"The dogs being out or one of them being killed?" Blackstone asked.

"Both!" Came the annoyed response.

"I don't know how the dogs got out," Blackstone widened her eyes. "When Major Jefferson told me he wanted to take their nightly walk, I personally went down to the kennels and informed the handlers. I don't know what happened after that."

"Have you talked to the handlers this morning?"

"No, sir, not directly. I only received a brief report about the condition of the dogs. I haven't had the chance to follow up on it. Perhaps either you or Captain Webster would like to debrief them."

"Yes, I would, but I'd like to visit with our three survivors first. Do you know where they are?"

"I believe Davis and Reynolds are in the DEFAC getting breakfast. Major Jefferson checked out a car and left the facility about twenty minutes before you arrived … you might have passed one another on the highway."

"Do you know where he was going or for what reason?"

"No, sir, I do not. I was busy doing paperwork regarding last night's episode."

"Anything else?"

"Only one of the helicopters will be here at 0730, the smaller one. Evidently, there seems to be a minor problem with the other one. Orion Air informed me it should be here before the 1300 briefing and the pilot hopes this won't be an inconvenience."

"It shouldn't be. I don't think anyone was planning to go out to the Backskatter site this morning. Thank you for the report, Lieutenant … you may return to your duties. I'm going down to the

DEFAC. Let me know if anything else develops."

"Will do, sir."

Roberts left the young woman standing in the hallway and proceeded directly to the DEFAC. He not only wanted to know what the two investigators and the engineer were up to, he also wanted to get a clear picture what had happened with his guard dogs. On his way, he heard the distinctive sound of a helicopter fly overhead. Right on time, the major thought to himself.

Neither Davis nor Reynolds were in the dining facility. When asked, one of the cooks replied the two had finished their breakfast and left the area approximately fifteen minutes prior. Roberts went directly to the office assigned to the two investigators. Coming up empty there as well, he checked their quarters next. That too, was empty. Not knowing where else to look for them, Roberts checked the lab in hopes of at least finding Reynolds.

Aside from the usual workday crowd of engineers, technicians and the like, Roberts came up empty in his search for the troublemaking engineer. No one he talked to had seen the man since earlier that morning.

If Roberts had decided to walk down to the building's south end and visit with the dog handlers, he would have found Capt. Devon Mitchell, his chief of base security ... along with everyone else he was looking for.

Frustrated with how his day started out, the major returned to his office to prepare for Jefferson's afternoon briefing and the arrival of his boss from Colorado.

~

T.J. Rutledge picked up Col. Kelly at his residence shortly after 0930, MDST. Both men wore their standard dress blue uniforms for the occasion. The normally twenty-four minute drive from Schriever AFB to Peterson AFB took Rutledge under twenty minutes. On several occasions, Kelly had to remind his junior officer he was exceeding the posted speed limit.

Once they had cleared Peterson's main gate, Rutledge followed the directions to the building containing the flight dispatch department. Once checked in, the pair were escorted out to the flight line where a master sergeant verified their identities, credentials, and documentation before boarding them on the recently returned JetStar.

Both officers removed their caps and uniform jackets then made themselves comfortable while the aircraft's First Officer/co-pilot gave them a standard safety briefing. Partially out of curiosity and partially because he was trying to be friendly, Rutledge thought to ask the officer where their first trip that morning took them. "Oregon" was all the young woman said before she disappeared toward the aircraft's cockpit.

CHAPTER 64

COTEF Facility
Early Afternoon

With the help of a high-altitude tailwind, the C-140 JetStar made the trip from Peterson to Oregon in two hours and ten minutes. The sleek executive jet landed at Bend's municipal airport shortly before noon, taxied to the main ramp area, and shut down. The flight crew were instructed to stay on station until the "big meeting" ended, then fly everyone back to Colorado. Unbeknownst to Rutledge and Kelly, the return manifest listed no fewer than six Air Force officers.

By prior arrangement, the two colonels were met at the airport by two security people in a SUV and driven directly to the COTEF facility. Upon entering the complex, they couldn't help but notice the small white helicopter sitting in the parking area.

Waiting for them in front of the main security gate was Maj. Derick Roberts and Capt. Mark Webster. After introductions, the four officers made their way inside, then walked directly to the DEFAC where Maj. Roberts had a special lunch waiting for them. In terms of the chain of command, Colonel Kelly was now the senior ranking officer, followed by Lt. Colonel Rutledge, then Maj. Roberts, and finally Capt. Webster.

After the better-than-average, military-grade meal, Maj. Roberts and Capt. Webster gave the two colonels a quick tour of the facility. Having never been to the classified site himself, Colonel Kelly was fairly impressed by what he saw. The group made its way to the main conference room at approximately 12:50 p.m., PDST.

Already seated around the large, oval-shaped table were Lt. Logan Davis, Brian Reynolds, Capt. Devon Mitchell, and a uniformed Oregon State Police officer. Sitting along a side wall behind the conference table were Lt. Jennifer Blackstone, the two Backskatter survivors, two technicians from the lab, one of the dog handlers, and the unnamed civilian "project advisor." Everyone stood when the COTEF commander and the two colonels from Colorado entered the room. Derick Roberts' gaze went immediately to the OSP officer.

Maj. Roberts narrowed his eyes and asked Lt. Davis, rather incredulously, who the officer was and why he was at this meeting. Davis introduced Trooper Shields to the recently arrived officers and said he was exclusively invited to attend the briefing by Maj. Jefferson. The Lieutenant explained the trooper was conducting an active civil investigation which involved the Backskatter accident; hence, his reason for being at the meeting. Roberts wanted to know who escorted the officer onto the classified property without his prior knowledge or approval.

"I did ... sir," Davis said.

"Lieutenant," Roberts barked, "you and I, along with Major Jefferson, will have a serious conversation regarding your unacceptable actions after the briefing! You two have grossly exceeded your role and authority!"

Logan Davis stood tall and looked directly at Roberts. "Yes ... sir."

Roberts, caught off guard by the presence of Shields, was obviously embarrassed and was putting on a display of "I'm in charge here" for the two visiting colonels.

"Speaking of ... where the hell is Major Jefferson? He arranged for this meeting!" Roberts snarled, openly displaying his annoyance with the young lieutenant and the whole affair.

Before Davis could respond, the distinctive sound of Orion Air's MD 500 making its landing approach thrummed through the building. All eyes turned toward the windows in time to see Chance Barclay make his customary, spot-on landing on COTEF's primary helipad.

"I believe the major is back from his flight out to Backskatter ... sir," Davis observed.

Roberts stole a quick, glaring glance at the lieutenant before turning back toward the windows.

Everyone in the room now watched the helicopter as it took its time spooling down to ground idle. No one, except for Logan Davis and Matt Shields, expected what came next.

Colby Jefferson climbed out of the still-running 500's right front seat. He said something to the pilot before shutting the door, then opened the door to the back seat. Two uniformed Air Force officers with briefcases climbed out and glanced around. Even with the distance separating the helipad from their vantage point, everyone in the conference room could see both men were colonels with a ton of service ribbons on their uniforms.

"What the hell?" Roberts muttered as he looked over at Rutledge and Kelly. The two shrugged and exchanged quizzical looks. "I'm going to get to the bottom of this … right now!" Roberts barked as he headed for the door.

Rutledge and Kelly quickly followed him out of the conference room, looking none too happy themselves. Something was going on neither knew anything about, and they were just as anxious as Roberts to find out who these two officers were and what they were doing at Backskatter and COTEF.

Colby Jefferson buzzed his two guests through the security gate. They were admitted through the front door by the guard manning the desk in the lobby. The recently arrived officers were met there by Roberts, Rutledge, and Kelly.

"Major … you have some serious explaining to do!" Roberts demanded, looking directly at Jefferson.

"Good morning, sirs." Jefferson looked unfazed while acknowledging the group of the three officers standing together. "Allow me to introduce Colonel Stryker of the regional JAG Corps office and Lt. Colonel Colletto from the regional Office of Special Investigations. Both of these officers flew in earlier this morning from Peterson. They are here as a result of a phone conversation I had last night with Colonel Colletto. I had some procedural questions concerning my investigation. On their own initiative, they decided to fly out early this morning to see the situation for themselves and attend my briefing."

CHAPTER 65

COTEF Facility
Early Afternoon

A JAG officer was the Air Force's equivalent of a prosecuting attorney. Every branch of the U.S. military had its own JAG Corps, which stood for "Judge Advocate General." The standing orders for all these specialized units were to investigate, prosecute, and/or defend illegal actions on the part of military personnel per the Uniform Code of Military Justice. Colonel Stryker's presence at COTEF could only mean he was investigating any number of several serious allegations. Any one of which, could be punishable by reassignment, reduction in rank, discharge, court-martial, and jail time in a military prison.

Lt. Colonel Colletto's attendance was further testament the Air Force was deadly serious about the outcome of the Backskatter accident. The OSI group was not only responsible for assisting the JAG Corps with major criminal investigations, but also tasked with conducting major accident investigations. The group had the additional responsibility for protecting critical Air Force technologies. OSI officers were the Air Force's equivalent of FBI agents.

Stepping forward, T.J. Rutledge tried to take control of the situation. This was, after all, his project, and his responsibility. "With all due respect, I would like to see identification from the two of you … if you don't mind."

Stryker and Colletto pulled out their credentials, flipped them open and held them up for Rutledge and company to see. There was no denying who or what they claimed to be. The three project officers were temporarily at a loss for words. Rutledge, Roberts, and Kelly looked as if they had just been served with unexpected divorce papers. Rutledge again took the initiative and asked the two colonels by whose authority gave them permission to be at Backskatter and COTEF.

As the senior officer and JAG representative, Col. Stryker spoke for the two of them. "We are here, Colonel Rutledge, Colonel Kelly, Major Roberts, under the authority of General Wheeler." The highly decorated, no-nonsense, two-star general was no stranger to anyone in the group. He was the top officer in charge of all Air Force installations and activities in the western region. "Aside from that, you know when it comes to accident investigation and possible criminal activity, our authority will supersede that of any ranking officer in charge … which also includes you, Lt. Colonel Rutledge, as project manager, and you as well, Colonel Kelly."

Before Rutledge, or anyone else could speak, Stryker continued. "And with all due respect, gentlemen, we fully understand the work going on here is of the highest security and secrecy classifications and was initiated by a presidential directive. Still, you of all people, Colonel Rutledge, should know the nature of this project does not give you or anyone else 'carte blanche' to sidestep procedure when an accident of this extent happens. You may protest, file an official grievance, or call General Wheeler if you want, but the fact remains we are here to perform an official follow-up to Major Jefferson's preliminary investigation. Any interference, in any form or from anyone, will be considered by us to be an obstruction of justice. Do you understand?"

Lt. Colonel T.J. Rutledge stiffened, having had been squarely put in his place and everyone present knew it. The presence of the two new investigators meant the seriousness of the accident had been revealed to higher authorities and was not about to be swept under any rug.

Rutledge tried to play the "this is a matter of national security" card, but Stryker and Colletto weren't buying it. Stryker said this was an internal matter and everything disclosed would be kept in house and classified. Rutledge said that would not be possible if Jefferson's briefing went off as planned. Stryker asked the Colonel to explain what he meant by that.

"We have a civilian law enforcement officer present for the briefing," Rutledge answered curtly.

"Yes, Colonel, I am aware that Officer Shields of the Oregon State Police is to be present for the briefing," Stryker said. "His presence and participation have already been cleared by me and Colonel Colletto. It is my understanding he is actively investigating several civilian deaths, disappearances, and damage that appear to be the direct result of your accident. I want to hear what he has to say."

Following those remarks, everyone clustered in the small lobby fell silent. Undoubtedly, Col. Stryker was now the officer-in-charge of the situation and wasn't going to be intimidated or challenged by anyone. He had a job to do, and he fully intended to get all the facts and to make the proper call.

"So, it's now 1320 hours and we're late for a meeting," Stryker announced looking at his watch. "Gentlemen, I suggest we proceed to the conference room and get started. There are a number of things we need to sort out and we're burning daylight."

As the group filed back into the conference room, everyone automatically rose to their feet. All the Air Force people present stood at the expected position of attention. Colby Jefferson, the last to enter the room, took up station on one end of the oversized table. He began by first, introducing Colonels Stryker and Colletto to the group. Next, he went around the table and introduced all those individuals to the two colonels. Finally, he introduced, as best he could, the people sitting along the side wall. All told, the meeting included fifteen men and three women and consisted of two colonels, two lieutenant colonels, two majors, two captains, two lieutenants, two Backskatter survivors, two lab technicians, one enlisted dog handler, one civilian "project advisor," laser engineer Brian Reynolds and OSP Officer Matt Shields.

As everyone sat, Lt. Blackstone went around the room, handing out bottles of water to everyone. Stryker and Colletto each parked their briefcases on top of the table and took out notebooks and small tape recorders before setting their gear down on the floor beside them. Within a few moments, everyone had settled and were now looking at Jefferson, who was finishing arranging his notes.

The major welcomed everyone but instead of taking the lead, invited Col. Stryker to explain his and Colletto's presence and set the ground rules.

Stryker cleared his throat and reiterated what he'd said to Rutledge, Kelly, and Roberts in the lobby about why they came to be at this meeting. Looking around the room for any reaction from the assembled group but only getting a few concerned looks, Stryker continued with procedural items.

Although this was not a formal hearing or a courtroom, everything said would be entered into the official record of the session. In effect, the colonel emphasized, everyone involved would be making the equivalent of a formal statement which could follow them into court or a board of inquiry. He also reminded everyone that perjury was a serious offense and would be treated as such, regardless of rank or status. Stryker finished by stating this meeting was now an official Air Force proceeding and that everything said in the conference room was to stay there. In effect, the colonel was issuing a "gag order" on briefing. He pointed out this also applied to Officer Shields and the mysterious "advisor." Stryker took a few seconds to survey the faces of all those present before asking if anyone had any questions regarding this. No one did.

"Alright then," Stryker said. "Let's get this show on the road. Major Jefferson ... you're up."

CHAPTER 66

COTEF Facility
Early Afternoon

Major Colby Jefferson began his briefing by asking Lt. Davis to hand out copies of a timeline to everyone. Jefferson and his partner kept good notes during their three-day visit to Oregon and had prepared a detailed account for everyone to refer to. The first notation was for Saturday morning, October 16, 1999, 0800 hours (8:00 am), PDST. The scheduled time for the botched experiment to begin.

The six-page, double-spaced document included a daily time log which contained not only entries of what Jefferson and Davis had experienced, but also the observations of Officer Shields, the staff at Central Oregon Regional, and the pilots from Orion Air. Everyone present took a few minutes to scan the information before Jefferson continued. A few low whistles could be heard when some of the attendees read the last couple of entries.

For the benefit of Stryker and Colletto, Jefferson started out by asking Lt. Davis to give a brief history of the project. This was followed by Jefferson explaining how he and Lt. Davis got involved in the initial investigation. Brian Reynolds spoke next. Jefferson asked the engineer if he would give the group a brief overview of the COIL laser ... including the history of its development, technical aspects, and capabilities. Reynolds spoke longer than either Jefferson or Davis, talking for almost twenty minutes. The three were interrupted multiple times during their brief by Stryker and Colletto to get clarification on some details.

At the end of his narrative, the engineer looked over at the two lab technicians sitting by the side wall and asked them if they would care to add anything. Both men looked down and shook their heads no.

Next, Jefferson outlined the accident itself, walking everyone through how he envisioned things must have played out. He asked Brian Reynolds to supplement his presentation by further explaining, in non-technical terms, exactly how something like this could have happened.

Nothing was left out, the change in gases, the change in power settings, the forgotten computer upgrades, the runaway, the accelerated timeline, and the lack of adequate safeguards. Without naming names, at least for the time being, Reynolds also alluded to unauthorized and irresponsible decisions made on the part of one or more individuals as the underlying factor. Stryker and Colletto made note of that comment for later follow up.

When Colletto questioned the engineer about the nature of the explosion and what may have happened to all the equipment, Reynolds reiterated what he had described to Jefferson and Davis the day before. It was, in no uncertain terms, a graphic and ugly picture of the level of destruction. At this point, Jefferson asked Capt. Mitchell to show the video of what he and his first response unit found when they got to the Backskatter site on Saturday morning. No narrative was needed, the visuals were enough.

Following the showing, a subdued pallor settled over the room. Stryker shook his head, took a deep breath, then asked about the missing staff members. Lt. Davis spoke first, recounting everything he knew about Aaron Thomas; his recovery from the desert, what became of him at the hospital, and how he was eventually identified. Jefferson followed his junior partner, describing the condition of the ten bodies found at Backskatter.

Matt Shields spoke next, adding what he witnessed in the desert and at Christmas Valley. He also mentioned the on-going search for two missing hunters. Capt. Mitchell followed up by recounting the efforts to rescue the two surviving staff members, both of whom sat along the side wall. Col. Stryker asked the women to give an account of their experience, which they did. The emotionally charged description of their ordeal in the bunker and eventual rescue made a visible impression on the two colonels.

"So …" Stryker said, looking down at his notes. "Out of a staff of what … twenty-five people, we have ten mummified bodies, one cremated engineer, and two living survivors. Can someone explain to me what happened to the remaining twelve people?"

"Perhaps … I can," Brian Reynolds offered. The room fell silent again as all eyes turned to the engineer.

Stryker extended his hand towards Reynolds as if giving him permission to proceed.

"Given the nature and volume of gases used for the experiment," Reynolds began, "coupled with the extreme amount of microwave energy channeled into the laser … I would venture to guess the subsequent explosion was extremely intense. I think the unaccounted-for staff members who were anywhere near this at the time, were instantly and literally … vaporized."

"You can't be serious!" T.J. Rutledge scoffed. "Something like that can only be created by a nuclear weapon!"

"Well … this would have been the next best thing, only on a more confined scale," Reynolds said. "I see no other plausible explanation. No additional bodies or remains have been found. There have been no reports of accident victims showing up anywhere. Everything I've salvaged from the accident site tells me this is what happened to our people. One minute they existed, the next minute … poof."

"Thank you, Mr. Reynolds," Col. Stryker finally said, after taking a moment to absorb the engineer's presumption. "I appreciate your technical … description on this matter. Does anyone else have a theory about what happened to these people?"

Capt. Devon Mitchell said he would have to concur with the engineer's theory. The captain said his first response unit was diligent in searching for survivors from the moment they first got on site. Once the ten withered and naked bodies were discovered well outside the blast area, his people had extended their search efforts to cover most of the property by Monday afternoon … without results.

When asked about Aaron Thomas making it all the way to the Lost Forest, Reynolds and Mitchell could only speculate the lead engineer must have been somewhere outside when the runaway and explosion occurred … possibly monitoring the test from somewhere else on the property. Capt. Mitchell also speculated the ten bodies they found were probably working somewhere outside the blast area as well. Other than that, the engineer and the first responder had nothing else to offer.

The room fell silent once again, everyone seemingly lost in thought. Most tried to imagine what it must have been like for those caught in the explosion and its aftermath.

After jotting down a few notes, Lt. Colonel Colletto turned to Rutledge, who was sitting next to him, and asked about the value of the destroyed equipment and property. T.J. Rutledge didn't know the exact figure but gave his best estimate, trying to minimize the amount. "Somewhere between two and three million dollars."

"More like closer to five or seven million," Brian Reynolds interjected, correcting Rutledge.

"Don't forget the damage to individual property, as well as the probable loss of civilian life," added Matt Shields.

T.J. Rutledge visibly bristled at the two remarks, his face turning a bright, rosy color.

Things were growing tense in the conference room. Col. Stryker asked everyone to settle down and stop interrupting when someone else spoke. He didn't want to lose control of this briefing; he still had a number of items to cover.

"Okay," Stryker announced in an authoritative manner. "What we are dealing with here is a serious 'Class A' accident. We have damages in excess of two million dollars with multiple loss of life, not to mention what has happened outside of our areas of authority. According to the DoD instruction manual regarding accident notification, investigation, and reporting … as well as our own Air Force protocols regarding the treatment of accidents, we have a number of serious missteps to account for. First of all, this accident should have been reported … properly and immediately. That being the case, the 'preliminary' investigation by Major Jefferson will be elevated to a full-fledged, formal board of inquiry when we return to Peterson."

"Now, having established that," Stryker continued, "I would like to determine who is responsible, directly or indirectly, for causing this mess."

CHAPTER 67

COTEF Facility
Mid-Afternoon

With that perfunctory remark from Stryker, all eyes turned to T.J. Rutledge. The project manager for the COIL laser's field-testing program was the apparent "goat."

"I was not consulted, nor did I authorize any changes in the gas medium, power settings, or any of those other things mentioned ... period!" Rutledge leaned on the table, glaring at those staring at him. "Furthermore, I resent any implications ... from anyone ... that I could have, somehow, been responsible for this catastrophe."

Everyone's gaze shifted back to Stryker, wondering what the JAG officer was going to say or do next. Although no accusations had been directed toward anyone yet, Stryker seemed surprised by Rutledge's quick rebuke. He decided the best approach to finding out what he wanted to know was to initiate a subtle line of questioning, starting with Colby Jefferson.

Stryker asked Jefferson if, at any time during his investigation, he'd found a clue as to who may have ordered the changes that led to this disaster. Jefferson said yes. He asked Brian Reynolds to explain what he had discovered so far. Reynolds cleared his throat, then glanced down at his notes before returning his attention to Stryker.

"According to the notes left behind by Aaron Thomas and what I've been able to determine in talking with the other engineers and technicians, I believe Captain Webster may have authorized the changes."

The room erupted into a cacophony of comments, side conversations and noisy gestures. It took Stryker almost two minutes to get everyone quieted down and refocused. Once everyone settled, he asked the engineer if he had any proof of the accusation. Although he did not, Reynolds said he did, thinking the circumstantial evidence he had would be enough. Before the meeting, Jefferson took the engineer aside and coached him into implicating Webster. If for no other reason, than to bait him into revealing who was actually responsible.

Mark Webster took the bait hook, line, and sinker. He stiffened and glared across the table at the engineer. Brian Reynolds didn't even flinch. He never liked the pushy captain and neither did anyone else on the technical side of the project. Webster's arrogance, along with his cavalier approach to safety concerns made for several heated exchanges over the past several months. Everyone considered him a "loose cannon" and had tried to convey their concerns to Maj Roberts and Col. Rutledge on several occasions, without results.

"Well ...Captain?" Stryker demanded, raising an eyebrow. "What do you have to say?"

"With all due respect, sir." Webster replied, folding his hands on top of the table. "My duties at this project require me to keep everything working together and on track. This also means keeping things on schedule. Which, I believe, I've done a damn good job of. As we started to fall behind and weren't getting the results we hoped for, the engineers wanted to experiment with a new combination of gasses and power settings. I supported them. Since we were behind on our timetable and everyone wanted results, I authorized the changes ... with one caveat: the test scheduled for last Saturday still had to be at the fifty percent mark. To get back on schedule, we needed a laser blast of 5,000 KW."

"Did you clear this beforehand with either Major Roberts or Colonel Rutledge?" came the obvious next question from Stryker.

"Yes, sir, I did."

"That's bullshit!" blurted Rutledge, pointing a finger at Webster. "If I, or Roberts had authorized any of these changes they would have been in writing! I don't recall ever signing off on anything of the sort!"

"I distinctly remember asking you if I could authorize this, sir." Webster looked directly at Roberts, "you said to do whatever it takes to get the field testing back on track. So, I took the initiative and did my duty. I told the engineers to go ahead with the changes."

Maj. Roberts glared at the young captain, not knowing what to say in his own defense.

"Am I to assume then ... Captain Webster, Major Roberts, Colonel Rutledge ... that these proposed changes to the COIL laser were not run up the chain of command, and there is no written record giving anyone the authority to make them?" Stryker asked.

"It seems that would be the case Colonel," Roberts answered sheepishly.

"Am I to further assume, that the engineering staff was not allowed to experiment with controlled or lower power settings beforehand?"

"Yes, that's exactly what happened!" Brian Reynolds looked relieved that he finally got to say what had been on his mind.

Col. Stryker glanced at the engineer, then looked directly at Rutledge, Roberts, and Webster before lapsing into a moment of thought.

"The three of you are all culpable. By virtue of your rank and responsibilities, you all know this is not how we do things in the United States Air Force," Stryker stated, alternating his gaze between the three officers. "Is there anything else going on here I should know about?"

Colby Jefferson cleared his throat and said there were a couple of items he'd like to bring up. Stryker asked what they were.

Jefferson said he believed there was a conspiracy regarding the laser's intended purpose, as well as a coverup regarding the accident itself.

Stryker asked Jefferson to explain. The major said he and Lt. Davis suspected they had been under constant surveillance and their movements monitored since their arrival in Oregon. In his opinion, the COIL laser was being developed for covert and offensive purposes as well as for defensive reasons. He believed this was such a closely guarded secret this wasn't even known to many who worked on the project. Furthermore, he believed the scope of the accident was intentionally minimalized to prevent discovery of what the laser was actually being built for.

"Major Jefferson, can you prove any of this?" Colletto asked, now thinking the COIL technology was something his group should have been more involved in from the beginning.

"No … no actual proof, I'm afraid," Jefferson replied, being careful with his words and mindful of the two tape recorders sitting on the table. "I am of the belief … there is so much at stake here for so many … that someone deliberately tried to end my investigation last night."

"How did that come about?" Colletto prompted.

"Someone tried to kill me, Lieutenant Davis and Mr. Reynolds to shut us up, stop my investigation, and bury this accident."

CHAPTER 68

COTEF Facility
Mid-Afternoon

Instead of the room erupting into gasps, side conversations and miscellaneous comments, everyone fell silent, in a state of shock. Though all were aware of the previous night's "accident," Jefferson's revelation stunned them. Attempted murder was a serious allegation, and all eyes were now locked onto Jefferson, as if everyone wanted to ask the same question: "Are you serious?"

Stryker, narrowed his eyes, looking back and forth at the three men sitting across the table from him, then asked Jefferson to explain. The major drew everyone's attention to the second-to-last item on the timeline. The date was yesterday, Monday, October 19. The time was approximately 2120 hours (9:20 p.m.). While he, Davis and Reynolds took a stroll around the inside of the perimeter security fence, the outside lights suddenly went out. Shortly thereafter, the two investigators and the engineer were attacked by four, free-roaming Doberman pincher guard dogs.

With additional details provided by Davis and Reynolds, Jefferson walked the group through every step of the eleven-minute encounter. He omitted nothing, including the extent of their wounds and the delayed arrival of the security guards and dog handlers. He concluded by asking the dog handler, who was present at the briefing, to tell what happened from his perspective.

The handler said Lt. Blackstone came down to the kennels at approximately 2055 hours (8:55 p.m.) to inform them Maj. Jefferson, Lt. Davis and one of the laser engineers would be taking a walk around the inside of the security fence. He and his partner secured

the dogs in their kennel as requested then, following a suggestion by Lt. Blackstone, took a break and headed for the DEFAC where a newly-brewed pot of coffee and freshly baked cookies awaited.

The handler said both he and his partner were unaware of a problem until the alert horn went off and security people started rushing outside. The young man further described what happened when the group reached Jefferson, Davis, and Reynolds. He couldn't believe the three men not only survived an attack carried out by four highly-trained Dobermans, but that all the dogs had been injured in the process. The handler finished by saying he was the one who took two of the dogs into town for emergency medical treatment and that one didn't survive.

Col. Stryker asked the young man to describe how the dogs were kenneled and if their enclosure was secure. He wondered if the animals were smart enough to figure out a way to release themselves. The handler said that was an impossibility. The door latches were of a style to prevent such a thing from happening; they could only be opened from the outside and by a person.

Stryker took a moment or two to jot down a few notes before looking back up at the faces around the table. His list of potential charges against a variety of the officers present was steadily growing. Then he singled out Lt. Blackstone and asked her if she saw anyone roaming about in the vicinity of the kennels after she left. She said no; after talking to the dog handlers, she went directly back to her office.

"Well, someone sure as hell opened those kennels!" Stryker finally commented. "This was no accident."

Logan Davis raised his hand to be noticed. "Perhaps I can shed some light on this, sir."

All eyes focused on the young lieutenant as Col. Stryker gestured for him to speak.

Davis shifted uncomfortably in his chair and looked directly at Stryker and Colletto.

"At the suggestion of Major Jefferson, earlier this morning I went into the security station and asked the guard on duty if I could see last night's video tapes of the kennel." Davis spoke loud enough to be clearly heard by everyone in the room. "According to the time stamp on the video, at approximately 2110 hours, it clearly shows all of the dogs in their kennel, barking furiously to get out. Then, a hand can be seen reaching up and unplugging the camera. There was no more footage after that."

"Can you describe what the hand looked like or anything about it, Lieutenant?" Stryker asked.

"Only that it looked small, like a child's or woman's hand, and it had what looked like some type of a ring on the little finger."

All eyes shifted toward Jennifer Blackstone, who immediately covered up her right hand with her left.

"Lieutenant Blackstone, please stand up and raise both of your hands," ordered Stryker.

Blackstone hesitated, then did as she was commanded. She wore no rings on any of her fingers, but on the pinky finger of her right hand they could all see a pale band of skin.

"Lieutenant, I am going to ask you directly … did you unplug the surveillance camera in the kennel last night?"

Blackstone maintained her composure and said nothing, obviously considering her response.

"Lieutenant Blackstone, did you unplug that camera to hide the fact you were the one who released the dogs … knowing what would happen next?"

Before she could say anything, and to everyone's complete surprise, T.J. Rutledge jumped to his feet and yelled at her not to answer the question. The room went completely silent. Rutledge instantly regretted his spontaneous reaction. Blackstone sank to her seat and stared at Rutledge. The colonel stood still for a few seconds with his mouth open, looking at the faces around the table, trying to figure out what to say or do next.

Col. Stryker shifted his gaze between the two for a brief period after the unexpected outburst. Everyone in the room recognized there was something going on between the colonel and the young aide to Maj. Roberts. Realizing he had just implicated himself and identified his secret operative, T.J. Rutledge slowly sat back down without saying another word.

The JAG officer rocked back in his chair, gazing up at the ceiling as if temporarily lost in thought. Finally, he looked around the room at the assortment of anxious faces and said it was time to take a break. He ordered everyone to reconvene in exactly fifteen minutes.

As the others took their time filing out of the room, Stryker and Colletto stayed behind, locked in a quiet discussion.

CHAPTER 69

COTEF Facility
Mid Afternoon

After the short break, everyone filed back into the conference room and settled in their seats. When all side conversations ended, Stryker cleared his throat and addressed the group.

"When Colonel Colletto and I return to Peterson ... I will have orders issued for you, Lieutenant Blackstone, as well as for Captain Webster, Major Roberts, and Colonels Rutledge and Kelly to attend a formal Board of Inquiry ... where all of you will likely face a variety of charges stemming from what I've heard today."

Stryker looked alternatively at the five officers he just identified. Their faces were blank and none of them said anything.

"Furthermore, consider yourselves temporarily relieved of duty. Lieutenant Blackstone, consider yourself under house arrest until you get to Peterson. The individuals I have just named have forty-eight hours to get your affairs in order. I will arrange to have all of you picked up at the local airport and transported directly to Peterson Thursday afternoon. Colonel Rutledge, Colonel Kelly ... you two, along with Major Jefferson and Lieutenant Davis will be flying back to Colorado with me and Colonel Colletto immediately following this meeting."

After a short pause to let his announcement sink in, the colonel continued. "Captain Mitchell, I am putting you in temporary command of COTEF. Be advised, both you and Mr. Reynolds here will also be required to testify at the inquiry. I'll arrange for your transport at a later date. Officer Shields, I want to personally thank you for your help and especially for your discretion regarding this matter. I trust your report will not disclose what was covered in here today. I also want you to know that we will hold all those responsible for this incident ... accountable."

Col. Stryker concluded his remarks by asking Colby Jefferson one last question, "Do you have any more ... 'surprises' for me Major?"

"No ... no surprises, Colonel," remarked Jefferson. "But I do have one unresolved question."

Stryker waved a hand for him to continue, showing a little impatience.

"I would like to know who this unnamed 'project advisor' is, and why he's here." Jefferson looked directly at the man in civilian clothes sitting along the side wall.

After an awkward moment of silence, the serious-looking man slowly rose to his feet and looked directly at Jefferson. "My name is Smith, Major Jefferson. Just like you, I work for the U.S. Government. I am here to determine if the COIL laser project should be managed and controlled by someone other than the Air Force."

"That's it?" Jefferson's tone was laced with obvious skepticism.

"That's it ... Major," the man replied. "Now, if you'll excuse me, I have a plane to catch."

With that remark, the "advisor" headed for the door. Capt. Webster moved to intercept him but was stopped by Colletto.

"Let him go Captain. I'll take care of this when we get back to Peterson,"

Col. Stryker once again asked everyone to settle down, he had a few remaining things to cover. He went around the table and asked everyone if they had anything else they'd like to add to the proceeding ... or the record.

Jefferson and Davis each said no, they believed they had covered everything. Brian Reynolds asked about the COIL laser project itself and what would happen to it. Stryker said he supported Maj. Jefferson's recommendation that everything here be cleaned up, packed up, and moved back to Kirtland Air Force Base in New Mexico. A move that would essentially close down the "Oregon Project" for good.

That being the case, Reynolds was curious about the staff who were working on the project. Stryker said the military people would be reassigned. The civilian engineers and technicians would go to Kirtland and resume their work on the COIL laser there, including Reynolds if he wished. Any remaining civilians would be given opportunities to work elsewhere.

Devon Mitchell asked about the security of both sites until that happened. Colletto said he would arrange to have specialized teams from several bases come in to deal with a phased shut down. He added it would probably take at least a month to pull off the move and until that happened, Capt. Mitchell would remain in charge.

Matt Shields asked about possible compensation to the Christmas Valley cattle ranchers for the loss of their livestock. Col. Stryker said he would look into it but could make no guarantees. He said reimbursing the ranchers would be tantamount to an admission of guilt and, as a result, not only expose the classified Air Force project, but establish a "liability precedent" for other accidents. Shields said he understood but still had to ask.

No one else had anything else to offer, so Stryker concluded the meeting by thanking everyone in attendance for their cooperation and participation. He added that, although the COIL laser was an enormous technological achievement and he had high hopes it would have a future in the Air Force, the way the project was mismanaged in Oregon was a travesty. Looking directly at Brian Reynolds, he asked the engineer if he would write up a detailed plan to address all safety concerns surrounding the development and testing of the COIL and present them at the inquiry. Finally exonerated from the reputation as a time-wasting troublemaker, Reynolds smiled and nodded.

As everyone filed out of the conference room, and headed to wherever they were going next, Colby Jefferson went up to Matt Shields and asked him to walk out to the parking lot with him. Logan Davis went back to their temporary quarters to start packing.

Col. Stryker instructed Lt. Blackstone, Maj. Roberts, Capt. Webster, Lt. Col. Rutledge, and Col. Kelly to remain in the conference room. After everyone had left, he prepped them as to what to expect next. A team of JAG lawyers would be assigned to represent them either collectively or individually for the official accident inquiry as well as any follow up needs. He also advised them not to do anything irresponsible that could exacerbate their situation. In other words, be a professional and don't do anything stupid.

As Jefferson and Shields cleared the security gate at the fence, the Air Force trooper asked the Trooper what he intended to do next. Matt Shields said as far as he was concerned, this case was closed. He would write up his report, being careful not to disclose any more than promised, and present it to his supervisor. He also said he needed to get back to the deputy and the veterinarian in Christmas Valley and tell them what the outcome of his investigation was. Again, not divulging any classified information. Jefferson asked him if he also wouldn't mind following up with the staff at the hospital, saying they deserved to know the whole story. Shields said he'd be happy to do that.

Before they went their separate ways, Jefferson felt compelled to personally thank the officer for his service. In response, Shields had one last question for the major. "What about our pilots and the service they provided?"

Jefferson looked over at the two Orion Air helicopters sitting side by side. Chance Barclay and Trent Westbrook were busy cleaning the windshields of their machines in anticipation of their next flight.

The Air Force officer and the Oregon State Game Warden smiled at each other, nodded, then started walking over to where the two Orion Air pilots had been dutifully standing down with their aircraft since early morning.

EPILOGUE

The official Air Force Board of Inquiry regarding the Backskatter tragedy convened on Monday, October 21, 1999, at Peterson Air Force Base in Colorado.

For the three-day period leading up to the formal hearing, Lt. Jennifer Blackstone, Capt. Mark Webster, Maj, Derick Roberts, Lt. Colonel T.J. Rutledge, and Col. David R. Kelly spent time on base consulting with the JAG attorneys assigned to them. Capt. Devon Mitchell, Brian Reynolds, the two Backskatter survivors, and one of the dog handlers were flown in on the day prior to the hearing.

The board of inquiry lasted three and a half days. Upon its conclusion, Blackstone, Webster, Roberts, Rutledge, and Kelly were individually charged with a variety of "high crimes and misdemeanors" per the Uniform Code of Military Justice.

Col. Kelly was charged with failure to adequately supervise and was relieved of his command at Schriever. He was demoted to the rank of Lt. Colonel and reassigned to Minot AFB in North Dakota, the "Siberia" of North American Air Force bases. He quietly retired after one year at Minot.

Lt. Colonel Rutledge was also relieved of his command and charged with abuse of authority, misuse of assets, failure to adequately supervise, failure to report a serious accident, conspiracy, conduct unbecoming an officer, and thanks to Jennifer Blackstone, accessory to commit attempted murder. Rutledge was stripped of his rank and forfeited all pay and military privileges. He was dishonorably discharged from the Air Force and was sentenced to seven years in Leavenworth. Because of his combat service in Iraq, the judge reduced his sentence to five years.

Maj. Derick Roberts was relieved of his command and stripped of rank and military privileges as well. In addition to the primary charges levied against him, he was additionally charged with failure to adequately supervise, failure to report a serious accident, conduct unbecoming an officer, and conspiracy. He received a bad conduct discharge and received a reduced sentence of eighteen months in a minimum security military prison.

Capt. Mark Webster was additionally charged with command irresponsibility, misuse of assets, destruction of government property, conspiracy, conduct unbecoming an officer, and twenty three-counts of involuntary manslaughter. Webster received a dishonorable discharge and was stripped of his rank and military privileges. He would spend the next five years in various military prisons.

Lt. Jennifer Blackstone faced additional charges of obstruction of justice, conspiracy, conduct unbecoming an officer, and three counts of attempted murder. Her punishment resulted in a formal court-martial where she was found guilty on all charges. She received a dishonorable discharge, was stripped of rank and all military privileges, and sentenced to four years in a special military prison for women.

Capt. Devon Mitchell, as a result of his new responsibilities as acting COTEF commander and coordinator of the salvage and asset transfer operation, was promoted to major. After the two-month-long project was completed, he was reassigned to Beale Air Force Base in northern California as deputy chief of base security.

Brian Reynolds was offered a top job at the Air Force Weapons Laboratory at Kirtland Air Force Base in New Mexico. He became one of the principal engineers on the further development of the COIL laser. The envisioned system never lived up to its expectations of being a long-range weapon and was eventually downsized and re-engineered to be an active airborne system.

The doctors and caregivers at Central Oregon Regional, along with Coroner Michael Clark, having been briefed on the outcome of the accident investigation by Matt Shields, continued with their regular duties. Per their agreement, none ever spoke of their knowledge or involvement in the incident.

Oregon State Trooper and Game Warden Matt Shields completed his investigation, wrote his summary report, and submitted it to his supervisor. The document left out any classified details as agreed. No follow-up action was required, and the report was subsequently filed away in the State Police archives. As promised, Shields contacted the sheriff's deputy and veterinarian at Christmas Valley, telling them only what they needed to know to satisfy their paperwork as well. Matt Shields returned to his normal duties as a game warden, and on several occasions, called upon the services of Orion Air to help him out.

The remains of the two missing hunters from Christmas Valley were never found. After a week of looking, the official search was called off, but went on for another two weeks by friends and relatives without success. The cattle ranchers were denied compensation by the government for the loss of their animals.

Maj. Colby Jefferson testified at the Board of Inquiry and at the trials for the five accused Air Force officers. He received several commendations for his work on the Backskatter accident and returned to his previous job as chief of base security at Schriever AFB. Upon completing his enlistment requirements with the Air Force, Jefferson decided to make a lifestyle change and left military service altogether. In short order, he found a new home with the Federal Bureau of Investigation.

Lieutenant Logan Davis also testified at the Board of Inquiry and at the trials for the five accused Air Force officers. His emotional testimony on the dog attack was so compelling it completely derailed Blackstone's and Rutledge's defense strategy. At the recommendation of Colby Jefferson, Logan Davis applied for, and attended the Air Force's school for OSI officers. After graduating from the program with high marks, he was assigned to Pederson Air Force Base and went to work for Lt. Colonel Colletto. Citing the need for on-going "therapy" after his harrowing dog experience at COTEF, the newly-minted captain adopted a beautiful Australian shepherd from a local animal shelter, whom he named Colby.

The Backskatter radar site was completely disassembled. Its various components sent to wherever they could be put to use. The razed site resembled something akin to a ghost town for a number of years. Only the concrete footings for the radar arrays, several buildings, the substation, and parts of the fencing remained. It became a local curiosity for adventure seekers and conspiracy theorists. In later years, it would be considered as an ideal location for a solar farm.

Once vacated, and with all classified equipment removed, the COTEF facility was turned over to the Oregon National Guard. The Guard remodeled the complex and turned it into a special school for "at-risk" teenagers. The highly regarded program went on to win several national awards and set the standard for a residential-based school built on a military model. Boys and girls from all over the state of Oregon used the voluntary program for generations to get their high school education back on track and to make something of themselves.

After a profitable five days of flying for the State Police and the Air Force, Orion Air went on to enjoy an additional month of flying for the military. At the suggestion of Maj. Jefferson, Capt. Devon Mitchell retained the services of the small helicopter company for the decommissioning process of the Backskatter site. Trent Westbrook and Chance Barclay took daily turns at ferrying technicians and military people back and forth between Backskatter and COTEF in the MD 500. Trent Westbrook couldn't have been happier.

When the clean up and transfer process was completed, Barclay and Westbrook went back to doing their standard helicopter tours, flight lessons, and assorted commercial work. They honored their code of silence as well, and never spoke of what they knew about the Backskatter incident or the work they did for the Air Force. When asked, they simply said it was somewhat of a boring flying job … but that it paid well.

Backskatter

Tom Wangler

ACKNOWLEDGEMENTS

I owe a great debt of gratitude to many people in the writing of this story and the publication of this book.

Starting with my "Beta" readers. I want to thank them for their time, expertise, and willingness to make a valuable contribution to the writing of "Backskatter": Meredith Mason, Lt. Col. Pat Carpenter (Oregon Air Guard, ret.), Sue Tomcho, Fred and Lisa Kroon, and Connie Souther. I appreciate their help and encouragement more than they will ever know.

I am also deeply indebted to my principal editor, Kelly Schaub, as well as my publisher, Kim Cooper Findling. Both of these ladies were instrumental in keeping me on track with my story and for helping me navigate the maze of publication. Additionally, I would like to thank Todd Griffith of Dancing Moon Press for all the design and layout work he did, as well as Philip McDaniel for his graphic illustrations. I can't thank these individuals enough.

Finally, it must be said, this work would not have been possible without the support, encouragement, and patience of my wife Cheryl. She deserves a medal for all that she put up with in the writing of this story.

ABOUT THE AUTHOR

Tom Wangler was born and raised in the high desert country of Central Oregon. A graduate of Oregon College of Education (now Western Oregon University), with a BS degree in education and journalism, Tom initially embarked on a teaching career before joining the Peace Corps.

After a two-year stint in the west African country of Nigeria (the inspiration for his first novel), He obtained a master's degree with honors from Oregon State University. After enjoying a variety of careers, including commercially flying helicopters and teaching, Tom quietly retired from public service as a school administrator to finish "Backskatter".

He now lives with his wife Cheryl, and their two German Shepherds, in the resort community of Bend, Oregon.

Made in the USA
Middletown, DE
17 June 2022